The New Exploits of
Joseph Rouletabille

BY THE SAME AUTHOR

Exquisite Pandora

The New Exploits of Joseph Rouletabille

by
Martin Gately

A Black Coat Press Book

Acknowledgements:

Stories & Afterword Copyright © 2020 by Martin Gately.
Foreword Copyright © 2020 by Jean-Marc Lofficier.
Cover illustration Copyright © 2020 by David Rabbitte.

Visit our website at www.blackcoatpress.com

While inspired by a character created by Gaston Leroux, this work has not been authorized by his Estate.

TABLE OF CONTENTS

ROULETABILLE

LE MYSTERE
DE LA CHAMBRE JAUNE

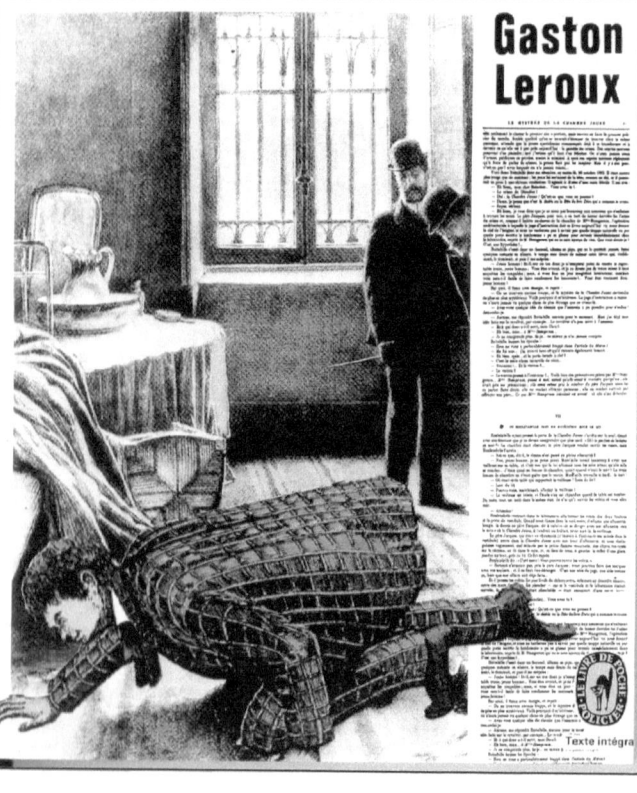

Gaston
Leroux

Foreword

The leading *feuilletoniste* of the Belle Époque was Gaston Leroux (1868-1927), a writer best known for his classic *Le Fantôme de l'Opéra* (1910),[1] the tragic yet murderous man-ape *Balaoo* (1911), and the adventures of *Chéri-Bibi*, a man unjustly pursued by a hostile fate (1913, 1919).[2]

Trained as a lawyer, Leroux was a renowned investigative journalist who even traveled to, and reported from, Russia just before the Bolshevik Revolution. His journalistic skills helped the French *fantastique* emerge from the melodramatic and romantic literary burdens of the end of the 19th century, and, by making it more real and contemporary, gave it a new lease on life.

In *The Phantom of the Opera*, Leroux skillfully mixed fantastic events with real-life facts. The same was true of *Le Fauteuil Hanté* [*The Haunted Chair*] (1909), a fantastic mystery novel in which a mad scientist used ingenious, murderous devices to rid himself of applicants at the French Academy who have uncovered his dark secret. Both novels read like sensational newspaper accounts of the surreal.

Leroux's eclectic curiosity conferred upon his *oeuvre* a wildly diverse nature. In his first novel, *La Double Vie de Theophraste Longuet* [*The Double Life of Theophraste Longuet*] (1903), a retired merchant found himself possessed by the spirit of notorious 18th century French highwayman, Cartouche. He goes on to discover a secret, underground society which has been living in vast caverns beneath Paris since the 14th century.

Later, Leroux shied away from purely supernatural themes, with a few exceptions: short stories such as the

---

[1] Black Coat Press, 978-1-932983-13-5.
[2] Stage play adaptation, Black Coat Press, 978-1-934543-43-6.

7

Hoffmannesque *L'Homme qui a Vu le Diable* [*The Man Who Saw The Devil*] (1908) and *Le Coeur Cambriolé* [*The Burglared Heart*] (1920).

When Leroux dealt with such fantastic themes, it was in ways that were resolutely modern, but often derivative of the works of other popular writers. His classic *Balaoo* (1911) was about a murderous ape-man *à la* Edgar Allan Poe's *Murder in the Rue Morgue*. *L'Épouse du Soleil* [*The Bride of the Sun*] (1912) was a Lost World story with pure H. Rider Haggard elements. Finally, *La Poupée Sanglante* [*The Bloody Puppet*] (1923) and *La Machine à Assassiner* [*The Killing Machine*] (1924) were a strange combination of classic horror and science fiction. In the first volume, the brain of Benedict Masson, a man framed for murder and later guillotined, is transplanted into the body of Gabriel, an android. In the sequel, Gabriel exposes a vampire cult–one without some of the more supernatural characteristics usually associated with vampirism–led by a depraved nobleman.

Leroux's literary idols being Alexandre Dumas and Paul Féval, the author of the seminal *The Black Coats* series, it was no surprise that he was equally comfortable chronicling extravagant tales of murder, revenge, masked men, swooning women, mysterious dwarves and secret societies meeting in underground caverns, with or without fantastic elements. Like their American pulp counterparts of the 1930s, these sagas were fantastic more in terms of their atmosphere than because of any specific supernatural concepts. In this vein, the ever-prolific Leroux penned *Le Roi Mystère* [*King Mystery*] (1908), a *Count of Monte-Cristo*-like story, *La Reine du Sabbat* [*The Queen of the Sabbath*] (1910) and *Les Mohicans de Babel* [*The Mohicans of Babel*] (1926), which both owe a clear debt to *The Black Coats*.

Leroux also wrote *Les Aventures Effroyables de Herbert de Renich* [*The Terrifying Adventures of Herbert de Renich*] (1917-20), an epic undersea saga which was his answer to Verne's *Twenty-Thousand Leagues Under the Sea* in which a Captain Nemo-like American designs a super-submarine to fight the Germans who are responsible for the death of his family. In chapter 7, the narrator, de Renich, says, speaking of the new generation of submarines: "they do things the *Nautilus* couldn't do... After all, that was only a ship... They, on the other hand, also drive at will on the bottom of the sea. Yes, they have wheels and can be either ships or vehicles."

Today, Gaston Leroux is best remembered as the author of a series of mystery novels starring the character of dashing young journalist, Joseph Josephin, a.k.a. Rouletabille, clearly an idealized projection of the author, and conceived as a direct challenge to Conan Doyle. Like C. Auguste Dupin, Lecoq, Sherlock Holmes and Hercule Poirot, Rouletabille solved his cases by pure deductive reasoning, what he called the "good end of reason." He drew a figurative circle around the facts that were known, and excluded everything that was not part of that circle, even if, to others, they appeared to be.

In the first Rouletabille novel, *Le Mystère de la Chambre Jaune* [*The Mystery of the Yellow Room*] (1907),[3] the hero solved an attempted murder in a locked room. In that book, Leroux revealed that "Rouletabille" is the nickname of 18-year-old journalist Joseph Josephin, who was raised in a religious orphanage in Eu, a small town on the western coast of France, near Fecamp.

It turned out that Rouletabille's father is none other than Ballmeyer, an international criminal of great repute and many identities. As Jean Roussel, Ballmeyer had married a rich American heiress, Mathilde Stangerson, the "Lady in Black," who was, therefore, Rouletabille's own mother. (For various speculations on Ballmeyer's ancestry, see our entry on Monsieur Lecoq.)

In a tragic twist of fate, Rouletabille unmasked Ballmeyer, who was hiding under the guise of French Surete detective Frederic Larsan, in 1902, and saved his mother from his father's evil designs.

---

[3] Black Coat Press, 978-1-934543-60-3.

There is an irreconciliable dating problem with the first Rouletabille novel: it was unarguably stated by Leroux as taking place in 1892, yet its sequel, *The Scent of the Lady in Black*, is said to take place in 1905, "three years later," so 1902 has therefore become the accepted dating for *The Mystery of the Yellow Room*.

Ballmeyer returned in *Le Parfum de la Dame en Noir* [*The Scent of the Lady in Black*] (1908). At the end of the story, which took place in a castle by the sea in Southern France, Ballmeyer died, freeing Rouletabille from the evil shadow of the past. Soon afterwards, in *Rouletabille chez le Tsar* [*Rouletabille and the Czar*] (1913), Rouletabille was summoned to Russia by the Czar, where he solved a murder at the Imperial Court.

Then, there is a break in continuity. In *Rouletabille à la Guerre* [*Rouletabille at War*] (often published as 2 volumes: *Le Château Noir* [*The Black Castle*] and *Les Étranges Noces de Rouletabille* [*The Strange Wedding of Rouletabille*]), which takes place contemporaneously, i.e.: circa 1914, the fearless journalist married the beautiful Ivana Vilitchkov and defeated the mad Turk warlord Gaulow, Lord of the Black Castle. The Rouletabille comic-book series (see below) made use of that break to insert additional Leroux novels rewritten to incorporate Rouletabille during that 1906-1914 interruption.

In *Rouletabille chez Krupp* [*Rouletabille at Krupp's*] (1917),[4] Rouletabille became a French secret agent and infiltrated the Krupp factories. Aside from John Buchan's Richard Hannay novels, this was one of the first, modern treatments of the espionage thriller. In the end, like a proto-James Bond, Rouletabille saved Paris from being annihilated by a German super-missile.

In *Le Crime de Rouletabille* [*The Crime of Rouletabille*] (1921), the detective was almost framed for Ivana's murder. There is a literary connection between *The Phantom of the Opera*, *The Double Life of Theophraste Longuet* and *The*

---

[4] Black Coat Press, 978-1-61227-144-6.

Crime of Rouletabille in that all these novels feature a police official named Mifroid.

Then, in *Rouletabille chez les Bohémiens* [*Rouletabille and the Gypsies*] (1922), Rouletabille helped recover a sacred book stolen from the gypsies and managed to thwart the evil schemes of the deadly Madame de Mayrens, aka *The Octopus*, the secret identity of whom we shall not spoil here.

The Rouletabille series included a few fantastic elements, but was filled with a remarkable gothic atmosphere, and today remains a classic of French detective fiction.

Martin Gately, who has sterling credentials when it comes to the field of popular literature, now takes over the character[5] and embarks on a new series of adventures, initially serialized in *Tales of the Shadowmen*.

Jean-Marc Lofficier

---

[5] Rouletabille had already been the subject of two authorized sequels by Noré Brunel, serialized in 1947-48 in *Le Soir*, novelizing two scripts written in 1928 by Pierre Lestringuez, both supervised by Leroux.

GASTON LEROUX
AVENTURES EXTRAORDINAIRES DE
JOSEPH ROULETABILLE
REPORTER

ROULETABILLE
CHEZ KRUPP

Rouletabille Rides the Horror Express

(Inspired by the script Horror Express
by Arnaud d'Usseau and Julian Zimet)

*The following report to the Royal Geological Society by
the undersigned, Alexander Saxton, is a true and faithful account of events that befell the Society's expedition in Manchuria. As the leader of the expedition, I must accept responsibil-
ity for its ending in disaster. But I will leave to the judgment of
the honorable members the decision as to where the blame for
the catastrophe lies...*

Professor Sir Alexander Saxton, FRS, MCIfA

Prologue - Outer Manchuria, winter 1906

It had been a hard trek across the ice fields, but Saxton's
spirits were high. The foothills were now in sight. And somewhere in those hills was the cave that a silk merchant in Pe-
king had described to him nearly five weeks ago. The merchant said that he had sheltered in a cave system during a
snowstorm and stumbled upon the partially decomposed body
of an ancient man-like creature encased in ice. The story had
fired Saxton's imagination, and the merchant's obvious sincerity had defused the geologist's natural cynicism. In addition,
the man had wanted no payment for the crude map he drew of
the cave's location; in turn, the local guides Saxton had pro-
cured in the nearby town of Xiang-Jing seemed well aware of
the cave and what it contained. Quite why they had not drawn
the authority's attention to the ice creature he did not know—
at this time.

Nearly two hours later, Saxton and his guides stood at
the ragged mouth of the cavern. He removed his thick fur mit-
tens and lit the portable limelight lantern he had brought with

him. The searing cone of silver projected by the lantern illuminated the interior almost as brightly as natural daylight; the harsh light glinted prismatically off the millions of tiny ice crystals on the cave's smooth walls.

Saxton allowed one of the guides to ease in front of him, and the man led him unerringly to where the creature lay. The silk merchant had not exaggerated. This was an anthropoid creature from out of the remote past. Saxton marveled at it. While it was not perfectly preserved, the level of protection created by the ice was extraordinary. Decomposition had twisted the waxy flesh of the thing's face into a terrifying sneer. And its eyes were still in place—remarkable! He was unaware of the discovery of any human-like creature with the eyes intact. This find would make his reputation, and the Royal Society of Geologists would surely agree that the diversion away from the study of alluvial deposits, with which he had been tasked, was well worth it. Of course, the matter did not truly fall within the field of geology; more properly, this was paleontology, or some weird offshoot of it. While it was quite obvious that the ice creature was flesh and bone, not stone, he resolved that he would refer to it as a fossil, particularly when speaking to the uninitiated and ignorant. Also, if the Chinese authorities misunderstood the nature of the find, and believed it to be a recently frozen man, he might be caught up in weeks of wrangling. Far better that it be thought of as a fossil by all concerned.

He turned to the guide.

"Fetch the tools from outside. We are going to have to cut it out of the ice and carry it back to the town," said Saxton.

Trans-Siberia Station, Russian Concession, Harbin - three weeks later.

In some ways, Joseph Rouletabille had never felt happier. The appalling affair of the Living Bombs was retreating in his memory; it was months now since he had become entangled with the affairs of General Trebassof. Following that, the

French journalist had been a little surprised when a call for his assistance had come from China, though he shouldn't have been since the Russian Concession had both Russian and French language newspapers which dutifully recorded his exploits. Yes, General Wang, whose role was a combination of military governor and minister for trade, had heard of Rouletabille, and required his assistance in finding the hidden den of a group of Dacoits allied to a certain *Devil Doctor.*

Rouletabille had worked more or less undercover with an Irish soldier, Captain Sean O'Hagan, who was serving in the concession's International Regiment. Ultimately, a raid had been organized on the tunnels the Dacoits had constructed beneath freight yards of the Chinese Eastern Railway. During his time in China, Rouletabille had concluded that the foreign concessions within the country were marvelous, cosmopolitan and egalitarian institutions. Perhaps they were even a blueprint for the future organization of society. After all, crime was very low and the corruption of public officials almost unknown, or was he just viewing this particular jointly administered enclave through rose-tinted *pince nez?*

In the office of the Trans-Siberian Rail, the calm was rapidly disappearing from the voice of Professor Sir Alexander Saxton. He pointed speculatively at a filing cabinet with his walking cane, while addressing the station master.

"My name is Alexander Saxton. If you check your records, you will find the telegram I sent you three weeks ago requesting both a single private berth and space within a freight car."

"I'm sorry," replied the official. "There isn't a single seat left."

Saxton's outburst of fury was delayed by the arrival of Dr. James Wells, a fellow academician and acquaintance of Saxton's. The doctor was accompanied by a rather portly and matronly woman of about sixty, who generated the aura of that rare creature: the female scientist. Wells' extraordinarily gaunt face relaxed into a friendly smile

15

"Professor Saxton, I presume," greeted Wells, in mock imitation of Henry Morton Stanley.

"Dr. Wells," said Saxton, coldly. "What the Devil are you doing in Harbin province?"

"I might ask you the same... Actually, I'm here collecting both zoological specimens and bacterial cultures," said Wells, who then gestured in a chivalrous way in the direction of the lady at his side. "This is my assistant, Miss Jones. She is a superb technician."

"For a woman, he means," said Miss Jones, self-deprecatingly.

Miss Jones extended her hand and Saxton just about managed to shake it politely; inside, he was still seething that he had not been allocated a private berth and space in the freight car.

Miss Jones looked Saxton up and down. Why, he didn't seem English at all; he looked more like a displaced Italian nobleman. He was six feet five inches at least, and his face was adorned with a thick, dark moustache. He was compellingly handsome, and so very obviously as volatile as a volcano.

Suddenly, Wells seemed to have the attention of the station-master.

"I realize that I'm asking the impossible, but I need two private berths on the next train to Moscow and space for three animal crates." As he said this, he passed the man a thick bundle of pale turquoise Chinese banknotes.

"Of course, sir," said the station-master, immediately returning to his desk to write out the travel warrants.

Wells turned back to Saxton.

"In China, it's called 'squeeze,' I believe," said Wells.

"And in Britain, we call it bribery and corruption," condemned Saxton.

Saxton advanced on the little station-master's desk with fury in his eyes, clutching his walking cane as if it were a club. With a single sweeping action, he knocked the typewriter, desk lamp and document basket off the desk and onto the floor with a crash. The official recoiled in fear, anticipating that he was about to take a beating from this madman.

The door into the office opened yet again. This time a platoon of International Regiment Soldiers in their distinctive peacock blue uniforms marched in; leading them was a European officer with a flaming red moustache.

"Captain O'Hagan, sir," said the officer to Saxton. "General Wang asked me to find you and see if I could make myself useful."

Saxton knew the seemingly omniscient General Wang only slightly, and had not thought to rely on him for favors, though he had, as a matter of courtesy, sent him a message describing the importance of the ice creature fossil find. He was extremely pleased that International Regiment troops would be on hand to move the crate and guard it.

Saxton noticed that the station-master was now filling out a reserved ticket travel warrant for him, just as he had for Wells.

"Your ticket, Excellency," said the little man, assuming expediently, although incorrectly, that Saxton had some form of diplomatic status because troops had been deployed to assist him.

Saxton shook Captain O'Hagan's hand warmly.

"You're a sight for sore eyes, Captain. I have an extremely valuable archeological find for transportation aboard the Express. Your men are just what I need."

Rouletabille had not seen O'Hagan, arrive on the station platform because he had been paged loudly to the local telegraph office. The message was from the French Diplomatic Bureau located within the French Concession in Shanghai. The telegram used plain text, but was couched in such a way that it was obvious that he was being asked to undertake a mission which would greatly benefit his government.

He considered it for a moment, then surreptitiously burned the telegram whilst lighting his pipe. Further along the crowded platform, a man caught the journalist's attention. His body language was furtive, and this stood out quite noticeably in the hustle and bustle of ordinary passengers and merchandise sellers. The man now loitered by a large padlocked and chain wrapped crate. Rouletabille could not see his hands, but the movement of his shoulders was highly distinctive. The man was picking the padlock.

Rouletabille continued to move nearer. Then, he became aware that there was another man at his side, keeping pace with him. It was a tall bearded Russian dressed in the distinctive black robes of a *strannik*—a religious wanderer. The holy man had obviously noticed, or sensed, what the brazen thief was now doing, and he, too, was moving in to apprehend him.

Rouletabille and the Russian exchanged a look; seemingly, they were allies on the side of right. But before they could reach the man picking the lock, he suddenly cried out and collapsed face down onto the rough flagstones of the platform.

Rouletabille suspected that the thief was shamming, and felt for his pulse. But the man was dead. The holy man turned over the body. The journalist wondered how he could have been so horribly mistaken. For the man could not have been a thief—he was blind! He had no pupils, no corneas. Both eyeballs were just a mass of white scar tissue, as if his eyes had been seared or cauterized by a red-hot poker.

The holy man began chanting incessantly in Russian, praying for the thief's soul. After a few minutes, the curious crowd parted to allow a policeman to approach the corpse. This was Inspector Pavel Mirov of the Trans-Siberian Express Constabulary Force.

"Why pray for *his* soul, *strannik?*" asked Mirov. "He was just a filthy sneak thief."

"You knew him?" said Rouletabille. "Yet surely, he could not really have been a thief. He was blind."

"He could see well enough when a policeman was after him!" spat Mirov. "It is Grashinski, the failed locksmith. His father was Russian and his mother Chinese."

Mirov moved closer, and was obviously shocked by the dead man's blank white eyes.

"I'll be damned," said Mirov.

"This *is* the work of the Devil," said the holy man.

Simultaneously, Rouletabille and the *strannik* started to pull the chains from the crate in order to get it open and see what was inside it. In his mind, the Frenchman was already forming a hypothesis: it was quite possible that someone was inside the wooden box and had squirted acid through the small rectangular aperture that he had now noticed in the side of the crate, and it had gone into Grashinski's eyes.

Saxton, who had just come out of the office, was appalled to see the two men seeking to open up his precious crate.

"Get away from my property," he bellowed.

Again getting ready to wield his cane as a weapon, he had completely forgotten that O'Hagan and a platoon of armed men were standing ready to back him up.

"Is this yours?" queried the French journalist. He had imagined the crate as belonging to some local crime lord, perhaps smuggling a wanted confederate out of the concession to the comparative safety of Moscow.

"It reeks of evil. Whatever is inside this box is unholy and must be destroyed," said the *strannik*.

"What is in the crate, Excellency?" asked Mirov.

"Merely fossils," said Saxton. And then adding by way of explanation, "Ancient bones that have, over time, become stone by way of a natural process of molecular petrifaction."

Mirov and the holy man both looked unconvinced, but Rouletabille was fascinated.

"What sort of bones? Animal bones?" he inquired, but his question went unanswered.

"It's just a laboratory specimen, of no value to a thief," assured Saxton.

"Everywhere there is a place for God," said the holy man, enigmatically. "Even on this stone floor," and with that, he stooped down, removed a small piece of chalk from his pocket and drew a cross on the flagstones. "But where the Devil is, the cross cannot be marked."

The holy man reached up to the wood of the crate, pressed hard and attempted to draw the cross again. This time, no mark was made at all. Mirov's face registered surprise, but Saxton was merely appalled at this display of charlatanry and superstition.

"A puerile conjuror's trick," said Saxton. "Captain O'Hagan, would you get your men to put the crate onto the train as carefully as humanly possible?"

While the troopers strained with the box, O'Hagan took the opportunity to say a proper farewell to Rouletabille.

"It has certainly been a pleasure working with you, Joseph. I hope you don't mind if I look you up if I'm ever in Paris?"

"My friend, I will show you all of the sights," promised Rouletabille. "A man who has not seen Paris has not lived."

Rouletabille wrestled his wallet out of his pocket to check his travel warrant reservation, and then started to make his way along the express train, looking for his carriage. He glanced back down the platform and saw that Mirov's uniformed men were already carrying away the body of Grashinski the locksmith. It looked as if he would have to place the mystery of the blind thief into the 'unsolved' section of the filing cabinet in his study.

In the freight and baggage car of the Trans-Siberian Express, Dr. Wells was already inspecting the placement and integrity of his animal crates and the smaller cases of culture specimens. Everything seemed to be in order. At that moment, the troopers carried the large crate containing the ice creature up the ramp and into the car under Saxton's watchful eye.

Without warning, a deep roar reverberated through the train car. It came from nowhere and everywhere—permeating every iota of Saxton's being. He looked suspiciously at Wells' small live animal crates. But rats, hares and juvenile deer do not roar. He moved closer to the crate, but the sound had stopped.

Bidding Saxton farewell, O'Hagan led the troopers away, leaving Saxton to his puzzlement. The scientist unlocked and swung open a rectangular door at the top of the crate which revealed the ice creature's head. Wells was at the far end of the freight car, feigning a lack of curiosity. Saxton put his hand to the anthropoid's face. The thing was starting to thaw.

Wells approached as Saxton was re-locking the door in the crate.

"What are you going to astound the scientific world with this time, old boy?"

"You'll read about it in the Academy's annual report. It is a most unique and remarkable fossil," said Saxton.

"You're joking! It's not a fossil! You've got something alive in there. A moment ago, it was growling," said Wells.

"You're badly mistaken," said Saxton, condescendingly.

"Well, if it's a fossil, you won't need to feed it," Wells teased.

"The occupant has not eaten for roughly two million years," said Saxton.

"That's one way to economize on the household food bill, I suppose," grinned Wells.

Wells exited the freight car just as two more people entered and the train started to move. The first was Maletero, the baggage man; the other an unfettered vision of loveliness, the Countess Irina Petrovski, an extraordinarily beautiful noblewoman in her late twenties. In one arm, she clutched a small white poodle, and with her free hand, she gently held a long red velvet bag—the sort in which a lady might place her most treasured valuables.

"You have a safe place for valuables?" she asked the quietly whistling Maletero.

"Yes, Countess, I shall make you out a receipt," said the baggage man, hurrying off towards his corner desk.

The Countess commenced to walk past the ice creature's crate, at which moment her little dog started to whimper horribly.

"Excuse me," she asked Saxton, "something is making Alinka afraid. What do you have in that crate?"

"Nothing that would interest Alinka, Madame," said Saxton.

"Then perhaps it is *you...* but normally she likes Englishmen—all we Poles do" smiled the noblewoman rather charmingly. "Oh, yes—England, Queen Victoria, Sherlock Holmes, crumpets…"

"I admire Poland, Ma'am," said Saxon. "I believe that there is a bond between our countries."

"Yet, we Poles also have long memories—my husband the Count often mentions how your King Henry sided with the Lithuanians against King Jagaila of Poland in 1389."

"I hope that you and your husband will accept my profoundest apologies for that betrayal," said Saxton with grandiose sincerity. He had become totally entranced by her beauty.

Rouletabille had paused at the restaurant car only long enough to order soup and a sandwich, and then made his way along to his berth. The *strannik* had also been in the restaurant car ordering food, and the Frenchman was able to learn that his name was Father Pujardov, and, perhaps more surprisingly, that he was a passenger in a private first class coach allocated to Polish nobility.

At the moment Pujardov walked past Rouletabille, the express crossed a set of points at high speed and the holy man momentarily stumbled against him. The journalist could not resist satiating his curiosity regarding Pujardov's trick with the chalk, so he picked the pocket of his robe and relieved him of the item. Pujardov, oblivious, simply apologized and strode off to his coach.

Once he was out of sight, Rouletabille paused and examined the chalk. At first, it seemed perfectly ordinary, but then he saw that one end of the chalk had received a thick hard coat of white enamel paint. Pujardov was perhaps little more than a harmless charlatan. The trick had been a pre-rehearsed one, and the journalist could not help wondering in what other circumstances he had used it, as well as what else was in his repertoire.

Rouletabille slid open the door into his berth and found a blond man in his mid-thirties already settled in at the little table playing chess with himself.

"I hope you don't mind company, my friend," said the man. "This train has been overbooked and the conductor is doubling up everyone in what were supposed to be private berths."

"Not at all," said Rouletabille. "And I see that you play chess. What better way to pass the time as we journey through the Siberian wastes? I am Joseph Rouletabille."

"And I am Oleg Yevtushenko, an engineer," said the blond Russian. "Now will you play red or white?"

Back in the freight car, Wells pressed several turquoise Chinese bank notes into the hand of Maletero, the baggage man.

"If someone were to drill a little hole in this crate in the night and see what was inside, I'd be very grateful," said Wells.

The woman had no ticket and was therefore desperate to avoid the relentless advance of Conductor Konev up the train. She knew that the Express was completely full, but was desperate to find some hiding place. The door to Berth 8 was partially open and there was no luggage at all inside it. That meant the passengers must've missed the train, for everyone was in their respective carriages by now. Possibly if she hid in, or under, one of the bunk beds she would escape Konev's attention?

She stepped swiftly into the berth and shut the door behind her. Should she lock it? No. That would only arouse the conductor's attention. The berth had a small cupboard for luggage; she might be able to squeeze into that. But before she had a chance, the door was opened again. Through the portal stepped a gaunt, kindly faced man with smiling eyes.

"You must help me," she implored.

Wells shot her an admiring glance and did not allow himself to be distracted from storing his suitcase on the rack.

"My dear young lady, what could I possibly do to help you?" he asked.

"You see, I have no ticket," said the woman. And her eyes widened as if to emphasize her extreme helplessness; while as the same time, she arranged herself to show off the nubile form that lay beneath the tight blue silk of her Chinese-style suit. The transaction offered was most apparent: "Cover for me and I'm yours." Wells was instantly aroused at the thought of it. For the price of a sheaf of turquoise notes pressed into Konev's moist palm, he could be spending himself inside her all the way to Moscow.

Tears welled up in the woman's eyes. She was obviously just about to lose control. She pressed herself into his body for comfort.

"There, there…don't cry," said Wells.

The woman's scent was intoxicating. In another few seconds, he would have to start maneuvering her towards the lower bunk. He wondered idly if there was a do not disturb sign for the door.

"I had to get out of Harbin…there is a man there, an evil Chinese Doctor… I barely escaped with my life from his women's quarters," said the woman.

Suddenly, the door opened again and this time Saxton entered and immediately started securing his luggage on the rack.

"Sorry, dear fellow, you're in the wrong pew," said Wells, rather diplomatically. "You see: Berth 8," he continued, showing his ticket.

"I have a ticket for Berth 8 also—for the upper berth," Saxton confirmed, as he ascended into his allocated top bunk, after putting his case and hunting rifle in the luggage rack.

"This young lady is in trouble," explained Wells.

"Well, what would you like me to do about it?" asked Saxton. And then, realizing that it would be ungentlemanly to cast out a damsel in distress, he added, "I am sure we shall get along swimmingly."

He unfolded a French language copy of the *Harbin Times* from under his coat and started reading.

In the comparative warmth of the freight car, the thaw of the Ice Creature's body continued and its brain became more active with each minute passing.

Back on the platform, it had sensed the presence of the locksmith Grashinski and scanned his mind. It might not have bothered to absorb him, except for the ability to open locks, which was one which might prove essential before the night was out.

Experimentally, the Ice Creature moved its right shoulder. With the state of decomposition of the muscle tissue and the degraded nature of the nerves, this movement virtually amounted to an act of telekinesis. The Ice Creature slid its hand out of the small rectangular door in the crate and felt along the chains until it reached the steel bulk of the padlock. It extended the long brown decaying limb as far as it could out of the crate until it lighted on Maletero's work table. The hand, like some great hairless spider, explored the table, selecting and discarding potential tools with which to pick the padlock. The fingers found a steel nail. That might be of use. And then, with strength that Grashinski would never have been able to muster, the nail was bent in the center at a ninety degree angle to make it into a more effective lock-pick. Accessing the whole of Grashinski's experience, the Ice Creature started to work the lock. Almost immediately, the shank clicked open, and the chains fell away.

Maletero rushed from his corner desk towards the crate and looked into the rectangular aperture with alarm registering on his face. The set of fiery red eyes within it transfixed him. His brain seemed to boil, his eyes started to bleed profusely. Then his eyes turned milky white. He was dead. Eerily, the dead lips of the Ice Creature strained into a pucker. And the thing started to perform the tuneless ditty Maletero had been whistling earlier in the evening. Finally, it was free of the crate!

The effort of absorbing a psyche, the effort of killing, had put a considerable strain on its system. What if it were discovered now? What if it were cornered? It might be destroyed by the soldiers or the policemen on this train. It now devoted all of its remaining psionic power to regenerating its bodily functions. It had not waited with insane patience for two million years to have its life snuffed out now. It had to make it to a city. It needed not a train full of people, but millions of humans; only then would it be able to recreate its hive mind and extend its consciousness to the god-like proportions that were required. It flexed both its hands. It was starting to regain proper control of its body. The hominids had progressed well over the last two million years; yet, where might they be now if they'd had the benefit of guidance from the cosmic demiurge soul which dwelt inside the Ice Creature? They might already be traveling amongst the stars...

The Ice Creature placed Maletero's body inside the crate and re-chained it before finally snapping the padlock back in place. This would stall the humans for a while. They would simply waste time looking for the baggage handler. And all the time, the express train was moving relentless across the Siberian tundra, every second bringing Moscow nearer. The Ice Creature created a space at the back of the freight car, hunkered down and hid itself beneath canvas and old blankets and waited to regenerate.

Hours passed, and with its brain thawed and repairing itself, the thing experienced sleep—proper sleep—rather than just the suspension of it consciousness for the first time in epochs. Naturally, it dreamed of its ultimate return to the interstellar depths.

Eventually, the sound of raised voices caused the Ice Creature to awake. Using its telepathic powers, the being scanned the vicinity. The Siberian-Express Policeman, Inspector Mirov, was quizzing the two British passengers—Saxton and Wells—trying to ascertain the whereabouts of Maletero.

Wells admitted bribing Maletero to open the crate. Mirov demanded that the crate be opened, but Saxton impetuously threw the padlock key out of the freight car window, infuriating Mirov, who then placed the scientist under arrest. Then Konev, the conductor, was called upon to smash open the front of the crate with a fire axe.

Within moments, they had discovered Maletero's corpse within the crate. The Ice Creature was impressed with the humans' reasoning. Even though they were facing a being returning to life from suspended animation, something totally outside of their experience, they had drawn the correct inferences and conclusions from the information at hand. These modern-day hominids were promising. It must not underestimate them.

Mirov directed two armed Siberian Express guards to lock up Saxton.

"We'll search this train and find it—and destroy it," he said. "We mustn't alarm the other passengers."

Later the Ice Creature eased itself from its place of concealment, stretched its taut limbs, and walked out of the freight car into the train proper. It needed a strong and vital new body to transfer its consciousness into until such time as they reached a teeming metropolis. The ape-man that it currently inhabited had served his purpose. What he needed now was to be able to blend in. He briefly considered transferring its consciousness into a sleeping child, but how much better would it be to become a figure of authority in this new world. Almost without warning, the armed guard was right next to it in the corridor and was already starting to un-shoulder his rifle. The Ice Creature's eyes burned again. The guard fell. Blank eyes staring, and blood flowing from his eyes, nose and mouth.

Yevtushenko and Rouletabille had decamped to the restaurant car, not so much because they were hungry, but because they wanted to drink some champagne. And they were not the only ones. A gaunt-faced Englishman and a Russian beauty in a blue silk suit were also quaffing champagne. Somehow, Yevtushenko and Rouletabille had got onto the subject of religion—something the journalist normally avoided. And he had made the somewhat unsettling discovery that the Russian engineer was an atheist.

"Why so surprised my friend?" asked Yevtushenko. "In another hundred years, religion will be all but dead. Faith will be replaced by science. No proper scientific theory requires the involvement of God. There is no room for God in Newton's work on gravity. Likewise, there is no need to involve God in our thoughts and theories about how life arose on Earth. The answers lie in Darwin's writings, not a Bronze Age book of fables."

"But when you look at the beauty of the world and the goodness that man is capable of, how can you doubt the existence of the Almighty?" asked Rouletabille.

"When I look at the world, I see a desperate and savage battle for survival by all the creatures within it. And when I read the Bible, I see the handiwork of primitive men, the beginnings of a basic moral framework. Why, the Ten Commandments themselves don't forbid the keeping of slaves, or even the act of rape. Moreover, it is a random collection of contradictory writings with no insight into the true nature of the universe. Not one. If it just contained one or two revelatory facts... I don't know... that the sun is really a star, or that the earth rotates around it, then I would be more hesitant perhaps. But as it is, I can see that it is a book of ignorance rather than wisdom," said Yevtushenko.

"The theory of evolution seems to me immoral," observed Rouletabille.

"Yet it is a fact. And there is no morality in a fact," said Yevtushenko.

Somewhat dumbfounded, and with his head slightly aching, Rouletabille glugged the contents of his champagne goblet.

At that moment, Inspector Mirov strode rather anxiously into the restaurant car and went up to the gaunt Englishman. A brief conversation ensued during which Mirov ascertained for certain that the Englishman, whom he called Wells, was a doctor. Dr. Wells was not enthusiastic about leaving his meal of boiled salmon, but ultimately he did so. To Rouletabille, this could mean only one thing, a crime—most likely, a murder—had happened aboard the train. The hairs on the nape of his neck stood on end. While his main interest was always to serve justice, it occurred to him that enormous kudos might be gained from being the first amateur detective to solve a murder on a moving express train before it arrived at its destination.

Wells knocked and then slid open the door to Berth Six.

"Miss Jones, I shall need your assistance with an autopsy," he instructed.

A storage car was partially cleared and the dead baggage man, Maletero, and the dead guard were laid out side by side. Miss Jones held the swinging electric light still while Wells sawed open Maletero's cranium with Mirov looking on. As had happened with Grashinski on the platform, Miss Jones had to be assured that Maletero was not a blind man—the white eyes struck her as possibly some kind of genetic abnormality. Wells levered off the top of the skull and Miss Jones gasped.

"Smooth as a baby's bottom. Not a single brain convolution. He has lissencephaly," said Miss Jones.

"Yet, I saw this man earlier today and his mental functions were perfectly normal," said Wells. "Which is quite impossible if he'd been born with this disease, plus he'd have been unlikely to have lived past the age of two. No, something did this to him—today. And if Saxton's living ape-man fossil is really responsible, then it is capable of attacking people and severely damaging their brains. I'm not sure how. I suppose a virus isn't out of the question, but shouldn't we all have been affected?"

Wells closed his eyes momentarily and visualized the scene in the baggage car.

"After it killed Maletero, it locked him in the crate using the chains and padlock. How would an ape-man know how to do that? And before that, it escaped from the crate. But even Maletero didn't have the key. How did it get out?" asked Wells.

Mirov considered the problem fast and was horrified by his own deduction.

"It had the skills of the first man it killed—Grashinski, the thief—the locksmith!" he whispered.

"My God," began Miss Jones. "It's capable of leeching thoughts and memories from within the human brain—if it gets closer enough."

The Ice Creature clung with all its strength to the roof of the train. The humans had not yet thought to check the outside. Perhaps they were not quite so advanced as it had first thought. But after a couple of hours, the thing regretted its decision to climb out of the train. It was starting to refreeze. Its limbs becoming stiff, it was getting more difficult to think. It had to get back inside. And carefully, very carefully... If it fell into a chasm, or landed in a bank of snow, it might be frozen for millennia again. The thought horrified it. It had to make it to where there were more people. The hive mind must be restored.

With Saxton now arrested and held under guard in a different berth, Wells wasted no time attempting to seduce the ticketless woman who called herself Natasha. A more willing seductee, he could not have wished for. As soon as she saw him move in for the first kiss, her hand went to the belt of her blue silk pants. A moment later, she sloughed them down to her ankles and stepped out of them. Wells tugged open her jacket. She wore nothing beneath it. As they kissed, he rubbed her left nipple hard between thumb and forefinger, erecting it. She broke away from him, turning her back to her eager lover as she braced herself between the side of the bunk and wall against the movement of the train. Her gorgeous smooth behind was being proffered to him. She was ready to be taken.

Afterwards, she dressed swiftly and excused herself to the bathroom along the corridor. She performed her ablutions perfunctorily and then headed for the freight and baggage car. Wasting not a second, she removed from her pocket a notebook and set to work opening Maletero's safe where the valuables were kept. Inside was the small velvet bag the Countess had asked the baggage handler to lock away securely back at Harbin Station. She grabbed it, closed the safe and got ready to leave.

The cold dark hands of the Ice Creature grabbed her arms, restraining her with immense strength. The thing's eyes glowed like cherry-hot metal in a blacksmith's forge as it leaned in to consume her mind. The Ice Creature commenced to drain her memories… first the mundanity of her mission for the *Devil Doctor* to steal from the safe, then the overwhelming intensity of her orgasm with Wells just minutes ago...

For the first time since its release from the caves, it paused in its desire to attack. It remembered its own last coupling with a female some two million years ago. Mounting the coarse-haired ape woman from behind and thrusting deep into her. Ejaculating explosively, then finding that her vaginal muscles had clamped down and locked them together. They had been cleaved together as one until the sun rose. It would have to tear the human apart to get her off if that happened now.

The Ice Creature pulled open the woman's jacket and took Natasha's left nipple between clawed thumb and finger and rubbed it hard in imitation of the memory it had devoured. Despite terror and partial brain damage, it erected. The Ice Creature was aroused too. It was secretly pleased that its generative organs still functioned. The claws ripped away the silk and then forced her thighs apart. There would be time to filch the rest of her memories after coition. It turned her to face the wall...

"Natasha? Natasha, are you there?" asked Wells as he entered the semi-darkness of the freight car. The horror of what he saw then would stay with him always. The Ice Creature had pinioned the girl to side of the carriage and was violating her in the most appalling way imaginable, grunting repetitively as it did so. She was close to death.

Wells turned to flee, but the ape man took hold of his arm with phenomenal strength, and it felt like it was going to be torn out at the socket. Wells felt the thing's baleful red eyes turn upon him.

Suddenly, a shot rang out. The bullet struck the creature, and it released Wells from its grasp. The Doctor ran out into the corridor, past Inspector Mirov, who stood there, clutching his smoking automatic.

The Ice Creature continued to advance. Mirov fired again, this time aiming for the anthropoid's brain—and hitting one of its eyes.

The thing's mind was thrown into turmoil by this attack. All of the regeneration of the Ice Creature's body was being undone by the impact of the bullets. With a supreme effort, the thing's consciousness started to abandon the body that had served it so well for so long. Scintillas of thought flowed from it and out towards the only available vessel within range: Mirov.

Almost immediately, the consciousness detected the weakness of this body, as compared to that of the ape-man. Huge amounts of genetic material would need to be rewritten to make this form more robust. It started with the arm. The cells divided and divided; a swiftly commenced metamorphosis, and easier that it had expected—the modern hominids and the Ice Creature were, after all, very closely related.

Just seconds after the transference of consciousness had been completed, the skull of the Ice Creature exploded in a welter of blood and whitish matter.

Rouletabille lowered his revolver, and stepped forward to feel for a pulse on the girl's throat. There was nothing.

"Are you all right, my friend?" he asked Mirov.

Mirov simply nodded, and thrust his disproportionately large claw-like hand into his jacket pocket before the Frenchman could see it. The Inspector replaced the automatic in his shoulder holster and then picked up the velvet bag with his human hand. He could feel a heavy rectangle of metal within the bag. This was something important.

"You," he almost growled, unaccustomed as he was to using human vocal cords, "are the French journalist. This… is something important. The dead girl was trying to steal it. Come along, let us take it to Count Petrovski. Help me, I am feeling weak."

Rouletabille assisted the Russian policeman along the train to the luxurious carriage where the Count, Countess, and their personal *strannik*, Pujardov, had their quarters.

Count Petrovski weighed the metal in his hand.

"Steel—harder than diamond. That's why thieves and spies are after it. The French, the Germans, the English—even a Chinese criminal organization. But they are wasting their time. What matters is the formula, and that is up here." He pointed to his temple.

"What happened to the girl—the spy?" asked the Countess.

"The creature… the fossil, or whatever it was, killed her. It was quite horrible," said Rouletabille.

"But there is no more danger. Between us, the young Frenchman and I killed the monster," said Mirov.

"You think evil can be killed with bullets? Satan lives," smiled Pujardov. "The unholy one is still among us."

With the creature dead and the danger over, Saxton was released from custody and co-opted into assisting in an autopsy on the anthropoid.

Saxton jabbed a scalpel into the left orbit of what was left of the creature's skull and popped out the eyeball.

"What are you hoping to find within its eye?" asked Miss Jones.

"Perhaps the means by which it attacked and absorbed memories and abilities as per Mirov's theory," replied Saxton.

"Yes, its eyes were glowing when it attacked Natasha," said Wells.

Saxton swiftly removed part of the aqueous matter from within the eyeball with a syringe, squirted it into the petri dish, and then viewed the result through Wells' miniature brass microscope.

"I recall that a similar experiment was done with the last of Jack the Ripper's victims—to see if the eye had recorded the image of the killer. But it was not successful. Here however… look for yourselves…" said Saxton.

"Good Lord," said Wells. "I can see Mirov and the young Frenchman. But the image is flickering, changing, now great fields of ice… other ape-men and prehistoric creatures— like something out of the Pliocene. Now, some sort of map of the world. No, wait… it's an image of the Earth from space. The whole of the thing's memory is recorded on the fluid in its eye."

"And perhaps not just its memory," broke in Miss Jones. "Perhaps the last surviving vestiges of its consciousness. We must be careful."

"The consciousness within the creature was undoubtedly alien. It obviously journeyed here through the trackless depths of the interstellar void countless millions of years ago," said Saxton.

The door to the carriage slid open and Pujardov entered.

"What are you doing?" he asked.

"You may find this interesting, holy man," said Saxton. "Through the microscope, you can see a view of the Earth from the heavens."

Pujardov looked through the microscope's eyepiece and was amazed.

"Where does this picture come from?"

"From inside the creature's eye," said Saxton, pointing to where the eye lay abandoned on the table.

"It is as in the holy writ. Before the Fall, Lucifer was in Heaven, looking down upon the Earth. It is the Eye of Satan! It must be destroyed!"

And with that, Pujardov grabbed the eye and ran from the carriage, frantically chanting prayers as he went.

"Is he quite mad?" asked Saxton.

"I'll go talk to him," said Miss Jones, "and see if I can get that eye back."

Miss Jones headed for the baggage car, which seemed to her an obvious place for the *strannik* to hide.

Mirov spotted her and was curious as to what she was doing. He followed her into what had once been Maletero's domain.

"What are you looking for, Miss Jones?" asked Mirov.

"Not what—who. Father Pujardov ran off with the anthropoid's remaining eye. He thinks it's the eye of Lucifer or something. There's a thousand rubles in it for you if you help me get it back," said the female scientist.

"A thousand rubles for an eye?" queried Mirov.

"There's something in it... Pictures, images of long ago and of the Earth from space."

"Who else has seen such pictures?" asked Mirov.

"Just Dr. Wells and Professor Saxton," replied Miss Jones.

Mirov pulled down the blind on the baggage car's only window. Even in the semi-darkness, Miss Jones could see that the hand Mirov used was not human.

It was to be the last thing she saw, apart from Mirov's glowing red eyes.

Miss Jones' corpse crumpled to the floor—her eyes boiled white by the process of the removal of her memories and knowledge. Blood flowed freely from every visible orifice. Standing over her, Mirov became aware of someone kneeling next to him in the darkness. It was Pujardov, offering to him the anthropoid's eye on a white handkerchief.

"Have pity… have pity," begged Pujardov. "Are you going to kill me?"

"Fool," condemned Mirov, "there is no knowledge in your head worth having—just paltry fables and parables which impede rational thought. You would be a pollutant in the hive mind."

Mirov took the handkerchief-wrapped eye from Pujardov and threw it into Maletero's stove. He left the holy man kneeling there and went to find Wells and Saxton to tell them of the death of Miss Jones.

Moving through the restaurant car, Mirov found that the passengers were in a panic. There had been too much death on the train, and many were demanding that the train be stopped so they could get off. Notwithstanding that they would freeze to death, or if they survived the cold, be at the mercy of wolves and bandits. They had to reach Moscow. Mirov needed hundreds of thousands of people at least to form the hive mind properly, to create the beacon that would bring his own kind back to collect him. So he did the only thing he could and threatened shoot anyone who spoke of leaving the train.

Rouletabille re-entered his berth.

"What's all the fuss out there?" asked Yevtushenko.

"Passengers wanting to stop the train. There's some talk of another death caused by the Ice Creature. Though I can't see how. I shot it through the head. Anyway, the police inspector seems to have it well in hand," said Rouletabille. "Hmmm. This is a mystery that needs solving. I'm going to see if I can find the two Englishmen."

The journalist paused only to light his pipe and then was gone. Yevtushenko went back to playing himself at chess. Red was moving in for the kill on the opposing king.

Rouletabille found Saxton and Wells in a booth at the far end of the restaurant car.

"Gentlemen, *has* there been another death?" asked the Frenchman, sitting down with them

"Yes, my assistant, Miss Jones," replied Wells, ashen-faced.

"Is the creature responsible? Is it alive or dead?" pressed the journalist. "Do you have any idea?"

"I don't," admitted Saxton. "But I've wired ahead for the express to be stopped at the next station."

Suddenly Mirov was looming over them.

"You had no authority to stop the train!" screeched Mirov, almost hysterically. Then he rushed on down the carriage and out of sight.

It occurred to Mirov that he might be able to counter-mand the instruction for the train to be stopped if he got to the telegraph room quickly enough. As he neared the door, he saw that Pujardov was loitering in front of it, then he started to feel the train decelerate. It was approaching the station. It was all too late. The sudden transference of consciousness into Mirov had been too traumatic. He was still nowhere near ready to create the hive mind, even in an embryonic form. He had now to seem as inconspicuous as possible to those who arrived on the train. If they discovered that he was responsible for the deaths, he would undoubtedly be executed and his conscious-ness would be snuffed out forever.

"Tell me who you are. Tell me, and I will serve you," pleaded Pujardov

"I am the Devil," said Mirov. "And you are my acolyte. I have come to reclaim this world and enslave everyone on it. They will all become part of me." It was only a partial lie, tailored to the holy man's pre-existing beliefs.

"I knew it. I knew it," said Pujardov to himself.

If the Devil had come to take over the Earth, he would have to ally himself with the Dark One, at least for the time being, simply in order to survive. If it looked as if God was going to win, he would switch sides. Better yet, perhaps he could engineer the redemption of Lucifer. The Devil had been an archangel once, and perhaps he would be again. If he could turn the Devil back to righteousness, his own place at the right hand of God was assured.

Rouletabille, Saxton and Wells continued to ponder how the Ice Creature could have killed Miss Jones after it had been shot through the head.

"The best we can surmise is that, millions of years ago, something, some form of intelligence, came to Earth from another planet, perhaps another galaxy. It entered the body and brain of an Earth creature—the ape-man—in order to survive," explained Saxton.

"And this thing from another world survived in the fossil and came alive again?" asked the Frenchman.

"Exactly," confirmed Wells.

"Then it seems to me that the animal I killed was only the host. The alien intelligence transferred somehow to another host. It's inside someone... somewhere on this train," deduced Rouletabille.

"You're a damned clever detective for a journalist," said Wells. "But the difficult part will be discovering who is now the host."

"That's our next step," said Saxton.

"But what if one of you two is the monster?" asked Rouletabille.

"Monster? We're British, you know," reassured Wells.

Awaiting the arrival of whoever in authority was going to board the now-stationary train, Mirov had taken refuge in Yevtushenko's berth. The engineer had welcomed the visitation, and the two were engaged in a game of chess. To his surprise, Mirov found he was winning.

"You know how to measure Earth's gravity?" asked Mirov, conversationally. "I mean, what I want to know is: can gravity be overcome?"

"If you mean, can man get beyond the gravitational field of the Earth into space—not yet, but one day soon," replied Yevtushenko. "There is a mathematics professor called

Tsiolkovsky; he has ideas about rockets, machines that can fly free of Earth's gravity."

"You know him?" asked Mirov, intrigued.

If instead of creating a hive mind beacon, he could build a vehicle, perhaps marshalling hundreds of thousands or even millions of people under his control in the attempt, as well as all the industrial resources of this planet, he could get back to his own kind even sooner.

"Know him? He is like a father to me. But tell me, why is a man such as yourself..." before the engineer could finish, Mirov was reaching to pull the blind on the door into the berth and turn down the lights.

"This is just supposition, but from everything you have told me, the eyes are always the key. The creature's memories were recorded in its eyes... the eyes of the victims go white... just like the ones of the boiled salmon they serve in the restaurant car," said Rouletabille.

"Hmmm. I noticed that too," said Wells. "It's the only thing we have to go on. Let's check the eyes of all of the passengers. I have a magnifying glass somewhere in my case."

Saxton looked out on the snow-covered station platform. There were a handful of Cossack soldiers covering all the doors of the train with their rifles.

"What are they waiting for? We've been here for ages," said Saxton.

"They're probably waiting for the arrival of the local garrison commander. He won't be based here, but some distance away," surmised Rouletabille.

"Let's get on with this quickly. Can you imagine what a Cossack officer is going to make of a quest to find a creature from outer space by looking in people's eyes? He'll think we're all certifiable," said Wells.

Methodically the three of them worked their way through the train with a bogus story of checking for a highly contagious, but easily treatable, eye infection. There was nothing unusual about anyone's eyes. But the journalist was concerned that two people could not be found: Yevtushenko and Mirov.

Then, suddenly, about twenty Cossack soldiers boarded the train. They searched Rouletabille and confiscated his revolver, before forcing people out of their berths and herding them towards the restaurant car, where the immense swaggering figure of a Cossack captain waited in his braided coat, cutlass at his side and a cheroot between his lips.

Count Petrovski and the Countess were also manhandled at gunpoint. The Count presented himself immediately to the Cossack commander.

"I am Count Marion Petrovski, and this is the Countess Irina."

"I am Captain Kazan of the Imperial Siberian Regiment. Please return to your carriage, Excellency. You are, of course, exempt from my investigations. Two of my men will escort you."

As the two Polish nobles left, Mirov was ushered into the restaurant carriage by a soldier.

Two things occurred to Rouletabille: firstly, the Express had moved off and was accelerating powerfully. It seemed to be moving faster than on any previous stretch of the journey. The other thing was that practically everyone on board was now together in the restaurant car. The journalist leaned in close to Saxton to whisper in his ear:

"What if the host's eyes look different in darkness? We are all here, pretty much. I can test the theory instantly. I'm going to back away for the light switch... after that, I'm heading for the engine. Monster or not, my every instinct tells me this train is running out of control."

Saxton merely nodded.

Bizarrely, Captain Kazan seemed to be trying to interrogate the passengers en masse, as if the solution to the mystery might somehow present itself.

"Who are the killers?" began Kazan. "Who are the troublemakers? Who are the foreign influences?"

Mirov relaxed. This fool was not going to be able to expose him. All he had to do was remain quiet. Mirov was perhaps looking too pleased with himself since suddenly he seemed to have the Cossack captain's full attention.

"And who are you? The police inspector?" asked Kazan.

"Yes, Captain. Mirov is my name."

"Mirov, Mirov... A good Russian name. How excellent to have a reliable man at my side."

At that moment, Rouletabille reached the far end of the restaurant car. He placed his hand against all four light switches and flicked them off. The journalist didn't wait to see the result of the experiment. Wells and Saxton would have to be able handle the host. The Express was now going so fast he feared it would derail at any minute. Slipping between two Cossack soldiers in the darkness, he disappeared out into the corridor.

In the restaurant car, Mirov's eyes glowed demonically in the darkness. He was caught. The game was over.

Kazan was aghast. Everyone in the carriage could feel the palpable waves of malevolence emanating from the thing which inhabited Mirov's body. Every human mind present had some semblance of precognition of what the creature wanted to do to the human population—the hive mind, the enslavement, the construction of the vehicle to escape gravity, and more particularly, satiation of the carnal lusts it had developed while in corporeal form. The visions of what the creature had in mind caused a good portion of the women to faint and the men to vomit at the thought of the mass degradation and orgiastic depravity.

From somewhere, Pujardov cried, "Beware the wrath of Satan!"

Shots rang out from rifles and Kazan's automatic pistol. Terror reigned.

With the way to the engine car blocked by Cossack soldiers, Rouletabille opted to climb out of his berth's window and onto the roof of the train. He might've been surprised to learn that this was one of the creature's favorite methods of moving about the Express.

He crawled on his belly along the snow-crusted metal of the carriage top with the train juddering beneath him. Within seconds his fingers were numb. If he survived, he was going to have severe frostbite. After what seemed an age, but could've been no more than four minutes, he reached the end of the carriage. It was the penultimate carriage before the engine car. In less extreme conditions, and had he felt rather more swash-buckling, he might've jumped the gap between the two in heroic fashion. Instead, he descended the steel ladder carefully. Twice the skin of his palms stuck to the frozen metal of the rungs, and he had to wrench his hands off painfully.

Finally, he ascended the ladder of the last carriage, then wormed his way along towards the wood tender. He dropped down as quietly as he could into the heap of split logs. In the engine car, he could see the engine driver and stoker lying dead—their eyes blank and rimed with blood.

Yevtushenko was controlling the train, moving like a man possessed, stoking the fiery boiler and checking the controls. Instantly, he seemed to sense the Frenchman's presence. He turned. And even with the wildfire light of the boiler, Rouletabille could see that the Russian engineer's eyes were glowing like branding irons.

"Rouletabille! There is a brain worth feeding on. Your ability to solve problems... your deductive skills... you will be an essential component of the hive mind. Come and be one with me..." shouted the creature within Yevtushenko.

"I thought you'd be inside Mirov! He was alone with you just before I killed the ape-man."

"I can be in more than one place, human. I can be *two* people. I can be everyone. As you will see, my friend."

Rouletabille jumped down from the tender car and attacked the thing.

Ten minutes ago now, the dying Mirov, shot multiple times by the Cossacks, had crawled away into the baggage car and found himself reunited with Pujardov. Saxton and Wells, crouched by the door, had heard the chilling words from Pujardov:

"Come into me, Satan! Thy will be done on Earth as it is in Hell!"

And then they heard no more.

"Rouletabille, was onto something when he made the link between the creature's eyes and darkness. I think it can only use its power to drain minds in darkness. Every single attack it had made has been in darkened conditions," said Saxton. "I'm going back to the berth to get my limelight and hunting rifle."

Yevtushenko cracked his head hard against the boiler hatch door, knocked off his feet by the journalist's sudden onslaught. Rouletabille recovered the shovel from the deck and smashed the engineer across the face with it. He was fighting for his existence, his very soul, as well as for the souls of every human being on Earth. He tossed the shovel to one side. The creature was stunned, if only momentarily.

An idea formed in the Frenchman's mind. In other circumstances, it would have been horrible, and yet here, he had no choice. Lifting up Yevtushenko with both hands at his collar, he started to shove the engineer's head into the furnace-like interior of the boiler.

The creature began to recover itself. Its eyes tried to glow brighter. Rouletabille could feel the alien being raking the surface of his mind. He could feel his tear ducts starting to hemorrhage...

And then it was over. Yevtushenko's hair caught fire. His eyes were scorched by the flames from the boiler. The burned and blackened eyes sealed the creature's malign consciousness in the dying body. This part of the thing had been defeated.

Captain Kazan addressed Saxton as he returned to the restaurant car with the limelight and his rifle.

"We are just soldiers… How can we be expected to kill the Devil?" asked Kazan.

"It isn't the Devil, just a kind of living contagion. We must stop it from reaching a population center or it will over-run the Earth. Yet, perhaps I can reason with it. It is a rational creature. Give me five minutes then send your men in to rush it," said Saxton.

In the darkness of the baggage car, Pujardov stood stock still, his eyes crimson coals. Saxton swung the funnel-like beam of the limelight onto him, keeping him covered with the rifle in a single-handed grip.

"Who are you?" demanded Saxton.

"In words, it's difficult," said the thing within Pujardov. "I am a form of energy occupying this shell. I came with others like myself. I was left behind. An accident. I survived in protozoans, fish, vertebrates. The history of this planet is part of me. Pull the trigger and you will end it."

"Then what am I to do with you?"

"Let me go. I can teach you how to end disease, pain, poverty…"

"I wish I could trust you," said Saxton.

But the creature was already reaching for the limelight, and then smashing it to the floor.

Kazan's strong hands grabbed Saxton and pulled him away from Pujardov and out of the baggage car. Kazan drew his saber and charged Pujardov, simultaneously discharging his automatic.

"Attack it!" shouted Kazan, and his men unhesitatingly piled in behind him with bayonets fixed to their rifles.

"No, don't confront it in darkness!" begged Saxton.

Rouletabille had discovered that all of the locomotive's controls had been deliberately jammed by Yevtushenko. He could find no way to apply the brakes or slow the train down. The boiler was banked up with fuel, so he decided to uncouple the engine from the rest of the train. The journalist watched from the caboose of the passenger car as the driverless loco shot forward like a rifle bullet. Then he ran to the telegraph room since Russian trains always have a map of the route there. Tapping the Morse key, he requested that the points be changed about two miles ahead. He calculated that the train's momentum would take it at least that far, and it would come to rest in the small rail yard of a salt mine.

Meanwhile, Saxton and Wells were barricading the door of the baggage car while the rest of the passengers milled around in a state of near hysteria. Pujardov was killing the Cossacks. They could hear everything. There were shouted profanities, whispered prayers, and finally Kazan begging for his long-dead mother to rescue him with a quality in his voice that is reserved for the doomed and the damned.

Rouletabille rushed to the assistance of the Englishmen. He looked past the barricade and through the little window into the baggage car, he could see an army of red eyes. All of the Cossacks were under the creature's control. In a few moments, they would be seeking to break out. There was only one course of action. He partially depressed the baggage car's emergency locking brake. At this speed, the brake shoes would be worn away in a few seconds, but it would slow the car down. Then he disconnected the baggage car from the restaurant car. The car dropped back.

They crossed the points into the salt mine freight yard. Rouletabille leaned out to see if they were about to strike the buffers at the end of the line. What he saw struck him with horror... He had potentially brought them all to their deaths. The train line was heading straight over the edge of a crevasse into a salt pit.

"Everyone! Jump for your lives!" shouted the Frenchman.

By the time it reached the edge of the abyss, the train was going only a little more than a moderate running pace, and all the passengers made it off safely. Pujardov succeeded in smashing through the barricade at almost the exact moment the baggage car sailed into empty space, before impacting on the great blocks of rock salt below.

A little later, Saxton, Wells and Rouletabille stood on the lip of the salt pit.

"There's another one," said Wells.

Saxton shot at the broken bodied Cossack who was crawling through the salt and snow. Even at this distance, they could see his blazing eyes.

Rouletabille put his hand in his jacket pocket. For a moment, he thought he had lost it in the jump from the train, but no, the ingot of super-hard steel was still there. At least, his mission for the French government had been a success.

Most of the passengers were warming themselves by the fires in the miners' quarters, but the Countess Petrovski was wandering around the rail yard.

"Alinka! Alinka!" she called plaintively.

Hiding crouched beneath a salt truck, some distance away, the little dog ignored her mistress. Alinka did not want the Countess to see her eyes.

Rouletabille at the Old Bailey

London, 1909

Standing on the pavement opposite, Rouletabille looked up at the grand palace of Judgment that is the Central Criminal Court to see Lady Justice herself appeared to be looking back down at him beneficently from atop her dome. He checked his pocket. Yes, he had his notebook, a couple of pencils and the credentials which identified him as a representative of the French press. This would be his first time covering a case at the Old Bailey, and he felt a frisson of unaccustomed excitement. British justice was swift, and the entire murder case might not take more than a couple of days. And if an appeal was not lodged in a timely way, and there was no intervention from the Home Secretary, then execution by hanging was likely to follow equally swiftly.

The reporter crossed the street and saw for the first time the words engraved on the front of the building's portico: *PROTECT THE CHILDREN OF THE POOR AND PUNISH THE WRONGDOER.* A fine motto, and, to some extent, the very words he lived by. He joined the throng of people seeking admittance to the court building. Once inside, the black uniformed guardians separated journalists and witnesses from the general public. The public were ushered up a staircase towards the public gallery access corridor. Rouletabille and a handful of others—after the most perfunctory of security checks—were directed up a wide, green-flecked marble stairway up towards Court 4. Everything about this place seemed fresh and new, for although it had been built in a splendid and ancient architectural style, the building was actually less than two years old. Like some other courts he had been in, it seemed to combine the hustle and bustle of a railway station with the calm of a cathedral.

Rouletabille strode almost up to the door of Court 4 in order to examine the list sheet tacked to the courtroom notice board, on it; it simply said *Regina Versus Schellenberger - 10:30 a.m.* He removed the pocket watch from his vest to check the time. It was just before ten. There was time to repair to the cafeteria to get a drink, and since he found English tea to be virtually undrinkable, he hoped they served good coffee. The reporter located the cafeteria, got served at the counter, and then grabbed one of the small booths where he lit his pipe and sipped at the sweet strong coffee. Several of the booths and tables were occupied by barristers, unmistakable and re-splendent in their powdered white wigs and long black robes, their garb unchanged since the 18th century. Each barrister had a bundle of papers tied with a blue or red ribbon—this was their *brief*—all the information they needed to defend or prosecute a case; officially, their job was to be "Master of their Brief," totally conversant with all of the facts and argu-ments involved in the matter to be tried. Some of the barristers also had with them huge red-bound volumes of *Archbold,* the criminal barristers' bible of evidence and pleading practice, and just as a devout man might be able to quote a large num-ber of passages from the Bible, so too a senior barrister, or *King's Counsel,* would have committed to memory great swathes of *Archbold.*

Sticking out like a sore thumb in the cafeteria was a boy of about twenty, dressed in a long grey raincoat and sporting a wide-brimmed felt hat. The boy removed from his pocket a meerschaum pipe and chuffed on it studiously. He looked a little nervous, and Rouletabille wondered if he was a witness in a forthcoming trial. He was unlikely to be a defendant since only the most serious criminals were tried at the Old Bailey, and most were not bailed.

The Frenchman had been sent to London to report on the trial of the infamous Gustav Schellenberger, a German immi-grant who had murdered his French wife, Antoinette, and also two other people in what had become known as *The Pigeon Loft Murders.* These crimes had taken place in Bethnal Green in the heart of London's East End, a mere stone's throw from Whitechapel where Jack the Ripper had once plied his deadly trade all those years before. Bethnal Green was an area of great deprivation; there, crimes were commonplace and life was cheap. Yet, the people who dwelt in that cultural melting pot had a marvelous resilience, a determination to survive coupled with a desire to assist their friends and neighbors in doing the same. It meant people there had a community spirit, and a sense of collective identity to rival any urban citizenry anywhere in the world.

It was almost half past ten now, so Rouletabille drained his coffee cup and headed back towards Court 4. As he walked out of the cafeteria, he was aware the boy with the meer-schaum pipe had gotten up to follow him. His instincts told him this young fellow was a witness in the Schellenberger case; whether that was correct, only time would tell. As the reporter approached, the usher unlocked the door to the court-room and the interested parties commenced to flow in. There were four barristers, their accompanying solicitors, and a handful of policemen: three uniformed constables and a cou-ple of plainclothes Scotland Yard men. Fellow journalists, all from London's Fleet Street newspapers, numbered about half a dozen; these were easily identifiable in their trademark loud checked suits. Just a handful of witnesses had been warned to attend on this first day of the trial; among them was a tearful and plump middle-aged woman, a man of about sixty who looked to be unaccustomed to wearing a suit, and a girl of about twenty. They all waited on a hard, wooden bench direct-ly outside the courtroom.

Once inside, Rouletabille attached himself to the phalanx of Fleet Street journalists and followed them into the press box. The reporter drank in every aspect of the windowless courtroom. Dominating the chamber was the Royal coat of arms—the lion and unicorn device—gilt and almost two me-ters across; it hung from the wall directly behind the judge's red leather chair. Just in front and to the right of the judge's raised dais was the witness box. Then there were the barristers' benches. The senior barristers were already setting up the little portable lecterns they were entitled to use due to their status as *King's Counsel*. Rouletabille struck up a conversation with Ben Bates of the *London Star*, something of an "Old Bailey Hack."

"That's Sir Wilfrid Robarts, KC, the prosecution leader," said Bates. "He's scarcely lost a case for years. And behind him is his junior, Mr. T. C. Rowley, a bright and shining young star in the legal firmament. Both of them are from the elite and somewhat legendary *Eleven Queen's Bench Walk* chambers. Now, over there we have the Defense: Mr. Edward Leithen, KC, Tory MP, and Mr. Impey Biggs. You'd never know it in here, but all four barristers are actually good friends; they can be seen frequenting the wine bars together and drinking claret. But, in here, they give no quarter and take no prisoners."

From this point, the day moved forward briskly. All rose and bowed to the judge, Mr. Justice Wargrave, upon his arrival. And then the jury was sworn in. Distracted by these formalities, Rouletabille had initially not even noticed the arrival of the defendant, Schellenberger—brought up from the cells far beneath the Old Bailey and up into the dock by bailiffs who now flanked him on either side. The reporter shot a few surreptitious glances at the big German. He was pleased to see he was heavily manacled, rather like a modern day Jacob Marley. Schellenberger was about forty and had a shaven head and a drooping walrus moustache. He was huge, bear-like and savage. There did not seem to be any question that he looked very much like a man capable of eviscerating his wife and cutting up her body in a rooftop pigeon loft.

Moments later, Mr. Justice Wargrave asked Schellenberger to stand, and then the clerk of the court read out the charges on the indictment—three charges of murder. Following this, the German was invited to make his plea.

Schellenberger's deep, guttural voice boomed across the courtroom:

"I plead not guilty by reason of insanity."

A murmur rippled across the chamber like the buzzing of bees. Judge Wargrave barked a demand for silence without ever looking like he was going to reach for his oak wood gavel. Then, he addressed the Defense leader.

"Mr. Leithen, will you be calling expert testimony to establish your client's insanity?"

"Yes, M'lud. In due course, you will be hearing from Dr. Rupert Grierson, the Director of Leytonstone House Insane Asylum. Dr. Grierson is a fully qualified independent forensic psychologist," answered Leithen.

"Very well. We will now proceed to hear opening statements. Sir Wilfrid, please commence."

Sir Wilfrid stood up and fixed the jury with his icy blue eyes.

"Members of the jury, you have just heard Gustav Schellenberger plead not guilty to the murder of his wife, Antoinette, Reginald Scott his employer and his acquaintance, Edward Cookson by reason of insanity. The Crown's case is that Schellenberger is as sane as you or I. We will seek to prove his every action was coldly and fully reasoned out. He is cunning, cruel and evil—but he is not mad. The plea of insanity is a cynical ruse, attempted in order to elude the hangman's noose, and live out his life in the comparative comfort of a padded cell," said Sir Wilfrid, his calm and even voice resonating in every corner of the courtroom and up into the public gallery on the level above.

"The defendant, Schellenberger is a brutish and jealous man," he continued. "His motive in this appalling crime was simple. He feared his wife was going to leave him for Edward Cookson. Although he cared little for her, and is known to have struck her on two occasions, he was reliant upon her financially. She had a successful bookkeeping business with a large number of local clients, while he was only ever to gain casual work as a market trader, selling fruit and vegetables.

Even in this meager occupation, he was a failure. He had quarreled with Mr. Scott, the manager of a variety of stalls on Bethnal Green High Street, regarding his poor attendance—apparently he would rather sit drinking bottles of beer on Wanstead Flatlands than work—and then, the two men came to blows outside the *Salmon and Ball* Public House, where Schellenberger beat his employer to death in front of witnesses."

Sir Wilfrid paused for a second and consulted a typewritten list on the right hand side of his lectern.

"I call Mavis Blythe," said the prosecution leader.

With swift and practiced efficiency, the usher brought in the plump and tearful middle-aged woman Rouletabille had seen waiting on the bench earlier. Mrs. Blythe, landlady to the Schellenbergers, was led to the witness box and sworn in. The Judge could see the woman was fair shaking with nerves, and he did his best to put her at her ease and invited her to take her time and think hard before each of her answers. Further prompted by Sir Wilfrid, she began to give her *evidence in chief.*

"I had not seen Antoinette, Mrs. Schellenberger that is, for nearly three days when I decided to have a word with Mr. Schellenberger regarding 'er whereabouts. He could be something of a beast, so it was with some hesitance I went up the stairs of our building—Waterlow Buildings on Wilmot Street—to the roof. The roof is a flat one, and Mr. Schellenberger had constructed quite a large wooden loft to keep his pigeons in—these birds were his pride and joy. And caring for them was the only thing which seemed to even his temper. When I got up there, I saw he was making quite a noise...flattening old bits of metal by hitting them with a hammer. Lord knows why. Anyway, I asked him where his wife was and 'e says she's gone to Hammersmith to look after a sick cousin and won't be back for a week. Even as 'e said it, I didn't believe a word of it. Just as I was going, I looked back at the pigeon loft, and against the white painted wood inside it, I could see a spattering of little red dots. 'E saw where I was looking and shouted that a cat had got in and killed a pigeon before he could shoo it out. Such nonsense I've never heard, but it was time to start cooking my husband's dinner, so I had to go back to my own flat for a while. But I resolved to creep up there and see what was what after the brute went out to the pub."

Mrs. Blythe paused for breath and to take a swig from the glass of water which perched precariously on the edge of the witness box.

"And what did you find when you returned to the roof of Waterlow Buildings later," asked Sir Wilfrid.

"Well, sir, I thought I'd heard him go out, but I still went up careful like. I went towards the pigeon loft because I was worried he'd done her in, and wanted to have a closer look at those little speckles of blood. I was about to step into the loft when I saw the floor was inches deep in birdseed. Every single sack of birdseed had been emptied onto the floor, and there wasn't a single sack in sight. What's more, the birdseed was all stained bright crimson…"

"Stained, Mrs. Blythe?" pressed Sir Wilfrid.

"He'd done her in all right. Chopped her into little pieces and put her in the birdseed sacks," said Mrs. Blythe, suddenly sobbing.

Mr. Leithen, for the Defense, rose slowly to his feet.

"M'lud, if I might be allowed to interject, since the body of Mrs. Schellenberger has never been found, it is not possible to know whether it was, as the witness suggests, cut up and placed in birdseed sacks. It is merely conjecture on the part of Mrs. Blythe. Indeed, the sacks themselves have never been found."

Judge Wargrave aimed a withering glare at the barrister.

"I had understood the prisoner had entered a plea of not guilty by reason of insanity. Are you suggesting Schellenberger is not guilty of the offence at all?" he asked.

"M'lud, my client admits to the murder on the basis of the circumstantial evidence, and the disappearance of his wife—but, very unfortunately, his mental condition means he has no recollection of events around this time. Nevertheless, there would seem to be little purpose in disputing the reality of the murder on the basis that the prosecution cannot prove evidence of a body when multiple witnesses saw my client murder Mr. Cookson and Mr. Scott. And these are murders he can recall."

Leithen sat down on the bench and Sir Wilfrid immediately rose.

"M'lud, the jury will also hear that the blood-soaked mulch of birdseed described by Mrs. Blythe contained fragments of human bone, human brain tissue and also blonde hair."

Rouletabille, unable to converse even at the level of a whisper while the court was in session, wrote a question for Ben Bates to read in his note book.

Why claim to be unable to remember the murder of his wife and yet admit to the murders of the two other men? Does it make any sense?

Bates scribbled his reply.

Who can account for the actions of a lunatic?

Rouletabille then wrote:

There is more to this than meets the eye.

But Bates only shook his head.

After this came the cross-examination of Mrs. Blythe, and while Leithen did his best to confuse the woman, shake her from her account, and generally muddy the waters, she stuck doggedly to her story. After this, Marie St. Claire, Mrs. Schellenberger's cousin from Hammersmith, gave evidence to establish she had not been ill, and had not asked Mrs. Schellenberger to come and look after her.

Next, Sir Wilfrid called someone named Harry Dickson. And Rouletabille was not surprised to see the young man he had spotted earlier in the Old Bailey cafeteria enter the courtroom. Dickson was sworn in by the usher.

Sir Wilfrid commenced questioning for Dickson's *evidence in chief.*

"Mr. Dickson, how did you first make the acquaintance of Mrs. Schellenberger?"

"The lady called at my consulting rooms in Baker Street with some concerns about her husband," said the young American. "I have recently started out in a small way as a detective, and had advertized my services in the East End newspapers with a view to drumming up business. She told me her husband had become progressively violent, abusive and secretive. He was having trouble holding down even the most basic forms of employment and seemed to spend a lot of time wandering on the Wanstead Flatlands. Although she could not be sure of the cause of this abhorrent behavior, she suspected another woman was at the bottom of it. Naturally, she hired me to follow her husband and give a full report."

"So you followed Schellenberger?"

"Yes, at the first opportunity, which was the following Monday. I donned common workman's garb so as to blend in with the populace as best I could. I followed Schellenberger when he left Waterlow Buildings in Bethnal Green and his first call was at an off-license on Cambridge Heath Road, where he bought half a dozen bottles of beer. He then took an omnibus to Wanstead and walked out onto the grassy plain of the flatlands."

"He did not see you?"

"People do not generally see me when I am following them. But in this instance, it was extremely difficult to avoid being spotted. Once past the oak trees that line the main road, I had to crawl through the long grass in the manner of a big cat stalking its prey. After a few hundred yards, he took off his coat and placed it on the grass to sit on, as if he was getting ready for a picnic. And there he stayed, largely immobile. I now saw he also had on him a pair of powerful looking military grade field glasses, and with these, he occasionally scanned the horizon. And sometimes he cupped his ear, as if straining to listen for something in the far distance. After about ninety minutes, I saw what he had been looking and listening for: a delicate bright yellow tri-plane with a droning engine that was little more than the buzz of a wasp. It was quite obviously one of the experimental planes constructed by the nearby A V Roe company."

"And you believed he had gone to Wanstead to observe this plane?"

"I could draw no other conclusion. Moreover, I almost immediately formed the strong suspicion he was a German agent. Aviation is bound to have military applications, and already some political commentators are saying war with Germany is inevitable. Mrs. Schellenberger had informed me during our short interview that her husband had been dishonorably discharged from the German Navy—that sounded to me to be rather a transparent ruse. Schellenberger had been sent to England on a specific mission of espionage. His job was to discover what progress A V Roe's company had made to produce a reliable and maneuverable aircraft. After he had watched the plane for a little while, he put down his field glasses and commenced to make notes and possibly sketches in a little leather-bound book. By this moment, I was already adamant whatever information he had gleaned would not fall into the hands of a foreign government. Mrs. Schellenberger had mentioned to me her husband had the hobby of keeping pigeons, and it seemed to me homing pigeons would be an excellent way of passing information to confederates. Why, from East London, a pigeon could easily fly across the Channel to German agents in Belgium, and there would be no way of stopping it," said the American detective.

"Sir Wilfrid," began the Judge. "The defendant Schellenberger has not been charged with espionage. I therefore have to query how directly relevant the testimony of Mr. Dickson is."

"M'lud, through Mr. Dickson's evidence, the Crown will seek to prove Mr. Schellenberger's apparently aberrant behavior was, in fact, a ruse. His actions are highly rational. It is true that, while there is insufficient evidence to charge him with espionage, his behavior on the Wanstead grasslands is hardly that of a drunken lunatic," said Sir Wilfrid.

The Judge returned to writing notes, and Sir Wilfrid took this as an instruction to recommence Dickson's evidence in chief.

"Mr. Dickson, you had determined you would prevent Schellenberger from passing any information to a foreign power. What action did you take next in this regard?" asked the prosecution barrister.

"I continued to crawl through the long grass towards where he was sitting. My intention was to grab his notebook and run off with it. I thought it might provide sufficient evidence for the police to effect an arrest," said Dickson. "However," he continued, "I had advanced to almost within ten feet when he spotted me. Lying in a prone position, I was now at a considerable disadvantage. I attempted to swiftly get up, but he struck me in the side of the head with one of his unopened bottles of beer, wielding it like a stumpy club. The bottle broke and cut open my scalp. A brief physical altercation ensued, during which I was able to strike him with an uppercut and disarm him of the broken bottle. Nevertheless, due to his great physical strength and fighting prowess, I was soon bested. I ended up back on the grass flat on my back. I made an undertaking to myself that if I survived this encounter, I would devote as much of my time as possible to the study of an oriental martial art, such as *baritsu.*"

"How were you able to escape, Mr. Dickson?" asked Sir Wilfrid.

"At this point, fate intervened. As I lay there in a semi-concussed daze, I saw Schellenberger had removed from his pocket a box of matches, and it seemed he would use them to set fire to the dry grass around me. But the miscreant's plans were spoiled when a dog walker—a retired man—came into view and challenged the German as to what he was up to. At this, he fled, muttering what I took to be curses in German. The retired man, Mr. Newcombe, then half carried me to the nearby infirmary at Whipps Cross, where my wounds were most efficaciously tended. And just as soon as I was patched up, I reported this matter to Scotland Yard. Little did I know then that Schellenberger was about to go on a killing spree," finished the young American detective.

With no further questions from Sir Wilfrid for the prosecution it was time for Dickson to be cross-examined by Mr. Leithen.

"Mr. Dickson, what formal qualifications or experience do you possess to qualify you as a detective?" asked the barrister. "Are you perhaps a former employee of the Pinkerton Detective Agency or an ex-Scotland Yard man?

"I have no particular qualification or experience of that type, but I have had practical experience of detective work from a young age, doing some spot work for Nick Carter," said Dickson, defending himself as best he could.

"In fact," said Leithen, "you are still enrolled at the University of South Kensington. What is your degree course at the university?"

"English Literature," answered Dickson

"Not Criminology? Nor Chemistry, nor indeed any subject even peripherally associated with the investigation of crime?" asked Leithen.

"No, sir," said Dickson.

"Why did you take rooms in Baker Street? What was the particular attraction?" asked Leithen.

"My student accommodation is shared, and affords little privacy when consulting with clients. I therefore found it necessary to also take rooms off campus," said Dickson.

"It is then, merely a coincidence that all four of London's greatest detectives—Sherlock Holmes, Sexton Blake, Sir Seaton Begg and Victor Drago—all operate out of the exact same street where you just happened to rent a room?"

"It is an extremely convenient location," said Dickson.

"Is it not the case that you are a mere dilettante imitator of the great consulting detectives of our time? A talentless amateur, a dabbler involving yourself in matters far beyond your abilities?"

"It is true my career is at an early stage, but my early successes speak for themselves. And regarding having a Baker

Street address—why, it is no different from surgeons congregating in Harley Street, or the accumulation of barristers in Lincoln's Inn. There is room in the market place for the novice in every profession—everyone has to start somewhere. As a novice, my fees are modest, sufficiently modest a respectable East End lady could afford them—and that, sir, is why I am here. I have nothing to apologize for. I am a good detective, and I expect to make my living in this job for many years to come."

Rouletabille smiled inwardly. Leithen had sought to provoke Dickson using his youth and inexperience as levers in order to discredit his evidence and it had backfired spectacularly. The young American had kept his cool. And although originally skeptical, Rouletabille had been won over to his way of thinking. He thought it highly likely Schellenberger was a spy. But questions remained: where was the body of Mrs. Schellenberger? How had the bags which had previously contained just birdseed for the pigeons (and now presumably contained the dismembered Mrs. Schellenberger) been disposed of?

This was the sort of puzzle to which the Frenchman was attracted, like a moth to a flame. The cross-examination of Harry Dickson continued for a little while longer without a great deal of incident, and when it concluded, Dickson went to the public gallery to watch the rest of the proceedings. The Judge directed the reporters not to place into the public domain details of the target of Schellenberger's alleged espionage on the grounds of national security. There then followed several more witnesses recounting the events around the publicly witnessed murders of Cookson and Scott. The first of these was Thomas Dewe, the landlord of the *Salmon and Ball* public house, who had tried to intervene during the fatal assault on Reginald Scott, Schellenberger's employer.

Lunchtime approached, the court would break for an hour shortly. Rouletabille's every instinct was that he would not solve the mysteries of this case while sitting down on a hard wooden bench at the Old Bailey. The answers were out there somewhere… in the alleys and tenements of Bethnal Green, or perhaps in the sparse woodland and grassy expanses of the Wanstead Flatlands, where an experimental airplane was probably even now under testing. Then it struck him. He scarcely knew London at all. It would be an arduous quest indeed to find and gain access to all of the important locations in this case without some sort of guide. Ben Bates was out of the question; his editor would expect him to attend every minute of the trial, whereas Rouletabille could, in theory, operate with rather greater latitude, especially if he was able to locate Mrs. Schellenberger's body, or prove the killer was also a German spy. The only option seemed to be to forge an alliance with Harry Dickson himself. He just hoped the American would agree to it.

When the lunchtime adjournment began, Rouletabille followed Dickson out of the court with a view to making his acquaintance.

Less than ninety minutes later, Rouletabille and the American detective stood on the flat, zinc-covered roof of Waterlow Buildings, close to the pigeon loft. The birds fluttered and cooed, their grayish feathers made iridescent by the bright afternoon sun. Rouletabille moved to the edge of the roof and looked to the east and south. They were adjacent to a primary school, but beyond that were more tenements. In the distance, the Frenchman could see the back of Bethnal Green Police Station, which was only just along from the *Salmon and Ball* public house. Looking to the west, there was a similar three-storey tenement across the street, and although he could not see it from this vantage point, Dickson had told him Weavers Fields—a large open play area, and one of the last expanses of greenery before the City of London proper began—lay on the other side of this neighboring building.

Dickson opened the door into the pigeon loft, and Rouletabille noticed none of the birds took the opportunity to escape. Then, on closer inspection, he saw why. The pigeons had their own exit—a little window opening to the sky, which could be closed if required. However, there were four little lockable nesting boxes in which a pigeon could be placed with just about enough room to turn around.

"These boxes must be where he kept the homing pigeons. The other birds are free to come and go as they please, as you can see," said Dickson.

Rouletabille looked down at the floor. The blood-soaked birdseed had long been cleared away, although some rust-like stains remained. Then his eye was attracted by a loose board in the wall of the loft. He bent down and picked at the edges of the board with his fingertips. After just a few seconds, he was able to tug it from its place. Concealed in the hollow of the wall was a battery, about twenty centimeters long and ten high, two brass terminals on its top.

"Well, the police missed that," said Dickson. "Logically, he must've had a transmitter too. But the police didn't find that either. Crucial evidence in this case just seems to vanish into thin air."

The Frenchman lifted the transmitter battery from its hiding place.

"It's heavy. Much heavier than it looks." He looked around the roof and spotted something that had been placed to the side of one of the building's chimneys—flattened sections of metal.

"The metal Schellenberger was flattening with a hammer. Mrs. Blythe mentioned it in her testimony," said Rouletabille as he picked up the pieces and examined them minutely. He considered every fact he had so far heard about this case, mulling the information over like a wine taster trying to identify a particular vintage.

"We are going to need meteorological reports for the night Mrs. Schellenberger was killed and the following couple of days," said Rouletabille.

Just as Dickson started to nod, a projectile struck the chimney brickwork at high velocity and ricocheted off, spiraling away like an enraged insect. The French Detective's swift eyes were able to see it was some kind of dart, most likely shot from a pneumatic rifle.

"Keep down!" shouted Dickson, and they both rolled for the cover available. It seemed to Dickson the dart must have been fired from the tenement opposite. Ignoring his own advice, the American raised his head above the level of the parapet to see if he could spot their assailant. A small black-clad figure was in the open stairway of the building across the street; a scarf obscured his features and he had a small carbine with a telescopic sight.

No sooner had Dickson seen him than he fired again, this time missing only by inches. The dart zinged off the stone of the parapet balustrade and fell into the street below. In theory, the two detectives were trapped on the roof, but Bethnal Green police station was a matter of only a few hundred yards away, and once the populace realized shots had been fired, the coppers would be summoned. Time was the enemy of the assassin. Rouletabille prepared to hunker down for a long period of concealment when he realized Dickson had armed himself, albeit with one of the smallest firearms the Frenchman had ever seen. It was some kind of Derringer, and Rouletabille suspected it had been concealed in the American's sleeve, like he was some riverboat gambler, though he had not seen him remove it. Dickson rapidly fired off two shots in the direction of the open tenement staircase, and then with practiced dexterity, deftly reloaded the weapon.

Dickson stole a look above the parapet stonework and saw that, although his shots had both missed, the marksman was fleeing the scene, running along Wilmot Street and heading towards an alleyway which ran between the tenement blocks before exiting onto Weavers Fields. Although he had little chance to aim, Dickson discharged an opportunistic round at the running figure; who stumbled momentarily, as if the bullet had just clipped his arm, then continued on his way with short irregular strides suggestive of someone not much given to physical exercise.

"We should get out of here too, my friend," said Dickson. "Technically speaking, I don't actually have a license for this thing."

It was early evening by the time Rouletabille presented himself at the Fleet Street offices of the *London Star,* Harry Dickson having gone back to his Baker Street lodgings. Ben Bates had returned from the Old Bailey and was typing up copy of the day's events at court. Nevertheless, he found five minutes to show the young French journalist down to the newspaper's morgue where he could examine the weather reports from the week when Mrs. Schellenberger was murdered. After, following some improvised calculations, Rouletabille had cause to send telegrams to his own newspaper's office, as well as a journalist colleague in the Netherlands.

Having finished his inquiries for the day, Rouletabille returned to the *Star's* bullpen, and sat with Ben Bates, adding plumes from his own pipe to the bluish grey fog of cigarette smoke which hovered above the desks of the loudly dressed London newsmen.

"So, who is on the witness stand tomorrow?" asked the Frenchman, over the general racket from the typewriters.

"It's Dr. Grierson, the head of the Leytonstone Insane Asylum; you'll probably recall him getting a mention this morning. His job is to give a professional forensic opinion on whether or not Schellenberger is really insane. But I've seen Grierson before. He's a nasty piece of work," said Bates.

Rouletabille's puzzlement at the idiom showed on his face.

"An unpleasant, sadistic-looking character. I wouldn't want to be subjected to his tender mercies... electric shock treatment and so forth. He has the look of a villain, bald as an egg and a face like a defrocked priest!" laughed the cockney journalist. "In some ways, it is the most important evidence of the case, because it determines whether or not Schellenberger will hang."

"I do not know if I would want to escape the hangman's noose only to live out my life in some lunatic asylum," considered Rouletabille. "I think I would rather suffer that short drop through the scaffold trapdoor and face my final Judgment than cling so very desperately to this world."

"But Schellenberger is almost certainly some brand of nihilist, and probably an atheist into the bargain. He does not have your sensibilities, nor your moral compass. If he's an atheist, he's putting off the blank emptiness of non-existence; if he has some semblance of religious belief, he's avoiding imminent damnation. Not so very long ago, we hanged people for every conceivable crime in this country—stealing a lamb, or even a handkerchief—right the way up to assault and bestiality. And so, I have to wonder just how much of a deterrent capital punishment is. More crucially, you have seen how courts work: some well-educated men ask questions in order to bring out certain points, while other well-educated men do their best to obfuscate and confuse the issues. Following that, twelve good men do what they can to decide the matter. The whole process is too susceptible to human error. No one's life should really be resting on it. In another fifty or sixty years, the whole business of execution will have been reformed. I doubt if they'll be hanging anyone except traitors," said Bates.

"Which brings us back to Schellenberger," said Rouletabille. "I have seen today the strongest evidence he is guilty of espionage, so I have caused inquiries to be made abroad—in both Holland and France, and I expect these investigations to reach fruition some time tomorrow afternoon. I have, as I believe you say in England, 'set the hares running.'"

Bates merely smiled at this and inhaled deeply on the remnants of his cigarette.

"My intention," continued Rouletabille, "in terms of London newspapers, is to give the story to the *Star* as an exclusive in thanks for all the assistance you have given me. Naturally, the story will also run in my own paper."

"You are pretty sure of yourself," laughed Bates.

"I suppose I am. But I should probably say no more at this stage; to some extent, the whole thing is in the lap of the gods, or more properly in the hands of the east wind," said the Frenchman, and although he was thinking about the wind, he could not get out of his mind's eye the image of hares running hell for leather across an open field, as if desperate to evade a monstrous pursuer.

The following morning, all of the main players had returned to Court 4 at the Old Bailey as the court went back into session. Rouletabille was again sitting next to Ben Bates on the hard wooden benches of the press box. Harry Dickson was up in the public gallery, and Dr. Grierson was being sworn in by the usher. Grierson was a gnome-like figure with thick-lensed glasses, small ears and his right arm held in a sling. Suddenly, Rouletabille was aware of Dickson waving to him frenetically from high up in the public gallery—the Frenchman gestured to him to desist. It was not a good idea to draw attention to one's self in the public courtroom, and depending on the mood of the judge, the slightest infraction could result in a charge of contempt of court, or at the very least removal from the courtroom. This was literally the last thing Rouletabille wanted to be party to. Whatever it was, it could wait.

Since Dr. Grierson was technically a Defense witness, the normal pattern of giving evidence was reversed, and Mr. Leithen took the first turn in asking questions in order to elicit the psychiatrist's *evidence in chief*.

"Dr. Grierson," began Leithen, "you have had the opportunity to examine the prisoner, Schellenberger, while he has been in custody?"

"Yes, on several occasions," said the doctor.

"And what is your professional opinion on his state of mind?" asked the Defense barrister.

"In layman's terms, he is morally insane. By which, I mean he is incapable of telling right from wrong. He is a perfect example of what has been described as the *moral imbe-*

cile. It means no more to him to kill his wife than it would to ring the neck of one of his pigeons," explained Grierson.

"What is your opinion of his apparent loss of memory in relation to the murder of his wife? Is he simply feigning amnesia?" asked Leithen.

"He has an extreme personality, and as such he would be highly susceptible to entering fugue states following episodes of excitement, passion or trauma. Put simply, a fugue state is something like a mental fog. It may lift in time, allowing memories to be recovered, or it may stay in place, becoming something like a permanent curtain within the mind. I have questioned him closely regarding his memory loss, and I have found his responses to be entirely consistent. Nevertheless, I think it is right Schellenberger has stood a full trial. The reason being it is highly disorientating for a disordered and amnesic mind to find itself suddenly imprisoned; in cases like these, it can actually be therapeutic for the patient to hear his recent story from the witnesses involved," said Grierson.

"You will be aware Mrs. Schellenberger engaged the services of a certain, Harry Dickson—an inexperienced young detective now resident in London. How do you account for the violent encounter which took place between Mr. Dickson and Schellenberger out on the Wanstead Flats?" asked Leithen.

"Through the application of commonsense and reason, it is quite easy to deduce Schellenberger's motivations. Nevertheless, he has confided in me during our sessions, and I can tell you it is no surprise to me that his deviant mind contains a strong attraction towards voyeurism. His sole intention in his pathetic meanderings on the grassland was to observe courting couples committing fornication. And being something of a skilled amateur artist, he drew the things he had seen. After his confrontation with Mr. Dickson, he burned the notebook. However, he was able to recreate some of the drawings for me during his incarceration. It is unusual for someone with homicidal tendencies to have a flair for illustration. Perhaps if this man had been born into a different strata of society he would've made his living as an artist," stated Grierson.

"Will you be placing these drawings into evidence?" asked Leithen.

"Well, I hardly think they represent suitable material to be placed before an English jury. They are, by their very nature, obscene. I would invite the court to simply take my word for it that such images exist," answered Grierson.

The Judge gave a perfunctory nod.

"The crucial thing is," continued Grierson, "that the prisoner's diseased mind certainly had no interest in aeroplanes. If he looked at them through his binoculars, then that is purely coincidental. They would've drawn his attention no more than they would've anyone else who just happened to be walking upon the grasslands."

The *evidence in chief* continued for just a little while longer and then Sir Wilfrid Robarts commenced his *cross-examination*. But Grierson proved himself to be adamant and immovable on every conceivable point. No matter where Sir Wilfrid directed the questioning, the psychiatrist remained calm and utterly professional. Perhaps only when he was quizzed on his academic qualifications did the mask drop just a fraction, and Rouletabille saw a man who clearly did not want to be troubled by any of this, a man who regarded himself as superior to all—there was a titanic ego cloistered within his stunted body.

It was almost lunchtime when a messenger boy unobtrusively entered the court and gave a large envelope to Ben Bates. Bates looked momentarily at the writing on the envelope and passed it to Rouletabille unopened. The Frenchman immediately saw it was addressed to him 'care of' Bates in Court 4 of the Old Bailey. Inside was a sheaf of telegrams which Rouletabille commenced to read.

TO ROULETABILLE:

REMNANTS OF DOWNED WEATHER BALLOON DISCOVERED EAST OF ARNHEM STOP BALLOON WAS CARRYING SMALL SACKS CONTAINING HUMAN REMAINS AND A RADIO TRANSMITTER IN WOODEN CASE STOP

Then Rouletabille read the clincher:

SOME BIRDSEED REMAINS IN THE SACKS STOP. EXAMINATION OF TRANSMITTER UNDERWAY BY EXPERTS STOP.

REGARDS, J FELDHEIM

INTERNATIONAL NEWS SERVICE BUREAU, ROTTERDAM

Rouletabille was jubilant. This was no time for hubris, but it was gratifying to know that even with the most limited of evidence—part of the examination of which took place while under attack—he was still able to reach a correct logical conclusion, one that had eluded the finest minds of Scotland Yard, as well as the promising Harry Dickson.

Rouletabille scribbled in his notebook and showed what he had written to Ben Bates. Bates blanched somewhat as he read it.

"How do I get to be a witness in this case?" was what the Frenchman had scrawled.

After the court had adjourned for lunch, Dickson rushed up to Rouletabille and addressed him in confidential tones while Ben Bates talked urgently with the instructing solicitors for the prosecution, trying to convince them to call Rouletabille as a witness.

"I've got the hunch to end all hunches that it was Grierson who shot at us on the roof of Waterlow Buildings. I'm pretty sure I winged our would-be assassin, and Grierson just happens to have his right arm in a sling," said the American. "His physical shape is also pretty unmistakable."

"Hunches are not evidence, my dear Dickson," responded Rouletabille. "If Grierson is part of a German espionage conspiracy, we are going to need more than a gut feeling to put him behind bars. He is one of the foremost forensic psychiatric practitioners in London."

"But don't you see? There are enormous ramifications if Grierson is one of Schellenberger's confederates. If German agents can be legally judged to be insane and placed in Grierson's custody at Leytonstone Asylum, he might spirit them out of the country after a period of time, and no one would be any the wiser," said Dickson.

Rouletabille's lunchtime was taken up being interviewed by Scotland Yard officers, who swiftly typed up his statement regarding the foreign investigations he had initiated. Naturally, the sheaf of telegrams from the International News Service was officially registered as an exhibit in the case and formally cross-referenced to his sworn statement.

Finally, the court was called back into session, but this time Rouletabille had to wait outside to be called in by the usher. Inside the court, there followed a short legal argument regarding whether evidence from the French journalist could be admissible at this stage. Once the legal wrangling was concluded, Rouletabille was summoned and sworn in. The court looked a very different place from inside the witness box, considerably more intimidating, and he stumbled a little over his oath through sudden and unexpected nerves—it seemed to him that to be a witness in a court is to be a bug under a magnifying glass, just waiting for the sun to emerge from behind a cloud and start the process of incineration. This sensation of scrutiny, combined with imminent doom, was made worse by the fact Schellenberger now had a direct line of sight to him, and was glaring at him like a gorgon. Perhaps even worse, on the fringes of his peripheral vision, he could catch glimpses of Grierson's face frowning down at him from on-high in the public gallery, looking every bit the malignant imp from some fairy tale, or fevered nightmare.

"You are Joseph Josephin, also known as Rouletabille, a French journalist assigned by your newspaper to cover this trial. Further to this, please tell the court the results of the enquiries you have caused to be made abroad," requested Sir Wilfrid Robarts.

"Yes, I am Rouletabille, and on the first day of this trial I heard, as we all did, the evidence of Mrs. Blythe and how she related the conundrum of the disappearance of Mrs. Schellenberger's body, which she suspected had been cut up and placed in small sacks of birdseed. These sacks were never to be seen again, at least not in this jurisdiction. Most crucially, Mrs. Blythe also related how Schellenberger had been bashing bits of metal on the rooftop with a hammer, flattening them. I investigated this and found these metallic fragments. They appeared to me to be broken up pressurized cylinders. More specifically, helium cylinders. The obvious conclusion was that, in dead of night, Schellenberger had released a helium balloon with the dismembered body of his wife as its cargo. I made calculations on how far such a balloon might travel in the prevailing weather conditions. My best estimates suggested it would lose buoyancy and come to earth somewhere in eastern Holland. And such has proved to be the case. Following inquiries, the downed balloon was discovered in a farmer's field outside Arnhem."

"So, did the balloon carry anything other than the human remains?" asked Sir John.

"Yes, sir, a wooden case containing a powerful wireless telegraphy transmitter. Ideal for use by a spy. In addition, a leather-bound notebook filled not with pornographic drawings, but rather with British military secrets gleaned by travels in and around the south east of England."

"I have no further question, M'lud," said Sir Wilfrid, suddenly sitting back down on his bench.

Flustered and somewhat ambushed by this new evidence, Mr. Leithen stood up to cross-examine Rouletabille with some reticence.

"A man might be a spy and also be insane, wouldn't you agree?" he asked. "After all, what sane man chops his wife up into little pieces?"

"Perhaps," admitted Rouletabille. "But he did not merely cut her up, he sent those pieces on a balloon ride. What I did not know when I made my initial calculations was that the helium balloon was fitted with a slow release valve. Schellenberger's intention was for the balloon to come down somewhere in the North Sea. While he had to find a way to dispose of his wife's body, in any event, she conveniently became the ballast to facilitate the permanent concealment of his transmitter. But the valve jammed—it was still jammed when the balloon and its payload were found. This act proves him to be sane. Only a sane man would seek to eliminate the evidence of his espionage in such a subtle and brilliant way."

"Is this not pure conjecture, Monsieur? The prisoner could just as well have used the birdseed as ballast."

"In which case, he would still have the body to dispose of. When the facts of this case are arranged in order, they can be read like a mathematical equation. Only one interpretation makes logical sense, and the level of conjecture is miniscule. Because of the actions of Mr. Dickson, your client was convinced he was being observed when he left his home. He thought the authorities were closing in. His wife must have revealed to him she had engaged the services of a Baker Street detective to investigate his behavior—many of whom have close ties to the government—in doing so she sealed her doom, and he killed her. Since he believed he was now under surveillance, he had to get rid of the body without leaving Waterlow Buildings. Options such as putting the body into a local canal or park were now out of the question. Whether he hit on the idea of using the helium weather balloon he had been issued with by his masters by chance, or whether it was part of a pre-conceived stratagem to put evidence of his espionage out of reach, we may never know," explained Rouletabille, pausing for breath.

"Then with the primary evidence removed from the scene, the pressure eased. Mr. Dickson is recovering from injuries—no longer following Schellenberger—his report of a German spy in the East End initially dismissed by Scotland Yard. Yet Schellenberger knows Mrs. Blythe has already noticed his wife's absence; soon the clients of her bookkeeping business will do the same. He buys himself a week with his lie about the sick cousin in Hammersmith, and uses that week to complete his spying mission; using the carrier pigeons in his loft to report back to his masters. Now what? The fear of arrest hangs over him like the Sword of Damocles, but still arrest does not come. He worries now there are sufficient human remains—fragments of skull, bone and brain mixed in with the bloody birdseed—to secure a murder conviction, but he dare not remove any of it from the roof for fear of being arrested with it on his person. He is merely a man who has murdered his wife, and for that he knows he faces capital punishment. But what if he can cheat the hangman by proving himself to be a lunatic? This he does by committing two appalling murders in public. For him, it is the safest course, much safer than attempting to flee the jurisdiction when for all he knew he might be placed on a watch list as a spy at any moment."

"I put it to you that your so-called evidence is pure froth and nothing of substance, and that you are simply an attention-seeking charlatan," said Leithen.

"No, sir. I am not a neophyte detective whose reputation you can cast doubt on. My work places me in the first rank of those who seek to explain so-called impossible crimes. Modesty normally prevents me from alluding to the fact that I solved the *Mystery of the Yellow Room*—one of the most famous cases in the annals of French crime, yet you force me to make mention of it. As for proof, all of the evidence I have described here this afternoon in relation to the balloon will be the subject of sworn depositions from the witnesses in Holland—they will be sent to the Old Bailey via courier just as soon as they arrive at the Dutch Embassy in the diplomatic bag," said Rouletabille, passionately.

Breaking his silence for the first time during the trial, Schellenberger made a bellow like a beast caught in the jaws of a trap and lunged to get out of the dock. Fortunately, the alert bailiffs were able to restrain him.

"Your client is going to the gallows," observed Rouletabille, somewhat coldly. "I swear it."

Two weeks later, Ben Bates and Rouletabille stood in the public entrance hall of Newgate Prison, shoulder to shoulder with two dozen other reporters. The Frenchman noticed somehow Harry Dickson had blended himself with the mass of journalists, and was trying to look unobtrusive in the corner.

"You owe me ten bob," said Ben Bates cheerily to Rouletabille.

"Eh? Ten bob? What is that?" asked the Frenchman, suitably puzzled.

"Ten shillings. They decide which four journalists will observe the execution by pulling names out of a hat. Let's just say the journalists from *The London Star* and *Le Temps* have their places pre-booked. Such things should not be left to chance," whispered Bates.

"Well, I don't really approve of bribery and corruption, but today I will abandon my principles for the sake of seeing this monstrous brute hang," said Rouletabille.

The Newgate Prison governor literally pulled the names of the journalists out of a hat on slips of paper, and then announced the "winners" to the assemblage. The other two august journals whose representatives would be admitted to the place of execution were: *The Times* and the *Daily Telegraph*.

All four men were led by the governor and the chief warden up a winding stone staircase to the top floor of the prison. On this top landing were dozens of cells, all with their doors looked and closed—all, that is, except one. Since public executions had been discontinued some years ago, this cell had been converted to be an execution chamber. It was next door to the condemned cell, and this was a fact kept secret from those due to be executed, they tended to anticipate a long walk to their final doom when, in truth, it was only a few steps away through a specially constructed adjoining door. The four journalists were guided to their positions opposite the condemned cell doorway. This meant they had to step onto and across the gallows trapdoor and this sent a chill up Rouletabille's spine.

Rouletabille took out his pocket watch. It was almost midday. In less than two minutes, the condemned cell door would swing urgently open and Schellenberger would be brought speedily into this room by the executioner, and before his mind would be able to process events, the noose would be placed around his neck. Even the normally cocky Bates looked nervous, a film of perspiration glistened on his upper lip. Rouletabille looked up at where the rope was attached to the ceiling via brass fixtures. In the small and airless room, the moments accumulated like flies gathering on rotten meat. These were the final seconds of Schellenberger's life before it would be snuffed out. A scintilla of pity started to form in the French journalist's mind, but before the thought could fully take on form, he exiled it to the recesses of his consciousness.

The heavy iron door of the condemned cell swung open as if had been kicked. Schellenberger already had the death hood over his head. The prisoner was propelled, almost carried, by the guards on either side of him who had tight grip of his arms, which were securely strapped behind his back. Very swiftly, the executioner put the noose around Schellenberger's neck, then almost immediately his legs were strapped together at the calves. He was standing on the trapdoor—what was left of the murderer's life would be over in the bat of an eye. As the executioner stepped towards the lever on the wall which controlled the trapdoor, Rouletabille was aware for the first time of the prison chaplain intoning a prayer. The words washed over Rouletabille. They seemed incomprehensible and irrelevant.

The explosion struck like a thunderclap, tearing away the masonry from this corner of Newgate Prison and exposing the noonday sky. A large section of the brickwork from the wall fell away and disappeared into the street. Rouletabille had been struck by flying debris in the chest and legs, yet he was certainly the least badly hurt of the four journalists. Ben Bates was covered with dust and blood. He lay almost immobile, but when the Frenchman crawled nearer to him, he could see he was still breathing. One of the other British journalists had been blown limb from limb, and the other hovered near death in a growing stain of crimson which was spilling from his throat. The guards and the executioner staggered about, as if drunk or blind. The chaplain must've been screaming something, but no words seemed to be issuing from his mouth. It was then Rouletabille realized the blast had rendered him deaf—temporarily, he hoped. All he could he hear was a sound like the roaring of a waterfall magnified a thousand fold.

Of Schellenberger, there was no sign. Then Rouletabille noticed the rope which was hanging from the exposed roof level down into the condemned cell. The murderer was escaping over the roof tops. In the moments after the explosion, someone had entered the cell and freed him. Summoning vitality, he had no right to possess, the Frenchman grabbed onto the mountaineering rope and started to haul himself up onto the roof of Newgate Prison. Immediately, he saw Schellenberger had not been immune to injury from the explosion; limping, he was being helped across the roof by a small figure whose face was obscured by a scarf and a hat with the brimmed pulled down. The disguised man pulled a nickel-plated automatic from under his coat and loosed a round at Rouletabille. The report from the pistol seemed muffled and unreal—yet his hearing was starting to clear. Rouletabille dove for the cover provided by a raised glass skylight. He wished to God that Dickson was up here with him.

Suddenly, it seemed to him someone was calling his name, far off and incredibly distorted—as if heard underwater. Rouletabille crawled to the bomb-damaged parapet and dared to look down. It was Dickson! He was sprinting from the far side of the street in a fashion that reminded the Frenchman of a cricket player—a bowler. When Dickson came to a stop, he hurled something small and silvery up towards the roof. To Rouletabille, it seemed futile; the claws of gravity would soon grab it and pull it back to earth. But on it spun, before clattering to the prison roof just yards away from him. It was Dickson's Derringer. He lunged for it and cocked the hammer. Aiming and firing at the same instant, he missed and struck brickwork near Schellenberger's head. The disguised figure—could it really be Grierson? —tried to urge Schellenberger on to escape, but instead, he wrestled the automatic from the hand of his benefactor and aimed it at Rouletabille. Rouletabille's shot passed directly through the murderer's left eye socket and into his brain. His reprieve from execution had been but a few minutes. Now at the end of his endurance, and with no further ammunition, Rouletabille could only watch as Schellenberger's would-be rescuer made good his escape.

Four days later, Rouletabille was escorting Dickson back to his Baker Street apartments after they had visited Ben Bates in Marylebone Hospital. The cockney journalist was recovering well, and was due to be discharged from the hospital the following week.

"It is my firm belief there is still a German espionage ring operating out of the East End of London. Our work is not yet done. In particular, there is the matter of gathering evidence against the traitor Grierson," said Rouletabille.

"Forgive me," said Dickson, "but I now have cases piling up which need my attention. Give me a couple of weeks to clear my desk, then I can devote myself more properly to the spy ring affair."

"Very well, but it will be difficult without you since I do not know London as you do," said the Frenchman.

A swirl of fog had descended across Baker Street like a physical barrier, and Rouletabille could see a group of partially obscured figures waiting ahead of them. He could not quite make them out or tell them one from the other, but there seemed to be four men—all of them wearing fore and aft caps and mid-length Inverness capes.

"They are outside my door. They must be waiting for *me*. Stay here, my friend. I'll see what the problem is," said the American detective.

Dickson approached the identically dressed men with some trepidation, and then, after a little while, it became apparent he was conversing with them in a good natured fashion, and so Rouletabille relaxed. And after a few moments more, Dickson walked back along the pavement.

"It seems extraordinary, but they have accepted me into their number. They regard me as an official Baker Street consulting detective, due to my recent success," said Dickson.

"That is marvelous news," said Rouletabille.

"It seems there is a short ceremony in a local hostelry, followed by toasting and dinner. Do please join us," implored Dickson.

"I think not, Harry. I would be out of place at such a gathering. This is your moment. Savor and enjoy it. Do not speak to them of our case, and I will see you in two weeks."

The two men shook hands, and Dickson broke into a run on his way back to the consulting detectives.

The fog had lifted a little, but even so Rouletabille could not tell Holmes from Blake, Begg or Drago. In some respects they were a single man—the archetype, and those he had inspired. They belonged to London. They belonged to everyone.

The House of Despair

London, 1909

Harry Dickson was in the most marvelous mood. The past month had brought him even greater success—and success is the best form of advertizing. More and more clients had been arriving at his recently rented Baker Street rooms. If it carried on like this, he would have to consider employing some sort of permanent assistant, or at least a secretary, to schedule his appointments and manage his diary. As it was, he was spending far too much time tied to Baker Street, taking notes of his meetings with those in need of his help when he really should have been abroad in London, gathering evidence and bringing villains to justice. That was his very meat and drink, the thing which gave him the greatest possible thrill. His instinct was that he would never tire of it.

Yet, perhaps the strangest thing for the neophyte consulting detective was how he had been taken under the collective wing of the *Great Men of Baker Street*—Holmes, Blake, Begg and Drago. He was never short of advice, for it was most freely given. He had been told the correct tailor to visit, the right attire to wear for town and when visiting the country, the best place to purchase a revolver (and which make), how much ammunition to carry, how to swiftly apply disguises, how to fight with a sword stick. He was also given a list of local dog owners who were prepared to loan their dogs to consulting detectives for the right price. Dickson was also taught various mnemonics to enable him to memorize the geography of London, street by street—almost building by building.

Perhaps most generously of all, he had been introduced to incredibly useful contacts within Scotland Yard, Whitehall, and various foreign embassies. Indeed, so much new information had been imparted to Dickson recently that, in the back of his mind, he had started to develop the odd feeling that he had forgotten to do something. It was a nagging doubt which never seemed to coalesce into a fully coherent thought. He had the vague sense that he had forgotten to turn up for an appointment or take a minor exam. Whatever it was, he comforted himself that it couldn't have been anything too important.

Dickson had been taken aback by how much the *Great Men* socialized together and enjoyed themselves when not working on cases. It was an unexpected strand to his new existence, and he fully relished it. The older consulting detectives took great pride in knowing obscure and secret watering holes, restaurants and clubs. It was on one of these outings that the young American first encountered the beauteous Judith Fraser, who had been dining with her aunt and cousin. The *Great Men* nodded to each other and winked furtively as Dickson sought to strike up a conversation with the young woman at the adjoining table.

At first the somewhat fiery aunt was appalled by this contravention of social norms, but only moments later the detective's earnest colonial charm and easy manner had started to win her over. Of course, Miss Judith herself had been smitten from long before the American first spoke. The nominal purpose of that particular evening had been to introduce Harry Dickson to the Praed Street Detective, Solar Pons.

Over liqueurs, Pons had confidentially whispered to Dickson:

"Don't let that girl get away! I have a feeling you may be spending the rest of your life with her."

And so, his single-minded pursuit of Miss Judith began, to the exclusion of all personal interests excepting his detective casework. He was completely intoxicated by her. At the very start, her Aunt Josette played the chaperone, but she approved of young Dickson so strongly that it was not long before the girl was allowed to take walks alone with her suitor in London's lovely royal parks.

It was odd, but these open public parks seemed to foster an unaccustomed anxiety within Dickson. Some sort of sub-merged half-memory sometimes seemed to cry out from the back of his mind. And there was an unbidden visualization, of sorts. In his mind's eye, Dickson saw himself crawling along the ground through thick grass towards a bearded and danger-ous man. The bearded man was drawing something in a small notebook. Dickson had to find out what was in the notebook, even at the risk of his own life—quite why he could never fathom. Essential linkages in his chain of logical thought seemed to have been smashed beyond repair. The more he tried to focus on it, the more it eluded him. Concentration on the issue brought only anxiety, and when he opened his heart to Miss Judith about the matter, the suggestion came that there should be no more walks in parks. They would meet at the Ritz or the Café Royal instead. To her, avoidance of the prob-lem seemed paramount—ignore it and it will go away was her philosophy.

The romance continued, and the things Dickson could not remember, whatever they were, took on less and less of an importance in his life. Had it not, he would almost certainly have mentioned it to one of his mentors. They might have known people, mesmerists perhaps, who could have unlocked his memory. But why bother? Why should he allow this minor unease to sabotage his happiness? Things were going so well for him. He was in love. His career was burgeoning. Some of the greatest men in London held him in the highest regard. His future looked entirely rosy. Yes, Harry Dickson was in the most marvelous mood.

The Journal of Dr. Rupert Grierson - Leytonstone House Asy-lum, 30th June 1909

The usual problems persist with the women inmates. One common factor for all of them is the overwhelming desire to do themselves extreme harm. One might be forgiven for think-ing that all of their intellectual energy, such as it is, must be given over to this end. Nevertheless, the ingenuity that they do display is alarming. Last week, Nancy Pearce, managed to secrete a piece of stale bread upon her person—her previous feigned good behavior meant that she had been allowed to eat in the communal dining hall. To the layman, an additional piece of bread in the hands of a mental patient might not have been thought to be a matter of concern, but over time the bread hardened. Before long it could be sharpened until it had a reasonably effective cutting edge. After a few trial strokes on her upper arms to test the implement, Pearce slashed open both of her wrists. Fortunately, she was discovered before she bled to death, and medical aid was administered.

However, this was not the case with Rosemary Andrews. Andrews was a baby farmer convicted of killing nineteen of her charges, but saved from the hangman's noose by virtue of her insanity. Andrews repetitively and determinedly injures herself with whatever comes to hand. She was to be fully restrained in a straitjacket and strapped to a table, for when she is confined in a padded cell, she strikes her head repeatedly against the wall with sufficient force to damage her neck vertebrae, irrespective of the padding. This means that she is often restrained for a week or more at a time. When she pleads and offers that her behavior will improve, ultimately my staff have little choice but to allow her out of the straitjacket for a probationary period. After all, she could not be restrained in that fashion on a permanent basis. As this pattern played itself out recently, Andrews was released from restraint, but, within a few hours, had torn apart her teddy bear and pushed a handful of its stuffing into her trachea in an effort to asphyxiate herself. She was saved from death by medical staff, but before she could be placed back in restraints, she ripped out her own eyes. Treatment was quickly given, but she remains in agony, and will be for some time since I have ordered minimal analgesics. Let pain be her tutor for a while—it may break down the mental barriers that reason and therapy cannot.

I therefore move onto the male inmates, the most remarkable of these is *JJ*. He may be the most extraordinary mental patient that I have ever encountered. He was brought

81

here by the Metropolitan Police in a highly agitated and psychotic state only a couple of weeks ago. He is devious, highly intelligent and extremely violent. Four orderlies were badly injured on the first day when they placed him within his cell. The patient would not give his name, and he seemed terrified of me. Some of his clothing was marked with the initials *JJ*- and so that is what I decided to call him.

JJ seems to be willing to speak to some of the more junior staff, but his ravings merely reveal severe and grandiose delusions of the most serious nature. He is, by turns, a famous journalist, the world's greatest detective, and possibly some sort of secret agent. A monolithic conspiracy operates against him; he is the victim of attempted assassination and actual poisonings. He says it was after he was poisoned that he was found half-naked on the streets of Bethnal Green. However, the arresting officer told me he was delusional and foaming at the mouth, to the extent that one younger constable wondered if the man had rabies.

He claims to be French, though I am not certain of this. He has not spoken in French to any of my staff. I have read of cases where psychotics will affect a foreign accent, and some stroke victims also speak with an unaccustomed accent during recovery. While being taken to a room for a medical assessment, *JJ* broke away from his escort and was at large within the main asylum building for something like four minutes. When recaptured, the orderly searching him discovered secreted on his person an asylum door master key and a pair of scissors. I have ordered him to be temporarily placed in a straitjacket. I am not particularly given to prescient feelings, but in the back of my mind is the notion that he will find some way to escape again. His orderly reported to me that while being placed back in his cell, *JJ* announced that he was the "King of the Locked Room." No doubt his gibberish is meaningless, but still it fills me with an odd disquiet.

I have given some consideration to possible treatment for this patient, and I have decided that, after a brief period to allow him to acclimatize to life in the asylum, I will commence with intramuscular injections of camphor. The pain from these will be severe, but nevertheless cathartic; it may allow for the re-emergence of his original personality, which I strongly suspect is not that of a French journalist or detective. I will follow up the camphor injections with cold water immersion hydrotherapy. In the most severe of cases, this can be quite successful at resetting the brain's normal functions. But there is the likelihood of the side effect of amnesia. In this case, I hope the unpleasant delusions of persecution will also be erased. I will have freed his mind, and in that I will take great pleasure.

It was the third time little Alfie had made a delivery to the asylum since the strange man had started appearing at the window. Alfie's father had explained to him all about the sort of people who were locked up in asylums. There were two sorts: lunatics and imbeciles. Imbeciles were none too bright, and lunatics were dangerous—or, at least, that was how his father had explained it to him. The strange man seemed clever, though he spoke with quite a thick foreign accent, therefore Alfie deduced that he was a lunatic, and likely to be dangerous.

"Little boy, do not be afraid. I mean you no harm," said the strange man to the rotund boy wheeling the bicycle.

The strange man was high up at a barred window on the second floor of the asylum. The wire reinforced glass of the window had been flung wide by one of the man's keepers to ventilate the cell during this hot spell. Alfie did not see how the strange man could possibly harm him from so far away, so it seemed an odd thing to say, and as the boy drew nearer he could see the man's arms were enveloped in some sort of binding of tough canvas which kept them tight against his torso.

"Just come a little nearer... a little nearer," said the strange man. "I need to tell you something."

"I can't stop to talk. I need to deliver the groceries in my basket to the kitchen," said Alfie, who knew, because once again his father had told him, that the high quality fruit and vegetables from his family's grocers down on Leytonstone High Road were destined not for the consumption of inmates but rather for the table of the Director of the asylum, Dr. Grierson.

"It will only take a moment," said the strange man. "Take out your pencil and notebook."

Alfie looked up at the man with narrowed and suspicious eyes. How had he known he always carried writing materials on him? Most boys did not. Could the man be some sort of mind-reader? Had he somehow been locked up because he was a mind-reader? Alfie decided to stand his bicycle carefully against the asylum wall and take out the notebook and stub of pencil from his apron pocket.

"Write this down: *To Harry Dickson, Baker Street. I have been captured by Grierson and placed in his asylum. I am being tortured. Effect rescue immediately. Yours in despair, Rouletabille*," commanded the strange man.

The strange man had to go through the message twice more before Alfie had all the words down and the spelling correct.

"But what am I supposed to do with it now?" asked Alfie. "I can't ride all the way to Baker Street."

The strange man seemed to consider for a few seconds.

"Then take it to the nearest police station, or give it to your parents," he said.

Alfie shrugged and went back to pushing his bicycle towards the kitchen delivery door just around the corner. The boy had something of a suspicion of policemen which the strange man obviously did not share. He very much wondered how much weight they would place on a note from a madman in a cell in the local asylum.

When the doorbell rang, Harry Dickson leapt up from his desk in anticipation. His own housekeeper was on holiday in the Highlands of Scotland, and so he had Mrs. Bardell on loan from Blake, since Blake was out of town on a case.

He could hear voices from the floor beneath, and as he had expected, Miss Judith had now arrived.

"You just keep on with your knitting, Mrs. Bardell," the girl was saying. "I am quite capable of making a tray of tea and carrying it up to Harry."

"Oh, Miss Fraser! What a fine wife you will make for him, and not before too long, I hope," said the housekeeper.

The American continued to listen, and a few moments later, it was plain that Mrs. Bardell had withdrawn to her parlor and shut the door. Dickson therefore drifted downstairs with a view to surprising her in the scullery. As he rounded the corner, he saw that she already had the kettle on and the best bone china cups and saucers on the tray, but he was surprised to see that her delicate fingers were dropping a tiny soluble white tablet into one of the cups.

"What are you putting in my tea, darling? Not bromide, I hope," joked Dickson.

"Hardly," said Miss Judith. "But you've been looking so run down lately. I thought you might need some kind of tonic to just pep you up a little."

"Why, Mrs. Bardell is right, you are going to make a fabulous wife," said the detective.

"Is that a proposal of marriage, Harry," laughed the girl.

"Well, I guess it is at that—but let me try it again properly. Judith Fraser, will you marry me?"

"Of course, I will. But being a gentleman, you'd better get permission from my Uncle Rupert. You remember how I told you he was my legal guardian until I came of age last year?"

The two of them went upstairs to the sitting room, and once the tea had time to steep they drank it and each other in. To Dickson, she seemed to be more than merely beautiful— she was transfigured, as if lit from behind by some great arc light. The radiance seemed to emanate from beneath her skin, to pass through her being. He was captured by her gaze like a specimen impaled on a pin in a display case. Her burnished copper hair framed her face like a ruddy halo. Her eyes were sea green, but with flashes of sudden fire deep within.

The girl gestured at something on the carpet.

"I've dropped my sapphire earring on the floor, Harry. Would you mind picking it up for me?" asked the girl.

"I… I can't move," said Dickson.

He strained as if at invisible bonds, but could not get up from his chair. '

With a sinuous movement, she reached down to retrieve the item of jewelry and then knelt in front of him.

"It is a beautiful stone isn't it?" she asked, not waiting for, nor seemingly wanting a reply. "It was a gift from my Uncle Rupert. Look deeply into the sapphire. You'll see that it is starting to glow."

The gem did indeed start to glow. At first, it seemed to be little more than the light which might be cast by a firefly, but after a few moments, the intense brightness outshone even the illumination that the transfigured girl seemed to generate. It was like a welding torch was being fired into his brain, His optic nerve overloaded, all was blank whiteness. To think the simplest thought was to marshal an effort akin to shoveling coal.

"You have never previously met my uncle," the girl insisted. "Have you?"

"I have never met your uncle," agreed Dickson, after doing his best to search his memory.

"And the name Joseph Rouletabille is unknown to you. You have never had any association with Joseph Rouletabille."

"I have never had any association with Joseph Rouletabille," the American intoned mindlessly.

"That is excellent," said Judith Fraser.

She stood up now and sloughed off her dress, undid her corset and pulled down her cami-knickers. Moving closer, she put her right nipple to his lips. He latched onto it. She fumbled with his clothes and then sat astride him on the chair. The reward for forgetfulness would be ecstasy. And yes, she thought to herself, she would make a good wife just as she'd made a good whore.

"If the message is from some loony Frenchman, why is it in your handwriting?" said Alfie's father.

"He had to tell me what to write. His arms wuz all bundled up in some kind of canvas," said Alfie.

"Oh? In a straitjacket was he?" Alfie's father asked, somewhat rhetorically. "They save that for the worst of 'em. But I'm still not sure I believe you. You can be a right little liar when you put your mind to it."

"He wants this message sent to a man in Baker Street, where all the detectives live. This Frenchie must be a detective himself, or maybe even a secret agent. Baker Street is too far for me to go on my bicycle. Will you take it for me in your van?" asked Alfie.

"You must be joking. I'm not trotting off on a wild goose chase as a result of one of your lies. It was bad enough when you told me you'd seen a woman with a butcher's knife hiding in our bathroom, and I spent an age searching the house and backyard for her," said Alfie's father.

"Oh, please Dad. Take the message round to Mr. Dickson, or the French detective might be angry next time he sees me."

"I need to take you round to Sergeant Arbogast at the nick," said the greengrocer. "If he puts you in one of his cells for an hour or two, perhaps you will learn to tell the truth."

This was a common threat from Alfie's father who was good friends with the desk sergeant at the nearby police station on Leytonstone High Road. But this time it seemed as if he really meant it.

"Quickly finish off loading those sacks of potatoes then we can be off down the station," said Alfie's father.

The two orderlies were large, burly men and they handled the weakened Rouletabille with great ease. The French detective was propelled down the stark corridor with his feet barely touching the floor. He did not bother to struggle; he needed to preserve what strength he had. Within moments they arrived at the white-tiled hydrotherapy room. The enamel bathtub in the center of the room was far larger than its domestic equivalent, and had already been filled with water and chunks of ice. Almost surreptitiously, Rouletabille began to take deep and rapid breaths in an effort to oxygenate his blood. He did not really know what good it would do. His fear at this point was drowning. He thought that the orderlies would be forcefully holding his head beneath the water until his lungs cried out for air. Instead, they pulled off his pajama bottoms and physically hurled him, legs first, into the great tub.

The shock of the extreme cold hit him like a shotgun blast. He was instantly numb and vested with a lethargy that bordered on paralysis. His arms were still tightly bound in the straitjacket, but his legs and head seemed to be beyond his ability to control. His mind retreated out of his body, as if observing the whole scene from a distance. The body, which no longer seemed to be his, was lifted out of the tub then plunged back into it a second time. Then a third, then with random repetitions that he ceased to be able to count; his brain merely registered their tediousness.

Before long, but he could no longer judge time—so it might have been hours—the water started to seem pleasantly warm. The rock-hard ice was starting to soften at the edges. He held this to be the most important secret he had ever known. He continued to wince and grimace each time he was dropped back into the water. He must give no sign to the orderlies that the shock of the freezing water had abated. At one point, he caught a glimpse of his bare legs, they were blue with cyanosis. The "warmth" of the water in the tub was obviously a relative thing. Maybe it had only risen in temperature a couple of degrees while he was being tortured. Then, he was overcome by a kind of drunkenness, and his body seemed burningly hot rather than cold. It was all he could do in these circumstances to hang onto his identity, to stop his coherent sense of self from fracturing. But from somewhere in the depths of closed-off mind, a single word burrowed its way through the permafrost to the surface: hypothermia. His organs were starting to shut down. Then it all stopped. It seemed to him that the orderlies were carrying him back to his cell just before he would have died.

In his cell, the orderlies gave him a cursory rub dry with a rough towel. The towel had been left on a radiator and was quite warm to the touch. What bliss! As they dressed him, Rouletabille thought what splendid fellows the orderlies were. He wondered for a moment why their kindness seemed to be the only human interaction he had known in his life, and then he realized. He had no recollection of how he had come to be in this situation. No clue of what had happened earlier in time. The cold water had washed away his life. That seemed absurd. There was surely no former life to remember. He had always been here.

Alfie had expected his father to come into the station with him; instead he waited outside and gave him a note to take in to Sergeant Arbogast. Alfie walked under the station's blue lamp and up the steps into its most forbidding interior. The station was as quiet as a lending library, and the desk sergeant was sitting studiously examining something in the immense leather incident ledger which was spread open across the countertop.

Arbogast raised his head revealing his rather florid, mutton chop bewhiskered face.

"Yes, young man? How may I assist you?" asked the sergeant.

Alfie felt that if he tried to speak he would simply be sick, so opted to stand on tiptoes and offer up the scrunched up note his father had written to Arbogast.

"It says here that you are a very naughty little boy who likes telling lies and needs to be taught a lesson," stated Arbogast. "Is that right?"

The urge to vomit had subsided slightly within only to be replaced by a feeling that he would very shortly lose all bladder and bowel control. So, in answer to the question, he merely nodded the affirmative.

"Come with me, then."

Arbogast came around from the far side of the counter and led the rotund boy down the white tiled corridor towards the cells. The officer removed a ring of keys from his belt and unlocked a cell door.

"In you go then, sonny. I'll let you out in the morning."

To Alfie, the six by ten foot cell seemed little bigger than a coffin. He had never experienced claustrophobia before, but it hit him now with the force of a ruptured water main. His consciousness refused to dwell within him, and he found himself looking down at his quivering form as if from the ceiling. He felt considerable sympathy now for the Frenchman locked in his cell up at the Leytonstone House Insane Asylum—they were almost kindred spirits. Nevertheless, he would never again risk his liberty to assist someone, and he would never, ever, trust a policeman. A permanent change had taken place in the boy as a result of this harsh and disproportionate punishment. He would never be the same again.

It had all come back to Rouletabille fairly slowly. The details of his past gradually took on more and more solid form. And though some of the recollections caused him to doubt his own sanity—such as his experiences just a few years ago aboard the Trans-Siberian Express—he could not doubt that these must be real memories. He'd had an existence prior to his incarceration. He was both a detective and a journalist, and he's been tracking down a German spy ring operating in East London. The spies had been trying to steal secrets relating the development of an experimental armed tri-plane which was being tested by the British government on the Wanstead Flatlands between the built-up sprawl of Leytonstone and Epping Forest. And he had not been working on this case alone, there was Harry Dickson too, the young detective he had met at the Old Bailey during the Schellenberger trial.

Dickson's success in the case had caused the neophyte detective to be accepted by the fabled *Great Men of Baker Street* and inducted into their number. Following the afore-mentioned induction, there was supposed be a short break from the espionage case while Dickson wound up his other outstanding cases. But Dickson had not kept his rendezvous with Rouletabille in Bethnal Green and the Frenchman had been left trying to follow up various leads on his own. This had been a disaster, for while questioning a woman in the *Salmon and Ball* public house, it had become apparent that she was a member of the spy ring. But the woman had already poisoned his drink with some sort of hallucinogen.

When he'd come to his senses, he was incarcerated in the asylum run by Dr. Rupert Grierson—the very man Dickson and Rouletabille strongly suspected of being the leader of the spies; the man who had effected the release of Schellenberger from the condemned cell at Newgate by means of an explosive device.

Now, Rouletabille's memory had come back. But if the ice water immersion treatments continued. day after day. how long could his recollections realistically survive? He was felt pessimistic. His instinct was that it might take only one or two more treatments to fracture his mind completely. Then the thought struck him: could he really be sure this was the first ice water treatment? Could he trust his own memories?

He heard the cell door unlock and then swing open. From his prone position on the floor, he turned his head and saw Grierson enter the room. Rouletabille expected to be mocked, humiliated, or insulted by the doctor. Instead, he was almost entirely silent. The detective had neither the strength nor the will to resist. He saw that Grierson had a syringe and a bottle of yellowish liquid. The doctor opened the bottle and filled the syringe with its syrupy contents. The liquid in the bottle gave off a pungent aroma, which stung Rouletabille's eyes. He could not initially place this rather acrid smell… then it came to him. It was camphor!

Without further preamble, he was injected in one thigh and then the other. Within moments, he was wracked by convulsions, his body jackknifed again and again, fitting and spasming with exquisite pain. All of his nerves seemed to be on fire. After several minutes, the intensity of the pain started to diminish, and he was able to re-establish some sort of control over his muscles. Stillness brought him no comfort. He found that the only way to keep his mind off the pain was to keep hurling himself around the cell, weeping, screaming and babbling. He prayed that his rescuers would not arrive now, for if they saw him now, they could draw no possible conclusion other than that he had become a madman.

"It's such a pity that Mr. Dickson has been so ill recently," said Mrs. Bardell. "Nevertheless, I'm sure that, between us, we will be able to nurse him back to health."

"There really is no need for you to bother yourself with this, Mrs. Bardell," said Judith Fraser. "You know I have picked up more than a little knowledge of nursing from my time as a volunteer auxiliary nurse at the Royal London Hospital in Whitechapel."

"Funny that you should mention Whitechapel," said Mrs. Bardell. "I never told you my husband was a sergeant in the City of London Police before he retired the other year. He saw you leaving here the yesterday when he came to pick me up. He told me he knows you by a different name, 'Vinegar Judy'—the dirtiest tuppenny tart operating on the London Road."

"What! What did you call me?" stammered Judith Fraser.

"Vinegar Judy," said Mrs. Bardell, fixing the girl with a white-hot, Medusa-like, glare.

Without another word, Judith Fraser leapt at the older woman and gripped her throat in an attempt to strangle her. But Mrs. Bardell was surprisingly strong. With some ease, she broke the stranglehold and punched Dickson's lover square on the nose with a right cross that would have made a Bethnal Green prizefighter proud. She staggered back across the scullery with blood flowing freely from her nostrils. Mrs. Bardell lashed out with a sweeping kick which took Judith Fraser's legs from beneath her. The girl crashed to the floor and lay still, blood trickling from the back of her head.

Mrs. Bardell went over to the counter and tipped into the sink the milk from the china cup intended for Dickson upstairs in his sick room—the hot tea had not yet been poured into the cup. In the cup was just the evidence she had been looking for, a partially dissolved tablet. Her regular employer would know how to analyze it upon his return. She anticipated that, without being intermittently drugged, young Mr. Dickson would soon start to make a full recovery.

As Mrs. Bardell thought back, she realized that she had been suspicious of Judith Fraser almost from the very beginning—irrespective of her husband's revelations. The girl had seemed too good to be true. And, inevitably, anything that appears to be over-endowed with goodness will be hollow, false and poisonous—like a perfect white chocolate Easter egg stuffed with putrescence and maggots.

Then Mrs. Bardell heard the sound of footsteps on the stairs. They were light, quiet, almost tentative, something like those of a small child. She rushed out into the hall and saw ascending the stairs a dwarfish, baldheaded figure dressed in a smart dark suit.

"Judith? It is your Uncle," called the little man.

Mrs. Bardell stepped briskly back into the scullery and inadvertently allowed the door to slam behind her. She had only seconds now to find a weapon. Her instincts told her and both she and Dickson would be in great danger when the "uncle" discovered the current condition of his "niece."

She wrestled a butcher knife out from the drawer, and grabbed unconscious Judith by the hair before kicking back open the scullery door.

The little man was now almost back at the bottom of the stairs, having come to investigate the noise from the scullery.

A look of shock played momentarily across his face at the sight of the bloodied girl in the hands of the ferocious looking knife-wielding woman. Mrs. Bardell was a strong woman ordinarily, but right now, a substantial amount of adrenaline was fizzing through her system. She dragged Judith along behind her as if she weighed little more than a mannequin, and then threw her along hall to land on the carpet near the feet of the dwarf, only a yard from the front door. The girl moaned, as if coming around, and rolled onto her back.

"Get out of here!" commanded Mrs. Bardell. "And take this unfortunate baggage with you!"

In response, the little man swiftly removed from his jacket pocket a powerful-looking repeating air pistol, and shot Judith Fraser once in each eye. Mrs. Bardell considered hurling her butcher knife directly at the man, but there was a moment of hesitancy, during which he calmly opened the door and stepped out onto Baker Street—re-pocketing his weapon as he did so.

Mrs. Bardell stepped over Judith's body and watched the killer saunter off down Baker Street with a strange, undulating gait. She looked down at the girl and found that she pitied her. What chance had she had in life? Yet someone had picked her off the street and removed her from a life of debasement, only to turn her into a weapon against the forces of good.

She knew that she needed to notify Scotland Yard straightaway, but they could hardly be relied upon to actually catch the dwarfish killer. But to whom should she now turn for help? She took the opportunity to run upstairs and check on Harry Dickson. Yes, he would doubtless recover in time, but for now, he was still lethargic and feverish. Her own employer was unlikely to be back before the end of the week. That left perhaps three of the *Great Men of Baker Street* available to answer her call for help. And if all of them were otherwise engaged, then she would just have to deal with matters herself.

Of course, everyone knows that, in order to escape from a straitjacket, you have to dislocate your shoulder. The question is, what do you do once you've got your shoulder out of its socket? Rouletabille had bashed his right shoulder against the wall perhaps only four or five times when there came a crunching sensation, followed by the feeling that the interior of the joint had been packed with broken glass. Nauseous from the pain, he stood stock still, considering what to do next.

After a few minutes he experimentally moved his arm and discovered the higher he moved his arm up his chest within the straitjacket, the greater the slack, the greater his field of movement. Nevertheless, it was excruciating. Fortunately, his arms had only been crossed rather than folded. He doubted he'd have been able to withstand the agony of unfolding them, since this would've involved pulling his arm across his torso laterally rather than just pushing it up. Oddly perhaps, as he forced his right arm over his head, the pain eased. He realized that this was because his shoulder joint was close to going back into position, but he couldn't allow that to happen, he still needed the slack to continue in order to be able to work himself to freedom.

Getting his head through the tight gap formed by the crook of his arm felt like threading a camel through the eye of a needle, but once that was achieved the tightness and restriction seemed to go out of the jacket completely. Rouletabille dropped to his knees, exhausted and in a cold sweat. His arms were still within the canvas of the straitjacket, and his hands were firmly buckled together, but he was able to move his arms quite freely now. A series of swift pendulum-type movements loosened the tongue of the buckle sufficiently that he was able to work at it with his teeth. Then, in an ecstasy of flailing, he was able to free himself completely from the straitjacket, only to collapse exhausted to the floor before losing consciousness completely.

Rouletabille awoke ready to put into action the next phase of his improvised plan: escaping from his cell. And then, he fought to stifle the sobs which emanated from him so uncontrollably, for while he had been unconscious, the orderlies had discovered him, forced his shoulder back into position, and put on a fresh straitjacket that was tighter than ever. This time, his arms were closely folded, and it would be much more difficult to get free.

Summoning up the final vestiges of his resolve and his stoicism, he started to beat his shoulder against the wall once more.

Since his time in the police cell, Little Alfie had visited the grounds of the asylum twice. Neither of these visits had been part of his duties as a delivery boy. His father had sent him everywhere in the vicinity except Leytonstone House. He'd therefore developed a spurious excuse for his presence in the grounds of the mental hospital—which were extremely extensive and heavily overgrown. His concocted excuse was that he had taken a fancy to building dens, as he was given to understand some boys did. So far, he had not come close to being caught, but if he was, he'd most likely be let off with a light warning or a cuff round the ear—nothing so imaginative as his incarceration in the police station at the hands of Sergeant Arbogast.

And so, against both his interests and his instincts, he constructed not one, but two dens, concealed within the grounds. Since he was a large and rotund boy, the dens themselves were generously sized, put together from skeletal frames of fallen branches and covered with bracken and evergreen fronds. Purely by the virtue of being assembled from these materials, in combination with the neglect and overgrowth of the grounds, the dens were invisible, unless being deliberately searched for. The second of the dens was in the shadow of an old beech tree, and the interior was actually quite cozy. The grounds were seldom patrolled, and the view from this particular den—through a small aperture he had created, which somehow reminded him of a feature a birdwatcher's hide was likely to have—allowed him to see the drive leading up to the asylum and two of the main pathways leading through the grounds. Most importantly, he could also see the barred window of the strange Frenchman. Little Alfie munched on his chocolate bar, swigged his lemonade, and wondered if the absent Frenchman would ever appear at the window again.

The boy's mind wandered back to what had happened when he was released from the police cell. There had been three men in the police station that he had never seen before. A man in the sort of hat one might wear for shooting in the country; he had one of those mid-length tweedy capes on too; a fellow who seemed to be a doctor, who sported a droopy moustache, and finally a grey-haired man so fat he seemed to have trouble walking.

They had questioned him quite briefly after having spoken to the sergeant, and seemed quite accepting of the information he gave about the Frenchman, so much so that they gave him a shilling. And the boy had been left wondering why he had been punished for lying, when some grownups thought he was telling the truth.

On his way out of the police station, he paused. He was just out of sight, so they carried on talking in loud voices. Devoid of any context, he had to interpret what they were saying as best he could. Spies. There were German spies operating in the area. The Germans were seeking information about the trials of a military tri-plane which was being tested very nearby on the Wanstead Flatlands. The Frenchman was apparently some ally of the British, and they would now seek get him released, since he was most assuredly not a madman.

Later on, he had watched from a distance as the men left, after having visited the asylum. The three of them walked out of the gates without the Frenchman. So where was he?

There was an odd conflict within Little Alfie. His new philosophy of life forbade him from assisting others if it meant that his own liberty might be curtailed. On the other hand, he could not properly know peace of mind until the Frenchman was freed. The boy's eyes continued to scan the grounds and the paths to the asylum building. The three men from the police station had left empty-handed the other day, and as far as he knew, they had not bothered to come back. He looked again at the barred window for some sign of movement. Nothing. But the Frenchman had said he was being tortured. Perhaps they had gone too far and killed him.

Suddenly, an ice-cold hand snaked around Little Alfie from behind and clamped over his mouth. His first thought was that he had been grabbed by some kind of monster, something that had clawed its way out of a grave. Twisting his head, he found himself looking into the vacant, glassy eyes of the Frenchman. His face was milky-white, fatigue and pain had scraped the life from his features.

"It was Hell, but I have escaped," said Rouletabille, before collapsing onto the floor of the den.

For half an hour, Little Alfie crouched over Rouletabille, wondering how to wake him up. His mum was always saying sugar was reviving, so after much thought, he gently opened the Frenchman's mouth and poured in some of his own lemonade. Rouletabille spluttered, but then opened his eyes widely. The boy looked at the man's right shoulder, and it was immediately apparent that it was badly dislocated—high and contorted, like a badly designed marionette.

Little Alfie did not want to see the Frenchman recaptured, he had decided. His principles on this point seemed to have become as pliable as India rubber. He no longer feared the loss of his own liberty because the real authorities wanted to free the injured man. It seemed to him that he stood on the threshold of vindication. He had not lied; he had never lied; and he would soon be in a position to prove this to Sergeant Arbogast, and his father; his father most of all since he seemed to think so very little of him.

He wished he had one of those moving picture cameras in order to record all that was happening around him so he could and make his father see and understand. Perhaps, one day, he would be able to get the whole world to see things from his point of view, to understand his fears and preoccupations.

"We need to get you away from here," said the boy. "They aren't looking for you yet… There's no-one searching the grounds. But I need to get home before it is dark."

"My shoulder is agony… I won't be able to climb the walls. Doubtless they will find me soon, but the pain of the escape was worth for even an hour or so of respite from those torturers," said Rouletabille.

"You won't need to climb. I still have the key to the kitchen delivery gate from when I bring up food. Once we're through that, we're almost home free. There's a bit of loose masonry under the metal railings of the boundary wall. I get in by moving the bricks and then putting them back. There'll be plenty of room for you to squeeze through. Come on!"

Harry Dickson was waking from his drugged and hypnotized state, like a man coming around from years in a coma. Mrs. Bardell ministered to him most effectively, giving him sips of milk and spoons of pureed food as if he were an infant.

There was a period of feverishness and sweating as he suffered withdrawal from whatever addictive filth Judith Fraser had been slipping to him, but just as soon as he was able to vocalize a coherent thought, he started ask about Rouletabille.

The elusive, nagging, forgotten thing from the back of his mind was now at the forefront. He had promised the French detective that he would spend a couple of weeks concluding the cases currently on his desk, and then collaborate with him on the German spy ring case. To have "forgotten" such a commitment was mortifying. Yet, he had not simply forgotten; he had been drugged and subjected to some sort of sinister mesmerism—worse, this had been done by a woman he had believed to be the love of his life. The most horrifying realization was that Rouletabille never turned up to chide him for not coming to his assistance. Where had the Frenchman been all these weeks? Who had him?

"Where is Rouletabille?" screamed Dickson in despair, suddenly sitting bolt upright in his bed.

"Do not concern yourself, Mr. Dickson," said Mrs. Bardell. "The *Great Men* are looking for him. They will find him, and they will save him. So don't you fret."

As he heard those words, he sank back onto his bed, and before long, had returned to a fitful sleep.

It was dusk now out on the Wanstead Flatlands, and Rouletabille had parted company with Little Alfie. He had turned down an offer to be taken to meet the boy's father. His instincts told him to keep away from the streets. There would be too many people, and he was not sure he could tell friend from foe. Once he had recovered slightly, he wanted to see if he could force his shoulder joint back into position.

Somewhere in the air above him, he could hear a droning sound—as if from a far off angry hornet. It was an aircraft engine. Of course! He was walking through the proving grounds of the very aero-plane that the German spies had sought to obtain information about. He could see it now, a delicate yellow and black tri-plane, circling high above him like a buzzard. He could not judge the precise altitude, but it looked to be spiraling lower. Then an inspiration struck him. The plane must be coming in to land. If he simply followed it, he would arrive at a section of the flatlands designated as an airstrip. At the landing site there would be military, and perhaps police representatives, and engineers from the AVRO Company. If he made himself known to them, they would doubtless assist him.

The yellow plane continued to lose altitude; as it did so, the sound of its engine grew more and more and more insistent. The plane was coming nearer and nearer, lower and lower, directly towards him. And yet, there was no landing site in view. The Frenchman had expected the plane to start making towards the horizon, but it did not. On the horizon was a stand of trees, and he had reasoned that these must be blocking his view of the airstrip. The descent of the tri-plane was now accompanied by a kind of screeching or whistling. He had never before heard quite such a sound. It was haunting, almost banshee-like. The plane was entering a dive. Something just behind the propeller started to flare and glow. Searing phosphorescent streaks traversed the hundreds of feet between the plane and the ground upon which Rouletabille stood in just the blink of an eye. There were little explosions of dust and dirt all around him as the machine-gun bullets struck the earth. Only now did he hear the dreadful, repetitive staccato sound of the weapon itself. He ran as best he could, but his attempts at sprinting provided no greater speed than that of a staggering drunkard.

He dropped to the ground as the plane passed overhead, perhaps no more than ninety feet above him. At this point, the firing ceased and the pilot started to execute a turn in order to make another pass at the pathetic stumbling figure below him. Ignoring the lightning bolts of pain in his shoulder, as well as the way that the limb flailed uselessly behind him as he moved, Rouletabille got up and soldiered on. He was gradually nearing the line of trees. Now, he was close enough to see that they were oaks. He kept going, daring to sneak a look back.

The plane had turned and decreased in altitude even more. Now it was perhaps only sixty feet above the ground, but flying straight and level. Coming in for the kill. In the dusky twilight, he was finally able to make out what was beyond the trees. It was a small area of water, much too small to really be called a lake, more of an oversized pond—albeit one with little islands where he could see waterfowl starting to hunker down for the night.

Just as the Frenchman started to reach the shelter of the trees, the machine-gun struck up again. He could hear bullets hitting the bark of the tree trunks, but this time, he did not dare to look back. Instead, he flung himself headlong into the water of the pond. Too late he realized that the water was far colder than he had expected it to be. He had accidentally recreated the cold water torture given to him by the orderlies. He cursed his bad luck as his mind started to unravel into the black incoherence of a fugue state. It was as if he could actually feel his ego leaving his body, being pushed sideways to somewhere else completely, leaving only fragments... crumbs... where his original identity had resided. He clung to those remaining morsels, more precious to him than any diamond: Rouletabille. French. Journalist. Detective. Room. Something about a locked room. The rest was lost now.

From his position of concealment in the undergrowth on the far side of the flatlands, Little Alfie had seen a surprising amount of what had transpired. He really hoped that the Frenchman had gotten away, but perhaps even more than that, he really, really, wished he had a moving picture camera.

The yellow plane came around for one last pass, zeroing in now on the water of the pond where the pilot guessed that Rouletabille was. The pilot was an instant away from ratcheting down the lever that would start the machine-gun spraying death when the presence of the plane startled the geese and other wildfowl on the little island, causing them to erupt into the air in a confused mass of flailing wings and snaking necks.

The frightened birds were so dense that they formed a sudden and dangerous barrier in the air. The pilot dragged back hard on the joystick to avoid them and plane soared away with its engine whining in protest. The plane did not attempt to fire on Rouletabille again. Instead, it headed back to its landing site. The sun had set, and darkness had spilt across the flatlands like a bottle of ink carelessly tipped over on a blotter.

Later, a bedraggled Rouletabille walked in circles across the grass and woodland, devoid of purpose, deep in his fugue state—a weary somnambulist. He came close to the plane landing site and heard voices speaking a language he did not properly understand. Although he did not consciously realize the peril he was in, some submerged instinct urged him away from these men. And yet, he needed some refuge, some sanctuary.

In the moonlight, he saw a grandiose building, almost like a palace, and wondered if it was some sort of mirage. It was not; it was Snarebrook Crown Court, the suburban sister to the Old Bailey which nestles unexpectedly, almost surreally, in the woodland on the edge of London.

Again, his most primal instincts directed him away from the great sightless windows of this darkened edifice. His peregrinations continued and he saw a more modest dwelling. On the periphery of its grounds were a group of men with bulls-eye lanterns. He moved nearer. They appeared to be looking for something, and he wondered what. He could see the nearest of the men was dressed in a deerstalker hat and some sort of mid-length Scottish style cape. Rouletabille had absolutely no idea who the man was.

The house was Theydon Grange, part of the Lord Chancellor's estate, and used as a lodging place for judges conducting cases at Snaresbrook Crown Court. Yes, the French detective had been found by one of the *Great Men of Baker Street,* just as Mrs. Bardell had predicted. And medical attention was swiftly administered. Indeed, it was Dr. Watson himself who reset Rouletabille's shoulder. The injured and amnesic detective was given quarters in a small cottage in the grounds of Theydon Grange called the Gatekeeper's Lodge, and Mrs. Bardell was moved in to minister to him with her other charge, Harry Dickson, who was by now greatly improved and free of the pernicious withdrawal symptoms from which he had been suffering.

Rouletabille was fed with Mrs. Bardell's warming broth and provided with soothing poultices for his still swollen shoulder. But there was an urgency and impatience about the many visitors who came to check on the recovering Frenchman over the next few days. And although they did not pester Rouletabille himself, the question was whispered in hushed tones to Harry Dickson again and again: "When will Joseph Rouletabille recover his memory?"

The question was a weight pressing on Dickson's shoulders. It swirled around the American's mind day and night. How can memory be recovered? How can memory be evoked? Particularly when Watson had said the young Frenchman was too mentally delicate to undergo hypnosis. Yet, within Rouletabille's mind would be a myriad of clues to crack this case. Perhaps even the whole solution to this labyrinthine conundrum.

The little sitting room at the cottage had small display cases of mounted butterflies. Rouletabille found these relaxing to look at and would sit in his chair for hours with one of the cases on his lap scrutinizing the multi-colored wings of the insects. Late one morning, Dickson bit the bullet and decided to start questioning his friend.

"Can you remember anything about your time in the asylum? How did they torture you?" he asked.

"Some things are starting to come back. I remember being plunged in cold water. I remember painful injections... of camphor," said Rouletabille.

"Camphor?" repeated Dickson with furrowed brow. And an idea began to take shape swiftly in his mind. "Mrs. Bardell! Could you please light the fire here in the sitting room?" he cried with an odd desperation in his voice.

"Whatever for, young man? It is the height of summer, and really quite hot enough already,"

Then Mrs. Bardell saw the grim set of Dickson's face and realized that there was more to this than some idle request. She hurriedly collected kindling, old newspapers and matches from the kitchen, then commenced to lay the foundations of the fire over the hearth grate. Without another word, Dickson rushed upstairs and they could hear him rooting about in drawers and opening the squeaky doors of wardrobes. In the end, he found what he was looking for. Whatever he had found, he kept secretly in the palm of one closed hand. As Mrs. Bardell decamped to the kitchen to prepare lunch, Dickson put down on the hearth directly in front of the fire a couple of crumbling crystalline spheres. Rouletabille watched with interest.

"What have you got there, my friend? *Boules de naphtaline?* Mothballs?" asked Rouletabille.

"Yes, and mothballs contain camphor..."

The American paused. The heat from the fire was already causing the mothballs to soften, and a sickly, somewhat irritating, aroma was starting to pervade the atmosphere of the room and tickle the back of his throat.

"…and what is more evocative of lost and forgotten memories than something which stimulates the sense of smell?"

Rouletabille breathed deeply, and the disrupted connections within his brain started to re-establish themselves – neurons fired and ganglia pulsed with the fresh flow of information.

"You are right. It is coming back to me in a deluge," said Rouletabille. "And, by God, I will have my revenge on Dr. Grierson."

The Yellow Terror

London, Summer 1909

The great iron gate of Newgate Prison clanged shut be-hind Dr. Rupert Grierson making a sound eerily like that of a single toll from a lonely funeral bell. Before the resonance had died, Grierson showed his credentials to the guard and then was swiftly admitted to the inner courtyard. Grierson confi-dently assured the guard that he would be easily able to find his way to 'A' Wing North from previous visits, and would require no escorts. The guard recognized this little, bald-pated, gnome of a man to be a prominent medical practitioner—the head of Leytonstone House Asylum for the Criminally Insane, but his breadth of knowledge was insufficient to know that Grierson was also one of the foremost forensic psychiatrists in the country. He would therefore have been surprised to dis-cover that Grierson's entry papers were complete forgeries, and he had no legitimate business to conduct within the gaol. on this day. But the guard had no reason to suspect any of this, so he retreated back to his little wooden sentry box, where a chipped enamel mug of hot tea rested on the shelf, awaiting his return. He perched back on his stool, took a swig of tea, and then went back to reading the latest issue of the *Police Gazette*.

Grierson tramped his way up the steel stairway on the north side of the gloomy courtyard. He could see that the building work around the condemned cell area to repair the bomb damage was now largely complete. That was where he had made his abortive, and rather desperate attempt to free Schellenberger just before his execution. Schellenberger had been killed by the French journalist, Rouletabille, during the break-out. Grierson gave an audible bark of cynical laughter.

It was quite plain now that this Frenchman was merely using his position within the fourth estate as a cover. He was obviously one of France's top intelligence operatives. Rouletabille's interference during Schellenberger's trial for the murder of his wife had proved fatal to Grierson's plan to have the killer certified insane. An insane man is not placed on the gallows, he is locked away in an asylum. And in this case, it would have been all too easy to make Leytonstone House Schellenberger's place of incarceration. Later, no-one would have known if the German had been replaced by a similar looking street derelict and spirited back to the Fatherland. Yes, Rouletabille had seemed dangerous from the very beginning—his deductive reasoning matched, or perhaps even exceeded that of the legendary *Great Men of Baker Street*—those four consulting detectives who had now been joined by the irritating American neophyte, Harry Dickson. Dickson too had become embroiled in the Schellenberger affair at an even earlier stage than Rouletabille, since the American had been hired by Frau Schellenberger to investigate her husband's odd behavior. The reason for his odd behavior was simple enough, Schellenberger was a German spy tasked with finding out as much technical information as possible about the new British tri-plane being tested out on the military proving grounds on the Wanstead Flatlands.

And so, the German spy neglected his wife and his job—and was ultimately forced to murder his spouse when she revealed she had put a Baker Street detective on his trail, such sleuths were infamous for their close contact, nay allegiance, with the upper echelons of the British Government. Schellenberger then fell back on a standing protocol used by his spy ring: when the authorities are closing in, feign insanity. He beat Reginald Scott, the owner of the fruit and vegetable stall where he sometimes worked, to death in the *Salmon and Ball* pub in front of witnesses, and also killed Edward Cookson, an acquaintance after spreading rumors that the man was having an affair with Frau Schellenberger. In the end, it was perhaps Schellenberger's own over cleverness which carried him to the gallows. No madman would be able to think of procuring a weather balloon and using it to carry off the dismembered remains of his murdered wife. On this point the Old Bailey jury had agreed with Rouletabille—especially after the brilliant young French detective calculated the likely landing area of the balloon and had its shredded remnants and bloody cargo recovered by his colleagues in the International News Service bureau in the Netherlands. Yes, without the involvement of Rouletabille and Dickson things would have looked very different.

Grierson reached the North Wing and the heavy door was opened by a prison officer to admit him to the landing. After an even more cursory check of his documents he was directed to Cell 19, where Klaus Eschmann was incarcerated. The prison officer opened the small metal viewing slot near the top of the door and called through.

"Visitor for you, Eschmann."

The only response was an animalistic grunt.

The door swung open and Grierson entered without hesitation. He looked Eschmann up and down, insofar as was possible in the gloom of the cell. He seemed like he had lost even more weight—his skin was tight across the bones of his face. Yet still, it was obvious the man was highly dangerous. It was so very apparent to Grierson who had seen many caged men that this specimen would kill to escape the moment the opportunity presented itself.

"I hope you have good news for me," rasped the prisoner.

"A point of culmination has been reached. The mission of your team—the mission you failed to complete, will soon be brought to a suitable conclusion by two individuals I have corrupted. They are very close to the *Yellow Terror*—closer than your agents with their note books and stopwatches, making futile attempts trying to ascertain the plane's secrets from hundreds of yards away by means of schoolboyish observation."

"Have a care, Grierson. I am well thought of by our superiors, my long history of covert action against the Fatherland's enemies speaks for itself. You know it is true or you would not be here. Now what are your orders?"

"Naturally, I am to help you escape. You are to be broken out of prison before you stand trial," said Grierson.

"Well then, I hope that you are of greater assistance to me than you were to Schellenberger. Personally, I can't think of a more idiotic plan than trying to rescue someone from jail a split-second before they were due to be executed."

"It was a daring plan, and it would have worked but for the interference of Rouletabille and Dickson. The former is a dangerous genius, and the latter a young bumbler with the luck of Satan himself," said Grierson.

"What have you done to ensure that the genius and the bumbler are well and truly out of the picture?"

"It has not been easy. If I had taken direct action against Harry Dickson—had him killed—it would immediately have attracted the involvement of the *Great Men of Baker Street* en masse. Can you imagine such a situation? They would have descended on us like enraged furies to take vengeance on whosoever had harmed their protégé. Instead, I neutralized Dickson by placing him in the tender care of a woman I believed to be one of my top operatives—Judith Fraser, also known as *Vinegar Judy.* I had previously schooled her extensively in the practice of hypnosis. And so, with the American kept permanently half-drugged with a mild scopolamine derivative it was possible to use hypnotic suggestion to prevent him from recalling his relationship with Rouletabille. This state of affairs continued for some weeks, and perhaps I was overoptimistic in thinking that it would remain the case until the conclusion of the espionage mission," said Grierson.

"I expect your so-called 'bumbler' broke through the wall of his hypnotic conditioning."

"That would have almost have been too predictable. No, Dickson's salvation came from a rather more unexpected quarter. I arrived at Dickson's Baker Street lodgings one afternoon to find that his temporary housekeeper had gotten the better of *Vinegar Judy* in a rather brutal physical confrontation. She must have given herself away through some inadvertent slip, possibly while administering a dose of the drug. I could not see any way to rescue Miss Fraser inconspicuously from Dickson's rooms without placing myself in severe danger of arrest. I therefore drew my repeating air pistol and shot the girl once in each eye, before retreating out of the front door and hailing the nearest hansom cab. I had hoped to prevent her from revealing anything during interrogation. But only today I discovered that a surgeon at Marylebone Hospital had served her life, though not her sight. It can only be a matter of time now before she recovers sufficiently to tell everything she knows," concluded Grierson.

"Your catalogue of incompetence grows ever longer. To be honest, I am having difficulty keeping track. But if you could not stymie the bumbler, I daresay the 'genius' Rouletabille was able to outwit you. Pray, what became of him?" asked Eschmann.

"I had another of my female agents drug Rouletabille while he was at large in an East End pub conducting his investigations. The drug induced symptoms similar to the sudden onset of psychosis. So while he raved and foamed at the mouth, my men were called from Leytonstone Asylum to cart the lunatic away. He had only been incarcerated in the asylum for a few hours when he almost managed to escape. I ordered him restrained in a straitjacket, and he escaped the straitjacket twice. The second time he absconded from the grounds completely, though precisely by what means I am yet to discover. If I did not know better, I would suspect that he had assistance from someone within the asylum. Yet I am sure none of my men would risk such a betrayal—they all know the medical interventions I have planned for those who dare to oppose me," said Grierson.

"I shall not bank too heavily on being rescued by your machinations, Grierson. I would be better advised to steal a spoon from the refectory and commence digging a tunnel.

"Your sarcasm is understandable, but misplaced. We are arriving at the end game, the final reckoning. Before very long, all of the secrets of *The Yellow Terror* will be ours, and you, my friend will be back in your beloved Berlin—making plans for that technological hierarchy which you are so keen to see running the world. The zenith of my achievement will be the final destruction of Rouletabille and Harry Dickson. They will be drawn to their doom by the single thing they cannot resist—an impossible mystery. Already the trap is primed, and once it is sprung, we will see not only the end of this pair of nauseating meddlers, but of all of the *Great Men of Baker Street* too," said Grierson.

Eschmann looked hard at Grierson's face. Yes, there was confidence written upon it. But the eyes stared a little too wildly, the grin was inhuman—almost shark-like. Grierson's reputation as an infallible master-planner had taken some near-fatal hammer blows since he went up against these two young men. He did not doubt that Grierson was capable of anything, and was also fired up to get the better of adversaries he had underestimated. Yet, Eschmann wondered at Grierson's levels of mental resilience—knock back and frustration at his defeats had affected him. And would it not be a supreme irony if a man in charge of an insane asylum was tipped over into insanity himself?

Inspector Hopkins approached the door of Theydon Grange House's little lodge keeper's cottage with some trepidation. He knew that Joseph Rouletabille and Harry Dickson were now fully recovered and impatient for action. He used the knocker to rap loudly, and within a few seconds the door swung open. Mrs. Bardell's face broke into a welcoming grin as she recognized the veteran Scotland Yard detective who had assisted Sherlock Holmes himself in the *Case of the Three Music Boxes*. She showed him into the cottage, which was filled with a most delicious aroma of baking. Bread, cakes and sausage pie were Mrs. Bardell's particular areas of expertise. In the small sitting room, Rouletabille was in an easy chair gorging himself on a great slice of chocolate cake. The gauntness caused by his imprisonment in the asylum had now vanished, and the roses had returned to his cheeks. Harry Dickson was neglecting a great slab of steaming hot sausage pie which was sitting on a plate on the dining table. Instead, he was sawing off the long barrel of a shotgun with a hacksaw he had purloined from the garden tool shed, in order to make it into a more effective close-quarters weapon. Hopkins looked on this activity with growing horror.

"Good God, Harry! That's one of the Lord Chancellor's Purdey shotguns. Have you any idea how much those things cost?" asked the Scotland Yard man.

"Nope. And I don't care. We're spoiling for a fight and hit by cabin fever. When are we going to raid the asylum and grab hold of Grierson?" demanded the American.

"When Special Branch executes warrants to search Leytonstone House and arrest the offenders within, I'm sure you will be informed. But as a private citizen with an interest in the matter you most certainly will not be invited to participate. Nor will you be allowed to take possession of other people's firearms," said Hopkins, assertively relieving Dickson of the sawn-off shotgun.

"You know I am perhaps not so hot-headed as my American friend," began Rouletabille. "But this long delay is equally incomprehensible to me. Why is Dr. Grierson allowed to retain his liberty when we know that he is an agent of a hostile foreign power? Even if you do not believe that, he unlawfully imprisoned me and attempted to kill Miss Judith Fraser."

"Grierson is being kept under extremely close surveillance. Why just today he was followed when he made a visit to Newgate Prison to see Klaus Eschmann," said Hopkins.

"And what more proof do you need? Eschmann is to stand trial for espionage at the Old Bailey later this month," barked Dickson.

"His guilt has not yet been established. And a state of war does not yet exist between England and Germany...perhaps it never will. For the purposes of diplomacy we must tread carefully and avoid exacerbating the situation," said Hopkins.

"If Grierson has been to see Eschmann it can only be because he intends to break him out just as he tried to do with Schellenberger," said the Frenchman. "We foiled him before and we must stand ready to do so again."

"The primary reason for holding off action against Grierson is that the remnants of the Schellenberger spy ring are still at large. We have no idea where they are. But, if he makes a move to contact them, we can round the lot of them up. At the moment, no one has come near the secret AVRO workshops close to here on the Wanstead Flatlands in the way that Schellenberger and Eschmann did," said Hopkins.

"They have merely changed their tactics. They'll be lurking around here somewhere…," said Dickson.

And then Rouletabille realized that he had been struck with a sudden headache. He had suffered from these a lot since his escape from the asylum. Somehow, it was the mention of the AVRO workshops that had brought it on. He had thought that all of his memory had come back to him in a flood—but this was not entirely true. Something was still being held back, and he was not sure what. Something had happened to him immediately after his escape. After he had said goodbye to the boy, Alfie, and trying to bring it to mind was like trying to grasp wisps of smoke. Every time it eluded him and sent a knitting needle of pain probing into his frontal lobes.

A few hundred yards away, Captain Oliver Treadwell arrived at Theydon Grange House and pulled hard on the doorbell. The eagle-eyed would have noticed that Captain Treadwell's smart Royal Engineers' uniform bore an unusual shoulder flash—a modest black badge with red lettering bearing the legend 'Pilot.' Treadwell was one of handful in that vanguard of officers who were learning to fly in the British armed forces. In the years, and then decades, to come, that cadre of officers would become the Royal Flying Corps, before finally taking pride of place as the Royal Air Force. But right here was their point of genesis, brave, yet inexperienced men testing the limits and capabilities of highly experimental aircraft built in the wake of the Wright Brothers' triumph at Kitty Hawk, North Carolina. Naturally, such dashing and valorous men were almost irresistible to women, especially perhaps to the daughters of judges raised in the rarified atmosphere of the Lord Chancellor's judicial lodgings within the Snaresbrook Crown Court Campus.

The door swung open and a beauteous vision met Treadwell's eyes. This was his fiancé, Berenice Munro, the only daughter of His Honor Judge Aloysius Munro, that ogre of the assizes who ate inexperienced young barristers for his breakfast, yet had taken such a shine to this handsome captain. She practically dragged him inside the hallway and after a quick look behind her to see that no servants were in sight she delivered an intimate and arousing kiss. And while she could've easily done the same within the comparative privacy of the drawing room, part of the thrill was the possibility of discovery.

"Surely, you do not wish your father to happen upon us and think that I'm here to take your virginity before our wedding night!" chided the young captain.

The girl laughed coquettishly.

"Since we are to be married in less than a month, it would hardly seem to matter what anyone thinks. Besides, I would hear the creaking of my father's wheelchair a mile off, and I know for sure that he is locked away in his study reading the case papers for that awful murder trial he is presiding over next week."

They moved into the sitting room where her slim hands moved to his waistband and began to unbuckle his belt. At this, he lost his temper and slapped away her hand.

"Cool your ardor, my dear. You are like a bitch in heat," said Treadwell.

Berenice dropped herself onto the couch in mock anger and crossed her arms, her desires frustrated for now.

"Very well. I suppose you want to talk about that silly little toy aeroplane of yours instead," said the girl.

"The Empire's greatest and most secret weapon is hardly a toy. There was a nasty cross-wind over the Hackney Marshes this afternoon, and I nearly ended up in the sewage treatment works, instead of my refueling stop near the cricket pitch. I daresay I'd have been court-martialed for damaging government property, but if I'd splashed into that noisome morass I'd probably still carry the stench, and that might be enough to keep even you away!" said Treadwell.

"You may be sure of it. I'd have had Jenkins the gardener hose you down in the yard before you were admitted," teased the girl. "But whatever is the point of all this? I hear the interminable drone of your engine overhead...I hear the clatter of your dismal guns as you reach the proving grounds—typically disturbing my afternoon nap. And the next day it's the same. Will you be testing the plane here forever? I, for one, certainly hope so. I have no desire for you to be posted elsewhere following our marriage. I would get so...lonely."

"There are some things which must remain secret. As it is, I tell you far more than I should. Let's just say that I will be around here for at least a little while longer. And now, before you call for tea in the conservatory, I really must pay some attention to your dear mama. I have been rather neglecting her of late. Is she upstairs in her room?" asked the young officer.

"Of course, the old dear is suffering dreadfully with her hay fever. She sniffles and sniffles both day and night. I will be the most enormous relief to her when summer is over. What a martyr she is..."

Treadwell ascended the stairs, and on the landing encountered another of the young beauties closeted away in the judicial lodgings, Lara Haining, the younger child of His Honor Judge Thomas Haining, her elder sister had just recently married and she was beginning to find life on the Snaresbrook Crown Court campus stifling and isolating. She was pleasant enough to him, but she could be haughty and aloof when the mood took her. A keen horsewoman, he often saw her exercising her mare on the Wanstead Flats while he was piloting his plane. There was something rather unobtainable and imperious about her, he mused for a moment that the chase had been rather too easy with Berenice. Perhaps he had gone after the wrong girl, though there was little he could do about it now, gentlemen were still sued sometimes for breach of promise when they failed to follow through on their stated intention to marry a young lady.

Lara put her fingers to her lips.

"You'd best be quiet up here, Captain. My father has just reprimanded me for disturbing him while he was studying papers for his new Old Bailey case."

"I was just going into see Berenice's mother, and wish her well. Why don't you join us in the conservatory for tea in a few minutes?" he more or less whispered.

"Yes, I'll be down shortly," she confirmed.

He moved silently down the corridor and rapped ever so gently on the third door he came to. A quiet feminine voice asked him to identify himself and when he did he was bade to enter.

Treadwell entered Mrs. Munro's bedchamber and could not help but smile. Berenice often made reference to her mother as if she were an old woman, while, in fact, she was barely forty, and looked much younger. Her youth had somehow been mysteriously preserved, she was just as vibrant and lovely as her daughter. A pang of illicit desire rose within him and he quashed it, this was no time for dalliance, but there was always time for flirtation.

"How lovely to see you again, Oliver," said Mrs. Munro, huskily, her throat much affected by the terrible hay fever which always afflicted her at this time of year.

"And you are looking as radiant as ever," he flattered. Though, in truth, it was the bedchamber in which the woman lay which seemed radiant. It was illuminated by every conceivable means, a cluster of incandescent bulbs in a newly installed modern style chandelier on the ceiling, the flickering gas lamps on the walls as well as a host of candles. The room seemed as bright as it did in daytime, light from those various sources seemed to bounce off the multiplicity of mirrors, including the enormous gold framed one which hung over the marital bed.

"Sit down a moment, why don't you?" urged Mrs. Munro, patting the side of her bed. He needed no further encouragement and placed himself down on the edge of the bed. Now there was the usual fight he had with himself to look into her remarkable hazel eyes instead of at the contents of her extraordinarily sheer negligee. Her full breasts were exactly like those immortalized in those rather filthy dog-eared French lithographs which were constantly being re-circulated around the barracks back when he was a cadet.

"I wanted to ask if you were feeling well enough to join us in the conservatory for tea," said Treadwell.

Mrs. Munro's hand strayed onto his thigh. His whole body tensed. Now was not the time…now was not the time. His inappropriate dalliances with his future mother-in-law could not be discovered now, that would ruin everything. He was struck by a powerful premonition that as soon as his finger tips caressed Mrs. Munro they would be walked in on. His mind played out in vivid detail the embarrassing aftermath of such an occurrence, and Mrs. Munro interpreted his sudden qualms as a lack of interest; the expression on the older woman's beautiful face hardened somewhat.

"If it is my daughter you wish to be with then go to her."

"Only if you are sure you do not desire to join us," he said.

She kicked back the bedclothes suddenly and rather lasciviously, revealing her long legs as well as the fact that the action had caused her negligee to ride all the way up her smooth flat belly. She was exquisite.

"I cannot imagine you will find anything of greater interest on offer in our conservatory. But if you do, then I am disappointed," she chided, waspishly.

The display had been crass and unladylike, yet monstrously tempting.

He got up to leave.

"Do not pursue me onto the landing and create a scene. Judge Haining is hard at work reading his papers," said Treadwell.

A few minutes later in the conservatory, the Earl Grey tea had been poured and Berenice was sitting with arms tightly folded, unappreciative of the presence of Lara Haining. But now that he was back downstairs Treadwell was starting to feel more relaxed. While Berenice stared out of the window into the darkening garden, his mind wandered too. He was a slave to his own desires, he wanted to strip practically every woman he met of both clothing and inhibitions. He wished to could somehow hypnotize both Lara and Berenice and make love to them both right now, wiping clean their recollection afterwards like a wet sponge across a slate. Such feelings had grown and grown in him recently, like some kind of weird addiction. And the more he tried to satiate them the more they increased.

From somewhere outside and faraway came a persistent whine. It was the sound of a straining engine.

"That sounds like the noise of your…," began Berenice.

Immediately Treadwell cut her off.

"It can't be…it just can't be," he got up suddenly and then stood stock still, waiting, listening. Then came the clatter of machinegun fire, and the high caliber bullets started to rain down on the house.

Inspector Hopkins almost battered down the door of the lodge cottage, fortunately Mrs. Bardell unlatched the portal before his fists burst through the wood.

"C'mon, you two! If ever you were needed it is now," shouted Hopkins. "Get your coats and hurry. You must have heard the shots!"

Although it was not late, Rouletabille was laying on his bed resting. Dickson was smoking in the living room and reading a Dickens novel. Perhaps this would not be the precise clarion call to action they had desired, for they were both desperate to participate in a raid on the insane asylum. But they had been cooped up in the cottage for so long that any diversion was a blessed release.

Rouletabille skidded to a halt at the bottom of the stairs and demanded to know what had happened.

"It's the AVRO experimental plane—*The Yellow Terror.* We thought it had been stolen since not ten minutes ago Theydon Grange House was attacked from the air, and Judge Haining killed. But the Special Branch officers guarding it have just told me that the plane is still in its workshophangar," explained Hopkins. "There is no other plane in England armed with machine guns. How did the perpetrators steal *The Yellow Terror* and replace it without being discovered?"

"If you are certain of this plane's uniqueness, then that is a mystery indeed," said Rouletabille. "Fortunately, impossible mysteries are our trade."

Outside the Gatekeeper's lodge cottage were two armed constables with bull's eye lanterns. They guided Rouletabille and Dickson through the gloom to the far side of the Crown Court campus towards Theydon House, with Hopkins dragging along behind. Truly, the two foreign detectives were in their element—like a pair of terriers being led to a rats' nest. As they walked they reminded each other in hushed tones that a man had died, and after that their levity became muted; their mood deliberately made somber. Nevertheless, it was a relief to be outdoors in the warm summer night and away Mrs. Bardell's rather stifling benevolent supervision.

As they neared the rather grandiose regency dwelling that was the Judges' lodgings the two constables shone their lamps onto the upper storey to pick out the damage they had seen earlier. It was evident that the bricks and rendering around one of the bedroom windows had been hit by a volley a high caliber bullets - deep, precisely circular pockmarks abounded. The glass and mullions of the window itself had also been struck. Hardly any glass remained, and a dark green curtain flapped occasionally in the breeze, like a restless spirit.

Without further ado, Hopkins led them directly upstairs to the scene of the murder while the two constables stood guard outside. Their eyes began drinking in every detail from the moment they crossed the threshold. Every scintilla of information would be absorbed and cross-referenced by Rouletabille's extraordinarily analytical mind, and this made Dickson feel slightly competitive. The Frenchman had solved numerous mysteries and had well and truly made his name in the annals of detection. While he was under the wing of *The Great Men of Baker Street* he also had to become 'his own man'—and perhaps this was the case in which he would be fully able to demonstrate his acumen, especially if he could beat his friend, Rouletabille, to the punch. But when Dickson found himself starting to visualize newspaper headlines celebrating his success he was forced to rein himself in—now was not the time for counting his chickens, there was work to be done.

The two detectives stood in the doorway to Judge Haining's combined study and bedroom and surveyed the scene. The body had been covered by a spare sheet, and the still fresh blood had soaked through in numerous crimson patches that were even now trying to amalgamate themselves into a single awful stain. The Frenchman's keen eyes scanned the floor of the room and settled on a scuffed area of partially coagulated blood over by the desk.

"What has been removed from the floor over there, Inspector?" he asked, pointing.

"The Judge was reading confidential case papers for his forthcoming trial at the Old Bailey," replied Hopkins. "They were dropped to the floor during the attack, and ruined by the amount of blood that was over them. I picked them up and disposed of them in the basement incinerator."

"Nothing should have been removed from the room before our arrival—nothing!" rebuked Rouletabille in hushed tones.

For another ten minutes, Rouletabille examined everything in the room—the carpets, the furniture, bullet strikes on the internal walls, and most particularly, the bloodstains and spattering of blood. Dickson was no slouch at detective work, but here he learned, as if at the feet of a master, lessons he would remember for the rest of his life. Finally, Rouletabille announced that he was ready to meet residents of the house (not servants) who had been present during the attack. Hopkins informed Rouletabille that Lara Haining, the judge's daughter, had been in such deep shock she'd had to be sedated. Judge Munro's wife, Adelaide, was in a state of extreme hysteria—due to a bullet passing through an internal wall and hitting the chandelier in her bedroom. She had refused sedation and was currently being comforted by her husband. This left available for interview the couple's daughter, Berenice, and her fiancé, Captain Oliver Treadwell, who was also - by coincidence—the test pilot of *The Yellow Terror*. In fact, this suited Rouletabille, because though it was of primary importance to interview these firsthand witnesses, he was extremely impatient to get to the 'real' scene of this impossible crime—the nearby railway arch workshops from which the aeroplane had been stolen and then returned without raising the suspicions of the uniformed Special Branch officers assigned to guard it.

Inspector Hopkins ushered Rouletabille and Dickson into the conservatory where Miss Munro and Treadwell were waiting. Her face was tearstained, and his pale and bloodless. Hopkins explained to the traumatized couple that these two private detectives had been temporarily seconded to Scotland Yard's Special Branch.

Dickson utilized his gentle charm to put them at their ease and then encouraged them to relate exactly what had happened.

"We were sitting here with Lara just about to have tea," began Berenice. "When suddenly I heard the sound of the plane's engine, but it was much louder and much closer than it normally is. Usually, it's just a far off whine."

"And I was perhaps even more shocked when we heard *The Yellow Terror's motor,* for I know I am currently the only person authorized to pilot it," stated Treadwell.

"And to fly it presumably takes a great deal of skill?" asked Rouletabille, somewhat rhetorically.

"Why, yes. I suppose this is not the time for false modesty. It is a tricky beast to fly. It takes some practice, particularly because it is easily blown off a precise trajectory by crosswinds," said Treadwell. "And the thing is, I would balk at flying it in twilight or nighttime conditions, but that is precisely what the pilot who has stolen it has done."

"What is so unusual about this plane? What makes it so secret?" asked Harry Dickson.

"Am I allowed to reveal technical details to these two foreign gentlemen?" asked Treadwell.

"You are," said Hopkins. "I have written authority from Whitehall which allows them access to all secret information relating to the German spy ring...and in my estimation this murder and the espionage case are inextricably connected."

"Very well then, *The Yellow Terror* has twin front mounted machine guns which fire *through* its propeller. This allows the pilot unparalleled ability to aim, and then shoot with pinpoint accuracy. After the attack I ran outside and it was obvious to me that only *The Yellow Terror* could have fired on the house with quite such accuracy. Most of the shots hit the Judge's window or the area of brickwork just around it," said Treadwell.

"So you actually saw the aeroplane still above the house?" asked Rouletabille.

"No, not really. It had pulled up and was starting to execute its turn—already quite a long way away. But Miss Munro did see it too," replied Treadwell.

"Yes, I did. And I could still hear its engine quite clearly," she said. "I was very worried it would return, but it just kept on drifting away."

"Something should be done immediately about the men who say that the plane was never stolen, for that is quite impossible," demanded Treadwell. "They must be in league with the German spy ring. That plane could only have been stolen and returned by an expert pilot. And there is absolutely no way to remove it from the workshop hangar, let alone replace it, without someone outside noticing."

"It is certainly pretty darn perplexing," said Dickson. "I guess we'd better go and see for ourselves."

Dickson hastily concluded the diagram of the house and environs he has been drawing in pencil in his notebook. He noted that the plane had approached from the west, and that the conservatory was built onto the eastern side of the house.

As they left, Rouletabille whispered to Dickson, "We are not done here by a long way. I have an instinct that we should return to search the bedroom of the hysterical Mrs. Munro. Something is not right here."

Hopkins and his two uniformed officers led Rouletabille and Dickson beyond the confines of the grounds of Theydon Grange House for the first time in a few weeks down towards the railway embankment a few hundred yards away where *The Yellow Terror's* hangar had been constructed inside a large brick archway which was part of the support structure for the railway above. It was common for the spare space in a bridge or embankment to be utilized by local businesses in this way—nearer to London there were car repair garages or machine shops housed in railway arches, and on the approach to the country it was sometimes a blacksmith's forge. Typically, the railway arch was bricked up at the far end, and a set of wooden or steel doors fitted at the remaining opening. Additional ventilation or chimneys were added as required. The uniformed officers' bull's eye lamps illuminated the locked steel doors upon which were painted in letters almost ten feet high the legend 'AVRO'—short for A.V. Roe, the embryonic aviation company which would one day go on to become a major force in the world of aircraft construction.

"The workshop has been left unguarded," judged Rouletabille as he strode forward. "Let us try to imagine how the miscreants were able to remove the plane from the archway without alerting the watching officers."

"Have a care, m'sieur," warned Hopkins. "You take your life in your hands by approaching this facility unannounced. It is indeed guarded, by my fellow Special Branch officers, and they have instructions to open fire on anyone who is not known to them personally."

Rouletabille was aghast, but now he saw there were figures in the shadows of railway embankment archways, and lurking in the undergrowth, as well as in the shelter of nearby trees. There were perhaps seven men in all, and they were all armed with heavy Webley revolvers.

Then Hopkins raised his voice and shouted, "This is Inspector Hopkins with constables Willis and Matthews. Also with us are two private detectives seconded to Special Branch: Joseph Rouletabille and Harry Dickson. Please allow us to approach."

The men guarding the AVRO workshop stepped out from cover and holstered their weapons.

"Get the doors opened quickly," ordered Rouletabille. "There may be some trick or illusion in place, making it look as if the plane is in the workshop, when in reality, it has been stolen."

At a nod from Hopkins, Rouletabille was obeyed and the great doors swung open. Inside, *The Yellow Terror* was most definitely still in its home. The tri-plane was delicately constructed, yet it looked positively vespine in its yellow and black painted livery—a lethal and gargantuan wasp ready to spew forth death. Instinctively, Harry Dickson put his hand to the barrels of the machine guns and then onto the engine housing.

"Cold," said Dickson. "The plane hasn't been used for hours, and the machineguns have not been fired."

"I suppose that could be achieved by means of deception," mused the French detective. "Perhaps cold, wet rags could've been applied to the engine cowling and the barrels of the guns."

"I am more interested in how the plane was removed," said Dickson. "We need to check if an aperture has been created at the rear of the railway arch—maybe all the bricks were cut away and then replaced. It wouldn't be possible to do that without leaving at least some sign, surely?"

But the two men looked for such an opening without success. More out of desperation than conviction, Dickson suggested that the railway ties above the workshop had been removed and the plane craned out of its home. This caused a little confusion because in England railway ties are known as 'sleepers.' Nevertheless, whatever you call them, a close examination of them—following a climb to the top of the embankment by all of the investigators—found no indication at all that they had been removed and replaced.

"All these men guarding the workshop hangar could not be in the employ of a foreign power," ruminated the Frenchman. "That would be ridiculous. And yet not one of them saw the tri-plane removed. However it was removed there would have been some sign…some noise. To do the job invisibly and inaudibly it is either the work of phantoms or angels."

"What if each of them had a relative or loved one held hostage by this gang of Teutonic spies?" wondered Dickson. "They could have been compelled to assist by means of blackmail."

"And what would be the point? If you wish to steal an experimental plane, then why not just steal it? Why use it to commit a murder and then replace it as if nothing has happened? Who exactly were they trying to fool?" questioned Rouletabille, almost ranting.

"Can we even be sure that this is the real *Yellow Terror?*" asked Dickson. "If it is merely a good facsimile how could we know? We need Captain Treadwell to take it aloft and test it out in the morning, to see if it handles and performs exactly the same as the genuine tri-plane."

"If a burglar breaks into your house and replaces all of your possessions with exact duplicates, are you the victim of a crime or not? Is the perpetrator a criminal genius or a performance artist?" laughed Rouletabille hollowly. "This is a similar conundrum, my friend. This unique vehicle is used as a murder weapon in circumstances that are quite literally impossible. My head is starting to hurt—and I do not mean that metaphorically—it does not hurt from the effort of thinking, but rather because something is gnawing away at the inside of it. Painful thoughts and recollections summoned up by the plane itself...I am reminded of the torture I suffered at the hands of Dr. Grierson, and parlous mental state in which I found myself in the aftermath of my escape from the asylum. Something from that time still eludes me. There is a memory that would make sense of this whole narrative if only I could access it."

"Come now, we have taken this as far as we can tonight, surely. Let us return to the Lodge Keeper's Cottage and rest," advised Dickson.

Rouletabille had anticipated that he would wake up early the following day, at the first crack of dawn. He surprised was when he picked up his borrowed pocket watch from the bedside table to find that it was five minutes after nine. Mrs. Bardell had allowed him to sleep in, and the delicious aroma of frying bacon was wafting up from the kitchen. He took his dressing gown from the back of the door, pulled it on and padded down the stairs.

"Good morning, Mrs. Bardell," called Rouletabille cheerily, as he looked about the cottage. "Where is Harry?"

"Oh, he made himself some toast hours ago, and then went out for a walk. I think he was just going to Theydon Grange," said Mrs. Bardell.

The Frenchman was not entirely sure what to make of this. Had Harry decided to solve the case on his own, or was he just giving Rouletabille additional opportunity to rest? Either way, he had enjoyed the extra couple of hours sleep. The nocturnal ramble to the railway arches had taken more out of him than he really wanted to admit. He took a leisurely breakfast, followed by a long soaking bath on the basis that this mystery was not the sort that would take flight and elude him.

No, its various constituent components were anchored here in the court buildings, their environs and a comparatively small envelope of the surrounding countryside.

The day was already very warm as Rouletabille set off on the short walk to Theydon Grange House from the cottage. The machinegun damage to the side of the house seemed somehow worse in the day time, and a carpenter was just arriving to board up the window. The police must've felt that all of the available clues had been identified. Although neither of the two uniformed constables guarding the property had seen Rouletabille before, they had a clipboard upon which was a typed a list of people with permission to enter the house, and he was gratified to find that his name was third on the list after Inspector Hopkins and Harry Dickson.

Once inside he went straight to the conservatory on the far side of the house which was where the occupants seemed to congregate and drink their tea. There he found only Berenice Munro—her face pale and tear-streaked. And while he had very little to go on, it did not seem to him that her suppressed sobs were being caused by the death of Judge Haining. Some other force was at play here.

"Hello Miss, I am very sorry to intrude," began Rouletabille. "Is my American associate, Mr. Harry Dickson, here in the house?"

She took a moment to compose herself and then said, "Yes, he is upstairs, examining where the bullet went through the wall of my mother's room."

"Then your mother is with him?" asked Rouletabille.

Miss Munro had to force from her mind the image that was so powerfully scorched there. The image of what she had seen when she suddenly walked into her mother's boudoir, and found her mother engaged in a shameless and filthy act with Captain Treadwell. Her mother had fled the house almost immediately upon discovery leaving the Royal Engineers Officer to refasten himself and mouth hollow apologies. It was strange that she might never see her mother again. Even stranger that she would never kiss her, and had no desire so to do.

"My mother has gone. Somehow, I doubt if she will ever return. My father does not yet know his marriage is over. He went to his chambers early to study the papers for the case he's had to take over from Judge Haining."

Then anticipating the Frenchman's next question she said with some venom, "Captain Treadwell is not here. He is no longer my fiancé, and I have no interest in his whereabouts."

And with that she threw herself down on the conservatory's chaise longue and emitted a maelstrom of howling sobs such as Rouletabille had never heard. He withdrew.

Upstairs in Mrs. Munro's bedroom, Harry Dickson had turned on the electric light, lit all of the myriad oil lamps and was examining the great mirror which hung over the head of the bed and a slightly odd angle, as if tipped forward. Upon even closer examination he noticed it was the surface of the wall itself that had been built at the strange angle.

"She liked it very bright in here. I wonder why?" said Rouletabille, looking around. His eyes lighted on the dressing table and he walked over and yanked open one of the drawers. He was taken aback to find drug taking paraphernalia hidden beneath a small, neatly folded pile of lace handkerchiefs.

"I am forced to make the conclusion that Mrs. Munro is a hopeless cocaine addict," said Rouletabille. "A strange state of affairs for a judge's wife. She was caught *in flagrante delicto* with Captain Treadwell, and that is doubtless the only reason the equipment and powder is still here. In her haste she fled without it."

"What do you make of the mirror over the bed?" asked Dickson. "Why is it at that weird angle?"

"Let's see, shall we?"

Rouletabille picked up the poker from the small fireplace and wielded it like a sword at the mirror. The glass immediately started to break apart, and some of the jagged, dagger-like fragments fell down onto the cotton sheets of the bed, while others dropped noisily to the floor of the secret space - too small, surely, to be called a room—which was hidden behind the mirror.

Gingerly, Dickson stepped up onto the bed doing his best to avoid the glass.

"Yes, it's a moving picture camera, angled to be able to film whoever was in the bed. There's not really enough space for a cameraman. Oh, I see. There's a concealed switch allowing her to activate the camera from within the bed," said Dickson.

"And so, what we thought was merely a lodging place for itinerant judges for this legal term is instead a den of debauchery and corruption. Blackmail too must be part of the equation, with Treadwell as the victim," decided Rouletabille.

"Treadwell's involvement links it back to *The Yellow Terror*. There is only one villain of this piece, and that is Grierson—all roads lead to him," said Dickson. "To control the pilot of *The Yellow Terror* is to control the machine itself."

"Where is Inspector Hopkins?" asked Rouletabille. "We must tell him what we have discovered here and what it has led us to suspect."

"I saw him here first thing this morning, but he has gone now to make the arrangements for the Eschmann trial. The trial will take place here at Snarebrook Crown Court instead of the Old Bailey," explained Dickson.

"Why? Why is that?" demanded the Frenchman, suddenly horrified.

"Well, the trial is now allocated to Judge Munro following the death of Judge Haining, and this is his primary residence. It's all easier for him here because he is wheelchair bound."

"My God, the pieces of the puzzle have finally dropped into place. What incredible arrogance Grierson has to think we would not see through his plans. And the appalling sleight of hand distraction he planned for us—that whole business of *The Yellow Terror* being stolen and impossibly returned all seems so transparent now."

"Is it? Well then I sure wish you'd explain it to me," laughed the American.

"The 'impossible' mystery concerning the theft of the aeroplane was merely flypaper. We were supposed to devote all of our time and mental energy to solving a conundrum that did not, in fact, have any substance to it at all."

"Well, I guess the removal and return of the plane did bother me from the first. Captain Treadwell was *The Yellow Terror's* test pilot. He must've logged dozens of hours flying over the flatlands and testing the weapons. But he was also hesitant to fly at night, and thought it was a tricky beast to keep in the air. Also, he was present here in the conservatory during the attack which killed Judge Haining, so he can hardly have been the one who piloted the stolen plane. Even if he is being blackmailed, he must be innocent of the murder," reasoned Dickson.

Rouletabille creased his face and momentarily shut his eyes as he tried to summon up every fact, every contradictory impression connected with this affair and assemble them into something resembling the truth.

"My friend, that is not true. I strongly suspect that he is guilty of that murder—I just cannot prove it—yet. Don't forget how he insistently led the women to the conservatory for tea. The conservatory is precisely on the opposite side of the dwelling to Judge Haining's bedroom study. Treadwell knew of the attack and was attempting to take to comparative safety those who were not its intended victims. In the case of Mrs. Munro, he tried and failed. She was supposedly confined to her room with a case of hay fever, when in reality, she did not wish to stray far from her drugs; such was the state of her addiction," said Rouletabille.

"Which begs the question, what did attack Theydon Grange House? Is there a duplicate of *The Yellow Terror?* And, if so, what is the purpose of the espionage ring, for if they can build a duplicate then there is no good reason to spy on the original," said Dickson.

"No, no. The question is not what attacked the house, but rather why?" started Rouletabille. "And now we know the reason. Quite plainly it was in order to change Eschmann's trial judge, for changing the judge changed the trial venue. We must turn our minds back to Grierson's failed attempt to rescue Schellenberger. He personally undertook the jailbreak just moments before the man was due to be hanged and failed—barely escaping with his own life. We know of his monstrous ego, and he will have been bruised by this failure. Now he will undertake a similar rescue, but he has given himself more time, and he will act at a distance through his agents and those under the influence of his blackmail. In this endeavor he will perhaps take a backseat—be the spider at the center of the web—he is not willing to risk his personal liberty this time."

"We need to return to the cottage to properly plan our next move and to arm ourselves," said Dickson.

"And also get word to Inspector Hopkins," agreed Rouletabille.

Suddenly the two men became aware that Miss Munro was standing in the doorway to the bedroom. Curiosity about the source of the sound of breaking glass had overridden her emotions and now she saw the shattered mirror and the moving picture camera that had been concealed behind it. They eased past her in the doorway without attempting to engage her in conversation. They were partway down the stairs when they heard the sound of her retching, it had only taken her a few moments to realize the significance of the camera and its positioning.

Back at the Lodge Keeper's Cottage, the two detectives considered their best course of action. Rouletabille noticed that at some point Inspector Hopkins must have replaced the sawn-off shotgun Dickson had created in the gun cabinet. He took this for himself and secreted it under his jacket, then filled his pockets with cartridges. Dickson settled on another beautiful double-barreled Purdey. There would be no time to take a saw to it and he had little desire to invoke the Lord

131

Chancellor's wrath, now that he knew who the weapons belonged to.

From the sky above them they could hear the persistent drone of *The Yellow Terror's* engine. Treadwell was already in the air. Ostensibly it was just another day of flight tests, but this was also the first day of preliminary hearings in the Eschmann trial which meant that the prisoner would be present, having been transported in a secure wagon from Newgate Prison. Rouletabille was insistent that *The Yellow Terror* comprised a vital part of the plan to spring Eschmann. After all, it would be capable of mounting a devastating attack on the prison wagon.

"Yet still we have so little real evidence," bemoaned the French detective. "I am more reliant on instinct and guesswork than in any case I've ever been involved."

"Sometimes you just have to play your hunches," smiled Dickson. "I know I haven't been a detective for long, but it seems to me that instinct can be just as valuable as brainpower."

"Well then, my instincts tell me this. I should go out onto the flatlands in an effort to catch Treadwell at a refueling stop. If I capture him there then the attack will be over before it begins. You, my friend, just warn Hopkins and protect the wagon," said Rouletabille.

"I think it would be much better if I went with you," said Dickson. "I am not sure we should split up."

"I originally thought that my memory had fully come back, but I am increasingly aware there is a single piece of it missing. It is lost like a physical object—dropped somewhere on the rough grass of the flatlands like a pocket watch or a ring. I am convinced that if I go looking for it alone, I will find it," said Rouletabille.

"I'm sure you will, Joseph," said Dickson. "You're the one person I know who can do anything you set your mind to."

They shook hands, and then Rouletabille put on a borrowed hat Mrs. Bardell had obtained for him previously. He walked out from the cottage with a feeling of dark finality, as if he would not be coming back this day, or any day. He was headed for a reckoning with Dr. Grierson—or at least his machinations, and it would be a very great pleasure indeed to thwart them.

After walking in the hot sun for just forty minutes, Rouletabille regretted not bringing a canteen of water, or one of the stone bottles of fiery ginger beer Mrs. Bardell was always trying to force on him. But ahead of him was a small copse of just a handful of trees, if he lay down there for just a few minutes in the shade it would serve to revive him. During his recuperation in the cottage he had kidded himself that he had completely recovered from his dreadful incarceration in Leytonstone House, but it was not really true. He was still much weakened. As he wearily trudged his way into the middle of the small copse he encountered a strange, camouflaged barrier. There was canvas and netting into which had been interwoven leaves and twigs—the general purpose of all this was to mask a sort of tent or den. Rouletabille poked his head into the den's opening and looked inside.

"Oh, hello Mr. Frenchie. Would you like some lemonade?" asked Little Alfie.

Rouletabille glugged at the sweet cloudy liquid while the rotund boy made his explanations.

"I didn't really realize planes were all that exciting until I saw that one chase you and try to kill you. That was very good. I'm glad you got away though. Mind you, I didn't tell anyone. Nobody believes what I say anyway. I'll always remember it though," assured Little Alfie.

This was the event Rouletabille could not recall—being pursued by *The Yellow Terror* and ultimately running into one of the Wanstead Flatland's little lakes. It made sense, but still the memory was locked away and seemingly irretrievable.

"I made a den here because this where they pull the other plane into the sky," and then, before Rouletabille could ask for further details. "Hush. They're coming."

Two men in mechanic's overalls and flying helmets approached. They stopped about fifty feet away and with practiced efficiency lifted up a series of concealed and camouflaged sections—they were effectively trapdoors in the ground. They then started to lift out the components that would go to make up a modestly sized one-man glider, albeit one with a generous wingspan. They swiftly bolted and screwed the components together and then fitted at the very front of the cockpit a pair of machineguns identical to those which fired through the spinning propeller blades of *The Yellow Terror.*

So, this was how it had been done. Treadwell had towed the glider into the air, and then it must have circled in the clouds for ages—allowing him sufficient time to get to Theydon Grange House—before commencing its diving attack with guns blazing. Then Rouletabille remembered that Miss Munro had heard an engine during the attack, this must have been just trickery, for surely the glider had no engine.

Moments later, Rouletabille heard the whine of *The Yellow Terror* as it came in to land, and then rolled close to the glider's assembly point. Treadwell extricated himself from the plane, resplendent in his glossy, horse chestnut brown leather flying jacket and blindingly white silk scarf. He looked every inch the hero—but the Frenchman recognized him for precisely what he was.

"Hurry and attach the tow cable," ordered Treadwell. "It is almost time to free Eschmann."

And while one of the mechanics hefted the tow cable the other topped up *The Yellow Terror's* fuel tank from a jerry can.

"Is the glider's machinegun fully reloaded?" Treadwell demanded to know.

"Ja, all is as it should be," said the mechanic who was refueling Treadwell's plane.

Rouletabille cocked the twin hammers of his sawn-off shotgun.

"Then get into the glider and prepare for take-off," ordered the Englishman, to the German who was obviously both a mechanic and pilot.

"Ein moment, I must relieve myself first," confessed the German.

"Oh for God's sake, hurry," admonished Treadwell. And to Rouletabille's horror the German started to make his way directly towards the copse where the French detective and Little Alfie were crouching in the den.

"I wonder how Grierson is getting on with his bomb to destroy *The Great Men of Baker Street?*" wondered the second German mechanic.

"All I know is that he hired a delivery wagon from a local business and filled it with high explosive, he set off for Baker Street a while ago now. You never know, we might even hear the explosion—you'll certainly see the smoke plume from the air," said the first German just as he reached the copse.

Until this moment, Rouletabille had thought that when people referred to their blood running cold it was mere hyperbole, but now his blood was freezing in his veins at the prospect of some of the world's greatest minds being eliminated en masse. Nevertheless, he had an idea as to what he should do about it.

A couple of minutes later, *The Yellow Terror* jerkily pulled the glider and away from the flatlands, and then, at about one thousand feet, the towing cable connection was released and the glider started to soar even higher. Rouletabille was going to have to figure out the controls pretty quickly. While being towed it hadn't seemed to matter much what he did—it was as if the controls were locked off. But now he placed his hands around the joystick and found it highly responsive, likewise the rudder control pedals, upon which he was now exerting experimental pressure. It was undoubtedly the case that Treadwell would've expected the real glider pilot to participate in the attack to free Eschmann, but Rouletabille was incapable even of pretending to take that course of action. He felt lucky that he was even able to keep the glider in the air. He dipped the nose of the glider slightly with a view to opening fire with his machineguns on Treadwell's retreating plane which was moving fast out of sight, then he pulled on the triggers, but nothing happened. Whatever the means was for disengaging the safety he couldn't figure it out. Perhaps that was for the best. He would not be able to defeat so experienced a pilot in aerial combat. At the moment, Treadwell had no idea he had knocked the German pilot-mechanic unconscious once he reached the copse, exchanged clothing with him and taken his place. Treadwell would probably assume the glider wasn't taking part in the attack due to some technical malfunction. In fact, Rouletabille had now resolved to do his best to fly the glider towards Baker Street and warn of the bomb.

Rouletabille found himself in a cold sweat with an extremely elevated pulse rate and fizzing with adrenalin which would avail him little in the circumstances. He must calm down and he must start to think. It was nauseatingly vertiginous to look down out of the cockpit at the parched Wanstead grasslands and the streets of terraced houses where London's suburbs began, but really he had no choice. He had to orientate himself and then commence to fly this craft straight and level. Baker Street was in Marylebone, roughly southwest of his current position. He could only guess the distance since there were no maps on board. Dredging up from his memory all he knew of the geography of the metropolis he would say it could not be much more than ten miles away. The question was— did he have enough altitude to undertake such a journey? He wasn't sure. He pulled up gently on the joystick and the glider spiraled upwards like some dark and malevolent gull.

It all looked very different from the air, but within minutes he was passing over a London park, the thin dirty ribbon of a canal nearby led him to think this was Victoria Park on the edge of Bethnal Green. He was heading roughly in the right direction and still managing to keep this thing in the sky. Yes, he has started to relax a little, but a creeping dread about the descent and landing. How in God's name was he going to land the glider in a built-up area like Baker Street? He dismissed the idea of attempting to land on rooftops—it would be suicide. Or was this whole thing just suicidal? What had he been thinking?

As St. Paul's Cathedral and the River Thames came into view, he realized he needed to correct his course—there was no compass, so it had all been guesswork, but he was now much too far south and was rapidly losing height. He dismissed the idea of crash landing in the river and made the necessary correction. The open spaces around Lincoln's Inn looked too small to land the glider in. If he survived a landing that far from Baker Street he was bound to be questioned by the police, and it would take time to establish his bona fides. All of this would slow him down. He had to land as close to home of the *Great Men* as possible for he had no idea how much time he really had. He craned his neck to see that he was just going over the British Museum, there was still no open space to land in—just little square parcels of green—and he was far too low. In another couple of minutes he would be skimming the roof tops. Then, finally, his hoped for landing space came into view over to the North West. He had not remembered that there was a public park so near to Baker Street. What was the name of it? He strained his memory. It didn't matter. It didn't matter. He wrestled with the joystick. Then he noticed for the first time an odd brass handle on the right hand side of the cockpit. He turned it swiftly just in case its function was connected with landing the glider. In fact, it was a kind of siren, adjusted to emit a sound like the noise of the *Yellow Terror's* engines. The Germans really had thought of everything.

He lined up the glider to the park's emptiest open space and pointed the glider's nose slightly downwards. No! That was too much. He adjusted, but was still coming in too steeply and too fast. He pulled back and the glider made as if to ascend then simply belly-flopped onto the grass before cartwheeling. The cockpit split open like an egg and Rouletabille was hurled out onto the ground—injuring his right knee, and wrenching his only recently healed shoulder joint. Every bone in his frame ached from the jarring impact. But after only a few moments he leapt up and commenced a limping run in the direction of Baker Street. It was imperative that he not get caught up in a crowd of gawkers, nor be arrested by the police. Where was he? Regents Park! He was within yards of Grierson's intended targets. He had used up the luck intended for a whole lifetime in a single morning.

Rouletabille limped his weary way along the pavements of Baker Street looking for Grierson. His only clue was that a business local to the asylum had hired him a horse drawn wagon. When he saw the delivery van it looked so ordinary, so mundane, that he discounted it. But then he saw the dwarfish figure who was bundled up with a scarf around his face on such a very hot day.

The French detective did not hesitate. He pulled the sawn-off shot gun out from inside of his overalls and fired at Grierson as he was parking the wagon which bore the legend "Hitchcock Greengrocers, High Road, Leytonstone. The wagon's horses reared up momentarily at the sound of shot then settled back down making dismissive snorts. The unbelievably wide spread from the sawn-off peppered Grierson with buckshot, and some innocent passersby into the bargain. He cried out in a strangulated mixture of surprise and agony. He was bleeding from multiple small injuries, but not too badly hurt.

"You! How can you be here? How can you know of my plans?" he screeched, while yanking his lethal air pistol from his coat pocket.

Grierson loosed a couple of rounds at Rouletabille which hit him in the forearm and leg.

"Run you fool! It is only a matter of moments until the detonation…" shouted Grierson, as he himself quit the wagon's driver's seat and fled away from Baker Street.

Reeling from the fresh injuries, Rouletabille staggered to the doors at the back of the wagon. There was a heavy padlock which he set about with the only weapon he had to hand—the sawn-off. He dared not attempt to shoot off the lock in case it triggered the explosives. Holding the shotgun by the remaining section of its barrel he beat down on the lock repeatedly until it finally gave way. Flinging the doors open he saw a multiplicity of perhaps a dozen slow burning fuses. Grierson had lied. The explosion would perhaps have been two full minutes away. Rouletabille pulled the sputtering fuses out of the blocks of explosives.

Climbing out of the wagon to continue the pursuit, the Frenchman suddenly realized he had no strength, no energy, left. He was too badly hurt. One day he would catch up with Grierson, but today was not that day. He collapsed onto the pavement.

The Yellow Terror swooped down and unleashed a series of staccato bursts of crimson tracer fire at the armored prison wagon transporting Klaus Eschmann. The shots ricocheted off the vehicle's steel plates even as the driver and guard jumped away to cover. As the plane made a banking turn to attack again, Harry Dickson and Inspector Hopkins stood up from their positions of concealment behind Snaresbrook Crown Court's low boundary wall and opened fire—Dickson with his shotgun and Hopkins with a heavy Webley service revolver. This was followed by a fusillade of further pistol shots from the uniformed Special Branch constables.

A line of oily smoke started to trail from *The Yellow Terror's* engine, as it swiftly lost height. Anticipating where it would come down, Harry Dickson set off at a sprint, reloading his shotgun as he went.

Treadwell was already extricating himself from the crumpled plane's cockpit as Dickson approached. The American could see the traitorous pilot was holding a Mauser pistol in one hand as he jumped free of the plane.

"Going somewhere, motherfucker?" enquired Dickson. "Drop that pistol before I shoot you in the face."

Treadwell dropped the gun and momentarily reflected on the fact that he'd not had the guts to use it on himself. They'd hang him now for sure.

Epilogue

Naturally, it was Mrs. Bardell who was again given the job of nursing Rouletabille back to health at the Gatekeeper's Lodge Cottage. She limited the visitors and well wishers as best she could, but most of the *Great Men of Baker Street* made the pilgrimage to his sick bed to give him grapes or books with which to pass the time.

Dr. Watson had calculated that he and Holmes would both have been killed instantly by Grierson's bomb since the greengrocer's wagon was parked adjacent to 221B. By coincidence—or perhaps not, knowing Grierson's intricate plans—Blake had just returned from his case in Scotland, he would likely have been killed or seriously injured. Begg was away on vacation in his beloved Paris. The mysterious Drago's whereabouts are unknown, but his assistant, Spencer, is believed to have been in residence in Baker Street at the time of the attempted atrocity.

Little Alfie Hitchcock was also a regular attender. One afternoon, Rouletabille lay in bed, unable to concentrate on the latest issue of *Strand Magazine* and a thought struck him so he called out to his nurse and housekeeper.

"Mrs. Bardell? Could you go around to Theydon Grange House and get the moving picture camera from Mrs. Munro's room? I'm sure she has no further use for it, and I'd like Little Alfie to have it. Making films would be a most marvelous hobby for a boy like him."

Leviathan Creek

New Jersey, July 1916

Joseph Rouletabille had a few hours to kill before his appointment with the French Ambassador to the United States, and his fantasy had been to pass the time by dipping his toes in the cooling waters of the Atlantic. However, this was the hottest day, *so far*, of an oppressive heat-wave and it had driven thousands of the inhabitants of New York City to Spring Lake Beach on the New Jersey Shore with much the same idea. There was scarcely room on the beach for another soul; and the golden sands seemed more than two thirds concealed by the pseudo-geometric placement of picnic blankets upon which families feasted from their lunch pails.

In the hazy far distance, a good portion of the milling throng bathed shoulder to shoulder in the azure sea, while the hundreds who couldn't even get near the water just stood there trying to catch on their faces the moisture that rode in on the mild breeze. Rouletabille was thankful that he'd had the good sense to discard his usual tweeds in favor of a light linen suit. An obviously polite, yet rather overweight, lady in a summer dress eased a few inches along a wooden bench on the promenade so that Rouletabille could perch precariously on the very edge. Naturally, sitting in such close proximity to the fairer sex, he did not seek to light his pipe lest he spoil her enjoyment of the ice cream cone she was so ardently devouring. Ah, but what he would have given for a flagon of chilled French country cider! So much more refreshing than the tasteless suds that the Americans chose to call beer.

Then, it happened. Suddenly everything was different. The sound and mood of the packed beach altered. First, there were the screams, high pitched screams; the simultaneous screams of scores of women mixed with the outraged cries of men; then, the sound of retching, followed by the foul, sour smell of vomit on the air. Strangest of all, like a twisted parody of Moses' parting of the Red Sea—the crowd itself parted—what had been a tight wedged mass of humanity divided to make way for two men who carried a deathly pale human form towards the promenade. Great arterial gouts of blood hosed onto the sand. The injured man's life drained away from the bloody stumps that had been his legs with every step his rescuers took.

A middle-aged man ran towards them shouting, "Tourniquets! Quickly!" He pulled off his belt and another man did the same. They tightened the belts around the two ragged transfemoral injuries and lifted the poor fellow into a commandeered horse-drawn wagon. As they did so he shuddered and went limp... The corpse was soon transported at breakneck speed towards the nearest hospital.

Only a single thought inhabited the mind of Rouletabille, *What had done this?* He fought against the tide of people evacuating the beach and soon found himself by the water's edge. A girl of about 19, wearing a one-piece cotton swimming costume, stood looking out to sea and shielding her eyes from the glare of the Sun with one hand.

"Do you know what happened to that man...the man with the terribly injured legs?"

"He wanted to see the red canoe. There was a red canoe capsized in the water. When he swam over to it, something got him... bit away his legs... A shark? A barracuda? I don't know," she answered, her voice quavering with shock.

Rouletabille scanned the waves, shielding his eyes from the sunlight in the same fashion as the girl. Could a fish really sever a man's legs? Cut through muscle and bone? It seemed totally unbelievable.

"Look!" she cried pointing. "You can still see the canoe..."

She was right. Rotating gently in the surf about 15 meters away was what appeared to be a dug-out canoe of pinkish red hue, almost crystalline in appearance. The rip-current dragged at it, and it disappeared from sight.

The girl started to sob and walked away, but Rouletabille could not take his eyes from the ocean.

"The sea has teeth, I think," said Rouletabille to himself.

With his striking pure white beard and glinting jade colored eyes, Jean Jules Jusserand was foreboding in appearance, and yet avuncular in manner. Dwelling behind those eyes was a commanding, powerful dreadnought of an intellect. Indeed, Rouletabille was aware that the Ambassador had just been nominated for the Pulitzer Prize for History, but that sort of thing can be so very difficult to work into the conversation without appearing to be a fawning sycophant. Jusserand reached over his desk and liberally replenished the crystal brandy bloom in Rouletabille's hand.

"You still look a little pale, my young friend. Are you sure you are sufficiently recovered to receive the details of your mission?"

"Of course, Monsieur. I am more than a little preoccupied by what I saw…and intrigued to see if I can solve the mystery of the red canoe."

"Rouletabille, you must not allow yourself to be so distracted. Your mission here is vital to the future of France, and while the task is easy enough to explain, its execution will require the full dedication of your intelligence and skills."

"My apologies, Monsieur, I have something of an addiction to solving impossible puzzles, but I understand full well that a higher duty calls me now."

"Quite so, your mission is two-fold. Firstly, a ring of German saboteurs is operating unhindered here in New Jersey at present. Their base of operations is the summer residence of the German Ambassador; so, you see, it is not for the taking of sea air that I, myself, have temporarily moved to Spring Lake. The mastermind of the sabotage is likely to be the senior military attaché: a former U-Boat commander known as Mors, but that is a matter for you to fully determine."

Rouletabille pressed the tobacco firmly into the bowl of his pipe and lit it. "What has been the nature of the sabotage thus far?" he asked.

"The main targets have been armaments and pharmaceuticals bound for Europe. They have successfully planted small bombs on ships carrying munitions and stolen and destroyed consignments of salicylic acid from which analgesics such as aspirin are made. But they are not always successful, an attempt to make off with 2000 ampoules of morphine was thwarted by security guards and I have reports that the same men also hijacked a barge loaded with salt...presumably an error..."

"The agents of the Wilhelmstrasse are fallible mortals, I assure you."

"Secondly, your mission is not merely to bring an end to these attacks but to turn them to our advantage. The perpetrators must be exposed in such a way that it furthers French interests and increases the likelihood of American entry into the war," explained Jusserand.

The Ambassador pulled open the drawer of his bureau, removed a gilt-edged invitation card and handed it to Rouletabille.

"There is another factor to be taken into consideration, another piece on the chessboard of diplomacy and espionage that you and I inhabit. His name is General Herbert Brown and he could prove a powerful ally. He is a confirmed Francophile and, even though he is formally retired from the army, he still has the ear of the President in matters of foreign policy. Here is an invitation to a function at his mansion tonight. Be sure to attend it. He lives on Ocean Way just outside town."

"Monsieur, this is a costume ball! I will have no time to obtain suitable attire..." complained Rouletabille.

"You will find a most appropriate costume in a white box on your bed upstairs," Jusserand informed him.

"I've not yet established my cover..." spluttered Rouletabille. "How will I convince them that I am the new cultural attaché?"

"My dear fellow, I should not worry over much about that. Everyone will assume that you are a spy."

Rouletabille approached the mansion on Ocean Way already wearing his cloak and mask and with the invitation clutched in his gloved hand. The costume had not been the only thing in the white cardboard box. There was also a small collapsible Kodak camera and an 1892 Lebel revolver with a small carton of ammunition (the only tools that the French government seemed to think it necessary to issue to intelligence agents).

At the door, an immaculately uniformed, powerfully built black man of about 25 eyed him suspiciously before admitting him to the party after a careful scrutiny of the invitation. Inside, the revels seemed at full-throttle: maids circulated with trays overloaded with champagne glasses, handing drinks to a profusion of men dressed as knights, cowboys, highwaymen and even apes, with women masquerading as mermaids, witches and angels (amongst other things). The young spy had only stepped a few yards into the palatial entrance hall when he was accosted by a man in his mid-sixties with steel grey hair wearing the dark blue uniform of a Civil War era Union soldier. He fixed Rouletabille with a glare, as if trying to see through the mask he wore.

"Well, what have we here… a gatecrasher? You are the only one of my guests that I do not recognize, sir," said General Brown. "Who are you?"

"I am the Phantom of the Opera," said Rouletabille as he secretly sweltered beneath the mask and woolen cloak on such a hot night.

Brown laughed and then said quietly, "Your accent and choice of get-up mark you as one of Jusserand's boys. That means we should get on just swell. Let me get you a drink; my wife's got a craze on some new cocktail, it's got a whole bunch of fellas on their backs already. You're gonna love it."

"Elena, meet the Phantom of the Opera," chuckled Brown. The tall woman dressed as a Roman Empress turned from her mixing table. Rouletabille judged that she must be approaching seventy but she was still one of the most elegant and strikingly handsome women that he had ever seen; there was a vibrancy and joyfulness about her that the mere process of aging had failed to diminish.

Mrs. Elena Brown proffered Rouletabille a mauve colored drink in a frosted cocktail glass. "This," she intoned with a voice redolent of the uppermost echelons of English aristocracy, "will blow your little socks off. Gin, lemon juice, and crème de violette with maraschino—the general effect is like an army of archangels massaging your tonsils. It's called an *Aviation*."

Three glasses later Rouletabille understood what she meant. He sat down quietly in a corner under the fronds of a potted palm waiting for his system to find some way to metabolize the violet flavored lava he'd been drinking. Then something caught his eye, a man in a naval uniform wearing a domino mask was stealthily skirting the edge of the party crowd…making his way ever so nonchalantly towards a duck egg blue colored door in an alcove in the far corner.

The man pulled from beneath his tunic a golden cylindrical object roughly the size of a fountain pen. A flash of iridescent liquid sprayed out of the tube into the door's lock. Then, a moment later, the man opened the door; stepped into the room beyond and, just as swiftly as he had opened it, shut the door behind him.

It occurred to Rouletabille that he alone had just witnessed this fellow pick the lock by squirting some sort of concentrated acid into it. Now, if he were to catch this miscreant, General Brown would doubtless look upon him most beneficently.

As casually as he could, the spy eased his way through the revelers until he got to the door. Unhesitatingly, he pushed it open while tugging the Lebel revolver out from under his cloak. The stranger in the domino mask had been busy. A large oil painting of Abraham Lincoln had been swung to one side by way of its hinged connection to the wall. Behind the painting was a steel wall safe with a combination lock. The man had connected something that was perhaps some form of electrically-powered stethoscopic listening device to the door of the safe; he turned the combination dial waiting for the tumblers to click. With the earpieces of the device in place, he was quite oblivious to the presence of Rouletabille.

"I hate to interrupt your concentration, Monsieur, but I've been meaning to ask you, what is that costume you are wearing?" exclaimed Rouletabille in an unnecessarily loud voice. This caused the masked man to whirl around. Suddenly a pistol of unusual, almost futuristic, design was in his hand.

"This is how I usually dress," said the masked would-be thief in a German accent so guttural that it set the Frenchman's nerves on edge.

Rouletabille was conscious that the door had opened behind him, but he was unwilling to give the German even a momentary advantage by looking away; instead, he kept his revolver calmly leveled at him.

"What's all this?" said General Brown. "Not so much a Mexican stand-off as a Franco-German one." The General interposed himself between the two men and Rouletabille saw that he held a massive long-barreled Colt Dragoon revolver.

"I caught this gentleman trying to break into your safe," said Rouletabille.

"So I see. I expect you've had no time for introductions... Monsieur Phantom, allow me to introduce Kapitan Mors of the Imperial German Navy. Mors, this man is a French agent and perhaps it would therefore be best if you did not learn his name, nor see his face. At least, not tonight; tonight is for fun. Have you tried my wife's new cocktail?"

"Do not mock me, General," spat the German. "The contents of that safe are your property only by chance. By rights, it should be mine! It was never Smith's! It should never have been yours... I, and I alone, am the true heir to Captain Nemo."

"When I think you are in the same league as Nemo, my friend, I'll let you know. But for now, if you're done shouting, the party is outside…if you're *not* feeling sociable, I'll unlock the French doors out into my garden and you may take a hike. Either way, if I catch you in here again, I'll shoot you through the head. And I never miss." Brown stepped forward, produced a key from his pocket and opened the doors.

Still covering General Brown and Rouletabille with his odd pistol, the German officer backed out into the garden's inky shadows.

"Well," said Brown after a moment, "he's gone. I guess you'd like a crack at the safe. I'd much rather the French had access to its contents than the Germans. The papers inside were given to me for safekeeping by the President himself— though who may see them is at my discretion. They once belonged to Cyrus Smith and any engineer or scientist in your country would give his right arm for a look at them."

"Since you were once cast away with Captain Smith on that most mysterious of South Pacific islands, I can hazard a guess what might be inside," murmured Rouletabille in awe.

"You've got five minutes, then I'll drag you back to the party. I never met one of Jusserand's men who didn't have a nifty camera…please take pictures and leave the originals."

"But, General, I am no safecracker," explained the young man desperately.

"Oh, you'll figure it out," said Brown with a wink.

As Brown left, Rouletabille took off his mask and cloak and turned up the gaslight in the room to maximum. This was a forlorn hope. How was he supposed open the safe with no training...no idea at all how it was done? About the only thing he knew was that most modern British and American safe combination locks had to be rotated five times past a certain number clockwise, four times anticlockwise past the next number and so on until a single clockwise rotation past the final number was reached. He'd seen secretaries in embassies lose their tempers with combination locks even when they knew the numbers.

He swung the oil painting of Lincoln back over the safe door ready to give up before he had started and return to the party. The old man looked down at him with those kindly eyes and seemed to exhort him to try harder. Wait a minute… could it really be so simple?

Rouletabille looked around, the synapses of his brain opening and shutting fiercely like sparking electrical connections. From the bookshelf, he pulled down an old sea atlas and turned up the pages for the South Pacific and scanned the area around New Zealand. He could see no mention of what he was looking for… the atlas was too old, it predated the return of Captain Smith and his companions… but it had to be here somewhere in this room.

Rouletabille opened a cherry wood cabinet and found inside a collection of reasonably modern rolled up sea charts. He went through the same process again, looking minutely at the tiniest features of the South Pacific; looking for what once had been Lincoln Island: the island upon which Brown, Captain Smith, Pencroff, Gideon Spillett, Neb Dobey and Smith's dog Top had been stranded. Finally, he found what he was looking for… 1617 miles east of New Zealand: Ernest Legouve Reef—a scattering of fang-like rocks just peeping above the surface of the ocean—all that remained of the "Mysterious Island" following the cataclysmic volcanic eruption. The reef was subsequently charted by a French ship around the turn of the century.

Using a nautical rule and ready-reckoner, Rouletabille did his best to calculate the latitude and longitude of the reef. It had been a long time since a friend had taught him the rudiments of navigation during a Channel crossing, but he estimated the location to be 35° 12'S 150° 40'W. The 150 in the middle was the problem. Since there would be no 150 on the dial, Rouletabille would have to assume that this would be a 15 and hope that Brown had decided the same.

He swiftly turned the dial five times past 35 clockwise then even quicker, four times anti-clockwise past 12. No longer daring even to breathe, three times clockwise past 15 and finally twice anticlockwise past 40. Nothing happened. Rouletabille could hear the door starting to open behind him.

He had lost his chance! What embarrassment he would now face before the remarkable old General. The ignominy of it... Wait! The additional zero from the 150, perhaps it should be accounted for at the end of the combination. It was surely worth a try. He rotated the dial past 0 clockwise, just one solitary turn.

There was an audible click from the mechanism and the thick steel door eased open. Without pausing to turn to see who had entered the room, he removed the sheaves of paper from the safe and spread them on the desk in preparation for photographing them.

"I can see that the next time I set a test for the most famous detective in France, it will have to be a more difficult one," laughed General Brown. "Forgive my pretence of not knowing the Great Joseph Rouletabille... Of course, Jusserand told me who he was sending to my house."

Rouletabille carefully examined the drawings and blueprints from the safe. The first set were drawn in pencil on pages torn from a small notebook; they were intricate technical drawings of air pumps, torpedo tubes, some kind of combined periscope and camera obscura, water tight doors... and so on. Then the larger blueprints, these were orthographic projections and cutaways of a massive submersible vehicle...no prizes for guessing which one; the blueprints were marked *NAUTILUS*. The next set was completely different—silvery white ink on pale gold paper. The illustrated vehicle was like an elongated bullet on disc-shaped metallic wheels. Rouletabille took out his miniature camera, loaded the flash with magnesium powder and started shooting.

"The designs on the goldleaf parchment are by Robur, the self-proclaimed 'Master of the World,'" explained Brown. "Captain Smith was one of the few men to meet both Nemo and Robur. And Smith was an incredible engineer himself, he was able to hold his own; gain their respect."

Rouletabille turned over two drawings that were pinned together, one was one of Nemo's blueprints the other on the gold paper of Robur. In essence, what they showed was broadly similar – a long cigar-shaped craft with a metal riveted hull and wide nozzles at the rear. The differences between the two seemed largely aesthetic. Robur had drawn octagonal portholes, Nemo's were hemispherical. Rouletabille had no idea what the drawings were supposed to be of.

"What are these?" he asked quizzically.

"Hmm. First Nemo, then Robur and now Mors. All of them trying to develop the same thing—a craft that can escape the atmosphere of the Earth and head out to other planetary bodies. And where Nemo and Robur failed, Mors, I'm sure, will one day succeed. C'mon, let's get back to the party."

Rouletabille had expected to wake up in his quarters at the French Ambassador's summer residence. It took a few minutes for him to realize that he was still at General Brown's mansion on Ocean Way. Worse than that, it felt like the inside of his skull had been stuffed with coarse grade wire wool and fishing hooks; and that a violet flavored lizard had nested in his desert-dry mouth. Too many Aviation cocktails had left him trapped in a black vortex of a hangover. He climbed uneasily out of bed and poured water from a fish-shaped majolica jug into a blue glass tumbler. Just after his second swig, there was a perfunctory knock at the door. Before he could answer, General Brown marched cheerfully in wearing a robe and slippers.

"Ah good, you're awake," said Brown as he threw a blue and grey striped swimming costume onto Rouletabille's bed. "Get changed. We're going swimming…I expect you have a sore head and it'll do you a world of good."

"Swimming? In the sea? I saw a swimmer with his legs bitten off yesterday…"

"I swim every morning in summer and have never seen a glimpse of a shark. Hell's Teeth! I swam practically every day at Shark Bay on Lincoln Island without trouble. Anyway, I daresay most sharks don't bite harder than the average dog."

Rouletabille shrugged mentally. The problem with senior military men was they expected everyone to do everything that they said. He reached for the swimming costume.

Rouletabille and Brown exited through the garden onto the beach. It was only around 6 a.m. but the temperature was already pushing 75 Fahrenheit, it would be back in the 90s later in the morning. The young black man who'd admitted Rouletabille to the mansion last night was sitting on a drift-wood log nursing a type of Marlin Model 1893 rifle—a vari-ant with an extremely long barrel fitted. It occurred to the de-tective that it was the sort of weapon a sniper or an assassin might choose.

"This is Neb Jnr.," explained Brown. "He's my guardian angel. I relax when he's around because I know no harm will come to me."

Neb Jnr. nodded to Rouletabille and then pushed down the lever-action of the rifle as if to signal that he was ready for any eventuality.

The two bathers walked into the surf, which seemed al-most icy when compared to the growing heat of the day. As the cold water hit his calves, every muscle in Rouletabille's body tensed and his headache suddenly worsened, but then as he strode further and finally began to swim, the vise of pain clamping his skull slowly released.

"What further can you tell me about Captain Mors?" asked Rouletabille. "If he is a disciple of Nemo—who des-pised imperialist aggression—then why is he allied with Ger-many? Surely he should have forsworn allegiance to a nation-state?"

They paused to tread water and Rouletabille became aware that the morning tide was churning the sand and carry-ing in great swathes of seaweed. Visibility under the water was much reduced and, if there was a shark swimming be-neath him right now, he would never know it.

"Mors is a complicated character. He'd love to be like Nemo, but circumstance has dictated against it. A few years ago, he built a unique airship that was impervious to rifle and artillery fire. It was fitted with a ram and, for a while, he lived the Nemo or Robur lifestyle, calling himself 'The Air Pirate' and wrecking a few ships and balloons to very little purpose. But what Man could not bring crashing to Earth, God did. His airship was caught in a colossal storm in the Pyrenees and almost completely destroyed. He wasted his fortune attempting to salvage it and is now reduced to being a mere agent of the German government. Nevertheless, do not underestimate him, he is a quite brilliant man; though his eccentricity will be his undoing—he tells me he never removes that domino mask, like some penny-dreadful villain."

As Brown spoke, something caught Rouletabille's eye, a white spherical shape in the sky that was passing across the bay and losing height rapidly.

"Is there a weather station near here?" asked Rouletabille pointing.

"I think there's one over in Hunterdon County, but that's no weather balloon," replied Brown.

As the balloon came lower, Rouletabille could not help but agree. It carried no barometric instrument package, but rather a nest of cylindrical tubes festooned with electrical wiring. His heartbeat quickened with horror as he realized what the balloon's burden was strangely reminiscent of. In his mind's eye, he could see both the electric stethoscope and pistol belonging to Mors. Yes, they were all products of the same frustrated genius.

As the droplets hit the sea, part of Rouletabille's brain refused to accept that this was anything more than a rain shower. Why then was the rain red? Why then was it spraying down from the device slung beneath the balloon? It was blood. And every instinct screamed to Rouletabille that it was human blood. What terrible message was Mors trying to send after his humiliation yesterday? Rouletabille looked towards Brown and saw that his hair and face were covered in bloody spatters. The two of them were swimming in a crimson slick.

"Let's get back to the shore!" shouted Brown.

A crack of rifle fire from the beach drew their attention. Neb Jnr. had shot the Marlin in the air and was now frantically pointing to something in the water; something that lay directly between the swimmers and the shore. As the brownish grey finned back broke the surface, the detective prayed that the thing sharing the sea with them was something harmless. He remembered reading about how the largest sharks were quite innocuous—they ate the tiny things that floated on the surface. Unfortunately, his memory had been seized by raking talons of fear and was refusing to divulge the proper name for these tiny things. He was also concerned that the shark wasn't really big enough to be one of the harmless giants of the ocean. It was perhaps three or four meters long, at most.

He clung desperately to Brown's assurance that the bite of a shark was no worse than the bite of a dog, but with progressively less and less conviction that it was really true. His whole perception of the nature of sharks had shifted in less than a day. He'd thought them to be weak in every sense: weak jawed, cowardly, stupid... Something that might nip at a man's flesh in error, but incapable of taking away his legs in a deliberate attack. What if they were as cunning as wolves, or if their instincts were so perfectly adapted to survival in the hostile environment of the sea that it gave the illusion of tremendous guile? After all, what was intelligence but an appropriate response in any given situation?

His momentary reverie was broken by another report from Neb Jnr.'s rifle. The bullet blasted through the shark's dorsal fin tearing an untidy fist-sized hole more-or-less dead center. It was admirable shooting from that range—and what the Devil was he using for ammunition!—but he wanted to exhort Neb Jnr. to aim lower. The horrifying leviathan was hardly likely to die from having its fin shot; it was like shooting an axe-wielding maniac in the earlobes.

Without warning, Neb Jnr. unleashed a barrage of shots from the Marlin. Judging by the impact splashes as the bullets hit the water, Rouletabille guessed that the marksman had struck the shark in the nose or the top of the head. The great fish zigzagged away at astonishing speed heading out into the deep.

A few minutes later, Rouletabille and Brown were helping each other out of the surf.

"I need a drink," decided General Brown.

"I never want another Aviation as long as I live," declared Rouletabille.

"Who's talking about those silly cocktails? What we need is Kentucky Bourbon," said the old man.

"Let me shake you by the hand, Neb," requested Rouletabille. "You are the finest shot I've ever seen."

"But then, you never knew my father," smiled Neb Jnr.

"It's a pity that my guardian angel isn't going to be with me for much longer," explained Brown. "He's secured a position as a police officer over in Bay City."

"I'd been meaning to ask you, Monsieur Rouletabille, seeing how you're a famous detective, if you'd maybe give me a few pointers on that line of work," asked Neb Jnr.

"My dear friend, by the time I've finished with you, they'll want to make you Captain of Detectives; and probably your descendants too," laughed Rouletabille.

"My little Harold plays cops and robbers already..." added the future policeman.

Rouletabille looked back at the sky and the water. The balloon that had lost height so suddenly was now regaining altitude as if guided by an unseen hand.

In the following days, operating from within Jusserand's summer domicile, Rouletabille placed himself at the center of a web of surveillance on Kapitan Mors. Embassy "cultural staff," and paid informers dogged his every movement while Rouletabille kept himself carefully out of sight, planning to bring himself into play only at the final confrontation.

Mors' movements and clandestine meetings with his subordinates suggested that a major event was planned for sometime in the next few weeks, probably around the end of July, something that would take place in the vicinity of New

York Harbor. In addition, Mors was now in the habit of taking a prolonged early morning voyage in a small sailing skiff. Rouletabille deduced that Mors was making a rendezvous with a U-Boat, possibly the one that he had previously commanded. The question was, how to maximize this information to further French interests. A U-boat operating in US territorial waters could always claim it was there due to navigational error…it would have to be caught involved in the act of sabotage. It was really just a matter of giving Mors enough rope with which to hang himself; if Mors went too far and committed an extreme act, the game was essentially over—the Americans would enter the war. Yet if Mors' efforts were too ineffectual, his masters would put him under pressure to do more. Rouletabille did not envy Mors' position. Conversely, if Rouletabille uncovered a plot that meant likely death or injury to US citizens, he would be duty-bound to thwart it, even if that meant delaying American participation in Europe.

Rouletabille had also become very interested in sharks. Reports from ships arriving on the eastern seaboard indicated that there was a veritable plague of sharks about ten miles off the coast. The public mind had formed a link between German U-Boat activity and the presence of the sharks. In the popular imagination, the predators had come to feast on dead and dying sailors. The war was on America's doorstep, yet it was the sharks that everyone most seemed to fear. Coastal tourism was now blighted. Rouletabille could walk along the promenade alone, paddle in the waves to his heart's content… The concession stands were empty and abandoned. It seemed like the town was dying.

On the wall next to his desk, Rouletabille had thumb-tacked a map of the New Jersey shoreline. Ostensibly, it was for marking the surveillance of Mors, but he had also placed on it the locations of the two shark attacks that had taken place, albeit the first attack had been erroneously (if not bizarrely) attributed to a turtle. Charles Vansant was the first victim; killed in the early evening of July 1 at Beach Haven, Long Island. Over 40 miles from the second attack, that on

Charles Bruder at Spring Lake on July 6—the attack that Rouletabille himself had witnessed. Finally, the detective had marked the private strand of beach to the rear of the Brown mansion as well as some possible launching places inland for the murderous balloon.

It seemed apparent that this attack was merely an attempted assassination of General Brown, revenge for his humiliation of Mors the previous evening. The ingenious method of luring a shark to that location by way of the controlled balloon dropping human blood into the water was breathtaking in its audacity and infuriating since it left no physical evidence that might link Mors to the crime. Rouletabille had cogitated on the attacks for days now and concluded that the red canoe, like the balloon, was a device for attracting the sharks to where humans were bathing. Something that would go largely unnoticed by people yet would be an irresistible siren call to the largest and most dangerous of sharks... Mors was therefore responsible for all the shark attacks. And that was something that the detective had felt to be true from his first day here, even when there wasn't a scintilla of evidence to support it.

There was a brisk knock at Rouletabille's door and Pierre Galpin, the administrative under-secretary, strode in.

"Monsieur Rouletabille! We have just received word that, earlier today, there was a further shark attack. This one was on some young boys at Matawan."

Rouletabille consulted his wall map. Matawan was on Raritan Bay, only just south of New York.

"Do we know yet the exact location of the attack within the bay?" he asked the under-secretary.

"Monsieur, the attack wasn't in the bay—it was miles inland in a river creek."

"What! That is surely impossible... I must go there at once. Tell the Ambassador I am commandeering his chauffeur and roadster on urgent business."

Minutes later, Rouletabille was running down the residence's cantilevered staircase taking the steps two at a time.

Outside, he could see the Ambassador's yellow roadster with the engine already running. Then he heard Jusserand's booming voice call after him:

"Rouletabille! Attacks by sharks are not your affair!"

"They are when they are economic warfare!" he called back, not even bothering to slow down.

When Rouletabille got to Matawan Creek, they were already planning to dynamite it. The place was not at all what he had been expecting. A muddy, shallow and narrow creek, lined with reed beds and thick with flies, probably no more than 15 yards across at its widest point. It was also a good ten miles from the sea.

Earlier that day, a group of boys had been swimming in the dirty brown water. The shark had taken one of the boys and the body had not been recovered. Nightmarishly, a 24 year-old man called Stanley Fisher had waded out to try and find the boy's body and also become a victim of the shark. He was now dying at the Morgan-Lovell Infirmary in Matawan. It seemed appalling to Rouletabille that the boys had nowhere better to swim... they'd probably gotten into the habit of cooling off in the creek during this sapping hot spell. Yet, who could guess that a monstrous sea creature would, or could, venture so far upriver.

A boatman called Thomas Swann was holding court on the bank of the creek talking to a couple of Matawan newspapermen. Rouletabille noted that Swann reeked of whisky, which would be a minor point were he not also handling dynamite. He had a stick of dynamite in his left hand and a box of matches in his right; between the two hands, he was trying to wrestle a match out to light the magnesium fuse. Rouletabille had only had some basic demolitions training but the fuse looked very short. There were also onlookers, including children, scant feet away.

"Yeah, I seen a shark alright," began Swann. "They laughed at me then, said I was an old soak. They ain't laughin' now as little Lester got ate."

"So you actually saw the shark swimming upstream? How do you account for a salt water shark in a freshwater creek?" asked one journalist.

"Bull Shark, that's all. They's well known to swim in rivers. Ain't no mystery. It was a monster though; mebbe fifteen or twenny feet long."

Swann lit the fuse, and the sudden fizz as it took startled him. He tossed the caramel-colored stick away reflexively, but it only flew about three yards then struck the tops of some reeds and fell to earth at the water's edge. There were two girls in pinafore dresses only a few feet from where the dynamite had come to rest. Rouletabille leapt forward—a child had already died today, and he would damned if any other innocents would die while he could do something about it. He grabbed the stick and hurled it hard and low across the creek. It spun through the air and went about ten yards before hitting the water; it exploded almost the second it touched the surface, generating a broad fountain of muddy water.

The shockwave disturbed a metallic object that lay just under the water's surface. It was a long, segmented pole that seemed to run the full width of the creek. It rose up in the swell and then disappeared again. Rouletabille was puzzled by this sight immediately. Once again, the nerve endings inside his brain were firing furiously; theorizing, constructing explanations and dismissing them just as quickly. Was the pole the top of some sort of barrier, a net or an underwater fence? And if so, on which side of the barrier was the shark?

Rouletabille crouched by the water and scanned the surface of the creek. He nearly jumped out of his skin! The head of an enormous shark suddenly protruded from the swirling brown water not eight feet from the bank. The jaws extended as if trying to escape from the creature's head and snapped at him twice. The shock of seeing its pink fleshy maw and triangular teeth was more terrifying and alarming than it had been when he was actually swimming in the sea with such a creature the other week.

The beast broke the surface heading downstream towards the pole barrier. Rouletabille saw the dorsal fin quite clearly. The jagged hole in it was unmistakable. This was the same shark that Neb Jnr. had blasted with the Marlin rifle. His heart was beating so fast it was starting to hurt; it felt like every muscle in his body was soaked with adrenaline.

Knowing what little effect Neb Jnr.'s rifle had had, Rouletabille did not pull the Lebel from his shoulder holster. Instead, he yanked out the camera and hoped that the creature resurfaced. The shark's head came out of the water again as it rammed into the pole. He clicked the shutter and hoped he'd managed to capture it on film. The shark dove, and there was a thrashing as if it was fighting its way through something. Then it was gone. One thing was for sure, Swann had exaggerated its length. The great fish could not have been more than about twelve or thirteen feet, at most (to use the Imperial measurements which Rouletabille personally disliked).

"Wow!" said one of the journalists as he approached the young detective with notebook in hand. "You sure are a man of action! And if that photo comes out, the *Gazette* and just about every paper on the East Coast will want to buy it off you…who are you anyway?"

"Oh, I'm just a tourist…but I really don't like publicity," lied Rouletabille, who then tried to melt away in the crowd, but ended up jogging back towards the roadster to escape the newsmen.

He returned to complete his investigations at 6 a.m. the following morning. The bank of the creek was deserted now. His first port of call was the metal pole that traversed the width of the water. It was slim, telescopic and made out of a light steel alloy. It was attached to a motor that was half buried in the mud, and atop the motor were both a timer and some sort of wireless radio receiver. The purpose of this arrangement was to extend a fine metal net across the creek. The barrier could probably be set to be deployed at a certain time of day, (perhaps to match the tides?) or to keep captive or release the imprisoned leviathan by radio signal. The shark had wrecked the net by ramming it after the dynamite had gone off. Rouletabille suddenly felt nauseated. Those boys had not been subject to a terrible cruel whim of nature…the shark had not stumbled upon them while they were swimming. They had gone swimming in the shark's enclosure.

Rouletabille looked upstream where something had caught his eye. Of course, Matawan Creek was still tidal at this point and now it was low tide. This revealed something that he had not seen previously: a metallic disc perhaps four feet or so across, like a wide flat buoy sitting in the water, presumably anchored in place. It had the look of one of Mors' inventions. There was also a decaying, leaky row boat tied up to a post in the reeds.

He unhitched the boat, jumped in and pushed it away from the bank with its rotten oars. Nearing the disc, he reached over the side and laid his hands on it, bringing the boat's movement through the water to a halt. The disc had a section with a hinged lid. Rouletabille half expected it to be locked or welded shut, but it wasn't. He lifted it and saw that inside were open compartments packed with salt. A small electrically powered Archimedes screw type arrangement fed the salt gradually into the water. It was a device to salinate the shark's enclosure. From this, two things were apparent: the saboteurs had not stolen that consignment of salt in error, and, secondly, the creature held captive here was no mere Bull Shark; it was something larger, more deadly and something quite without the ability to exist in freshwater. Rouletabille headed back to the bank.

Rouletabille stood in the crowd at Raritan Wharf watching the little man with a mixture of curiosity and admiration. He was probably no more than five feet four inches tall and sported a droopy walrus moustache. One thing was for sure, he exuded, or perhaps broadcasted, a palpable aura of utter fearlessness. Amongst the onlookers were the same Matawan journalists that Rouletabille had encountered during the incident with the dynamite several days before.

"Yes, ladies and gentleman, I had no fear of the King of Beasts when I worked as a lion tamer so I certainly have no hesitation in taking on that jackal of the sea—the shark."

"Mr. Schleisser," began one of the journalists, "will you be hunting for the creature alone?"

"No, Monsieur Joséphin of the French Fourth Estate will accompany me. He offered a considerable sum for the privilege, but I've invited him to give that money to the family of the little boy who was killed in the creek."

It seemed strange to Rouletabille to hear his former name, his *real* name used, that name belonged to a different life. It had so little connection to him that it might as well be an alias.

"Monsieur Joséphin provided a photograph of the creature that has allowed me to identify it as a Great White Shark, the most dangerous man-eater in the ocean. It is not an adversary that I will be underestimating... and I will not be satisfied until I have defeated it."

Schleisser and Rouletabille climbed down into the little boat that Schleisser had hired for the expedition. It was scarcely bigger than the decayed row boat that he had used when he examined the salination disc. Rouletabille took up the oars with a steady determined stroke, and the two men slowly moved away from the wharf into the choppy waters of Raritan Bay.

After about half an hour they traded position, and Schleisser started to row. He instructed Rouletabille to break open the first of a series of three sealed zinc pails that were stored in the stern. Rouletabille recoiled at the appalling odor as he took the lid off.

"Chicken guts!" he laughed. "Just throw it all over the side...sharks cannot resist blood. Soon we'll probably be surrounded by 'em. Including the big son-of-a-bitch that you saw in the creek."

In fact, it was nearly an hour before the shark arrived. Rouletabille lay dozing with his hat over his face. His first thought was that they had collided with another boat, so sudden and powerful was the impact. He leapt up and looked down into the water. The shark seemed to just be hanging in position relative to the boat about ten feet down. He dragged the Lebel from beneath his jacket, adopted a stance with his feet wide apart to steady his aim and then fired. He saw his bullet corkscrew through the water leaving a tight spiral of bubbles, and then go wide. He took his time and aimed again. This time, the shot clipped the front edge of the shark's pectoral fin. This was ridiculous! How many revolver shots might it take to kill it? Fifty? A hundred? He had four left in the cylinder, and twelve more in the box in his jacket pocket.

Schleisser jostled him out of the way. The lion tamer's arms were filled with a lead weighted wide-gauge fishnet which he hurled down into the sea very accurately towards the great fish.

"That peashooter's no use! We gotta net him and row to the shallows…find a way to beach him"

The weighted net caught on the top lobe of the shark's tail and on its right pectoral fin. This drove it to the surface and allowed Rouletabille to confirm its identity. Yes, it was the shark with the damaged dorsal fin that he had encountered twice before now. The shark's mouth clamped onto the sternpost and started splintering the timber.

My God, it's eating the boat, thought Rouletabille.

The fish's wide, brownish-gray head was high out of the water and thoroughly occupied with destroying the boat. Seawater overtopped the gunwales and started to swamp the craft. Rouletabille held the end of the Lebel's barrel against the coarse sand-paper skin of the shark's head, trying to make some sort of calculation as to where its brain might reside. He fired twice, punching neat bloody holes, but there was little other discernible effect. He dropped the gun and grabbed one of the oars. Leaning the oar against the deck at about 45 degrees, he kicked hard just above the blade, while yanking the top of the oar towards him. The last two feet of the oar sheared off leaving a sharp, spear-like point. Wielding it high above his head, Rouletabille brought the broken oar down like a harpoon and pierced the beast through its left gill slits.

As he encountered resistance, he plunged and pushed the point further, shoving on hard through the spiracle openings—the shark equivalent of a gizzard—and then by blind chance tearing through the aorta. He'd had no idea that a shark's heart was so far forward, but the frenzied spray of blood into the ocean revealed he must have hit the most vital organ of all. The shark immediately stopped moving and started to sink. Schleisser hurried to cut it from the net.

"Help me get this net off him or he'll have us in Davy Jones' Locker!" he shouted with astonishing cheerfulness.

As Rouletabille assisted the little man, he looked up at something crossing his field of vision; another Great White, this one only about seven feet long, was starting to circle the boat. Schleisser saw it too.

"We killed one, we can kill another. It's the business we're in."

Just over two weeks later, Rouletabille was in a boat again, a motor launch crossing New York Harbor. This time, he was not looking for sharks. Mors himself was his quarry. And tonight was the night when, according to every scrap of intelligence they had, that Mors would bring his plans to fruition. It was the early hours of July 30 and, like Mors before him, Rouletabille was heading for Bedloe's Island. The launch docked inconspicuously out of sight on the east pier where he was met by a single US Marshal.

"Is Mors definitely still on the island?" he asked the Marshal.

"His sailing dinghy is still tied up. He's been creeping around for hours thinking we haven't noticed him. Right now, he's up somewhere inside Lady Liberty."

Rouletabille sighed. Mors' plans had once seemed obscure to him, but now they were all too obvious. He meant to destroy the Statue of Liberty, that symbolic gift from the French to the American people. It would have to be rebuilt and that would deflect valuable men and materiel away from the war effort. He wondered if Mors now regarded American entry to the war as simply inevitable. Either that, or he had figured out a way for someone other than the saboteurs to take the blame.

"Do you want the arc lights on?" queried the Marshal.

The temporary lighting that had been installed for the recent July 4 celebrations was apparently still in place.

"No thanks, keep it dark. I'll use a bulls-eye lantern when I really can't see what I'm doing."

Rouletabille jogged towards the colossal plinth, then headed inside. He could hear booted footsteps echoing from above. Mors was somewhere high above him, still ascending the narrow spiral staircase. Rouletabille removed his shoes and crept silently upwards. In his overworked imagination, he saw Mors carrying a small but incredibly powerful bomb, perhaps no larger than an attaché case, possibly derived from Professor Stangerson's disassociation of matter experiments—something that could level this entire island.

Rouletabille entered the statue's crown and swiftly flashed around the beam of his bulls-eye lantern. The chamber was empty, Mors was in the highest possible part of the statue, the Torch of Liberty. Rouletabille pressed onwards up the ladder that rose 40 feet through the statue's arm. He cast his light out onto the torch viewing gallery, while also covering the visible area with his revolver. A lone figure in a full-dress German naval uniform was standing out on the torch balcony platform.

Mors turned to greet Rouletabille as he stepped out into the fresh air.

"Ah, the little phantom who has hounded my trail these last few weeks and slain my pets… You've come to observe my little experiment, eh?"

"I've no time for pleasantries, Mors. How long until the explosion?" demanded Rouletabille.

"It will be any moment now... Certainly within the next 90 seconds..."

"Then let's get out of here! Do you want to die when the statue is razed?"

"Your arithmetic is poor, detective. While I'd hardly say this was a safe distance, 100,000 pounds of TNT and three million pounds of munitions couldn't demolish Lady Liberty from so far away."

"What are you talking about? Where is the explosive device?"

"Why, on the Black Tom Pier amongst the dozens of railroad cars packed with dynamite... Where did you...?"

Over on the Jersey Shore, the gates of Hell opened. A pearlescent dome of white fire, hundreds of yards across, appeared for a split second and then consumed itself... It transformed into billowing black and red burning clouds; and the clouds, in turn, started to form something shaped like a titanic tree of ebony smoke which towered thousands of feet over Jersey City. The Black Tom Pier was the logistical node for all ammunition and explosives heading to the European theater. Only a madman—or a genius—would've set a bomb there. Rouletabille cursed himself for disregarding the possibility.

"You are insane!" screamed Rouletabille, though he could hardly hear his own words over the deafening booms that were agony to his eardrums. "You could not have calculated the effect; you might've destroyed the city!"

"Nonsense! I know exactly what I am doing..." shouted Mors.

And at that instant a wall of debris engulfed Bedloe's Island like a January fog. What might've have been a railroad tie struck the fine copper work and glass of the torch platform. Rouletabille felt suddenly nauseous and realized that his scalp was very wet; the wetness dripped into his eyes, then the platform deck lurched violently upwards to meet his face as his knees gave way.

When Rouletabille awoke on the U-Boat, the solution to the "Mystery of the Red Canoe" lay immediately in front of him. Accommodation on the submarine must have been at a premium, and he lay on a camp bed in the refrigeration plant, which was not currently in use. Beside him were a small wooden canoe and some buckets which still held a bloody residue. Mors' men had used the canoe as a mould to create a small gory iceberg which could be set on the incoming tide to attract sharks to bathing beaches. The man-eaters would follow it like homing pigeons.

A few minutes later, the steel door to the plant swung open and Mors swaggered triumphantly in.

"Your injuries have been treated with medicaments of my own devising. You will heal swiftly and with no scars," he assured the detective.

"Am I your prisoner?" asked Rouletabille.

"No. I have a proposition for you… American entry to the war has always been inescapable, and now I have fulfilled my patriotic duty to the Fatherland by perpetrating the greatest act of sabotage the world has ever seen. I intend to take no further part in this war. In fact, I intend to leave the Earth completely. Especially since my superiors will assume from my radio silence that this craft and all in it were consumed by the Black Tom Pier explosion. But I need your assistance…"

"You want Nemo and Robur's plans for the outer-space craft," concluded Rouletabille.

"Only for the purposes of checking certain calculations regarding the hull stresses that will be experienced as we leave the gravity of Earth. I have a duty to protect the lives of my crew in this hazardous endeavor."

"I thought you needed the designs to construct such a ship."

"No, my ship, *The Meteor*, is already built and stands ready on one of my secret island bases."

"I see. I can provide you with the blueprints on the proviso that you cease to participate in this conflict; but that is purely on the basis of my own country's national interest and the orders that I am compelled to follow. I must tell you that, if it was a matter of my personal discretion, I would seek to bring you to justice for the appalling crimes that you have committed—most especially causing the death of an innocent child. And if I could not obtain justice, I would settle for mere revenge."

"The death of the boy is a source of great regret to me... and while I cannot undo it, if you come with me now, I will try to prove my good intentions for the future."

And so, Mors and Rouletabille ascended to the U-Boat's deck. Lashed to the deck were two huge cylinders, each almost 25 feet long. Rouletabille initially mistook them for immense torpedoes.

"This was to be the next phase of my war on the United States. Each tube contains an immature Great White Shark in a chemically induced torpor. Inside, nutrients and hormones will grow the predators to fantastic size, and they will be anthrophagous—they will specifically seek out humans as their main food supply. This weapon I will sacrifice as a gesture of goodwill. The growth process cannot be stopped. The devices are booby-trapped and impossible to open prematurely or sabotage—sometimes I am overly cautious—but I will allow you to set the control mechanism so that the cylinders won't open until decades in the future, rather than in a few months as I would have. And if we dump the sharks here, they are many miles from the nearest resort in any event—there is nothing but fishing ports here."

Rouletabille knelt down and turned the stiff metal control wheel almost as far as it would go. Six hundred and ninety months... The torpid sharks would surely be dead by then, and if they weren't, then hopefully this craze for sea-bathing would be over by three quarters of the way through the 20th century. The German then stabbed at a glowing blue control stud and the cylinders fell into the sea, the backsplash momentarily inundated the deck.

Mors gestured to the small sailing skiff that was moored aft.

"You can use that to get ashore. I won't be needing it anymore. Rendezvous with me here in a week's time and bring the spacecraft plans...After that, I can assure you that you will never see me again... I shall be leaving this sphere or dying in the attempt."

"Very well. I hope for your sake that you are a man of your word, Kapitan Mors."

"I am a German officer."

At these words Rouletabille just bit his lip.

The detective climbed down into the skiff, and then Mors untied it.

"Head for the lighthouse," instructed Mors.

Rouletabille turned the boat so that the prow faced the Amity Point Lighthouse and set sail. He could just make out the twinkling lights of the little township beyond.

Rouletabille vs. The Cat (1)

Winter 1916

The man in the black robe lay on the ground amongst the thistles and itch-weed, not moving, scarcely even breathing. They'd be looking for him soon. They didn't realize that he was already in the grounds of the house. They thought he only came at night—these men in black uniforms, armed with shotguns. They were noisy, clumsy fools, and they were unlikely to catch him, except by luck. Yet, there were more and more of them each day. They might stumble upon the place where he slept, and conceal themselves nearby, waiting for him to return. That worried him for a moment. Then, he decided that he would perceive their vile scent as he approached. Like most of his kind, he had astonishingly acute senses. It had taken him a long time to grow accustomed to the aroma given off by ordinary people; that malodorous bouquet of stale cigarette smoke, liquor and cooked food could still cause him to gag in a confined space.

His thoughts were suddenly interrupted by the spluttering sound of an approaching boat engine. He crawled through the long, unkempt grass until he reached the edge of the steep bank. When he looked down at the sluggish grey expanse of the Hudson River below, he saw a small vessel with a long, covered cabin nearing the jetty. Could it be a police launch? It certainly looked like it. As it drew alongside the mooring pontoon, a nimble uniformed figure jumped out and used lines to secure the boat fore and aft. Then the cough of the motor died.

The launch was overshadowed by the other vessel tied up at the jetty—a sleek and luxurious forty-foot racing yacht with the soubriquet *Sea Silk*. A few moments later, the launch's passengers disembarked: three men. The first, a straight-backed man of about fifty in a long black coat, then a much older man, perhaps in his late seventies, and even at this distance it was possible to discern the aura of authority which he radiated—he was an ex-military type. The final passenger looked to be little more than a boy. His head was adorned with a thick mass of dark brown ringlets and he wore a thick, rather uncomfortable looking tweed suit cut in the European style. The three men walked to where the landing joined the bank. There, they had to start ascending the spidery steel bridge which carried them over the railroad line which ran along the bank of the Hudson between the boundary of the West Estate and the water.

He didn't like it. Three more sets of eyes with the potential to spot him as he skulked around. To begin with, there had just been Cyrus West, Missy-Lou Pleasant and a handful more house servants and gardeners. Now, more and people were arriving at Glen Cliff Manor. It had to be tonight. He had to get into the house tonight, before the security was increased any further. If only he hadn't botched his first attempt; he might have already retrieved the relic. His mind boiled with anger at the thought of his people's holiest treasure in the hands of their persecutor. He would kill Cyrus West, if he could. But he must get the Crown of Jovan Nenad back to the homeland at all costs. Absentmindedly, he began to sharpen his claws in readiness.

Herbert Brown paused as he reached the mid-section of the steel bridge—just a little out of breath.

"You can catch your first glimpse of the big house from here!" he called back to Rouletabille. "Look! You can see it through the trees."

The young Frenchman took a step forward and craned his neck. The higgledy-piggledy asymmetry of the gothic revival shortbread mansion hove into view. With its castellation, turrets and neat clusters of high chimneys, it looked like it should be home to some ancient family of vampires. Rouletabille noted too that many of the windows were fitted

171

with decorative iron shutters, and, on the ground floor, these were all closed and barred.

Immense grounds with formal gardens stretched away in all directions; there was a glasshouse the size of a railroad station and numerous other outbuildings, both decorative and functional, strategically placed around the estate. This was the famous Glen Cliff Manor—home of the reclusive millionaire Cyrus West. The estate took up a good chunk of land on the outskirts of Tarrytown, and had been originally called "Brockenhurst" when it was constructed back in the 1840s.

"Well, my friend," began Herbert Brown, "what can you deduce from the request for your assistance here today?"

"Very little, General," answered Rouletabille honestly. "The order came via diplomatic channels at the highest level. I was to be met by you at the French Consulate in New York and to proceed to the house of Cyrus West."

"And what can you tell me about the man, Cyrus West?" interrogated the elderly general.

"Once again, very little. Cyrus West is old and very rich. He made his fortune in marine cable laying, and his company laid some of the first trans-Atlantic telegraph wires."

"Rouletabille, you once deduced the combination of my safe in less than five minutes. Surely you can do a little better on the subject of Cyrus...West?"

No effort was required on the part of the young French detective. The obviousness of it now struck him like a thunderbolt.

"*Your* association with Cyrus West can mean only one thing. He is the same person as Captain Cyrus Smith, your former commanding officer and fellow castaway on Lincoln Island in the Pacific. With the benefit of hindsight 'Smith' is an obvious pseudonym. And if I recall correctly, some official records also refer to him as Captain Cyrus Harding—suggestive of a series of pseudonyms," reasoned Rouletabille.

"Not bad, my friend. But I guess it is a little obvious when you think about it. Cyrus ran away to join the army when he was very young and has actually served with distinction under a variety of false names including Smith, Norman and Harding. However, West is his real name."

"Gentlemen! Gentlemen!" admonished Roger Crosby. "We must not keep Mr. West waiting, and particularly we should not be caught in the grounds after dusk, lest we encounter the interloper, or are mistaken for him by the guards…"

Rouletabille and Brown picked up pace and were soon descending from the steel stairway and heading on into the woodland pathways of the estate. As they exited the woods, Crosby pointed out the enclosed swimming pool—an architectural gem in its own right—it looked something like a Greek temple. It was nearly twenty minutes before they reached the front entrance portico. Crosby tugged hard on the handle of the wrought iron bell pull, and was rewarded by a sepulchral tolling somewhere deep within the building.

Moments later, the studded oak door swung open revealing one of the most striking looking women Rouletabille had ever seen. The unthinking and insensitive might merely label her Creole or "half-caste," but these terms did not sufficiently capture the rich complexity or her racial origins. Her cheekbones were high—her eyes narrow—almost Oriental. Her skin was a lustrous dark golden color. There was about her the most extraordinary lofty arrogance; one might be forgiven for thinking that this was her house, and she resented the interruption. The most incongruous thing about her was her outfit—a short maid's dress with highly starched apron; sheer black stockings sheathed her dancer's legs with little patent boots the rather odd finishing touch. She looked as if she would more properly belong in the stately robes of some ancient queen of Egypt.

"Lawyer Crosby…" was her only condescension to a greeting.

"Missy-Lou, you know General Brown, and this is Monsieur Joseph Rouletabille. They are here to see the Master."

"Then, enter," she pronounced as she turned on her heels and click-clacked across the polished tiles of the vast hallway towards the library, which also served as Cyrus West's study. As they followed her, Rouletabille unlocked his gaze from her gorgeous form and drank in the beauty of the statuary which loomed over them. Most of the pantheon of Greek gods seemed to be represented: Zeus, Hera, Apollo, Athena, Hephaestus and many others besides.

Inside the library, Cyrus West sat behind a broad mahogany desk in a wheelchair. Rouletabille had forgotten that the man must now be well over ninety. His hair and beard were both long and white, his eyes milky with cataracts. Yet, he sat erect and alert, and smiled a secretive and self-satisfied smile as they approached, like a chess grandmaster undertaking a successful gambit.

West proffered his hand for each of them to shake in turn, and then gestured for them to sit in the three Arts and Crafts style chairs that had been set out by Missy-Lou before his desk.

"Gentlemen, thank you for attending me. It is much appreciated. Monsieur Rouletabille, you have traveled far, and I hope not to detain you from your war against the Boche for too long. But your reputation as the detective who solved the notorious *Mystery of the Yellow Room* has spread far and wide, and I feel I will have great need of your services tonight," West explained.

"I understand that you have had an intruder in your grounds several times who has eluded capture," opened Rouletabille. "Do you have any idea what this intruder might want? Do you have any enemies?"

"Well, I have, in my life, made many enemies—perhaps too many. Most of my own family probably wishes me dead. They visit here occasionally like cats looking into a canary cage—wishing I would get on and die. But this is nothing to do with them. No, my greatest enemy, to answer your question, is undoubtedly the arms-dealer Basil Zaharoff. For, like my old friend Prince Dakkar, I have developed something of a kink about War. I despise War above all things and have tried to frustrate his activities whenever and wherever I can.

Zaharoff wishes me dead a thousand times over, but this is nothing to do with him either—at least, I wouldn't have thought so," the old man paused for a moment as if entering a reverie and then said, "Where is my hospitality? Missy-Lou, best brandy for our guests."

However, Cyrus West did not partake of any of the brandy himself. Instead, his shaking hand reached for a crystal decanter which sat on his leather-topped desk. The decanter glowed faintly with a bluish light, and the azure liquor that poured forth from it emitted wisps of silver vapor. Whatever the drink was, it was for West's lips alone. Rouletabille inched forward in order to see what was written on the metal medallion on the neck of the decanter. The detective was none-the-wiser since the medallion simply bore two letters "*E.V.*"

"Monsieur, I have a fair idea who the intruder might be—in general terms—and what he wants. In addition to War, my secondary hatred is the Occult. Until my health started to deteriorate, which is something that occurred comparatively recently, I waged a kind of vendetta against the degenerate witch cults that operate in some of the remote and forgotten corners of the world. In the Caribbean, I fought against the vile Voodoo cult and disrupted its practices. Missy-Lou was once a high-priestess of that religion—a woman of the Obeah. Now, she is a reformed character and a pillar of strength to me. And in Serbia, in central Europe, I skirmished many times with the adherents of a pernicious cat worship cult. Only the other year, my agents rescued from the cult a girl-child designated as a human sacrifice. That child is now being raised anonymously here in Tarrytown by a foster mother under my supervision," West paused to drain his glass.

"Roger, you know the combination of my safe. Would you mind?"

Roger Crosby dragged along one of the bookshelf ladders until it was adjacent to the fireplace. Now, for the first time, Rouletabille noticed the painting above the mantelpiece. It appeared to be the original of Goya's *Don Manuel Orsorio Manrique de Zunica*—a depiction of a young boy dressed in

175

red satin with two cats and a bird cage filled with finches, or perhaps canaries. Possibly the origin of Cyrus West's verbal allusion to cats and canaries earlier. Crosby swiftly ascended the ladder and swung the hinged painting to one side, revealing a safe. This evoked in the detective's memory his first visit to the study of General Brown, where the portrait of President Lincoln also concealed a safe. Crosby started to work the dial with practiced ease.

"This witch cult call themselves *Neprijaltelji Jovan Nenad*—The Enemies of King John, in reference to King John of Serbia. Their most revered artifact is the Crown of Jovan Nenad, which they stole from the Serbian Royal Family centuries ago. My agents have relieved them of this object and brought it here."

"And you think that the purpose of the prowler is to steal back the crown," deduced the Frenchman.

"Of course, but even if he were to effect entry to my safe, he would not be able to purloin the crown. You see, I have had the gold melted down and sold, and the gems re-cut and mounted in the form a necklace," smiled Cyrus West.

With the safe now open, Roger Crosby stood atop the ladder with the necklace in his hand. The huge emeralds and diamonds glittered magically in the firelight as he descended. It struck Rouletabille that the cult adherents would be driven into the most obscene fury by the loss of the crown. Cyrus West had deliberately, and perhaps rashly, destroyed something of great importance to them.

"Missy-Lou, go and get Monsieur Rouletabille's uniform for him, will you?" instructed West.

"Uniform?" puzzled the detective.

"Well, it makes sense, my friend," interjected General Brown. "Two dozen edgy men running around in semi-darkness with shotguns is a recipe for a mishap. Cyrus thought it would be a good idea if you wore the same sort of uniform and had the same weapon. That way the guards are unlikely to mistake you for our unwanted guest."

With that, Brown walked to the wall on the far side of the library where there was a small decorative rifle rack; on the lowest rung was a Winchester '73, above that was a Winchester 1912 pump action shotgun, and above that an unusual custom carbine with a silver plaque on its stock which appeared to be engraved with the word *Nautilus*. Brown selected the pump action and strode back to present it to Rouletabille. Almost simultaneously, Missy-Lou arrived back with the freshly pressed uniform and accompanying black octagonal peaked cap.

"Don't be impeded by false modesty," chided Brown. "You can change right here. I can assure you that Missy-Lou has seen the unclad form of a man before."

At this, Missy-Lou snorted slightly, and Brown and the other men chortled a little mirthlessly at the young man's embarrassment as he complied; firstly taking off his jacket in order to remove his leather shoulder holster. The holster contained his customary Lebel service revolver, and Rouletabille placed it carefully on West's desk. As if inspired by the sight of the revolver, West eased open his desk drawer and dug out a stubby snub-nosed brass Very pistol and a handful of parachute flares.

"This is my old flare pistol, Monsieur. You are welcome to use it. The guards tell me that the intruder wears black robes and just vanishes into the shadows. These parachute flares are my own personal design and made by one of my companies. They have the highest and purest magnesium content commercially available—for 15 seconds they'll turn midnight into noon," explained West.

There was a knock at the door just as Rouletabille was pulling on the black pants of the security guard uniform. Missy-Lou opened the door and a callow, smooth faced boy of about sixteen strolled in wearing an easy smile. He colored slightly as his eyes met those of the maid; she was, for him, an impossible, unattainable desire. And didn't she know it. The boy colored again at the sight of Rouletabille.

"I beg your pardon, sir," he commenced, rather baffled by the scene before him.

"I feel like I'm changing in the middle of a railway station," joked the detective, "or perhaps I'm trapped in the early scenes of a French farce."

"This is my nephew, Charles Wilder. He fancies himself something of a poet, but I've told him there's no money in it. After he's been to college, I think he should try writing a play. I'll bankroll it for him and get it on Broadway. Charlie has been staying with me while his mother is recovering from a serious illness. When you've got a family as dismal as mine a charming boy like him pretty easily ends up as your favorite!" announced West.

Roger Crosby stepped towards Charlie. Proffering to the boy the fabulous necklace that had once been the Crown of Jovan Nenad.

"Your uncle's latest acquisition, my boy. The jewels are of incredible value—perhaps over $200,000," intoned the lawyer.

Charlie took the necklace into his hands and looked into the heart of the jewels. Perhaps it was no more than a trick of the firelight, but his boyish smile seemed to twist into an avaricious leer.

"So beautiful," he murmured - his tongue struggled to sound out the words in a mouth that had suddenly filled with saliva. The dazzling jewels had filled him with a physical hunger in the same way that the sight of Missy-Lou's lithe form sometimes did.

Rouletabille's sensitive ears detected the sound of creaking metal under stress, akin to the sound of a door being forced. Then, the central library window seemed to explode inwards, peppering those present with glass shards of various shapes and sizes, and long slivers of shattered casement timber.

A black, tigerish shape bounded through the gaping aperture emitting a weird growling shriek. The shocking suddenness of the event had frozen everyone in place, after the initial reflexive flinch. Everyone—with the exception of Joseph Rouletabille. His reflexes had been, not so much honed, as tested to the limits of mortal endurance by both the rigors of battlefield combat in the Great War and his work as an intelligence officer.

Before the young detective had consciously ordered his arm to move, the Lebel revolver had been recovered from the desk and was in his right hand. He aimed and shot in the same fraction of a split second. The advancing form was not an animal, as he had first thought, but a man dressed in blue-black robes. Rouletabille's mind processed a glimpse of a strange, misshapen bearded face and short close-cropped hair—the yellow teeth were pointed like miniature daggers (could they have been filed?).

The robed figure folded in the middle at the impact of the bullet—but only for an instant—the slug could not have struck anything vital, perhaps it just glanced off his ribs. As the Frenchman got ready to shoot again, he realized that young Charlie Wilder had now stumbled into his field of fire. The bestial robed man saw what the young man still held in his hand, and recognized it—or rather what it had once been. This elicited from the creature an agonized howl of pain.

Rouletabille found this ironic, since he had remained silent while suffering a bullet wound. The Cat Man's right arm swung back, Rouletabille saw that the filthy, black chitinous fingernails had also been sharpened to points. The taloned hand jerked forward almost faster than the eye could follow in its attempt to rip open Charlie's throat. But the finger nails never reached it. Brown bulldozed into the attacker with one of the Arts and Crafts chairs held in front of him at chest height, looking very much like a past-his-prime lion tamer as he did so.

The Cat Man was sent reeling to the floor, but he still found time to tug from Charlie's loose grip the necklace that had once been the Crown of Jovan Nenad. The intruder rolled away, regained his footing, and then accelerated back towards the broken window. Now, with a clear line of sight, the detective fired twice. He could've sworn that he'd hit him, but there was no discernible change in the intruder's stride or speed.

"Are you all right, Charlie?" West asked the pale and febrile looking youth.

"Yes... Uncle Cy," he answered, looking at his empty hand as if he expected the necklace to re-materialize there.

"We should get you to a greater place of safety, Cyrus," advised Crosby, shaken.

"Nonsense, Roger. He will not come back into this room again after the reception he received. He has what he came for. His job now is to escape," judged the old man calmly.

Rouletabille busied himself removing the spent cartridges from the revolver's cylinder and replacing them with fresh ones. The unmistakable sound of the hollow crack of shotgun fire leeched into the room via the wrecked window, and made everyone jump a little. The security guards had spotted the Cat Man somewhere out in the grounds and were blazing away at him—probably to very little effect.

"Monsieur, you have now encountered our enemy face to face, and I would therefore not think the less of you if you were to spend the rest of the evening here in my library drinking brandy rather than pursuing him through the grounds. As it is, I will provide you with a considerable financial recompense for your trouble. However, if you can recover the necklace for me... well, I shall give you something of far greater value than mere money," smiled the millionaire.

Unexpectedly, Missy-Lou stepped forward and put a slim, graceful hand to Rouletabille's face and caressed his cheek.

"You do not need what he has to offer, my handsome young Frenchman. You already have a long life to lead," she warned enigmatically, and then glanced at West's decanter with its electric blue contents.

"I will return the necklace to you, if I can," Rouletabille assured him. Then he picked up the Very pistol and jammed it and the flares into his jacket pocket; shouldered the shotgun and was gone.

The shooting had quieted now, but the guards were still chasing around the flowerbeds and shrubberies, their battery powered flashlights casting truncated cones of weak illumination into the overwhelming darkness. Rouletabille snapped open the brass barrel of the pistol and loaded it with a parachute flare. He dragged back the stiff, heavy hammer and extended his arm vertically upwards; with a muffled whoosh the pyrotechnic launched. At the zenith of its trajectory, the flare's magnesium core lit, bathing the tidy lawns, regimented flowers and maple trees with an intensely bright silver-white luminescence. The flare swung beneath its miniature fire-retardant parachute, sending the shadows into a wild gavotte. Nevertheless, the detective was able to see a spattered trail of blackish crimson showing against the brightly lit verdure. The Cat Man was bleeding badly.

The Frenchman commandeered an electric flashlight from one of the security guards and forbade the man to follow him. With the flashlight in one hand and the shotgun in the other, he sprinted as fast as he could along the trail of blood—it would be easier to follow while the flare still lasted. After around six hundred yards, the droplets terminated on the steps of the temple-like swimming pool building.

He crept nearer and saw that an improvised barricade of poolside furniture had been piled on the other side the glass door—a black shape lay by the edge of the water: scooping water from the pool with his hand and using it to bathe his seeping bullet wounds. So the Cat was cornered, but doubtless more dangerous than ever.

He put down the flashlight on the steps and blasted the door repeatedly with the shotgun. The door had pretty much disintegrated by the third shot, so he advanced gingerly over the daggers of broken glass and kicked hard at the barricade. He passed inside, and it was obvious from the first moment that the Cat Man had done his trick of melting into the darkness. Rouletabille pointed the barrel of the shotgun experimentally into the furthest corner of the building—at an aggregation of thick, inky shadows. He squeezed the trigger and the shot-

181

gun blast boomed deafeningly in the confined space. A couple of pellets also ricocheted straight back at him and struck him in the scalp, just above his hairline.

Sensing movement behind him, he spun and struck at the shape creeping up on him with the stock of the shotgun. The weapon was twisted from his grip with immense strength and sent clattering onto the poolside tiles. The terrifying, snarling form ploughed into him and he lost his balance. Rouletabille anticipated the smack of his own skull on the hard tiles...but it did not come. Instead, there was a watery impact as he was enveloped by the warm wetness of Cyrus West's heated swimming pool. And he was not alone. The Cat Man was in the water with him; spitting, coughing and mewling in distress. The Cat Man couldn't swim!

With a piteous scream, the intruder disappeared beneath the surface of the water. The detective kicked his way to the pool edge, and started to heave himself from the water. His waterlogged clothes made the task more difficult. Suddenly, there was a sharp pain in his right ankle and it felt like a ship's anchor was dragging him down. The Cat Man had him by the foot and was clawing and biting at him under the water. Rouletabille struggled like a madman to free himself, but to no avail. His nose and mouth filled with water, and only then did he realize that it was a saltwater swimming pool. Even in circumstances such as this, the deductive part of his brain was an unstoppable engine—collating and inter-relating facts; theorizing and drawing conclusions. But his deductions could do little to save him now.

He adopted a quiet and dispassionate acceptance of his coming death, and allowed his thought processes to continue their natural work. Of course, West's swimming pool would be saltwater. He'd want to duplicate the experience of swimming at Shark Bay on Lincoln Island. That was probably where he first experimented with constructing flares. Absolutely vital in case one wanted to attract the attention of passing sea vessels. West's flares had the highest magnesium content commercially available. That was very interesting, mused the detective's hazy, oxygen starved brain. The most fascinating attribute of magnesium was its ability to burn underwater...

More out of curiosity than desperation, Rouletabille reached into his jacket pocket and yanked free the Very pistol. Loading it and snapping it shut seemed to be the most complex task that the Frenchman had ever undertaken. More complex than advanced algebra, or memorizing great chunks of catechism. It would be an interesting experiment to see if the Very pistol would fire underwater; after all there was little else to do while he was waiting to drown.

"Where the Hell is he? Where the Hell is he?" cursed Herbert Brown. The old general led an unlikely skirmish line comprising Missy-Lou, Charlie Wilder and two of the security guards. Brown was armed with the pneumatic Nautilus carbine, Missy-Lou cradled the Winchester with an accustomed confidence, and somehow young Charlie had ended up with Rouletabille's Lebel, after he had abandoned it in the library.

Without warning, up ahead of this search party, the interior of the swimming pool building blazed like a white-hot blast furnace.

"There he is!" screamed Brown triumphantly. The others streaked past him. Missy-Lou's long legs made her the fastest runner, but Charlie was close behind. Brown huffed and puffed and kept up as best he could. By the time Brown got inside the pool building the security guards were already lifting Rouletabille's unconscious form from the water.

"He'll be fine. Just get him back to Mr. West in the library as quickly as you can," Brown ordered the guards.

Charlie shone his flashlight into the aquamarine depths of the pool, where a dark, fetal form was wrapped in a cocoon of black silky fabric. Missy-Lou was aiming the Winchester at the drowned Cat Man as if he still presented an immediate threat, and warranted a series of potshots.

"Charlie, Missy-Lou—I want him out of there. He might still be alive," the old man barked.

Charlie swiftly unbuttoned his shirt and pulled off his slacks while Missy-Lou removed boots, sloughed off her stockings and pulled her dress over her head before arranging everything in a neatly folded pile clear of any broken glass, with her cotton underwear placed on the top last of all. With her maid's outfit cast aside, Louise Pleasant resembled nothing less than a bronze statue of a goddess come to life. This was how she had stood before the Voodoo worshippers on her home Caribbean island—how she had appeared when she had commanded life, death and sacrifice. How she had appeared when she had both presided over and taken part in the most lewd and debasing sexual rites imaginable. Cyrus West had thought he had rescued her from that life—but she would return to it in an instant if she could; if she ever dared to turn her back on what he alone could offer.

"Hurry up, you two!" commanded Brown.

Missy-Lou dove in, her body cutting into the water like a knife; and Charlie jumped in clumsily a moment after. They swam down towards the still black shape, creating a hurricane of bubbles. Charlie caught up with Missy-Lou with one thing on his mind, and held position next to her in the water. They were too deep now for the old man to see. He placed his palm on her flat belly, and when she raised no objection to this pushed his fingers down into the tight mass of soft curls and the softer flesh they concealed. Then something better caught his eye. The necklace lay at the bottom of the pool—the jewels glittered and burned even in the gloom of these watery depths. He veered away from Missy-Lou, grabbed the necklace and shot to the surface, leaving her to propel the dead weight of the Cat Man up into the life-giving air.

Once on the side of the pool, the Cat spluttered and coughed violently. Incredibly, he was still alive. He still bled from several bullet wounds, and his life would soon spill away.

"Missy-Lou, get back into your clothes and send one of the guards to get Dr. Trifulgas from the village.

"I say, let him die," pronounced the Voodoo Queen.

"The Master will want to question him. Please do as I ask," said Brown, as if to a child.

Missy-Lou fixed Charlie, who had eyes only for the necklace now, all the time she was changing with a vile, withering look of hatred. Men had begged to touch her flesh, before now. And some who had known it had been driven mad when it had been denied to them. She *had* liked the boy, but now she had the measure of him. Having rejected her in favor of baubles, he would never know the glories of her sacred *punani* when he became Master of Glen Cliff.

Cyrus West had the guards place the sopping wet Rouletabille on his leather-topped desk. West removed the stopper from the decanter of blue liquid and poured a liberal measure of it into a brandy bloom.

"Roger, raise his head for me a little will you?" commanded the white haired man. The lawyer complied and West poured the strange burning liquor into the young man's mouth. He neither coughed nor choked—his eyes fluttered open and he tried to sit up.

"Don't try to get up, son," said West. "Just rest easy. You'll live. Probably for quite some time."

A few minutes later, General Brown arrived back in the library.

"Well?" queried West.

"The guards have the Cat tied up, and I've sent for Trifulgas to patch him up," relayed Brown.

"Good. And the necklace?"

"At the moment, Charlie has it. You'll need to find somewhere very secure for it. The enemy may try again," predicted Brown.

"I'll hide it away someplace, don't you worry. Of course, we'll need Trifulgas to certify the Cat insane—once we've finished interrogating him. That way, there'll be no trial, we can just have him put away in the Fairview Asylum, over the way."

"As you have so many others who've got in your way over the years?"

"Well, if it's good enough for members of my own family, why shouldn't it be good enough for my enemies?" queried West.

"There's a streak of insanity a mile wide in your family, Cyrus. Sometimes, I worry that it has affected you too. You aren't the man you were on Lincoln Island. The years have made you ruthless and capricious."

"Don't talk like that in front of my lawyer, Herbert," laughed West. "What are you trying to do? Invalidate my will?"

The New World Order

Dedicated to David Mcdaniel—
he paved the way for all of us.

Philadelphia, May 1926

1. Slow Train Missing

It was less than ten minutes since Rouletabille had left the P.R.T Trolley Station, and he had already spotted the man to whom he needed to speak. The crowds at the Sesqui-Centennial Exposition celebrating 150 years since the signing of the Declaration of Independence were thinner than he had anticipated. The sudden, sharp torrents of rain were scaring people away, and that was a terrible pity since there was so much to see in the exposition grounds.

He needed a picture of the giant illuminated reproduction of the Liberty Bell for his newspaper, but right now he didn't want to lose sight of James Worth. The man he had come to see was dressed as Robin Hood—Lincoln Green outfit, pheas-ant-feather cap, tights, quiver and longbow. He was with a gaggle of individuals who were masquerading as Robin's *'Merrie Men'* and to a man, they were soaked to the skin fol-lowing the last downpour. They huddled together under the canopy of the Exposition Administration Building and grinned widely at the press photographers who were snapping them.

The next group to parade into view was an orderly line of Plymouth Pilgrims; at least their wide-brimmed hats had given them some protection from the rain. Seeing then that James Worth was no longer required by the press cameramen, the Frenchman moved forward to introduce himself.

"Mr. Worth? I am Joseph Rouletabille," he said, extending his hand.

"I am most pleased to meet you, sir," said Worth. "Come let's head up towards my office. I really need to get out of these wet things anyway. All I can say is, I volunteered to play Robin Hood in the history pageant a good while before the long-range weather forecast came in."

Worth ushered Rouletabille into the entrance hall of the administration building, where he was immediately struck by a beautifully executed mural showing the history of the United States. Every significant event from Penn's treaty with the Indians, through Washington crossing the Delaware, to the Wright Brothers at Kitty Hawk was lovingly depicted. Above the mural the following words were written in gold: *"For I dipt into the future, far as human eye could see; Saw the vision of the world, and all the wonder that would be."*

"I don't recognize that quotation," admitted Rouletabille.

"Ah, then you don't know your Tennyson," said Worth. "It is a line from that poet's greatest work—Locksley Hall. And this administration building borrows its name from the title of the poem; you are now in Locksley Hall."

They took the elevator up to the fifth floor and passed the desks of dozens of clerks and press aides before finally reaching Worth's overly palatial office. The American invited Rouletabille to help himself from the cylindrical walnut cocktail cabinet while he disappeared into a private washroom to disrobe, towel himself dry and change into his suit. Obviously, prohibition was little enforced amongst the higher echelons of society. Rouletabille swiftly rustled up a matching pair of Rickety Scotch cocktails, using a generous amount of warming Talisker and probably a few too many drops of grapefruit bitters. After a gap of a few minutes, Worth emerged and gratefully sipped at the drink.

"That's one hell of a concoction, young man," said Worth, smacking his lips. "But let's get down to business. I am one of the organizers of this exposition; it's been many years in the planning and, because of the weather, we're losing money hand-over-fist."

"You need an Indian witch Doctor to improve the weather, not a detective," said Rouletabille.

"Don't think I haven't considered it," said Worth," but that is not why you are here. In an effort to promote the exposition, I laid on a series of special free trains to transport people who might not otherwise have been able to afford to come. Last Thursday, one of these trains disappeared with everyone on it. There is simply no sign of the train at all—it's like it vanished off the face of the Earth."

"Hardly, a unique problem, Mr. Worth. It puts me in mind of the case of the 'Lost Special' in which the great detective Sherlock Holmes was peripherally involved. If memory serves, the train was concealed on the disused railroad leading to a mine. I assume that this train too was lost in a mining area?"

"Yes, in fact, in the heart of anthracite mining territory, up in Luzerne County. But this train won't be concealed down a disused mineshaft or some such, since every single mine in that vicinity is open for business and busy as a beehive. No, someone wants to stop people from coming to the exposition by generating bad publicity. Doubtless they expected the story to break by now, but I can tell you that every newspaper publisher on the eastern seaboard is a personal friend of mine. The lid is on this story tight, just not forever. I want you to go to Luzerne and find that train. Your reputation as a solver of impossible crimes precedes you. Surely this is right up your alley?" said Worth.

"I don't know, Mr. Worth. The lack of uniqueness in this case is not attractive. Holmes and at least one of his successors have been involved in very similar puzzles. While I have every sympathy with the families of those who have disappeared in such circumstances, this is likely to be a case where manpower will be key to solving the crime and finding the locomotive. It is a matter for the official police, not a lone detective, even one with skills such as mine," said Rouletabille.

"Well, that certainly disappoints me. I won't insult you by offering you vast amounts of money. But I believe I do have something that could entice you to commit yourself. I know that you are greatly interested in the events that took place on the so-called 'Mysterious Island' some decades ago and that Cyrus West and General Herbert Brown were personally known to you..."

"They were, indeed. God rest their souls," said Rouletabille.

Worth moved to the area behind his desk and slid to one side a wooden panel revealing the portrait of a belligerent looking man with heavy side whiskers.

"This is my father, Adam Worth. He was an associate of Cyrus West, and like him he was a Civil War *bounty jumper*— a man who enlisted in the army under false names in order to claim a bounty and then deserted, only to re-enlist under another false name. I'm not proud of my father. In fact, he was something of a villain. But he never painted himself to be a hero in later life, like West and Brown. The Mysterious Island castaways were not what they pretended to be. And the tales of their adventures on Lincoln Island were a pack self-serving lies. I know this because my father was on Lincoln Island with them—although his name was expunged from all the stories," said Worth.

Worth then tugged open his desk drawer and pulled out a worn and water damaged leather-bound journal.

"This book is my father's record of what really happened on Lincoln Island and if you find the missing train for me, I'll happily let you read it," said Worth.

Rouletabille considered carefully, while reining in the surge of anger inside him. He could not believe for one moment that Cyrus West had been a dishonest man. In the case of his old friend Herbert Brown, it seemed even more unlikely. He was consumed with the desire to grab the book from Worth's hand and commence to read it now. He suppressed the urge and lit his pipe instead.

"Very well. I shall take on this case, in order to have access to that journal. You have succeeded in piquing my curiosity in a most extreme fashion," said Rouletabille.

"I am very pleased to hear that," said Worth. "Now I realize that this information has probably come as a shock to you. But there is really no need for you and me to fall out. Instead, why don't you show me how to make that cocktail? It really is delicious."

And so, after a few more drinks, Rouletabille came to find himself liking James Worth irrespective of the man's rather manipulative nature. He was, admittedly, a little superficial, but there was a high gloss of charm and a personal magnetism about him that was difficult to ignore. He had diverse business interests in pharmaceuticals, agriculture, armaments and tool manufacture. His knowledge of the history of the United States had the pedantic completeness of the self-educated man, and he made no reference to having attended university. Plainly, he was one of the richest and most influential men in Philadelphia.

"Tell me, Mr. Worth, why did you play the part of Robin Hood in the History Pageant; and more importantly, why was Robin Hood included in a pageant of American history at all?" asked Rouletabille.

"Robin Hood is more than merely my favorite character, he is an early embodiment of the spirit of rebellion, just like Ned Ludd or the Scarecrow of Romney Marsh. In that rebelliousness lies the genesis of the United States, just as much or perhaps even more than in the desire of the Pilgrim Fathers for religious freedom," said Worth.

"Ned Ludd?" queried the detective.

"Perhaps you're not familiar with him. His followers, the Luddites, destroyed machinery in an attempt to halt the creeping mechanization that has ultimately soiled this world and profaned the glorious rural idyll of the past," said Worth.

"You are a most unusual man, Mr. Worth. I don't think I've ever heard an American complain that there is too much mechanization."

"To be honest, my friend, I don't even like guns, let alone machines. I prefer a good longbow in my hand for hunting, especially when I'm stalking deer. Let's go down to the shooting gallery in the basement and I'll show you how good a shot I am."

They took the elevator down into the sub-basement, which opened up into an expansive area about the size of a football field. There was a trestle table sagging under the weight of various weapons, including crossbows and a full-sized six-foot longbow. Fifty yards away various targets had been set up and one of them was a metal suit of armor. Worth deftly picked up the bow and nocked an arrow to the string, pulled back effortlessly, aimed just for a moment, and let fly the arrow. There was a muffled clang, as if a bullet had struck an old galvanized bucket at extreme range and the suit of armor was impaled by the arrow. Now, as if to prove that this was no fluke, Worth shot three more, and the plate mail started to resemble Saint Sebastian at his martyrdom.

"You give it a shot," said Worth.

And so, with some hesitation the Frenchman picked up the bow and clumsily got the arrow into place. The draw weight of the bow seemed immense to Rouletabille's unaccustomed muscles. He drew back and drew back until his shoulder burned. It felt like at least 150 lbs of pull was required. His arm started to shake, so he released the string. The arrow flashed past the target: a miss, but perhaps not so wide as Rouletabille had been expecting.

"Not bad for a beginner," said Worth. "Now, I don't want to keep you here too late since you need to be at Vermissa Junction in Luzerne tomorrow. But if we just practice for a couple of hours, I think you'll be surprised how much your aim improves."

It seemed that Rouletabille had again encountered a man that one simply could not say no to. He sighed inwardly and reached for another arrow, rather desperately wishing that he had brought the makings of another Rickety Scotch cocktail down here with him.

The following morning, Rouletabille was in the restaurant car of the all-stopping slow train to Scranton. He'd finished up his late breakfast of bacon and eggs and was now savoring some strong black coffee. He'd already laid out a large-scale map of the county on his table and weighted down the corners with the salt and pepper shakers and a bottle of Hunt's tomato ketchup. Perhaps some inspiration would strike him soon. He could not imagine that anything would be possible other than simply narrowing down the territory to be searched as much as possible, disembarking to gather a posse with the local sheriff's office and roving endlessly, perhaps fruitlessly, over the terrain.

The detective took to staring out of the window, desperate for some sort of inspiration. The steady rhythm and movement of the train had the opposite effect on him to what he was accustomed. It did not lull or relax him; instead it set his nerves on edge and generated a feeling as if a ball of ice were slowly forming in his stomach. Lunchtime came and went, and he chewed without real appetite on sandwiches filled with blue-veined Chester County cheese.

The arrival of one particular man in the restaurant car burned off the mist of his despondency. The man was very tall, at least six and a half feet tall and built more powerfully than a circus strongman. He wore a tailored blue woolen suit with a white shirt and red tie, as well as sporting large wire framed spectacles which served to give him a scholarly, almost owlish appearance. Rouletabille wondered if he might be a fellow reporter. Yet, perhaps the most striking thing about this giant was the streak of white hair that ran through his otherwise jet-black tonsure from the center of his forehead hairline all the way to the nape of his neck. Rouletabille could not account for the sudden rush of goosebumps that originated somewhere near his shoulders and descended quickly to his forearms. He had seen this man before. He recognized not so much his face as his unique physiognomy and lithe, pantherish movement. Could he be mistaken? No, the more he looked, the more certain he was.

Rouletabille got up from his table and approached the bar, where the newcomer was ordering a glass of lemonade.

"Pardon me, sir," said Rouletabille. "I believe you are a veteran of the French Army. I too served under Captain Crouan during the Great War. I remember all too well the day that you carried an immense canvas bundle of rations and ammunition through no-man's land to relieve our position. You leapt in great bounds across the wire and the mud. It was almost as it you had the power of flight. Afterwards, they tried to tell us that it was all an illusion; some form of mass hysteria. But my eyes do not play tricks, not then or now. I remember you. You are Private Danner."

At first, Rouletabille thought that the man might deny it. But instead his weathered face cracked into a sardonic smile.

"Speak softly, my old comrade-in-arms and call me Mark Rainham—that's the name I'm currently travelling under," said Danner. "You will have to refresh my memory on your monicker. I'm afraid I cannot recall the names of all the soldiers I served with," said the Adonis-like warrior.

"You never knew my name. I was just one of many you helped that day. I am Joseph Rouletabille."

"Perhaps I did not know you then, but I know you now. The detective who solved the *Mystery of the Yellow Room* needs no introduction. Yet, you are far younger than I would have supposed," said Danner.

"I am here to investigate another mystery—the disappearance of Exposition Loco 481 bound for Philadelphia. Though I have little confidence that this is a puzzle that I can solve."

"Good Lord!" said Danner. "This surely cannot be a coincidence. I have been hired to travel on trains during the Exposition to guard against any nefarious attack such as may have befallen the missing train."

"And who has given you this commission?" asked the detective.

"Why, the organizer of the Philadelphia Exposition, James Worth," said Danner.

"It is curious that he did not inform me of your involvement. He did not seem the sort of man to allow something to slip his mind," said Rouletabille.

The two men sat together for half an hour or so, trying to imagine in what circumstances a locomotive could disappear from its prescribed route. The discussion went swiftly in circles. With no long tunnel on this track, the only thing that might account for the disappearance was the train being diverted onto a mining company track—the exact same thing that had happened to the 'Lost Special;' in effect, it was a non-mystery. Sherlock Holmes, according to the article in *The Times* which Rouletabille half-recalled, had not even bothered to leave his Baker Street rooms in order to solve the conundrum. The problem with a train was that it left traces of its passing, but to deduce how it was done would not necessarily result in the discovery of the missing train. In country such as this, with mines, slag heaps, industrial waste lagoons and foundries, a thousand men might look for a locomotive for weeks and never find it. And what if the locomotive was now hidden in plain sight? Repainted, disguised... The problem was maddening in its complexity. Where were the passengers? Had none of them escaped? What dreadful fate had befallen them?

As if in answer, a sudden whine emanated from the axles and couplings and the slow train to Scranton heaved to the left. Crockery and silverware slid to the floor, women squealed, then regained their composure with a giggle. Rouletabille looked around. There were certainly plenty of beautiful young women in the carriage.

"We took those points far too quickly," judged Rouletabille.

"Then it's begun," said Danner.

Rouletabille consulted his map for the last time and pondered the situation. Worth had been wrong to think that only trains heading for the Exposition would be targeted. The slow train for Scranton was quite plainly no longer bound for its original destination.

Danner downed the dregs of his third lemonade.

"No reason to alarm the other passengers," he said.

"No. But we need to get to the engine cab," said Rouletabille.

The two men got up without a further word and worked their way through the two first-class cars towards the luggage cars, where they could most likely converse without being overheard.

"So, we've been diverted off the main railroad onto a private track that runs North East of Wyoming Valley. This is very isolated anthracite mining country. We need to find out if the engineer and fireman are in on this, and if not, get them to stop the train or reverse it," said Danner.

"They didn't slow down for the points change. And they haven't stopped. We better go look and see," said the Frenchman.

Rouletabille opened the door onto the coupling platform. Smuts and cinders from the smoke stack swirled around him, but his view of the engine was blocked by the tender car. The detective ascended the ladder at the back of the car and readied himself to crawl over the coal down and into the cab. His suit was going to get ruined. As Rouletabille reached the top of the ladder, he saw that there was a man in a strange military uniform in the cab aiming a rifle at him. His brain barely had time to compute that the weapon strongly resembled the pneumatic carbines used by the crew of the legendary submarine, *The Nautilus*, when, with a spitting hiss, a projectile was launched at him. The bullet, or dart, clipped the fabric of the suit at the shoulder. Then Rouletabille was aware of a powerful pair of hands pulling him back to safety.

"I knew I shouldn't have let you go first," said Danner, with a smile. "Stay here, pal, I'll deal with this."

Danner leapt on top of the tender car and stood on the heap of coal, seemingly oblivious to the danger in which he was putting himself. He was a sitting duck target for the marksman in the cab. He was struck several times by bullets, which did little more than blast away the fabric of his suit and leave angry dark welts on his skin.

In fact, there were two oddly uniformed soldiers in the cab; aside from the one blazing away at Danner, there was one keeping the driver and fireman covered. Danner strode confidently across the coal, knowing that his steel-hard skin meant that he was virtually invulnerable to bullets. During battles in the Great War, there were times when he had been constantly raked by heavy machine gun fire, but had suffered little more than bruising. Then his hawk-like eyes noticed that the marksman was swapping the steel grey ammo magazine of his rifle for a light powder blue one which he had removed from a satchel at his shoulder. Shooting from the hip, the man fired at Danner again, just a split second before the veteran planned to jump down into the cab and smash open the skulls of the two soldiers.

Danner reeled back in the most agonizing pain that he had ever experienced in his entire life. The impact knocked him backwards and he found himself lying on the coupling platform, having fallen from the top of the tender. Danner could barely keep himself from screaming; the agony did not diminish one iota. Rouletabille rushed to his assistance and, immediately, saw the source of the problem. Sticking into Danner's skin was something like a tightly wound glowing glass corkscrew. He placed his fingers around it and tried to wrench it from his old comrade's flesh. Now it was Rouletabille's turn to suppress a scream. The glass corkscrew was white-hot and the Frenchman could smell his skin burning like meat on a griddle. He let go and blew on his scorched fingers.

"Lay still, my friend," soothed Rouletabille, although he suspected that the almost super-human warrior could no longer hear him. His eyes had rolled far back in his head and he was jerking like an epileptic.

A few moments later, Danner was quite still, unconscious and breathing shallowly. The detective theorized that he would need something like a pair of pliers to get the dreadful projectile out of his comrade's skin. There might be such an implement in the toolbox in the cab, but how on earth was he supposed to reach it?

As usual, the powerful engine that was Rouletabille's deductive powers worked away unbidden. The presence of the soldiers with a weapon that could immobilize a man as apparently unkillable as Danner suggested that his presence had been expected, and catered for.

Now the train began to slow, and Rouletabille looked up at the stark, blasted countryside of this anthracite mining area. It seemed as bleak and lonely as another planet. Incongruously, a painted sign with a cheerful motif and bold black letters seemed to welcome them to their final destination. The sign said simply *CATHARUS MINE*, and depicted on it was a rather deft and delicately drawn picture of a bird with a mottled breast.

2. Into the Mine

The locomotive slowed to little more than walking pace as it traversed the mine's railyard and neared the great man-made cave which served as the entrance to the mine. More soldiers in black and white uniforms, armed with *Nautilus*-style pneumatic carbines emerged from out of the workings. Some of them had shouldered their weapons and carried portable wooden steps to allow easy egress from the train carriages.

While Rouletabille did not jump down from the coupling platform to the black and dusty ground, he did take the opportunity to crane his neck and see what the other passengers were doing. Well, he might've been forgiven for thinking that the train had pulled in to Scranton Station. The other passengers were disembarking as if nothing were wrong. Taking their luggage with them, they cheerfully strode to the gaping stone mouth of the mine. He noted that about seventy percent of the people on the train seemed to be women. And from their appearance and mode of dress, he guessed they were young women, mostly under twenty-five. A sudden inexplicable fear took hold of him which manifested as more iciness in his stomach and the feeling that these were virgins about to be sacrificed to some Dark God.

When the passengers, guards and restaurant staff were gone, one of the soldiers called out: "M'sieu Rouletabille, please come down and do not be afraid. Medical attention has been arranged for Mr. Rainham."

For a second Rouletabille's mind was blank; then he recalled that Danner had said he was travelling under the name Mark Rainham. Two men in white uniforms, carrying a stretcher between them, were almost at the train. Rouletabille jumped down and the soldiers made no hostile move towards him. Then, without warning, the carbines cracked twice and the driver and fireman fell from the cab dead. Quite obviously, these men were neither needed, nor welcome within Catharus Mine. The Frenchman resolved that if he ever got out of this situation, he would go about heavily armed. The world had changed since the war, and it seemed that firepower was more important than brains. A regrettable state of affairs, but one that he could do very little about. He had not expected to have to go up against a foreign or private army here in the United States.

Rouletabille was escorted to the mine; he walked just ahead of the stretcher carrying Danner. Inside, he saw that the shaft elevator was huge, large enough to hold perhaps fifty or sixty men comfortably. They had to wait for three more lots of passengers to be taken down. While they waited, Rouletabille looked around. This was quite plainly no ordinary mine. He also couldn't help but notice that the lift smelt strongly of horses. Yes, of course, some mines still used 'pit ponies' in the same way that they still used canaries to check for gas, but here, it did not seem right. The sheer obviousness of it all was causing speculation to gel into assumptions—and much too quickly for his liking. All the circumstantial evidence pointed to the fact that this mine was not being used as a mine. It was being utilized as some sort of citadel or sanctuary. There was a whole population down there. He could feel it in his gut.

The elevator went down and down and down; into velvet darkness that was illuminated only by meager flickering light bulbs. He felt like Orpheus descending into Hades. The winding gears complained as the brakes engaged and the elevator car came to a shuddering halt. More soldiers appeared and dragged open the folding metal gates. They emerged into a well-lit tunnel, where they were met by a man in flowing black and gold robes. The robes had a hood, not dissimilar to that of a monk's habit, which obscured his features. The figure lifted both hands to the material of the hood and gently pushed it back.

"Welcome, M'sieu Rouletabille," said James Worth. "I hope that you are not too surprised. Welcome to the main enclave of the Catharus Society. This is where you'll be living for probably the next two years."

There had been very few times when Rouletabille was so thunderstruck that he couldn't speak, but this was one of them.

Just along the tunnel, a man in a white doctor's coat stood by a small metal trolley. As they processed by it, with James Worth in the lead, the doctor picked a syringe from the trolley.

"Stop and take off your jacket, and roll up your sleeve, please," said the doctor.

"No harm will come to you, my friend," said Worth. "Quite the opposite, in fact. You are receiving an inoculation. Hugo Danner will need to be inoculated too, at some stage. We'll need to figure out a less traumatic way to get something through his tough hide than using our new carbines."

Rouletabille winced a little as the needle went in.

"Inoculated against what?" he said.

"A particularly nasty strain of Viral Hemorrhagic Fever which we developed right here in our underground laboratories," said Worth.

The stretcher bearers and the doctor passed into a side-room that was some form of medical facility. Rouletabille was reassured by Worth that they would simply remove the white-hot corkscrew projectile, called a 'plasma dart' from Danner, following which he would be sedated and restrained. After receiving some medical aid for his finger burns, Rouletabille continued with Worth. It was getting harder and harder to remember that he was down an anthracite mine. The internal architecture was starting to resemble the dungeons of some medieval castle. They passed into a room which could only be called a throne room, and naturally Worth (or was he 'King Worth' now?) took his place on the ornate golden chair.

"You probably have many questions," smiled Worth.

"You plan is to release a deadly fever at the exposition. The attendees will leave with it, incubating inside them and return to their home towns—or home countries. Perhaps within a few weeks, all but the most inaccessible parts of the world will be struck down by the epidemic. The only question is, why? What could you possibly gain? And you seemed like a rational man. Have you issued a ransom demand? What could a man as wealthy as you possibly want?"

"There will be no ransom demand," said Worth. "I want nothing except a great winnowing of humanity. I have taken the time to consider precisely where the ship of history is taking us. There will be nothing but bigger and bigger wars with bigger and bigger weapons. Ultimately, there will be armaments that could threaten and destroy entire cities. If these proliferate, then the entire world might be rendered uninhabitable. Imagine the entire planet shrouded by phosgene gas. Someone has to take control now and steer us away from the rocks. Even if I'm wrong about the destructive nature of war, the alternative is worse—over-population. A hundred years from now, there might be ten or twelve billion people. There won't be enough food or resources. We need an alternative to the chaotic nature of so-called progress. We've already seen what works best. An agrarian society with a low technology base, governed by feudal overlords, just like England in the middle ages. It will be a return to the rural idyll. With over ninety per cent of the global population dead within two years, virtually all knowledge and skills relating to high level technology will be lost. Only Catharus Society enclaves like this one will have access to the old ways, the old medicines. And only our ruling elite will benefit from them."

"Then why bring Danner and myself here? We are nothing to do with your New World Order, and I, for one, would rather take my chances with hemorrhagic fever than hide in this hole while civilization goes to hell," said Rouletabille.

"My friend, your incredible problem-solving mind could not be allowed to be destroyed in such circumstances. You squander your potential by acting as a journalist, detective, spy or soldier. In my New World Order, as you call it, you will be one of my feudal overlords. Don't rule it out now while anger governs your mind. I will win you around eventually. I have preserved other extraordinary individuals in much the same way. Danner presents more of a problem—he could never be allowed to become part of the lordly caste. Yet, had I left him on the surface, with his super-powerful constitution. he might have survived the fever, and gathered around him an army of survivors. That could have been a threat. I needed to find an effective way to enslave him; so far nothing has presented itself," said Worth.

"You said that if I took on the case of the missing locomotive, you would show me your father's journal—an alternative version of the events on Lincoln Island—too perfect an inducement, surely. I am not easily tricked, but I believed you completely," said Rouletabille.

"You were right to do so. It was no trick, unlike the story of the missing train. The missing loco merely brought Catharus Society members to the mine, men whose skills I will need in the years to come. The second train brought a stock of willing, fertile women for them to breed with. But I'm sure you guessed that," said Worth.

"And your father's journal?" said Rouletabille.

"Adam Worth was a genius. A man whose inventions and scientific knowledge were at least 50 years ahead of their time. You already know almost everything about him, for you know him under a different name. Adam Worth is the true identity of Captain Nemo. Prince Dakkar was a ludicrous fiction invented by Cyrus West. The journal reveals everything—well, almost everything. We can only infer my father's ultimate fate. Cyrus West murdered him for his inventions, and registered patents on most of them upon his return to the United States. Many of the patent blueprints in West's name are noticeably signed with my father's initials. West was a brazen thief indeed. Other drawings that were too obviously recognizable as being components of the *Nautilus* were kept by Herbert Brown; until, for reasons that are not entirely clear, you allowed them to fall into the hands of the German Air-Pirate, Kapitan Mors. I will bring you the journal after my final trip to Philadelphia tomorrow."

The door to the throne room opened and a man in a wheelchair entered, he was accompanied by a couple of the black and white uniformed Catharus Society guards. The man would have been tall and spare had he not been confined to the chair, and although perhaps no older than his late twenties he was already balding. Nevertheless, there was an obvious intellectual intensity and, rather oddly, a certain friendliness to his demeanor.

"Rouletabille, this is Ward Baldwin, one of the senior officers within my organization, and, like you, a veteran of the Great War. The advanced surgery techniques here in the enclave will hopefully restore some function to the leg he nearly lost in the Macedonia campaign," said Worth.

"I am very pleased that you could join us," said Baldwin. "Your mind will be a great asset to the Catharus Society."

"I have not, by any definition, joined you. I am your prisoner. I will do my best to escape and frustrate your machinations, but keeping in mind your vastly superior numbers, I imagine I will die trying. I am quite happy to accept that," said Rouletabille, flatly.

"It is not possible to escape from this place. I understand how you must feel right now. But within a few days there will be nowhere worth escaping to, and then, a man of your unusually high intelligence will be forced to accept the reality of the situation," said Baldwin.

"Until then, take him away," Worth instructed the guards.

Rouletabille was marched through the mine past living areas, great kitchens, storage facilities and (as he has suspected) stables towards a secure holding area which oddly resembled a collection of zoo cages. Just before he arrived at the cages, the procession passed a combat practice arena in which two men in chainmail and surcoats fought with maces. It seemed the final proof that Worth and his band of madmen were deadly serious. The world was to be reduced to a state resembling the 13th century and held there in stagnant perpetuity. In a couple of years, the inhabitants of the mine would emerge to find an almost uninhabited United States. An empty landscape, to be restructured to their will. There would be fields to be ploughed and castles to be built. The handful of survivors would most likely be reduced to serfdom.

The cage door clanged shut and Rouletabille was left alone. He marshaled every cell of his brain, every scintilla of mental energy to a single resolute purpose: escape. Rouletabille thought back almost sixteen years to his adventure in London, reported in a certain popular metropolitan magazine of the day as *The Adventure of the Snaresbrook Assizes.* At that time, he had been captured by the fiendish German Agent, Dr. Grierson. Grierson was a psychiatrist and briefly had the Frenchman committed to an insane asylum. After receiving torture by means of electric shocks and intramuscular injections of camphor, Rouletabille managed to escape even though he had been placed in a straitjacket. The intervening years dulled the recollection the agony involved, and he felt slightly cheered that he had successfully executed a Houdini-like exit once before in his career.

Within fifteen minutes, the detective had succeeded in breaking apart his belt buckle and was using the pieces to try to pick the cage lock. He was having almost no luck with the tumblers, but even if he had been the exercise struck him as a particularly futile one. It was going to be far more difficult to get out of here than a London insane asylum. When the baton struck his hand, Rouletabille realized that he had been far too wrapped in his task to hear the approach of a guard.

"Gimme what you were usin' to pick at that lock or, so help me, I'll brain ya," said the guard.

Using his uninjured hand, Rouletabille picked up the fragments of buckle from the floor of the cage and tossed them towards the surly, smirking guard.

"Try that again and I'll break your feet!" the baton wielder threatened.

The lower ranks of the Catharus Society had obviously not been made privy to Rouletabille's importance.

A newcomer strode into the dim light of the holding area. He was a tall man, with a handsome and trustworthy countenance; yet unfortunately, he too wore the black and white uniform of the Catharus Society militia, with what Rouletabille took to be officer rank insignia on the epaulettes and sleeves.

"What's going on here, Maddocks? Are you antagonizing a prisoner again? I'll have you on a charge!" said the officer.

"Why no, Captain Rogers," said Maddocks. This prisoner was picking his cell lock. I caught 'im at it."

"What was he using on the lock?" asked Rogers.

"Little bits of metal—looks like part of a buckle," said Maddocks as he stooped to recover the pieces.

Without warning, Rogers kicked Maddocks in the head, just as if he was kicking a football off the tee. The guard rose up with the transferred momentum, then crashed down onto his back: out cold. Rouletabille looked at the Catharus Society officer in disbelief.

"Sir, I know that you've little reason to trust me, but I can assure you that I am not on the side of the people running this mine. I threw in with them under duress. I am Anthony Rogers of the American Radioactive Gas Corporation and I want to get out of here just as much as you do," said Captain Rogers.

Rogers knelt down and removed a ring of keys from the guard's belt, then after a moment selecting the right key, he inserted it into the lock of Rouletabille's cage and released him.

"If this is an attempt to break my spirit by allowing me to escape and then re-confining me, it would seem extraordinarily premature," said Rouletabille, somewhat mockingly.

"I'll be proving my good intentions with forceful action against our captors—let that alone convince you. Talk is always cheap," said the Captain, and with that, he removed from his holster a pistol of highly unusual design. Rouletabille was reminded of the pistol that he had seen in the hands of Kapitan Mors a decade ago; perhaps that weapon too had been derived from the designs of Adam Worth.

"The best way out of here might be the ruse that you are a captive being transferred to a different level. I have some handcuffs here somewhere," said Rogers.

"Forget it. I am not being cuffed. I'll need my hands free to fight when the opportunity presents itself," said the detective. "Let's just walk out of here very casually and see if we can make it to the elevator," said Rouletabille. "There are a lot of newcomers here; it may be that they'll assume that I am just another neophyte of the Catharus Society."

"Uh-uh, they are very fussy about who they let back up to the surface. Only James Worth and Ward Baldwin seem to be able to come and go at will," said Rogers.

"Well, I don't intend to stay down here for two years… there has to be a way," said Rouletabille.

"Nobody is going to be down here for two years. I told them, but they didn't believe me. There's a rich vein of carnotite in the lower levels of the mine. It's a hydrovanadate of uranium. It means all the air down here is radioactive. Anyone down here for more than a few months will become seriously ill," explained Rogers.

"Are you sure?"

"Mister, this is my business. I'm a mining engineer with a specialty in this field. The abandoned Vermissa Mine next door is even more badly contaminated, and Worth plans to extend into that. He'll flood the Catharus workings with even deadlier gas," said Rogers.

"How were they planning to break through into that other mine?" asked the Frenchman.

"Well, they should drill through gradually and prop as they go, but these guys are pretty crazy. They've been using dynamite to create additional tunnels. Maybe you can get away with that in a lead mine or something, but in a coal mine, sooner or later you'll hit a pocket of concentrated methane and that'll be all she wrote! Next stop, the Pearly Gates or…"

"The gateway that says 'Abandon hope, all ye who enter here,'" completed Rouletabille. "How thick is the wall between this mine and the Vermissa?"

"Maybe just two or three yards in some places… I see where you're going. We could make our way to the surface from the abandoned mine. You're not loco enough to want to blast through, are you?" asked Rogers.

"We won't need to blast through. We just need Danner," smiled Rouletabille.

Rogers walked into the medical bay very confidently, as if performing an inspection on behalf of James Worth himself. He then pistol-whipped the doctor who was standing over Hugo Danner rather mercilessly, sending him into a temporary dreamless oblivion. The attendant nurse sought to flee but had her exit blocked by Rouletabille. The two would-be escapers were both far too gentlemanly too engage in violence against women, but that did not stop them from threatening, restraining and binding her. Once the woman was taken care of, they both examined Danner's situation. The plasma dart had been removed from his chest and a dressing placed over the wound. Over his face a rubber mask was fastened in place, and from the mask a thick rubber tube led away to a black gas cylinder on which where stenciled the words DIETHYL ETHER. There was a small brass control wheel at the top of the cylinder which Rouletabille immediately started to turn counter-clockwise to the shut position.

"They're keeping him heavily anaesthetized," said Rouletabille.

"And how exactly is this man going to help us?" asked Rogers.

"Well, I know nothing of his origins, but I can tell you that he is a modern-day Samson or Hercules. He has the strength of a hundred men. "

Rogers raised an eyebrow.

"You asked me to accept your word. Now return the favor," said Rouletabille.

"I wonder how long he'll take to come round," said Rogers.

"His constitution is extraordinary: see, he is already starting to stir," observed Rouletabille.

Danner's hands moved slowly to the rubber mask at his face and pulled it off. Then his eyes snapped wide open and Rouletabille instantly realized the terrible danger that Rogers was in. The mining engineer stood before Danner in the uniform of his enemy—possibly Danner might even think that this was the same man who shot him with the plasma dart within his ether-clouded brain. Swift as lightning, Danner grabbed Rogers by the throat and commenced to throttle him.

"Danner! No, he is an ally," shouted Rouletabille.

Mercifully, Rogers felt the fantastic crushing pressure on his trachea suddenly cease. He dropped to his knees clutching a throat that would be black and blue in the morning—assuming they lived that long.

As Danner recovered, Rouletabille regaled him with the full details of his experiences within the Catharus Mine, summarizing each cogent fact with the skill of a highly trained journalist, until finally Danner was fully apprised of the plan to break through into the nearby mine—but this was not what concerned him.

"It is extremely strange that Worth tempted you with this journal telling the true version of events regarding his father, who just happens to be the legendary Captain Nemo, when he also offered me access to an extraordinary and far more incredible journal. He claimed he had access to a secret diary which my father, Professor Abednego Danner lodged in the archives of Indian Creek College, Colorado—officially not to be opened until one hundred years after his death; when the world might be ready for the information therein. Worth suggested to me that my father was, in fact, an alien from another world sent to this planet from a dying world about to suffer an imminent catastrophe when he was only a baby. His crashed miniature space-vehicle was discovered by my grandparents who raised him as their own," said Danner.

"That's very telling. A man might have access to one revelatory tome, but to have two so conveniently related to men he wants to influence smacks of cynical and manipulative fraud," said Rouletabille.

"Fellows, we don't have time for this," judged Rogers. "Anyway, aliens? Who believes in such fairytales? Let's just get out of here…"

The trio went out into the corridor and almost immediately encountered a pair of guards. Before the men could unshoulder their carbines, Danner had set upon them. A blind rage descended on him as he fought and the two guards fell to the dusty floor of the tunnel as sacks of splintered bone.

Rouletabille recovered one of the dropped pneumatic carbines and armed himself. They moved forward like an army patrol with Danner taking point, Rouletabille in the center and Rogers bringing up the rear. They made their way past a set of women's dormitories where the girls from the train to Scranton were still unpacking their luggage, chatting and giggling, as if they were on the most adventurous sleepover of all time. Finally, Rogers directed them to a spur tunnel which took them closest to the Vermissa mine.

They stopped in front of the blank, black rock face at the tunnel's end and Danner placed his huge hands on the wall in front of him as if considering how much of his tremendous strength to utilize. Rouletabille and Rogers turned to defend their position against a phalanx of approaching guards. Rouletabille switched the carbine to rapid-fire mode and opened up. He wished he'd picked up a spare magazine now. Rogers blazed away with his pistol and proved himself to be an excellent shot. Rouletabille aimed carefully, just as he had back in the Great War, and soon found himself able to compensate for the carbine's propensity to pull to the right. The black and white garbed guards fell back, found cover and sniped into the tunnel from their positions of semi-concealment.

Suddenly, pulverized dust filled their nostrils as Danner's fists whacked again and again into the wall of black-blue anthracite coal in front of him. Danner extended the spur tunnel like some superhuman mole, and the detritus from his efforts built up around the two other men's legs like a rising tide.

Less than a minute later there was a sudden blast of stale, warmish air: Danner had broken through into the Vermissa workings. Rouletabille and Rogers retreated through the newly-opened tunnel, keeping up a suppressing fire at their adversaries. Once through, Danner dragged them to one side, jumped up and punched the roof of the spur tunnel suddenly collapsing it. Away from the electric lanterns that were strung along the tunnels of the Catharus Mine, the three men found themselves to be plunged into total darkness.

"I wish we'd thought to bring a flashlight with us," said Rouletabille.

"Don't worry, my friend. I can see in total darkness just as easily as in noonday sun," reassured Danner.

"One of the benefits of your otherworldly lineage, no doubt," laughed Rogers. "I find it easier to believe now. If all this is real, and not all in my mind."

Danner took Rouletabille and Rogers by the hands and guided them through the foul blackness. After almost half an hour of wandering, Danner came upon the long out of service shaft elevator. He tore open the gate and then got his two companions to loop their arms around his thickly sinewed neck, then started to ascend the greasy steel cable, which was thankfully still in place. Once at the top, a few of Danner's punches destroyed the wooden boards which blocked the mine entrance, and then they were free.

All three of them paused to cough up the anthracite dust they'd been inhaling, and then Rouletabille took stock of the situation.

"They may come over to this mine to investigate, if they have a brain between them. After all, they know where we've gone," said Rouletabille.

"So what's our next move?" asked Rogers.

"We need to get away from here as quickly as possible and travel to Philadelphia. We must thwart the propagation of the hemorrhagic fever virus, if we can," said the detective.

Without a further word, Danner grabbed both Rogers and Rouletabille around the torso with a vise-like grip and then made a prodigious leap which carried them all many hundreds of feet into the air. This process was repeated many dozens of times. At first, the landings were traumatic, but as they progressed Danner became more accustomed to cushioning the impact. While grateful for the speed with which they would get to Philadelphia, Rouletabille was thoroughly nauseated by the acceleration and sense of falling. Rogers, on the other hand, loved it, and whooped as if he were riding an exciting Coney Island rollercoaster.

"This is the only way to travel," he had to scream above the deafening roar of the wind.

Danner's jumps became longer and lower over time as he perfected his technique. Ultimately, the arcs of the jumps were perhaps only one hundred and fifty feet high, but nearly three miles in length. Finally, Rouletabille could see the grounds of the exposition below them. He could just make out the stadium, and to the west, the Treasure Island Lagoon with neighboring Fine Arts building. For a second, Rouletabille thought that Danner intended to land them in one of the various bodies of water in that part of the Exposition. In fact, Danner had judged the descent perfectly and they landed with a not too elegant thud on the flat concrete roof of the administration building.

"This is where Worth briefed me on the disappearance of the loco," said Danner.

"Me too. His office must be directly beneath us," said Rouletabille.

Without a further word, Danner's fists smacked a ragged hole in the roof large enough for them to drop through onto the plush royal blue carpet.

"We have to assume that the virus has not been released yet—search everywhere—wait! A safe behind a portrait is a recurring theme in my life… let's try it here," said the Frenchman. Then he slid the panel behind Worth's desk to one side, to show again the portrait of his father. He wrenched it forward and it swung on concealed hinges revealing an old Brooker 440 safe.

"Take care of it, Danner," said Rouletabille.

The brass and steel of the safe were torn apart by Danner, and the accompanying sound could almost have been the screeching of some gargantuan and monstrous raven. Danner retrieved the papers and handed them to Rouletabille.

"Anything useful?" asked Rogers.

"It's just papers and correspondence about something called *The Maracot Expedition.* Worth seemed to be in negotiations with the Maracot Diving Company to charter their staff and equipment for an exploration in the Pacific, once they had concluded their own excursion to the deep Atlantic. Hmm. I seem to remember that there was due to be a Maracot mission to the Atlantic years ago, but it all fell through when one of their engineers embezzled virtually all of the company's funds—Ian Hassett was the miscreant's name, as I recall," said Rouletabille.

"That doesn't sound like much help," said Danner. "Is there anything more relevant in that sheaf of documents?"

"There are some blueprints of the Exposition attractions: the 1776 Street, the Treasure Island Lagoon, the giant Liberty Bell with all the light bulbs on it…" said the detective.

"Let me see that," demanded Rogers. He took the blueprint of the enormous Liberty Bell from Rouletabille and brought it closer to the lamplight. "Look at this cross-section of the Liberty Bell. Yeah, sure, it is full of electrical cables and wires, but these other things look like air-pumps and plumbing, with reservoirs for holding some kind of liquid. And look at these nozzles near the surface of the bell. You know what it reminds me of? It almost looks like a gigantic, electrically powered perfume atomizer. Probably ideal if they wanted to disperse some kind of airborne infection," concluded Rogers.

"Is viral hemorrhagic fever airborne?" asked Rouletabille.

"Don't forget that this is something the Catharus Society cobbled together in a lab. It could well be spread by the prevailing wind," said Rogers.

"Danner, this is your department," said Rouletabille. "Carry the bell into the sea and destroy it completely. The virus will not survive immersion in saltwater."

"Consider it done, my friend," said Danner.

"You don't suppose that Worth has already activated the mechanism?" asked Rogers.

"I don't think so. I suppose if he has then the Catharus Society has already won. But I think he was waiting for better weather, for capacity crowds.

The two men searched the office for hours hoping to find one or both of the journals that Worth had offered them as an inducement, but there was no trace of them.

Momentarily unnoticed by Rogers or Rouletabille, another panel eased to one side accompanied by the whirring sound of a small servo motor. Behind the panel was a prototype crystal tele-screen, which flared to life with an azure glow.

"Gentlemen," began Ward Baldwin. "I congratulate you on stymieing the plans of the Catharus Society. Mr. Worth underestimated your capabilities and made a terrible mistake by involving you in our affairs. The Catharus Society invited Mr. Worth to atone for his shortcomings by taking the honorable way out. He was allocated the usual period for calm reflection before his suicide by poison capsule; but he has now killed his guards and escaped. We will hunt him down in due course. In the meantime, all traces of his failure will be eliminated. This organization will return in time, most likely with a different name, and hopefully with other more effective schemes. But rest assured that one day, humanity will be subjugated to our will."

Before Rouletabille could marshal within his mind some sort of coherent reply, the image on the screen ceased to be Baldwin's face. Now the screen showed the interior of the Catharus Mine. Technicians and militia were walking along the tunnels, some purposefully, others as if taking an afternoon stroll. Rouletabille noticed that a few of the girls who had arrived on the train with him were now walking along hand in hand with men. Without warning, a powerful explosion rocked the scene. Bodies were blasted apart by high explosives. The roof commenced to fall and the moving picture on the screen flickered and died; then there was nothing but blackness.

"You realize that we can never tell the world of this?" said the detective. "It would be like waking a somnambulist on a cliff edge... the shock could cause the human race to never know peace of mind again."

"I had sometimes thought that a big enough war might bring about some kind of Armageddon, maybe destroy the world. But the development of the sort of weapons that would be necessary seems to be still decades in the future. Now to find that doomsday can creep up on you like a thief in the night, and that people want to bring it about is, well, sickening," said Rogers. "I agree that we need to keep our mouths shut, but I can't help feeling that the world needs a united network command of law enforcers to guard against the return of the Catharus Society as some kind of technological hierarchy for the removal of undesirables and the subjugation of humanity."

The two men left the office and strode through the lobby on the way out. Outside, the Sun was rising and the pink early morning rays were hitting the mural of American History. Rouletabille realized that a pair of wood and canvas freestanding screens were obscuring the very end of this piece of art, which it seemed had been added to very recently. He pushed the screens aside. The mural now foretold history that would never come: of the arrival of a great plague, with people dying in the streets. Of the coming of a new lordly caste of knights. Of the building of great castles and the forging of an empire, with contented serfs toiling in the fields. And above this tableau, words of incredible cynicism and hypocrisy were neatly painted in black.

> *"Till the war-drum throbb'd no longer, and the battle-flags were furl'd*
> *In the Parliament of man, the Federation of the world."*

There was a sound in the air like the tuneless whistle of an approaching shell; it was Danner returning. Rouletabille resolved to get him to destroy the new part of the mural and gouge out those dreadful words. He too was sickened by how close James Worth had come to erasing the human status quo and replacing it with his absurd and idealized Ivanhoe-type future. Yes, Rouletabille still looked young, but he was starting to feel old in his attitudes, starting to wonder if peace was the just the hiatus between wars that came about when people were too fatigued to fight. Tennyson's words chilled him. What force, what tyranny would it take to truly unite the world? With all the disparate brands of politics and religion on the planet, if they were to be brought under one banner, a lot of people would have to die to achieve that end. The Catharus Society had been right about that.

Rouletabille vs. The Cat (2)

Winter 1926

The limousine left the access road and passed onto the driveway proper; grey gravel was churned noisily by the insistent grip of the tires. Rouletabille looked up at the black, anvil-shaped clouds that were arriving overhead. A colossal storm front was pressing in from the west. Perhaps the largest storm the eastern seaboard had seen for a generation. The last ten years had gone by swiftly. Too swiftly. He had traipsed largely unscathed through many adventures—his time among the gypsies, his encounter with the seemingly indestructible superhuman, Hugo Danner, the Affair of the Octopus, and, of course, the death of his beloved Ivana.... Despite all this, he seemed outwardly unchanged by the decade or so since the closing years of the Great War. Indeed, some said that he had scarcely aged a day in that time. The face he saw in the shaving mirror was still somewhat boyish. But that was hardly supernatural—his mother had retained very youthful looks into late middle age.

Only a few months after his last visit to the West Mansion near Tarrytown, he had received a letter from Herbert Brown stating that Cyrus West had passed away. The letter also told him he was a possible beneficiary in West's will, but that—rather unusually—the will would not be enacted until ten years after the date of death. The detective was therefore to report to the West Mansion for the reading of the will on the given date in the winter of 1926.

A little under two years later, it was with great sadness that Rouletabille received notice from Elena Fairchild-Brown that Herbert Brown had died following a stroke. Rouletabille very much regretted not being able to attend the funeral personally, although he did arrange for attendance by the French Ambassador.

And so it was that Rouletabille and three other potential beneficiaries (some of West's blood relatives) came to be picked up from Tarrytown railroad station and conveyed to the mansion by a luxurious limo. The relatives were: a rather surly and volatile young man called Harry Blythe, an ebullient and endlessly cheerful young lady with rather a wholesome country way about her called Cicily Young, and finally, the mirthless pinch-mouthed spinster, Miss Susan Sillsby—who, judging by her advanced age, was one of the relatives who had gathered periodically to assess Cyrus West's wellbeing "like cats looking into a canary cage."

The quartet disembarked from the limo to be greeted by the banshee wind that was roaring up the Hudson. They ran for the shelter of the entrance portico. Rouletabille's umbrella was torn from his grip and somersaulted dizzily into the sky. He looked back at the limo to see that it was already drawing away. Fortunately, the mansion's oak door was now creaking open. Rouletabille had anticipated the familiar and enticing form of Missy-Lou Pleasant on the other side of the door, but instead the door was being opened by a monstrously obese black woman who looked as if she might top 400 lbs in weight. She wore a housekeeper's white cap and a dress of funereal black that might have doubled as a tent in a former life. The immense woman admitted the Frenchman and the two women, but then suddenly barred the way of the saturnine Blythe.

"Wait! I knows M'sieu Rootabby, an' Miss Cicily, an' Miss Susan. But this man is a stranger to me..." she announced accusingly.

Roger Crosby emerged swiftly from the library and called to her.

"It's all right Mammy-Lou, this is Harry Blythe—the only surviving son of the Master's youngest sister."

Rouletabille's jaw was hanging open. How had one of the most beautiful women he had ever seen been transformed into the physical travesty now before him? More mysterious still, how had Missy-Lou's precise, albeit Caribbean inflected, diction been replaced with a degrading "minstrel show" accent? What had been going on here in the last ten years? And if this was some sort of pretense on the part of Missy-Lou/Mammy-Lou, what could possibly be its purpose?

Every nerve, brain cell and instinct that he possessed told him the answer straightaway. Cyrus West had been murdered and Missy-Lou's out of character behavior was some sort of warning sign to put him on his guard. To those who saw her every week, the changes would've been barely noticeable and incremental. But she had known that Rouletabille would return this night. She had been compelled to stay here all these years, perhaps under some kind of house arrest. He would not let her down. My God, how he wished he had returned here years before!

"Yes, I'm one of the family..." confirmed Harry Blythe, barging past her.

"We aren't all yet here," said Crosby. "But the reading of the will must commence at midnight as per the Master's instructions.

He ushered them into the library, which had changed little in the intervening years. Rouletabille noted the window appeared to have been expertly repaired. Through it, he could make out zig-zags of far off lightning. The storm was getting closer. Already seated in the library was Charlie Wilder. He rose and greeted his female relatives and Rouletabille, then commenced to serve brandy. Miss Sillsby declined in favor of sherry. Blythe glared at Wilder as if he hated his guts and for a moment it seemed they would not shake hands. Then with a jibe from Crosby along the lines of "C'mon you fellows...," they did a passable impersonation of two reconciled enemies.

There was the sepulchral tolling of the doorbell in the middle distance and shortly afterwards Mammy-Lou opened the library door to admit a striking woman of about thirty with luscious chestnut colored hair.

"I guess I'm here just in time!" she smiled. "The train from Kingsport was delayed due to flooding. I was too late for the limousine, but I managed to pick up a cab…"

"Annabelle West!" cried Wilder, embracing the new arrival warmly. She forced her features into a smile, but her eyes betrayed her. She obviously regarded Wilder as no more human than a maggot. Annabelle broke away from him and shook hands in friendly fashion with her cousins—Harry Blythe, she graced with an almost sisterly caress to the cheek. All the surliness drained away from him and it was rather obvious to everyone that Blythe was totally in love with this woman.

Suddenly, a deep resonant chiming echoed through the house and steadily increased in volume. For a moment, Rouletabille mistook this sound for the aforementioned sepulchral doorbell. The sound continued to swell until it was akin to something like an enormous gong being repeatedly impacted by a battering ram. All in all, it sounded seven times. The women put their hands over their ears (all save Mammy-Lou) and the brandy decanter rattled in its wooden holder. Mammy-Lou seemed to be murmuring some kind of prayer that sounded like "waited so long…waited so long" quietly to herself."

Crosby shook Mammy-Lou.

"What is it, Mammy? What is that sound… what does it mean?" the lawyer demanded.

"The machines… it's coming from the machines," said Mammy-Lou, as if emerging from a trance. And then, remembering her pretence, "I dunno Lawyer Crosby, could be ghosts in the machinery… or perhaps…It's a death knell. Seven bells and eight souls hereabouts… one of us will die!"

"Nonsense," judged Crosby.

"What machines, Mammy-Lou?" asked Rouletabille, but the housekeeper only stared vacantly.

"She must mean the electric generator," answered Wilder. "Ignore her," he sneered, "she's only one generation down from the trees."

Crosby checked his watch.

219

"It's midnight. Please all be seated."

Crosby dragged one of the library ladders over to the mantelpiece just as he had more than a decade before, ascended it, swiftly swung the painting to one side and opened the safe. He descended clutching two envelopes. Rouletabille noticed immediately that the envelopes were already opened. Crosby contained it well, but quite obviously he was furious.

"I'm not sure how this has happened, since as far as I know, only the Master and I had knowledge of the combination. But these envelopes have been tampered with. Well, whoever did it wasted their time. I am fully conversant with the terms of the will and two further duplicate copies reside in my office safe in Manhattan," said Crosby, as he scanned the contents of the first envelope.

"Since no attempt has been made to alter the will, I shall proceed with the reading: 'I, Cyrus Canby West, being of sound mind, do hereby make minor financial bequests to all invitees to this will reading who have seen fit to attend at midnight on the tenth anniversary of my death to the sum of ten thousand dollars each…' " read Crosby.

"Well, better than nothing—but peanuts compared to the value of his whole estate," interrupted Susan Sillsby.

"The old man was hardly going to invite us all this way and leave us nothing," replied Blythe.

"You forget that he hated most of his close relatives; although he did have a fondness for Charlie and myself," she smiled.

"May we continue?" snapped the lawyer. " 'The residue of my estate, including all property, monies, shares and patents (currently estimated to be $112 million in value), I leave equally to all my surviving relatives with the surname West."

Annabelle West shot up out of her Arts and Crafts chair like a jack-in-a-box.

"That means I'm the sole heir to the residue of the estate! I'm the only person here called West…" she said breathily.

"I'm just happy to get the ten thou," put in Cicily. "The things I'll be able to get for the farm!"

"Just one moment… I have not yet concluded," said the lawyer. " 'I am aware that a streak of insanity runs in the West family…' "

Susan Sillsby nodded sagely.

"That's right. Charlie's mother was in and out of asylums for most of her life—poor thing. Then there was that scientist cousin of Cyrus' up in Massachusetts; he certainly should've been in an asylum the things he got up to. But they're not the sorts of things that can be mentioned in polite company," wittered Susan Sillsby.

"Should any of my heirs die or be found to be insane within 28 days of inheritance, then their share of the residue passes to the heir named in the second envelope. The identity of the secondary heir is not to be made public except in the circumstances of death or insanity of any of the primary heirs,' " concluded Crosby.

"And yet someone knows who the second heir is," observed Rouletabille. "This is potentially a crime waiting to happen. The second heir could murder the first," he added too quickly, and rather without thinking.

"Except that the second heir is known to me and is a person of good character. Please confine yourself to solving crimes that have actually happened rather than theoretical ones, Monsieur," instructed Crosby.

"That sort of money could turn anybody into a murderer… why, I'd probably kill for it myself…" admitted Blythe.

"Oh, you're taking this so melodramatically," laughed Annabelle. "To Hell with murder, anyone who wants some of this fortune could at least try proposing first!"

Crosby lit a candle on the small desk candelabra, removed the candle and used the melted wax from it to improvise a resealing of the second envelope.

"I'm resealing the envelope that contains the name of the second heir. I'll keep it on my person until I can arrange for a locksmith to reset the combination of the safe. I very sincerely hope that it need never be opened," said Crosby as he moved towards Annabelle. "Miss West, you are now the Mistress of this house. There will be many documents to sign before all Cyrus West's fortune is transferred over to you, and a trip to my office may be necessary."

Mammy-Lou grinned, as if with triumph, and pulled from out of the top of her dress a third envelope, identical to the others—albeit rather crumpled.

"The Massa gave me this envelope to give to the heir. It ain't been opened. I looked after it careful," announced the housekeeper proudly as she passed it Annabelle.

Annabelle looked questioningly at Crosby.

"Strange that I know nothing about it," Crosby mused.

"I'll wager it's about the necklace," suggested Rouletabille.

"What? That tasteless thing that Cyrus had cobbled together from bits of an old crown... he lost it years ago. At least that's what he said," recalled Susan Sillsby.

"I never believed that he really lost it. So careful a man would never lose something so valuable. No, he hid it here in this house... or perhaps out in the grounds," said the lawyer.

"Why, the grounds are like a jungle now," interjected Blythe. "Good luck finding something out there even with a treasure map!"

Annabelle went to open the envelope and then saw that it instructed her to read the contents alone in the master bedroom.

Mammy-Lou explained that she had provided a buffet in the dining room—a sort of midnight feast of Caribbean bouillabaisse—Crosby led the way and most followed, but looking back Rouletabille noticed that both Annabelle and Charlie Wilder had hung back in the library.

"So you still hate me, Annabelle?" opened Wilder. "You know that girl you found me with was nothing to me—just a whore."

"That doesn't help, Charlie. You and I could've had something, but you spoilt it before it began. You've had the run of this place for the last ten years, well now you can pack your bags and clear out," she commanded.

As Charlie slunk out in the direction of the dining room without a backward glance, her mind drifted back to three years ago. She'd met up with Charlie in town, and they had a few too many drinks. He had seemed wonderfully charming and handsome; and the budding playwright had fostered the impression that he stood on the cusp of fame and fortune. Another few drinks beyond that point and they were opening their hearts, and becoming forever soulmates. Charlie revealed that he had never made love to a woman because of his terrible phobia and repulsion of the hair between a woman's legs.

At the end of the evening, he pressed a latchkey into her palm and told her to drop by his Manhattan apartment anytime: that was where he was spending most of his time while his play was in rehearsal. A week later, she used her dead father's cold safety razor on herself and took the train from Kingsport to New York to make a man of him. The apartment turned out to be a tiny cramped hovel above a deli—she didn't mind that. But she was struck mute by the sight of the girl straddling Wilder on the bed. The girl might've been sixteen—just. The girl had looked over her shoulder with an expression that seemed to say, "Wait your turn, sister," while she continued grinding her hips. Annabelle staggered out of there and hailed a cab, at one point she had to ask the driver to stop so she could be sick.

The hollow crack of shotgun fire awoke Annabelle from the painful reverie and she rushed out into the hallway.

"Is that thunder?" Susan Sillsby hoped.

"There's a man in uniform taking potshots at something out in that wilderness of a garden," said Blythe, his face pressed close to the dining room window.

A few moments later, the doorbell rang. Crosby shooed Mammy-Lou away and answered it himself. A man in the uniform of a security guard, armed with a double-barreled shotgun filled the doorway.

"What are you doing discharging a weapon here? This is private property," questioned Crosby.

"Pardon me, sir. I'm Hendricks, the Chief Guard over at the Fairview Insane Asylum in Tarrytown. We've had a breakout and a dangerous prisoner has escaped."

"Who is this prisoner? What does he look like?" demanded Rouletabille.

"He's a case from the violent ward, sir. A John Doe who never speaks…but they call him the Cat. He has teeth filed to points, and he won't let anyone cut his nails. They're big as tiger claws. He's around forty, with a black beard and straggly hair—he has an odd heavy-set Slavic look about him too," said the guard.

Rouletabille put his hands to his forehead. Chills were running up and down his spine in icy ripples. Tonight, of all nights, the Cat had escaped. Twenty or so guards had not been enough to protect the house last time. He wondered if any of them would survive this night. He saw that all the color had drained from Crosby's face.

"I remember the man you are describing," began Wilder. "He attacked us here over ten years ago and was shot over and over. I can't believe that the poor fellow who was so badly injured could be much of a threat now."

"Don't waste your sympathy on that monster, mistuh. He's killed two of fellow inmates while he's been in Fairview—and tried to eat them," retorted Hendricks.

"Please, Mr. Hendricks—we have the fairer sex present," reprimanded the Frenchman.

Hendricks bowed apologetically.

"Just keep all your doors and windows locked. It's howling a gale out here and the Cat will probably want to seek shelter."

"You might want to check all the outbuildings. That was where I found him last time," advised Rouletabille.

"Thank you, sir. I will," said the guard and disappeared into the night. After a few seconds, all that could be seen was the dancing beam of his flashlight.

Rouletabille drifted back to the library while the others returned to the dining room. He was looking for weapons to use. The Winchester Rifle was no longer on the rifle rack. He checked the *Nautilus* carbine and shotgun, but both were bereft of ammunition.

Mammy-Lou walked quietly in.

"The new Mistress wants you. She's up in the master bedroom," she explained.

"Very well. Just one question, if I may, Mammy-Lou. I don't mean to be rude. But what's happened to you… your appearance… your manner of speech?"

She smiled at him and winked.

"Missy-Lou disappeared… changed over time in order to survive. This subservient manner is just a smokescreen—while I behave like this, very little that I do is questioned or scrutinized. They are too dumb to realize what a threat I am to them. And as for packing on the weight, well not being so easy on the eye has its advantages too. Charlie Wilder has stopped trying to knead my ass and rub my snatch."

Rouletabille blushed and Mammy-Lou giggled.

"I been looking at you, M'sieu. You are still looking very, very young. That was a powerful batch of the old *E.V.* that Cyrus poured down your throat. It might be another twenty years before you show any grey," she said enigmatically, caressing his cheek with an enormous hand. And with that, she turned slowly and led the way to the master bedroom.

Annabelle showed the writing on the crumpled letter to Rouletabille.

"I guess pretty much everyone has heard of your reputation for solving impossible mysteries and puzzles—what do you make of this? Is it the clue that will lead to the necklace Cyrus hid?"

The detective read from the letter:

"Keep in Mind, the Mother of Wine
There you will find the treasure that is thine.
Enemies abound, yet love never wanes,
The Beast is among us, his claws are stained."

"Well for a soldier and inventor, he still made a lousy poet," smiled Rouletabille. "It's as much a warning as directions to the necklace. The first line alone indicates the location of what was once the Crown of Jovan Nenad. We'll need to go out to the glasshouse or whatever is left of it. I'll need a gun and some ammunition from Mammy-Lou."

"No need. There's a gun right here in my bedside drawer," laughed Annabelle as she pulled the drawer open. Rouletabille was amazed to see his old Lebel revolver—now gold-plated courtesy of Cyrus West. Could Cyrus have predicted all this? In creating a puzzle, he had guessed that the heir would call for Rouletabille. Thus allowing the detective to protect the heir. But protect the heir from what? Cyrus could not have foreseen the escape of the Cat, or could he? Without explanation Rouletabille pocketed the revolver and helped Annabelle into her coat. Then they slipped downstairs and surreptitiously headed out into the blackness and driving rain.

The interior space of the glasshouse was roughly the same area as two football fields. Rouletabille found the master light switch controls and threw them. A mixture of heat lamps and ultraviolet bulbs gradually came to life, bathing the scene with a dim, but slightly eerie light. The glasshouse roses had run amok during the last decade and most of the pathways were completely overgrown. Rouletabille and Annabelle picked their way through, avoiding the thorns as best they could. In the center of the glasshouse was a huddle of Greek statues: Venus, Cupid and Psyche.

"Keep in mind—the note said. Cyrus West loved Greek statues. And the use of the word 'mind' suggests the statue of Psyche is the relevant one," reasoned Rouletabille.

"But the house and grounds are full of statues. How do you know this is the right one?" quizzed the heiress.

"We are to keep in mind the Mother of Wine. The Mother of Wine is the grape," said Rouletabille, as he pointed up to robust trellis behind the statue; on it grew a thick grapevine—though at this time of year the fruit was naturally absent. "Where else would you find a grapevine in this climate other than in a greenhouse?"

The detective rooted around in the growth at the base of the statue and then noticed on the pedestal an embossed tile bearing the image of a bunch of grapes. Without hesitation he smashed it and gingerly reached into the cavity behind. Annabelle was astonished when he withdrew a rather dirty velvet jewelry case.

She snapped it open revealing the glory of the diamond and emerald necklace. Impulsively she opened the clasp and put it about her slim pale neck. Rouletabille helped her to refasten the clasp—the jewels suited her well.

The Cat watched them go from his place of concealment. They had found the Crown of Jovan Nenad for him and soon he would relieve them of it, but now was not the time. The man was armed, clever and dangerous. The Cat would take his prize from the girl when she was alone.

On the way back to the mansion, Rouletabille noticed a bluish illumination coming from within the swimming pool building. They went inside to investigate and saw that the pool was now dry and disused. In the floor of the swimming pool a trapdoor had been installed—a trapdoor which had been left open. Rouletabille jumped down into the pool and peeked into the chamber below. The room was intermittently illuminated by the sparks from odd looking electrical apparatus. In the center of all this paraphernalia lay a hollow crystalline cylinder about seven feet long that was filled with an opaque, luminescent blue liquid. Rouletabille wanted to investigate further, but was unwilling to leave Annabelle alone. This could wait until the morning. Soon they were back inside the house. The other invitees and Crosby had retired for the night, so the Frenchman had some special instructions for Mammy-Lou. Annabelle also retired, but after the extreme excitement of the day she took the precaution of taking one of the mild sleeping powders which she kept in twists of paper in her handbag. She thought about waking Crosby so that the necklace could be put in the safe, then she remembered that someone had already illicitly opened the will envelopes. The best place for the necklace was therefore around her neck. Rouletabille had told that he would post himself directly outside the door in a chair and not go to sleep. That made her feel safer. She didn't even bother to change into her negligee; just peeled off her blouse, skirt, underwear and stockings and lay on the bed nude. Within moments she was asleep.

A long time passed, cycles of dreaming began and ended, and after a while she became aware of the generous hand of her lover caressing and teasing her body in the most intimate fashion. It was good to have a lover again, but in her sleepy state she could put neither a name nor a face to her new man. How had they met? Perhaps she would remember in the morning. Now he was becoming too rough, and his nails hurt—they seemed almost like claws. Claws! Her eyes were wide open now. The black clawed hand reaching over her was just barely illuminated by a sliver of light from the curtain chink. The claws dragged up her belly to her cleavage and then yanked at the necklace and pulled it from her. Surprising herself with the speed of her reactions she switched on the lamp just in time to see the Cat's hand and arm retreat into a yawning aperture in the wall directly behind her bed. Then the secret panel slammed shut. Annabelle grabbed the robe from her bedside chair and ran for the door clutching it in front of her.

"Rouletabille! The Cat has taken the necklace…there must be a secret passageway!" she screamed at him.

"Quiet! Quiet!" ordered the detective. He attempted to bundle her back inside the room, but failed.

The Cat was framed in the library doorway. He edged along the wall to the stairs. Rouletabille eased the revolver from his pocket and covered the black robed figure as he went.

"There is no escape that way… Charlie," called Rouletabille. "Mammy-Lou has locked all of the bedroom doors and window shutters."

"My God! Charlie! It can't be…" breathed Annabelle.

The Cat started to advance back down the stairs and the Frenchman saw that his face was, after all, just a rather realistic papier-mâché mask. So obviously created by someone with connections to the theatre industry who had seen the real Cat up close.

Charlie Wilder untied the black ribbons which held fast the mask.

"You think you're so smart, Rouletabille. But I haven't lost yet…if this place goes up in smoke and you all die, there'll be no witnesses and I still inherit. I am the second heir…if the old man hadn't lost his mind, I'd have been the first heir."

The sudden sounding of the intensely loud gong momentarily distracted Rouletabille, and then the stock of a shotgun slammed into the back of his head causing him to drop like a broken puppet.

"You ain't paying me enough for all this," announced the fake guard Hendricks, as he stood over the Frenchman's crumpled form.

"Shut up, and go and get the gasoline," commanded Charlie.

Hendricks obediently headed for the front door, but stopped in his tracks when Mammy-Lou loomed out of the darkness holding the Winchester rifle. Without hesitation she shot Hendricks straight through the head. Charlie froze.

"You insignificant little fool. You dared to try to turn Cyrus against me. Manufactured and planted evidence that I had returned to the practice of Voodoo, and that I was being unfaithful to him; for those things you should die ten thousands deaths. It's a pity I can kill you only once. But I'll make your death last as long as I can," spat Mammy-Lou.

"No Mammy-Lou, he's insane. He belongs in Fairview," rasped Rouletabille, as he fought his way to his feet.

Mammy-Lou lowered the Winchester and Rouletabille dared to exhale with relief. Only then did the detective realize that his gold-plated Lebel was in Annabelle's hand and was being leveled at Charlie.

"The most gullible slut I ever fed a line to," were Charlie Wilder's last words before Annabelle shot him six times. Eventually, Rouletabille was able to wrestle the empty pistol from her, but by that time she was almost catatonic.

"I'll get Dr. Trifulgas for the Mistress," volunteered Mammy-Lou.

In the morning, Rouletabille was looking for Mammy-Lou but could not find her. Crosby and West's relatives were taking breakfast in the dining room, almost as if nothing had happened—even though they must've tiptoed around the bloodstains in the hall. He saw Dr. Trifulgas ministering to Annabelle and the good doctor confirmed that she would make a full recovery. He couldn't quite place Trifulgas' accent—but the physician revealed he was originally from a place called Ulthar. Rouletabille assumed this was in the Netherlands but didn't like to show his ignorance. He wandered into the library and found a pale fair-haired bespectacled man who slightly resembled Charlie searching through the old Master's desk.

"Who are you?" asked the detective.

"My name is Herbert West, I was invited to attend last night but there was severe flooding in the Arkham area."

"West? The scientist from Massachusetts? Then you've missed out on a share of $122 million," sympathized Rouletabille.

"So I hear. But all I really want is this," said Herbert West pulling from the desk drawer the E.V. decanter which still had a few dregs of the glowing azure fluid within. "It will be useful for some experiments I have in mind and I should be able to synthesize more. You see Cyrus always kept the precise formula to himself." The pale man smiled and strode swiftly from the library; and then from the house.

Rouletabille thought for a moment. He thought about everything that had happened. It wasn't easy, the blow from Hendricks had given him a mild concussion and his vision kept swimming. Some of it was starting to make sense. Charlie had played in the house all his life, so he had known about the secret passageways. He couldn't find the necklace so he needed the heir to find it. Charlie had watched Crosby and Cyrus open the safe often enough to be able to memorize it. Yes, some of the details made sense, but overall, the picture was still blurred. Where the Hell was Mammy-Lou? And then he had it. He pulled a decorative sword from the wall and left by the front door into the bright morning. The storm had passed, but there were still a lot of overgrown roses to cut back before he got to the Hudson.

Thirty minutes later he was on the estate boat jetty. The racing yacht *Sea Silk* was still tied up there. He climbed aboard. Abandoned in the companionway was a huge black dress surrounded by great molded sections of some kind of soft foamy rubber. On a chair in the galley was Mammy-Lou's rubber mask. It had been a disguise worthy of Rouletabille's great enemy Larsan. The door to the cabin was open and Rouletabille saw the slim, dark bronze form of Missy-Lou slip out of bed and put on the light.

"Come in, Monsieur Rouletabille," said Cyrus West. "I'd like to say 'you must have many questions'—but knowing you, you've probably figured the whole thing out."

Rouletabille stepped into the cabin and looked at West as he lay in bed. His beard and hair were now jet-black, his eyes clear—his face with scarcely a wrinkle—like a man of less than thirty.

"You did not die…instead it was a process of rejuvenation, albeit a slow one. It took ten years of immersion in the *E.V.* fluid to rebuild your body. I saw the machine responsible. It was concealed beneath the now unused swimming pool in the pool house. Missy-Lou left the door to the secret chamber open when she went to the pool after the gong sounded. The gong was an alarm to tell her that you were almost ready to be removed from the rejuvenation machine. I deduce that your confederates in this affair were your relative Herbert West, a brilliant scientist, and the physician that you keep on hand, Dr. Trifulgas. The clearest indication that you were not dead was that you made no allowance in your will for Missy-Lou—a woman you plainly held in the greatest affection."

"I told you he'd figure it out," said Missy-Lou, before landing a passionate kiss on Cyrus West's lips.

Rouletabille realized it was time for him to leave.

Less than twenty-four hours later, Cyrus West and Missy-Lou departed in the *Sea Silk* and were never seen again. Annabelle subsequently married Harry Blythe, and they lived as happily as one can be expected to live in this imperfect world.

Rouletabille on Mysterious Island

July 2, 1927

The first thing that the detective was aware of was a searing pain on the right-hand side of his head, about two inches above his ear. He put his hand to it. Even the gentle touch of his fingertips on the wound was excruciating. He realized almost straightaway that the injury had been bandaged. Well, that was something. He propped himself up on his elbows and looked around. He lay on the sandy section of a small rockstrewn beach, roughly twenty or so feet from the gently lapping waves. And he had absolutely no idea how he had come to be there.

The most delicious smell emanated from almost directly behind him. He turned over to find that he had almost rolled onto a little campfire. Half a dozen silver fish, each about four inches long and impaled on bent sticks, were barbecuing over the blaze. A mysterious benefactor had prepared a meal for him.

Suddenly ravenous, he picked a fish from its improvised spit and greedily consumed it—scales, bones and all. It tasted marvelous, similar to whitebait. But the species was unknown to him. Yet, so many things were perhaps unknown to him. He knew his name—Joseph Rouletabille, and that he had been a journalist and a detective... also a spy and a soldier. He remembered something about a yellow room and the scent of a woman... That had been important. But it all seemed so long ago and far away.

The intense pain had formed a barrier in his mind, not merely disrupting his memories but also the routine pathways of cognitive thought. This much he knew: his mind had been an extraordinary one—swift and unerring, a computational machine that never fully rested. Now the linkages and chains of reasoning were snapped, useless. He... could... not... think... properly. It was maddening. He did his best to comfort himself. He had been awake for only moments. Perhaps, as the injury healed, his brain would return to normal.

He stayed by the fire until he had eaten all of the fish. He was unsure whether this was breakfast or dinner. The sun hung low in the sky and he could not tell for the moment if it was rising or setting. While he was considering this, and who might've lit the fire, he found, half-buried in the sand, a military-style water canteen. He took a few swigs of the water inside, then put it over his shoulder and began walking along the beach.

Within ten minutes, he had rounded a headland and the beach had almost completely disappeared; now there were just black volcanic rocks. He looked inland. There was a stubby peak that could almost be the shattered remnant of a volcano. He estimated that it was less than a mile away. He resolved to explore a little more of the coast and then head into the interior of the island—he supposed it to be an island, but until he had circled it, he could not rule out the possibility that it was a peninsula.

Up ahead, something was perched on the pyroclastic rocks—as if washed onto them during a tempest. As he got closer, he could see that it was the wreck of a boat, or more properly a yacht. The masts, rigging and sails had all been lost. The hull had been punctured by some of the more jagged pieces of basalt, and these rocks now held the wreck precariously like a clawed hand. The cabin was splintered as per the proverbial matchwood.

Rouletabille could only guess—was this the vessel that had brought him here? He moved closer and closer, seeking some clue. Finally, he climbed the great stones and approached the stern of the smashed craft. Hanging loosely was a wooden plaque bearing the name of the ship. He said it aloud several times. His tongue playing with the words, holding them in his mouth like he would with medicine he was not quite ready to swallow. *Sea Silk... Sea Silk... Sea Silk...* It was dimly recollected. But that was all. It was no key to his memory. He had seen it before. Seen it somewhere. The ship had been intact—but just how long ago was that? It felt like months.

"You've probably figured the whole thing out," the bearded man had said, as he lay there in the bed in the cabin.

And then, the visual and auditory recollection was gone. Impossible to retrieve. In its place was something else. A useless piece of information: sea silk is a rare fabric obtained from the pen shell—it is made from the fibers the mollusk uses to attach itself to the sea bed. He wished he could somehow trade that fact for something more relevant and helpful. But human memory cannot be bartered with at the best of times.

Rouletabille did not even seriously consider going aboard the wreck. It looked far too dangerous. He could imagine the deck giving way beneath him and toppling down onto the rocks. Or perhaps the grip of the rocks on the hull was not so firm as it seemed, and the whole thing would slide into the sea with him aboard. No, the answer did not lie in the wreck. His every instinct was that it was a doorway to death. He headed instead for the volcano, if, indeed, volcano it was.

So, he walked on, and soon realized that the pseudo-whitebait had been breakfast—the sun was rising. The morning was hot. He turned his mind to attempting to deduce his general location in the world. The vegetation was pretty sparse, just a few scrubby palms and hardy sedges. As he ascended the crumbling grey pumice slopes of the volcano, he was afforded a much better view of the island. It was small—perhaps a few hectares larger than a typical deer park—and largely barren. At one point, he thought he heard the bleating cry of wild goats in the middle-distance, but he never did see any, nor even saw any goat tracks.

He considered it most likely that he was somewhere in the South Pacific. There were volcanic islands in that part of the ocean. He knew that he was French, and it was not difficult to surmise that he was likely to be in a French Protectorate area, perhaps Boragora or Tagataya. Again, he had a fragmentary memory and another useless one. He had once been at a social function in Paris where he had been introduced to a criminal who had survived an attempted execution by guillotine and gone on to become a magistrate on an island in the Pacific.

It was getting even hotter; he was now perspiring freely; a wide-brimmed hat would've been advantageous. He paused to take a few glugs from his canteen. He also drank in the great sapphire vista of the ocean with one hand shading his eyes. And now, for the first time, he saw it.

There was a ship at anchor, perhaps only eight hundred meters from the northeastern shore. A large merchant vessel, some kind of cargo ship with two great cranes fitted to the stern. He was saved! It was a miracle that another ship had arrived here at the same time he had. Did he have the strength to swim out to it, or if it would be better to attempt to signal it from the shore.

He was about to turn around and start heading back down the slope when something stopped him. Not a memory, but something more akin to an instinct. There was danger for him down in that cargo ship, and a far greater one even than there had been aboard the rock-stranded wreck.

Now he was confronted by the gaping, uneven maw of the volcano. Fortunately, it seemed that it was inactive. While there was the aroma of sulphur, there were no more noxious fumes and no heat. The sun was high and shone like a searchlight into the depths of the thing. Far, far below was the suggestion of greenish blue water. There was a water-filled grotto within the volcano. More significantly, an intermittent throbbing sound emanated from the depths. There was something mechanical down there, an engine of some sort. The grotto was inhabited!

Better yet, his subconscious did not furnish him with any dire warnings about what might be in it. Quite the contrary. His anticipation was that it was a place of sanctuary and peace. Rouletabille looked gingerly over the edge of the volcano in the forlorn hope that there might be a way down other than a suicidal leap into the grotto's emerald waters. Without the climbing ability of a spider, it looked to be impossible.

He sighed and accepted defeat. He would simply have to head back down the peak and find another way in. There might be a cave or an undersea tunnel which could unite him with the grotto dwellers. He shot a last look back at the abyss and was astonished to see, now that the sun had reached its zenith, that a steel gantry was visible, perhaps five meters below the lip of the crater. He could not account for its presence or purpose other than it was obviously the work of the grotto-dwellers.

It was another hour before the detective had fully resolved and summoned up the courage to attempt to jump down to the gantry. He had spent a lot of that time squinting into the darkness beyond the steel walkway and he thought he could see a set of metal steps leading downwards. He stepped back a few paces and then launched himself over the edge. As his feet left the ground, he feared that the arc of his fall would not carry him as far as the gantry. Yet somehow it did, and the stairway railing whacked hard against one of his calves while the deck rose swiftly to meet his face. He was just able to bring up his arms, as one would for a break-fall in Baritsu or Judo, and this saved him from nasty facial injuries. Nevertheless, his palms and forearms were bruised. But it was a small price to pay for the progress he had made. He was convinced that he would soon be reunited with friends and allies.

He could see that there were electric floodlights far below in the water and on two craft. One was a long grey submersible with a horn-like ram on the bows, the other was tiny—some sort of metal sphere with trailing cables attached to it. Somewhat winded, Rouletabille stood up and only then began to understand how precariously the gantry and stairway beyond were attached to the inner wall of the volcano. His jump down had only served to loosen them further. The whole of the steelwork seemed to have been exposed to incredible temperatures, and some of it looked partially melted.

He started to pick his way down the stairs with great care, and with each step, they seemed more rickety. Down and down he continued. When he was perhaps seventy-five meters from the surface of the water, there was a sound like a gunshot, and his first guess was that he had been spotted by some enemy or guard and was being sniped at. But no, the noise was one of the supporting bolts from the stairway wrenching itself from the wall.

He instantly abandoned the idea of carefully traversing the stairs and began to run just as swiftly as he could. The more he ran, the looser and more disconnected the stairs seemed to become. The framework juddered and oscillated; the rhythm of the soles of his shoes on the steps was a hastening staccato drumbeat.

He dared not look back, but it was now obvious that the long section of stairs that he had already traveled was peeling away from the interior wall of the volcano. The steel was beginning to screech like a fearful woman.

Rouletabille decided to take his chances, vault the railing and jump into the green water below. He put his legs firmly together and pointed his feet so that he would make a smooth entry into the water. He just hoped he was executing his feet-first dive properly. The even greater danger seemed to be that the tangled mess of metal would land on top of him. But then, his ending would be so quick, that it seemed scarcely anything to worry about.

He maintained the diving posture for what seemed like an age as he dropped through the air. On the edge of his peripheral vision, the steel stairway tumbled away. The stairs hit the water first, propelling upwards a wide irregular fountain of the green-hued liquid. Then, it was Rouletabille's turn to slice into the grotto's watery depths.

The impact carried him a long way down. He held his breath and clamped his mouth shut. After another couple of seconds, he dared to open his eyes. It felt like he was still going downwards. All he could see was the all-enveloping milky jade froth, a churning mass of bubbles. He wondered if he was caught in some sort of tide or suction. As he tried to swim, he realized just how much his sodden clothes restricted him. Then, he cursed himself for a fool. He had become disoriented in the opaque water after the moment of landing. He was not being pulled down by suction, but rather rising in an inverted position. The movement of the bubbles around him now gave this away, as did the luminescence from the floodlights on the deck of the submersible. He righted himself in the water and began to kick upwards. Then he un-looped the canteen from his shoulder and discarded his heavy jacket. The ascent now seemed easier.

When his head came out of the water, he was surprised to see how close he was to the submarine. There was even a man on the craft with a boat pole trying to assist him, trying to help him from the water. So, the grotto dwellers were friendly. He had obviously made the right decision in attempting to come down here. Then the Frenchman's stomach turned to lead and ice. The man was no longer silhouetted by the lights. He was wearing a black and white uniform and sporting a black peaked cap with white trim. This was the uniform of the Catharus Society!

Rouletabille remembered about the Catharus Society and its plan to massively reduce the population of the world by means of a hemorrhagic fever pandemic. A plan he had just managed to avert with the assistance of the extraordinary super-human, Hugo Danner, and the courageous Captain Anthony Rogers (who had had no choice but to join the ranks of this villainous organization).

His ability to recall was returning swiftly, just not swiftly enough. He was probably here to thwart another scheme by the Society or the unnamed rogue offshoot of the same organization that was commanded by James Worth, formerly a respected Philadelphian businessman.

He closed his fingers tightly over the end of the boat pole, and was then gently towed towards a rope and chain ladder, which would allow him to climb up onto the deck. He could've quite happily lain on the deck all afternoon recovering from the shock of his fall from the steel walkway. Yet, now he was starting to form the definite realization that he had secret allies here within the grotto, and he should make every effort to reunite with them so that they could achieve their mutual aims. The man with the boat pole suddenly shouted back to a figure on the submersible's conning tower.

"Tell the commander we've found another one."

Rouletabille was taken down a hatchway into the interior of the craft. The airlocks and so forth were not entirely unfamiliar to him. He had once been an unwilling guest on a U-boat. That had been during the Great War, off the coast of New Jersey. Kapitan Mors had been the commander. But that craft was a paltry thing compared to this. This submersible was luxuriously appointed with gleaming brass at every turn and fixtures and fittings of coral and ivory. The walkways underfoot were of a material unknown to him—some kind of resin? He noticed that the raised lower bulkhead sections of the airlocks at floor level were highly polished as if by the passage of feet over many, many decades.

The guard ushered the detective into a grand state room where, incredibly, an organ had been installed. Somehow, it did not truly suit the room. It seemed new and garish compared to the other décor in the chamber. Then Rouletabille saw that two people were tied with ropes to two of the chairs. One was a handsome man of about thirty with black hair and full black beard, and the other was a dark-skinned woman of around forty. This woman possessed an extraordinarily beautiful face, albeit a haughty one. Yes, these were his allies. Although his imperfect memory would have it that it was months since he had last seen them. The detective's guard tied him to a third chair and then left the trio alone.

"Rouletabille! My God, how did you follow us down here in your wounded condition?" asked Cyrus West. "You should've stayed on the beach."

"I went along the pathway that led to the volcano and there is... or rather was a steel stairway down. I should say that I still have partial amnesia, from this head injury, but I know now that you are Captain Cyrus West—sometimes known as Harding. And that the lady is Missy-Lou Pleasant."

"Careful what else you say," ordered Missy-Lou. "The saying that walls have ears is not mere idiom aboard this ship."

"I'll remind you of the more salient points that it is safe to repeat," said West. "Following your experience in Philadelphia last year, you ultimately deduced that James Worth and his allies, an engineer called Hassett and a German scientist named Grierson, were trying to salvage Captain Nemo's ship *Nautilus* from the submarine grotto here on Lincoln Island. With the help of my lawyer, Crosby, you were able to trace Missy-Lou and myself to my property in the bayous of Louisiana. Traveling there to enlist my help, we eventually set sail for the South Pacific in my yacht. Unfortunately, during a storm... wait, someone's coming..."

Three men entered the room and the remaining mental barriers that had shrouded Rouletabille's mind melted away like an ice cube dropped on the ground during a summer party. Two of the newcomers wore variants on the officer's uniform of the Catharus Society, but instead of the Thrush emblem of that organization, they instead sported patches and epaulettes with a kraken or squid-like design.

One of the men in uniform was James Worth—the man who had bragged to Rouletabille that his father, Adam Worth, had been the real Captain Nemo, and that Prince Dakkar— regarded by many as Nemo's real identity—had been a fiction created by West to allow him to steal and patent Adam Worth's brilliant inventions.

The other man, he had only seen in police photographs, never in person. He as one of the most vile perpetrators in the annals of criminology: the infamous Ian Hassett. He had commenced his dreadful career by murdering his brother, and then his father. He had been deliberately entombed alive by the world's premier consulting detective within an old Roman lead mine adjacent to the Great Rutland Cavern in Derbyshire. But he had succeeded, eventually, in escaping this fate. He was arrested for murdering a street woman in London, but found insane.

And that, perhaps, explained the presence of the third man, Dr. Grierson. He was one of the French detective's oldest surviving enemies—a German master spy who frequently posed as a psychiatrist or asylum head. Once, long ago, Rouletabille had fallen into his hands in London, and was subject to the most appalling torture—agonizing intramuscular injections of camphor and electro-convulsive therapy. He had been lucky to escape with his life on that occasion.

James Worth fixed Rouletabille with his grey eyes and laughed derisively.

"Well, well, the little French journalist Rouletabille, and playing way out of his league as usual," said Worth.

The sadistic Grierson moved closer, grabbed the detective by the hair and examined his face closely.

"It is Rouletabille," he said, "or at least it looks like him, but he has scarcely aged since I last saw him more than fifteen years ago. He is still little more than a boy."

"Merely proof of his long and close association with West. He's been allowed access to what West's intimates call the *old E.V. fluid*—the *Elixir Vitae* of legend."

"Why are we wasting time on them?" asked Hassett, his voice sickening cold and detached. "We are fully occupied with cutting away the entire ocean door. Kill the men now, but keep the woman alive. I may wish to use her later as a plaything."

With a practiced accuracy, Missy-Lou spat in Hassett's face from almost three yards away. Mortified, he moved to strike her, but was restrained by Worth.

"You can't touch her," he said. "I need her in one piece most of all. Get back to supervising the divers on the cutting team."

"So, all these days here and you never did figure out how to open the undersea door into the grotto. You had to blow-torch your way in," said West. "You made a hole big enough for a diver or a Maracot bathysphere to get in, but now you need to get the *Nautilus* out."

"Yes," replied Worth, "but we both know that that portal is ancient in origin. It wasn't put there by Nemo, but rather by the advanced civilization that occupied this area ages ago."

"If you say so," said West, smiling secretly.

"Actually, there is something I want to show you, West. Something I can't really explain."

"Something aboard the *Nautilus* that you do not under-stand?" mocked Rouletabille. "How can that be when your father was Captain Nemo, and you know all of his secrets from reading that journal?"

"I invented the journal merely as a means of manipulat-ing you, Rouletabille. But I know many things about this 'mysterious island' that you do not. For instance, the journey by balloon from Richmond to the South Pacific was no acci-dent. And, of course, it did not take place in a Confederate observation balloon, but rather in a powered dirigible of my father's own design," said Worth.

"Is that truly what he told you?" said West. "It's non-sense."

"Was his father ever really here, Cyrus?" asked Rouletabille.

"Yes, but he sure as hell wasn't Nemo. In more pleasant circumstances, I'll tell you the story."

"I doubt if you'll ever be in pleasant circumstances for the remainder of your very short life," said Grierson, before adding, "I'll get the men to bring in the girl's body."

A few minutes later, two guards carried in a partially shattered transparent cylinder, set it down on the deck, and then left. Inside the tube was the body of a young blonde woman of about twenty-five. The remnants of an azure fluid—something like bluish, translucent mercury—still sloshed around in the bottom of the cylinder, just about half an inch worth. The girl had been dressed in a skin tight, futuristic looking golden fabric, but this had obviously been cut away by Grierson. And following that, a rib spreader had been applied. It was possible to see where the psychotic doctor had rooted around in her chest cavity with his scalpel.

"We had to smash the tube to get it open," said Worth. "There are a couple of others with men in them. This one was marked—*Mercurian Female—Rulu.*"

"And yet, I have examined her organs and she is definitely human," said Grierson. "What's more, she has dental fillings and bridgework of the exact type used in the United States. She has inoculation marks and an appendectomy scar. She is definitely of Earth. So what game was being played out on this island, West? What was really happening here?"

"You'll never know," replied West.

"Mr. Worth, would you do me the favor of shooting Monsieur Rouletabille in the head with your sidearm?" asked Grierson.

"Why not? He knows the least of any of us about the island and Nemo, so he is of little use," said Worth, tugging his automatic from its holster.

West paled. He had not fully anticipated the ruthlessness of Grierson.

"Very well," said West. "I'll give you the full answer, but it may stretch your credulity. Nemo had a machine which could erase a person's personality—essentially evicting it like an unwanted lodger—and install a new, better personality in its place. This woman was a prostitute, a thief and a murderess. But by the time she had been processed by Nemo's machine, she had no recollection of her old life. She was effectively a completely different person. She really did believe herself to be a woman from another planet."

"That's preposterous. What possible purpose could it serve?" asked Grierson.

"Nemo had a vision not totally dissimilar from that of the Catharus Society—although it didn't involve murder on an industrial scale. He wanted to remove the underclass from society and turn its people into hunter-gatherer tribes residing in very isolated locations. On this island, he succeeded in turning modern-day men into primitives, using his machine—he called them the *Volcano People*. They were pirates, criminals, the dregs of the Earth. But the conditioning was perfect; their original personalities never re-emerged. His biological experiments would've provided the megafauna upon which they could've subsisted. But that was not enough. He also wanted to create a group of ultimately beneficent overlords—the technological hierarchy so beloved of Mr. Worth here. So Nemo created another group who believed themselves to be aliens. And with access to Nemo's advanced inventions, that was exactly what they appeared to be. Their first job was to menace the primitives, but in the end, they would've become their moral guides and law-givers, had the experiment not been terminated by Nemo's death."

"I believe him," said Worth. "My father was a scientific wizard, not the criminal mastermind—*the Napoleon of Crime*—that some have painted. And it is from him that the concept of a ruling class with superior technology originates."

"Worth, you are an intelligent man under a strange delusion. What sign did Adam Worth ever give to you in his ordinary life that he was a genius?" asked West.

"Well, we had to live quietly and unobtrusively in Philadelphia. If my father had drawn too much attention to himself, his early life as a Civil War *'bounty jumper'* might've been exposed," replied Worth. "Besides, he told me so much about this island and it's all accurate—he must've have been here. And if he was here... then, he was Nemo."

"The world will be a better place when people cease to believe outrageous claims on bad evidence or on faith," said West. "Just because he was here—and I'll admit now that he was—that doesn't mean he was Nemo. And Nemo's real identity, I will take to my grave. Even the threat of death and torture of my friends would not pry it from me. It is too important."

"I would not torture you or your associates in order to ascertain something that I already know," smiled Worth. "We are about to leave this grotto in the *Nautilus* for the first time. Hassett's men have done a wonderful job in restoring power to the ship. This vessel will again be the terror of military and commercial shipping. Soon, no oceanic journey will be undertaken by any nation-state without proper tribute being paid to me. But I am a superstitious man, as are many of the men who serve on the crew with me. Many of them are adherents of Santeria and they are fascinated to hear that one of the most powerful women of the Obeah in the history of that great religion has come aboard this ship."

"And so...?" asked Missy-Lou. "What do they want from me?"

"They merely want to know if this is going to be a successful voyage, my dear," replied Worth. "They have prepared a *potion pour voir l'avenir,* so that you will be able to tell our collective fortune and see if we prosper in the future."

"It won't work unless I mix it myself... Besides, an Obeah Queen cannot drink of a Santeria sacrament. It is sacrilege for both religions," said Missy-Lou.

"Nevertheless, I would hate to disappoint them," said Worth. "Nezzar!"

Rouletabille twisted his head to see the doorway, a huge black man was entering the room. His face was covered with a satanic-looking mask fashioned from a goat's head. He was also stripped to the waist, and at his belt hung a vicious looking machete. Predictably, the container for the potion, which would afford Missy-Lou a view of things to come, was a human skull converted to be a bizarre ceremonial chalice. Less expected was the appalling odor emanating from the liquid— burnt hair, urine and candle wax could easily have been on the list of ingredients.

And then, from behind the goat-masked man called Nezzar stepped an Amazonian woman with red hair and sunburned skin. Her eyes were a cattish green, but there were two other notable things about her. Since her mouth was partially open, it was possible to see that her teeth had been filed to points, and her fingers were adorned with razor-sharp brass nails. This was Hell-Cat Maggie, an underworld enforcer recruited by the Catharus Society whose allegiance had passed to Worth.

"I helped cook it up, so I wants to hear what the Obeah bitch sez," said the woman with pointed teeth.

"Very well, Maggie," said Worth.

Rouletabille noticed that she was wearing a female equivalent of the Catharus Society officer's uniform, but with a rather immodest short skirt and black beret.

Nezzar got hold of Missy-Lou by the hair and pulled her head back. The Obeah Queen did not put up much of a struggle; perhaps she was more interested in finding out if the Santeria future-seeing potion worked. The liquid was poured into her and Missy-Lou gagged and spluttered.

"I don't know why you put any stock in this sort of thing, James," said Grierson. "It shows the lack of a scientific education. And it is wrong to encourage it in the crew. Rationality should be the way of the future. Not this sort of tripe."

The cold fury emanating from West was palpable. All now were silent. Waiting…waiting for Missy-Lou to do or say something. But she just rocked backwards and forwards in her chair—held fast by the restraints.

Then the silence was broken by a sharp whistle from the internal communications system. Worth put the brass listening tube to his ear. A few moments later, he related back to the room what he had heard.

"Well, ladies and gentlemen," he began, "Commander Hassett reports that the ocean door has been successfully cut away. He and his men are back on board. We are therefore about to maneuver carefully out of the grotto via the aperture. We will then surface and continue to run tests of the engines and diving systems."

Then came a powerful and rhythmic reverberation as the engine began to make revolutions. Within a few seconds, the propellers were engaged. It was a huge source of regret and shame to Rouletabille that he should be aboard the *Nautilus* in these circumstances, with this most marvelous of machines, under the control of his deadly enemies. Through one of the small portholes in the wall of the stateroom, he could see the now-unmanned Maracot bathysphere being left behind as the *Nautilus* commenced the short and shallow dive to the passable exit from the grotto.

At first, the detective did not understand why something, perhaps his subconscious mind, was drawing his attention away from the porthole and towards the rather out of place organ that Nemo had had installed in the submersible. There was something wrong... something even more out of place regarding the documents on the organ's music stand. There were several sheets of music on it, but in front of them was a small printed pamphlet entitled *The Polyphonic Motets of Orlande de Lassus.* The significance of this struck Rouletabille like a freight train.

"My God, West," said the detective. "As dire as our situation might already seem, it is infinitely worse. We cannot now make it out of here alive."

He glanced back at the porthole and saw that the vessel had cleared the tunnel from the grotto and they were in open sea. Then, unexpectedly, the nose of the submarine dipped and they headed down into the deep.

"We're supposed to surface, not dive," shouted Worth. "What the hell is Hassett playing at?"

Before Grierson could reply, Nezzar struck the scientist high on the forehead with his machete. The top of the German's skull was sliced off as neatly as a boiled egg on a breakfast table. Rouletabille saw the exposed cluster of grey matter from which so many twisted schemes had emanated as his enemy collapsed to the floor. His incomprehension was leavened with envy. Grierson was one of the few men Rouletabille would have killed without compunction.

Nezzar pulled off the goat mask. The Frenchman was astounded to recognize the face beneath, although it had been almost eleven years since he had seen it. It was Neb Junior, formerly the bodyguard of General Herbert Brown, latterly an officer of the Bay City PD, and, as Rouletabille would later learn, currently seconded to the US Secret Service.

Neb Jr. moved like a striking snake and freed Rouletabille from his bonds with a single stroke of the machete. Worth's reactions were slow. He was a talker, not a fighter. Nevertheless, his hand was already reaching for the automatic pistol in his holster as Neb Jr. commenced to cross the stateroom.

Far more dangerous was Hell-Cat Maggie, she of the deadly pointed teeth. Rouletabille launched himself straight out of his chair at her since she was obviously about to leap on Neb Jr. from behind. He tried to close his hands around her neck and throat, but his circulation had been badly restricted by the ropes around his wrists. Maggie shrugged off his pitifully weak grip.

It was at that moment that a sound like the cackle of a fairytale witch filled the stateroom. It came from Missy-Lou, who was now subject to the full influence of the *potion pour voir l'avenir*. Her pupils were so dilated that her eyes seemed to be swirling black vortexes. The voice from her lips was not her voice. She was in contact with something else, and it spoke through her. What it was or could have been was open to debate: was it the Goat of Mendes? The Lloigor? But what it said is not in doubt.

"You… are… all going to die," laughed Missy-Lou hysterically. "Soon the darkness will take you. You have boarded a ship of doom."

And while she said this, Worth was aiming his pistol at Neb Jr.'s face, and Hell-Cat Maggie's teeth started to break the skin of Rouletabille's throat. Cyrus West shook in his chair like an epileptic. He was undertaking a desperate and futile battle against the strong rope which held him in place. Time seemed to slow down. Neb Jr. jerked his head to one side while aiming a blow at Worth with his blade.

The pistol went off. The bullet excised skin and bone in the area of Neb Jr.'s right eyebrow, but was little more than a graze. Yet the muzzle-flash had caught the lawman in both eyes, and he was blinded by powder burns. Robbed of its momentum, the machete caught Worth in the shoulder, causing only a minor injury. Neb Jr. dropped his weapon and fell to his knees, clutching both hands to his eyes.

Rouletabille struck at Hell-Cat Maggie with all his strength. His palm connected with the underside of her chin, driving those deadly teeth away before they could do much damage. Still she was on top of him. And she was larger and stronger than he. In a moment, she had him by the wrists and had pinned his arms to the floor. He could feel now that her brass "finger nails" were cutting deeply into the flesh of his wrists. He arched his neck, looking to see if assistance was going to come from any quarter, but Neb Jr. was still incapacitated—now curled up in a ball. Missy-Lou, still bound, was just muttering gibberish—the same words over and over again, commencing with—*Ph'nglui mglw'nafh.*

Then he saw that Worth had slumped to the deck and put down his pistol in order to tend to his shoulder wound. He was dabbing at the gory cleft in his shoulder with a handkerchief, but it would not stop bleeding.

Rouletabille writhed beneath Hell-Cat Maggie, reaching as best he could for the abandoned automatic.

Now she was playing with him, as she had with so many of the men she had killed in the alleyways and brothels of Manhattan. She wanted to let him think he had a chance against her. She guided his hand towards the gun, almost letting him have it. Teasing him with it. Then she crooned and whispered into his ear the obscene talk and worthless promises that seemed to distract men even when they were on the brink of death. She could not bear to kill him quickly now—trapped in the tunnel-vision of the psychotic sadist, she only knew that she wanted to prolong their physical struggle for as long as possible. She could not bite into his throat now, so she sank her teeth deep into his shoulder.

"Get away from him," ordered Hassett. "I need to find out what they've done to this ship."

Hassett stood in the doorway with his firearm drawn, covering Rouletabille and Hell-Cat Maggie. But with her bloodlust boiling, the woman ignored the order to release her prey. She'd decided that she'd rather kill him quickly than not at all... and her teeth were now working her way to his carotid artery. Seeing this, Hassett calmly shot her through the head.

"The control surfaces have locked into a dive. The buoyancy system only allows descent. I've cut motive power, but we are still going down," he said. "How have you done it, and more importantly, can it be undone?"

"They can't have done it," interjected Worth. "We caught them before they got into the sub. But wait a minute! Nezzar is one of them. He could've sabotaged the *Nautilus* days ago."

"It's becoming academic," said Hassett, shooting a glance at his watch. "Unless we stop the descent in the next few minutes, we'll have exceeded the depth for a safe evacuation in diving suits... if the pressure doesn't kill us, the bends will."

"We're not evacuating, Hassett. I've gone to too much trouble to abandon the *Nautilus* now," said Worth, and his hand crept for his dropped weapon. "Get back to the bridge or the engineering deck, or wherever the hell you need to be and fix this. I pay you well, start earning it."

Without warning, Missy-Lou suddenly stood up—the ropes that had held her snapped with the accompaniment of loud cracks.

Rouletabille could not be sure if this sudden inhuman strength was as a result of the potion she had drunk, or if this was a manifestation of the Obeah woman's own strange powers. He stood ready to leap at Hassett to restrain his gun arm if he pointed the weapon at Missy-Lou. But Hassett suddenly dropped his hand to his side.

Missy-Lou's will permeated every atom in the room. She was a protean, irresistible force now, and everything was subject to her and her whims. The power broadcast from her was aimed primarily at Hassett, and his feeble mind and underdeveloped soul were no match for it. They were dust motes lost in the hurricane. Yes, the power was sexual in nature and, even as a secondary recipient or observer of the Obeah in action, Rouletabille would've gladly surrendered his eternal soul for just a minute alone with her. She was fully clothed, in her black blouse and snug black cotton trousers, and yet projected into his mind was an image of her naked. She was standing almost completely still, and yet, he could see her performing the most lewd, provocative and shocking dance—shaking dark tipped breasts an almost un-seeable blur.

No, nothing was happening. She was not moving. She was not speaking. It was all in his mind. It was all in everyone's mind. Then she stepped forward and took Hassett in her arms. Somewhere behind him, Rouletabille heard a choked whimper from Cyrus West—a man who believed himself betrayed by the love of his life. Rouletabille, too, was irrationally charged with jealously. How could he ever think of Missy-Lou in the same way now that she had sullied her lips with the flesh of the dreadful Hassett? A man who had killed his own family without any trace of regret.

Missy-Lou kissed him very passionately and their bodies melded hungrily together. The kissing continued. Hassett wanted it to continue forever. And then, Missy-Lou bit off Hassett's tongue. He staggered backwards and tried to staunch the flow of blood with his fingers, but it was no use. The thick crimson liquid was gouting everywhere. Hassett ran from the stateroom leaving a spattered trail behind him. The spell was broken.

Missy-Lou spat Hassett's tongue onto the floor, swiftly released Cyrus and then went to tend to Neb Jr. Rouletabille relieved Worth of his gun without him even noticing. The man was drooling and only half conscious, his head full of visions of Missy-Lou and her sacred *punani*.

"Help me get him out of here," ordered West.

The two allies manhandled Worth off the floor and onto his feet, then half-dragged him towards the air-tight door exit to the stateroom. West could hear in the distance approaching guards, doubtless coming to investigate what had happened to Hassett.

West slapped Worth hard across the face to bring him out of his reverie. He knew that those who lacked a basic moral core and principles were the most susceptible to the power of the Obeah.

"Worth, you need to die knowing that your father was not Nemo. Your whole life has been a lie... Adam Worth was there with us alright, under one of his many aliases... he was Captain Shard, the leader of the pirates," and without further explanation, West propelled him through the doorway and slammed the airtight door shut.

Missy-Lou noticed then how badly Rouletabille's wrists and forearms had been injured by Hell-Cat Maggie. She tore lengths of material from her own blouse to make improvised bandages, and did her best to clean the macerated shoulder with brandy from the stateroom drinks cabinet.

"How is Neb Jr.?" asked West.

"That bullet creased his forehead. I think he's only temporarily blinded by the flash burns, but he's in deep shock, and terrible pain," said Missy-Lou.

"That's no good. I need him in full working order right now. Even though he'll disapprove of my method of fixing him," said West.

West strode swiftly to the drinks cabinet and removed a crystal tumbler, then dipped the glass into the shattered cylinder where the body of Rulu, the Mercurian girl still resided. Scooping up some of the azure liquid at the bottom of the tube, he then dribbled it onto Neb Jr.'s injured eyes. Almost immediately the swelling began to abate and the tissue to regenerate.

"The old E.V. fluid!" exclaimed Rouletabille. "But what is it doing here?"

"Nemo suspended Rulu in it in an attempt to save her, but she was too far gone," replied West. "Those fools smashed open this healing cylinder—wasting the precious fluid. It would've taken decades to synthesize this amount, and I should know."

Rouletabille recalled how West had spent ten years immersed in the fluid in order to rejuvenate his entire body. He had once given some of the fluid to Rouletabille in order to speed his recovery from a near fatal drowning.

"If all four of us consumed some of the fluid before exiting via an airlock, might it allow us to survive the journey to the surface?" asked Rouletabille.

"Frankly, I doubt it," said West. "But I'll admit that the thought did cross my mind. However, we must now be hundreds of feet below the surface. I'd rather go out in a blaze of glory trying to retake this sub than by drowning or the bends. Which reminds me, you knew that the *Nautilus* had been most effectively sabotaged. How?"

"As soon as I saw the monograph on the *Polyphonic Motets of de Lassus by Altamont Sigerson*," explained Rouletabille, "I knew that Sherlock Holmes, Hassett's nemesis, had got here before us and sabotaged this ship. He must've deduced that Hassett's expertise in underwater operations would mean that he was likely to be involved in any criminal attempt to salvage the *Nautilus*. I can just see the great man now, persuading his brother that he needed to 'borrow' one of the Bruce-Partington E-Class submarines and its crew, travelling here and ultimately solving the mystery of how to open the ocean door. The *Nautilus* had become a trap for evildoers. He did not completely overlook the possibility that men on the side of law would enter the vessel. And his over-endowed ego provided the solution—any good man capable of finding a way into the grotto would have more than a passing familiarity with his work. The monograph was both a calling card and a warning."

Neb Jr. got to his feet, much restored by the ancient elixir.

"We've stopped sinking," he said, taking a look out of the porthole.

"We've reached a point of neutral buoyancy," said West. "Unless there are more tanks still to vent, we will just hang in the water now."

"Cyrus, there is something that I need to tell you," said Missy-Lou.

"What is it, my dear?" asked West.

"The Santeria potion nearly ripped my mind apart giving me a full understanding of the future and—oddly enough—the past. I have seen in my mind's eye how we get out of here, and it is in the way Rouletabille suggested. A terrifying swim to the surface… our blood bubbling from the pressure shift, our lungs rupturing… but our bodies and souls preserved by the power of the old E.V. fluid."

"I am no adherent of these cultish practices," said Neb Jr. "Like you, I would rather take my chances in a good scrap and trust to your engineering skills to fix this hulk and get her back to the surface."

"Don't listen to him, Master," said Missy-Lou. "I have seen the future so very clearly, you are re-enlisted in the US Army and again using the name Smith, promoted to colonel and fighting in a terrible war somewhere in Asia… albeit it will be long decades before all this comes to pass."

"I don't doubt that *will* come to pass, Cyrus," said Rouletabille. "But you are such a brilliant tactician that your final rank will, I'm sure, be general. You could be like a modern-day Alexander or Hannibal."

"Your flattery doesn't help my decision-making. It's a pity we had to lose the element of surprise. Otherwise we could win a fight on this ship easily."

And then it seemed that the decision was taken out of their hands. A smoking red spot appeared on the airtight door into the stateroom. Hassett's men were starting to cut through with their acetylene torches.

"In less than five minutes, they'll have cut a hole big enough to shoot a carbine through," said West. "C'mon, let's fall back towards the rear airlock, but let's carry Rulu's cylinder with us."

West picked up the crystal tumbler and led the way towards the airlock.

Less than two minutes later, they had all toasted Rulu and drunk a glassful of the viscous metallic liquid from the bottom of the cylinder. Rouletabille could feel the injuries to his wrists and shoulder itching as they healed almost instantly. Then they crammed into the aft emergency airlock—and it was a tight squeeze. They all stripped to their underwear, apart, of course from Missy-Lou who only ever swam in the nude, whatever the circumstances. Rouletabille had been smitten with her physical beauty since the first time of meeting her, but now he regarded her as one might an elder sister, though not without great admiration. She was not a regular imbiber of the elixir; however, for a woman of more than forty her physique was exquisite.

West shut the inner door and primed the mechanism for the outer door. Outside they could hear gunfire as the *Nautilus* crew sprayed the interior of the stateroom with shots from their pneumatic rifles. Effectively, they had now made good their "escape," such as it was; only a madman would cut open the inner door and risk flooding the ship. With the *Nautilus* crippled by sabotage, Worth and the crew would most likely face death from slow suffocation—but that was likely to take weeks; perhaps the rations would run out first. Hassett would likely expire from blood loss unless someone assisted him by cauterizing his ragged tongue root.

The airlock swiftly filled with water and they all took deep breaths. Then the outer airlock door slid open. They kicked strongly through the door and out of the ship. West had warned them to ascend slowly, although he knew it was rather pointless since they would be unconscious long before they were anywhere near the surface. It was a matter of surviving drowning rather than swimming to safety. Quite what the protection of the elixir would be in relation to the bends, he was unsure. That had never been tested before.

Rouletabille took one last look back at the *Nautilus*, though most of his vision was impaired by the sting of the saltwater. Something was written in huge letters on the hull. And it did not appear to be in the alphabet of any language of which he was aware. There were two very similar words with a short word in between. He felt he ought to know what they said already, but he could not recall it. Was this the last vestige of his amnesia? If he lived, perhaps he would ask West about it.

The pain in his ears was excruciating. His chest was already very sore. It felt like his heart would rupture. He didn't think he would be able to ascend a hundred feet before he lost consciousness. Perhaps that would be a mercy. Black fog was already forming in his brain. His limbs were no longer obeying the instruction to swim and were just flailing.

At that moment, an immense curtain of silver bubbles erupted from the hull of the submarine. The last of the buoyancy tanks had vented. The *Nautilus* sank into the abyss. And the water here was miles deep. Realistically, no one would ever be able to salvage the vessel. The journalist in him regretted that he was unlikely to live to get the story into print.

Then his eardrums burst. There was a sudden urge to vomit, but that passed as quickly as it had arrived. His lungs were screaming for oxygen and his flailing converted into uncontrollable fitting—the beginning of death throes. He felt something touch him. He couldn't open his eyelids since his eyes were too painful, but he assumed he was about to be victim of a shark. No, it was hands touching him—pulling him close. Strong, yet unmistakably female. Then came the open-mouthed kiss. It was Missy-Lou. Was she doing it to say goodbye, because she knew that he did not have the strength to make it to the surface?

His brain started to unfog. She was forcing air into his lungs. Yes, much of her exhalation was carbon dioxide, but there was enough oxygen in her breath to reinvigorate him. She was pushing his eyelids open, turning his face, making him see, making him look, not at her but at what lay perhaps eighty feet above them. Was he hallucinating? It looked like a brass and enamel cathedral bell, suspended above them on long, white tether cables which reached up all the way to the surface. And then he understood! It was a Maracot diving bell, and it had been lowered towards the *Nautilus* by the ship that lay at anchor off Lincoln Island in some sort of rescue attempt.

Swimming strongly up towards the diving bell and pulling Neb Jr. as he went was Cyrus West—his endurance was prodigious due to the long years of exposure to the *Elixir Vitae*. Missy-Lou looped her arms around Rouletabille's chest and commenced a powerful scissor-kicking action which propelled them fast towards the open bottom of the diving bell.

Rouletabille wondered if they might not be going too fast. Could this swift sprint to the sanctuary of the bell result in the horror of the bends? There was no time to ponder it. Within moment, he was being thrust up through the diving bell's moon pool entryway, and after that, the hands of Cyrus West reached down to him and hoisted him up onto the wooden bench which went around the inside of the bell. It seemed almost miraculous that the interior of the diving bell should be dry and full of air, and that the seawater remained at a low level just above the lip of the bell.

"*Venture* to Diving Bell One, *Venture* to Diving Bell One," said a crackling voice coming from a small speaker on the wall. "This is Captain Englehorn, can anyone hear me? Over."

Cyrus punched at the microphone button.

"This is Captain Cyrus West of the United States Secret Service, I have with me fellow special agents Neb Dobey Jr. and Louise Pleasant. Also with us is Monsieur Joseph Rouletabille, a French journalist. We are survivors of the *Nautilus,* all other hands are believed lost."

"That's good to know, Captain. We heard from our captors that there was a small opposing force aboard the *Nautilus*," said Englehorn. "My crew has reestablished control of our ship and placed all of the Catharus Society operatives in custody in the brig. Understand that we will have to bring you to the surface very slowly to avoid risk of decompression sickness... please be patient."

"I know Englehorn, he's a good man," said West. "Worth merely chartered the *Venture*, as film producers often do when they're making motion pictures in these parts. Englehorn has no real knowledge of this offshoot of the Catharus Society, and certainly no loyalty to it after his treatment at their hands."

Rouletabille's ears were itching insanely inside where the old E.V. fluid in his system was causing his ear drums to swiftly regenerate. Likewise, the explosive pain in his chest was starting to ease off. Missy-Lou huddled up to him for warmth—all four of them were shivering.

"Well, is anybody a conversationalist?" asked Neb Jr. "Seems like we're gonna be stuck here with not much to do for quite a while."

"So, all of you are Secret Service agents?" asked Rouletabille.

"Yes," smiled West, "and I have been since my earliest days posing as a fellow 'bounty-jumper' in order to catch Adam Worth. Which reminds me? What day is it today?"

Rouletabille considered for a moment.

"I don't know. I'm not sure how long I was unconscious on the beach. Thanks for breakfast by the way…" said Rouletabille.

"I believe it is July 2," said Neb Jr.

"I thought as much. It's my brother Jim's birthday. Naturally, he's a Secret Service agent too. I wonder if he got that new Derringer I sent to him? I'll cable him when we get topside," said West. And then, he added, "Now is anything else about this little adventure puzzling you? There is still something of a mystery for you to unravel… let's see if you can do it before we reach the *Venture*. Or has that knock on the head when the *Sea Silk* was wrecked addled your deductive powers?"

"The final mystery is the riddle of Nemo's true identity. I know that he wasn't Adam Worth, and I know that he wasn't Prince Dakkar. For the moment, I will assume that you, Cyrus, are not Captain Nemo—although there is some evidence in

259

favor of that, for I do believe that there are major time discrepancies in Aronnax's narrative and your adventures on Lincoln Island. I am beginning to doubt that your experience on that most mysterious of islands happened during the Civil War at all," said the detective.

"Go on then, you're on the right track. The enigma of Nemo's identity is akin to Mr. Poe's *Purloined Letter,* it is actually quite obvious. Direct then, your mind to the most obvious suspect," said West.

"I'm not sure I know how to do that, but I will tell you what I have noticed. The *Nautilus* is old. Very old. Ancient, in fact. It had the look of something refitted and refurbished many times, which I was not expecting. The walkways were worn smooth by the perhaps centuries' worth of passage of booted feet. Then I would guess that the craft is a product of the same ancient civilization whose remnants can be found both on the island and in the sea; the same society which constructed the ocean door into the grotto. And then we have Nemo's association with the old E.V. fluid—a product which takes decades to distill even in small quantities. I therefore deduce that Nemo is an extremely long-lived representative of that society and that the first iteration of the *Nautilus* was perhaps launched millennia ago."

"That's quite insane, Rouletabille. No one will ever believe you, so I suggest you keep your theories to yourself... However, you are quite correct," laughed West. "Then who is he? I want to hear you say it."

"I remember now, the motto of the *Nautilus*—*Mobilis in Mobile*—according to Aronnax's journal. But on the hull of the craft, it was not written in Latin. What language is it? Is that part of the puzzle?"

"It's Achaean," said West.

"My God, of course. The language of the proto-Greek sea-people," said Rouletabille.

The surface of the moon pool was violently broken by a figure emerging from the depths. He was wearing a self-contained diving suit with small cylinders of air strapped to his back. His face was obscured by his breath mask and he was brandishing a short divers' knife. The diving bell's occupants all sought to draw up their legs onto the bench to avoid the swishing arc of his blade.

As the diver got his bearings, he directed his attack at Missy-Lou. It could only be Hassett beneath the mask. But before the knife could reach her, Rouletabille jumped down from the bench and landed hard on the assailant, filling the interior of the bell with a high fountain of foam and driving Hassett back out of the pool. Rouletabille wrestled with the villain for the knife. When Hassett's grip stayed firm, the detective clawed at the mask and pulled the regulator from between his lips. Hassett's tongueless mouth attempted to scream, but instead projected forth a ribbon of blood.

Rouletabille uncurled the Englishman's fingers from around the handle of the knife one by one and then used it to at jab his adversary's face. The knife went straight through the glass of the visor and into Hassett's eye socket. He must've died instantly since he started to sink downwards straightaway. Rouletabille looked up and saw that the diving bell had risen to be quite a long way from him. He fought to get back to it.

Friendly hands met Rouletabille as he rose from the moon pool and helped him up to the bench. While the detective coughed up seawater, West spoke:

"A group of individuals with access to highly advanced technology inhabited the Mediterranean region several thousand years ago. They also had their own immortality serum, which they sometimes shared with their favorites. They were the original, the prototype of the technological hierarchy. And if you read the stories of the Greek Gods and the works of Homer in that light, you'll arrive at a very clear understanding of what was going on. There was a man of that era, a king, a great sea-captain, warrior and explorer... a man who had good reason to have a kink about war since he participated in one of the biggest wars of that time... and it ruined his life. Yes, there has only ever been one sea-captain using the alias Nemo, and he's been using it since he encountered the Cyclops."

At last Rouletabille understood. It was a truth that could never be told, because it would simply never be believed.

"The King of Ithaca... the father of Telemachus... he was and always had been Nemo," smiled Rouletabille.

Once aboard the *Venture,* Rouletabille, Cyrus West, Missy-Lou and Neb Jr. stood at the stern between the twin cranes and watched Lincoln Island retreat below the horizon as the ship steamed north eastwards.

"I wonder if any of us will return to that mysterious island," pondered Rouletabille.

"We will not," said Missy-Lou, emphatically. "But I have seen the future, and one day, a family will inhabit it. And just as Kapitan Mors' ship to the stars was launched from within a volcano, so this family will launch great red and silver rockets, and these rockets will bring succor to those in need."

Many days later, the *Venture* was docked at Puerto Baquerizo Moreno, on San Cristóbal, where Cyrus, Missy-Lou and Neb Jr. hoped to get passage on a freighter to Bay City in California. Rouletabille planned to continue with the *Venture* to Val Verde, where they would pick up an expedition from the New York Zoological Society. He wondered if they had encountered the strange and deadly creature which was occasionally reported in the jungles of that country, and if they had, perhaps he should pick up its trail; it might make for a good story.

Rouletabille waved to his trio of friends as they walked down the gangplank onto the docks. After a few yards, Missy-Lou and Cyrus stopped. They were talking about something. Oblivious, Neb Jr. kept striding on.

"Cyrus," said Missy-Lou, haltingly. "In the years to come, I am with him," and she pointed a long finger back at Rouletabille on the *Venture.*

Cyrus West merely nodded. She had waited ten years for him when he was little more than a corpse... waited to see if the *Elixir Vitae* would revive him. He could demand no further loyalty from her. The Santeria potion had shown her the life she was to lead, and it was not with him. There was no point arguing.

Rouletabille saw Missy-Lou turn and run back up the gangplank. He wondered what she had forgotten.

Rouletabille by David Rabbitte

Afterword
Locked-Room Adventures in a time of Lockdown

I stumbled on the idea of writing the new exploits of journalist, spy and detective, Joseph Rouletabille, largely by accident, but I have always been fascinated by locked-room mysteries and impossible crimes. From Jacques Futrelle's Professor S.F.X Van Dusen (a.k.a. The Thinking Machine) to Sir Arthur Conan Doyle's *The Lost Special* by way of Rouletabille's Essex Boy TV incarnation, Jonathan Creek. In fact, *Leviathan Creek* was the chronologically first story I wrote in this series (note the not-so-cunning pun on Jonathan Creek's name this title represents), but even before that, I'd had a hankering to write a story in which Rouletabille deduces that a man has vanished from a locked cellar by using a time machine. This idea was abandoned, since the scope of it was quite limiting, but it led me on to develop the plot of *Leviathan Creek,* what I like to think of as an 'outdoors' locked-room mystery, in which the great detective is placed in the midst of the real-life inspiration for Peter Benchley's *Jaws* – the New Jersey shark attacks of 1916, but with a twist since he also encounters Herbert Brown, now a retired US Army General, from Jules Verne's *Mysterious Island.* Indeed, the involvement of Rouletabille in the affairs of characters from this sequel to *20,000 Leagues Under the Sea* would serve to provide a lot of mileage, and hopefully excitement, as he makes his way through a labyrinth of events towards the long anticipated climax on Mysterious Island itself—the intention being to create a strange melange or, at least, meshing together of the worlds of Gaston Leroux, Jules Verne and Sir Arthur Conan Doyle, amongst others, with both acknowledgement and affection for the multiple adaptations of the story which have contributed many layers of gloss to the narrative.

So why Rouletabille? The attraction lies in a character who is largely cerebral—his brain is his weapon—but what happens when he is pulled farther and farther from the rather too comfy comfort zone of solving locked-room mysteries? The answer is a sort of fish out of water dramatic tension. He is made to fight for his life again and again, and oftentimes he seems poorly equipped to win through—so even as the writer, I wonder if he will survive. Sometimes it seems it could've gone either way, each story might've been his last. Secondly, it is an enormous pleasure to write the lead character from the seminal locked-room mystery story, Gaston Leroux's *The Mystery of the Yellow Room*, which John Dickson Carr's character, Dr. Gideon Fell, determined to be the greatest detective story ever written in his novel *The Hollow Man*. It is a deftly plotted classic, and if you have not yet read Leroux's own Rouletabille stories, then a magnificent treat awaits you. Incidentally, I have already alluded to the debt David Renwick's creation, Jonathan Creek, owes to Rouletabille, and this is painted large in the Jonathan Creek episode *The Letters of Septimus Noone*—first broadcast in 2014—in which Creek and his wife go to see the West End musical of *The Mystery of the Yellow Room.* Undoubtedly an allusion to the long-running *Phantom of the Opera* show, also based on a Gaston Leroux novel.

Of course, I also owe a debt to the authors of the public domain works into which I have unceremoniously inserted our French detective hero, the first being John Willard for *The Cat and the Canary* (with the addition to the recipe of Algernon Blackwood's Cat People from *Ancient Sorceries).* I have been fascinated by the plot of *The Cat and the Canary* since childhood exposure to the old Bob Hope movie, which induces laughs and fear in equal measure, and is probably the best comedy horror film ever made. Upon reading Willard's original play, I was surprised to find that the film had displaced the action to the bayous of Louisiana from the banks of the Hudson. I therefore have little doubt that the Willard's Glencliff Manor was inspired by the Lyndhurst Mansion, which was later used as the filming location for Collinwood in the daily soap *Dark Shadows* (and its spin-off movies). Likewise, the play's Cyrus West must surely have been inspired by American businessman and entrepreneur, Cyrus West Field, who died in Irvington, New York, not far from Tarrytown where Lyndhurst is located.

A similar debt is owed to Arnaud D'Usseau, into whose plot for *Horror Express* I have attempted to graft Rouletabille – rather like grafting an orchid onto the bole of a sturdy tree. His story is a beautiful exercise in paranoia and claustrophobia—*Murder on the Orient Express* meets *The Thing*, in fact. It is, by turns, unexpected and terrifying, so much so that I think it is probably the last film I ever saw where I hid my eyes because it was too frightening… you'll have to take my word for it that I was very young at the time. And while it is difficult to find a way to improve on such a strong narrative, I could not resist adding the twist ending the film foreshadows, but doesn't get around to delivering.

The last Rouletabille stories I wrote are the ones set in and around London. These are less indicative of my childhood pre-occupations and rather more inspired by my early life living and working in London, particularly as a Serious Fraud Office law clerk covering hearings and cases at the Central Criminal Court—the Old Bailey—and also the environs of Bethnal Green; including the Waterlow Buildings where I lived for many years. In my latter years in the metropolis I lived in Leytonstone, sometimes described as one of London's more unlovely suburbs. It is certainly true that I lost count of the number of unsolved or ongoing murder investigations taking place within walking distance of my house, one of them close enough for us to be part of door-to-door inquiries by the investigating detectives. One of the murders would've been worthy of being a case for our French sleuth—or at least for his sometime associate, Mr. Harry Dickson—a man was murdered while playing the children's game Ludo for high stakes. Of course, Leytonstone was the boyhood home of Alfred Hitchcock, his parents' grocery store long gone by my time, replaced by a petrol station. Yet his spirit still somehow seemed to inhabit the place—after all, the police station where his father arranged for him to be incarcerated in the cells was still there, and the Leytonstone Tube Station by then was decorated with mosaics depicting classic moments from his films. The dismal House of Despair from which Rouletabille escaped is also gone, to some extent, remodelled to be the supermarket where I did my weekly shopping. Though strangely the supermarket pharmacy resides within the recognizable asylum chapel – and has an atmosphere of surprising tranquillity.

Farewell then, dear reader. I hope you have enjoyed these new exploits of Rouletabille. This cycle of stories has reached a natural conclusion and I have moved on to mine gold ore from elsewhere. But who knows? Perhaps years or even decades hence a tousle-haired Frenchman in tweeds accompanied by his beautiful new sidekick, Missy-Lou, will knock on my door and tell me in hushed tones that they've had a new adventure, and this too must be recorded.

Martin Gately
April 2020

FRENCH MYSTERIES COLLECTION

M. Allain & P. Souvestre. *The Daughter of Fantômas*
M. Allain & P. Souvestre. *The Death of Fantômas*
A. Anicet-Bourgeois, Lucien Dabril. *Rocambole: Two Stage plays*
Guy d'Armen. *Doc Ardan and The City of Gold and Lepers*
Guy d'Armen. *Doc Ardan and The Troglodytes of Mount Everest*
Guy d'Armen. *Doc Ardan and The Abominable Snowman*
Guy d'Armen. *Doc Ardan and The Fall of Inramonda*
A. Bernède. *Belphegor*
A. Bernède. *Judex* (w/Louis Feuillade)
A. Bernède. *The Return of Judex* (w/Louis Feuillade)
A. Bernède. *The Shadow of Judex* (w/Louis Feuillade et al.)
A. Bisson & G. Livet. *Nick Carter vs. Fantômas*
V. Darlay & H. de Gorsse. *Lupin vs. Holmes: The Stage Play*
Harry Dickson. *Harry Dickson and The Heir of Dracula*
Harry Dickson. *Harry Dickson vs The Spider*
Paul Feval. *Gentlemen of the Night / Captain Phantom* (plays)
Paul Feval. *John Devil*
Paul Feval. *The Parisian Jungle*
Paul Feval. *Heart of Steel*
Paul Feval. *'Salem Street*
Paul Feval. *The Invisible Weapon*
Paul Feval. *The Companions of the Treasure*
Paul Feval. *The Cadet Gang*
Paul Feval. *The Sword Swallower*
Paul Feval. *The Companions of the Silence*
Paul Feval: *Bel Demonio*
Louis Forest. *Someone Is Stealing Children In Paris*
Emile Gaboriau. *Monsieur Lecoq*
Emile Gaboriau. *The Casebook of Monsieur Lecoq*
Arnould Galopin. *Harry Dickson and the Man in Grey*
Arnould Galopin. *Harry Dickson vs Tenebras*
Goron & Gautier. *Spawn of the Penitentiary*
Jean de La Hire. *Enter the Nyctalope*
Jean de La Hire. *The Nyctalope on Mars*
Jean de La Hire. *The Nyctalope vs Lucifer*
Jean de La Hire. *The Nyctalope vs Lucifer*
Jean de La Hire. *The Nyctalope Steps In*
Jean de La Hire. *Night of the Nyctalope*

Antonin Reschal. *The Adventures of Miss Boston*
Léon Sazie. *Zigomar*
P. de Wattyne & Y. Walter. *Sherlock Holmes vs. Fantômas*
David White. *Fantômas in America*
Pierre Yrondy. *The Adventures of Therese Arnaud*
Pierre Yrondy. *The Adventures of Marius Pegomas*